DIVIDED FIRE

JENNIFER SAN FILIPPO

CLARION BOOKS
Houghton Mifflin Harcourt
Boston   New York

Clarion Books

3 Park Avenue

New York, New York 10016

Copyright © 2020 by Jennifer San Filippo

All rights reserved. For information about permission to reproduce selections from this book, write to trade.permissions@hmhco.com or to Permissions, Houghton Mifflin Harcourt Publishing Company, 3 Park Avenue, 19th Floor, New York, New York 10016.

Clarion Books is an imprint of Houghton Mifflin Harcourt Publishing Company.

hmhbooks.com

The text was set in Adobe Caslon Pro.

Library of Congress Cataloging-in-Publication Data is available.

ISBN 978-1-328-48919-7

Manufactured in the United States of America

DOC 10 9 8 7 6 5 4 3 2 1

4500805489

To Mom, Dad, and Rachael

PROLOGUE

Five years ago

The hill they climb each year is steep. Father carries the straw rope, cooking pans, a faded quilt, but the two sisters are charged with heaving the large basket of kindling up the slope. In front, her arms full of vegetables collected that afternoon, their mother turns and hurries them with a wave.

"We're coming," Father says.

Miren, the elder sister, watches the other children scream and clamber up with only a twinge of envy in her stomach. Tonight will be her night; she knows it.

The sisters crest the hill and huff dramatically, dropping their basket with a clatter. The plateau shimmers green in the wind, cradled by whispering, rolling plains that reach past the edge of any map. Toward the east, Miren can see far beyond Crescent Bay, past the docks and over the shimmering Tehum Sea and even, on a clear evening such as this, the peaks of Avi'or: blue, snowcapped pillars of stone, their crags piercing the belly of the rising moon.

They are one of the last families to arrive. The fishermen and their wives chat with each other, sharing responsibilities. The blacksmith, flanked by his two burly sons, laughs heartily at a joke from the baker. And even the baron, whose motives and fashions are often a subject of gossip, chuckles with a couple of fishermen. Conversations are, as always, a blend of voices and signing hands.

Miren can't stop smiling; warm excitement pools in her stomach and hums in her veins. She imagines opening her mouth as heat rises up her throat, her Voice ringing out with Song, catching everyone midconversation as the bundle of kindling bursts into flame.

The blacksmith's elder son, only a year older than she, was able to Earth Sing at the gathering three years ago. Now he works with his father, apprenticed like most Singers his age, learning to Sing the more difficult Songs of metal. Miren sees him standing beside the blacksmith, his hanging arms and half-closed eyes part of a still, deliberate calm that she admires. Even his name, Jonath, feels like a cool stone in her mouth.

He catches her eye and grins, disrupting his stillness just for her. Her cheeks grow warm with a different kind of heat.

Mother, carrying a tray of sliced carrots and potatoes and sprouts, rushes over to the collection of food by the tall wooden structure: artfully arranged meats and vegetables and cheeses and bread of every shape—a spread fit for royalty, Miren is sure. She hopes her nerves will quiet enough to allow her to enjoy the food.

"Miren," Father calls. "The wood goes over there."

"Yes, Father." Miren grins, and tells her sister, "We'll put it by the fire."

"I know," Kesia says, but she's smiling, her hazel eyes lighting up. She has a bounce in her curls and a spattering of freckles that Miren secretly envies, but her complexion is pale, her rosy cheeks a bit clammy. She hasn't been feeling well lately, but she's excited too.

The two sisters haul the basket toward the sea of quilts strewn around the edges of the plateau. On the far side sits a haphazard tower of wood twice the height of a man, branches of varying length stacked and tied together: the center beacon of the Skyflame ceremony.

The people look up and cheer as the family approaches. "The lightkeepers are here!" a fisherman cries. "Now Ami won't have to cook!"

Everyone laughs appreciatively as Miren and Kesia set the basket down. Even timid Ami, huddled with her fellow fisherfolk, feigns a gasp of relief and brushes the front of her blue dress. Mother adds her tray to the spread and joins the group, signing excited greetings with her hands.

Beyond the adults, the children scuttle around the lush green. Those near the age of twelve are supposed to remain silent until the ceremony, but most of them scream and laugh, chasing each other or taking turns rolling partway down the hill. Kesia giggles as a girl flails wildly, her grass-stained dress billowing as she tumbles.

Miren spots one boy sitting on the grass alone, watching the other children with his head propped up in his hands. He is the baron's son, though she can't recall his name. He is about Kesia's age, perhaps eleven years old; he may try to Sing tonight.

A twinge of doubt creeps up Miren's neck. Already thirteen, her chances of finally Singing are slim. For the past year, there has been no denying that womanhood has come. The time to Sing—if there ever was one—is past. To attempt Song tonight would be childish, embarrassing.

But that can't be, she reasons. Her parents have been only supportive. Every time her mother Sings, Miren pauses to listen, to catch every note, every breath, every bend in the melody. If it's a Song she recognizes, one for lighting the fire or warming a pan, Miren will join in, her own voice nestling comfortably beside her mother's. Mother will look up, surprised, and smile through her Song. Father will grin and sigh. "I feel warmer already." Then Miren's laugh will bubble through her concentration, and she'll change notes, complementing the Song with harmony rather than competing with it. She will never bother to check if the pan is warmer than it should be, or if the wood in the fireplace smokes with promise.

And now, standing on the plateau, a creeping certainty tells her she's wrong. She's not a Fire Singer. All the heat of a moment ago drains from her.

"Want to go play?" Kesia asks, pulling Miren's attention to the other children.

Miren blinks in surprise. "Do you feel well enough?"

Kesia shrugs, shy about her constant poor health. "Well, just for a little while."

Miren glances at Mother and Father, but their attention is with the other adults, on the wooden frame for Skyflame and the pots of food. In light of their work, the scurrying children suddenly look like *children,* a distinction Miren has dreaded for moons now.

"You go ahead, actually," Miren says. "I should help Mother with the food."

Kesia frowns. "I want you to come."

"It's all right, have fun. Maybe ask the baron's son to play with everyone. He seems sad."

Kesia turns to follow her gaze, and Miren takes the chance to slip away.

She shouldn't be this nervous. This is a celebration. Miren heads for the adults around the food, chopping vegetables and sorting meats as they talk, but her eyes catch on her father, who is leaning over the pile of wood. He and the other men are tying the ends of branches together with string, securing the base for the Skyflame fire.

"It's almost time to start," a fisherman says. "We should light the torch."

"I brought some oil."

"Oil's cheating, Haro."

The men chuckle. Father reaches for a long, thick stick and searches for a cloth.

Miren darts over and grabs a rag from the pile of tools. "How about this?"

"Thank you, dear." He wraps the rag around his makeshift torch as another fisherman secures it with twine.

Something gnaws at Miren's stomach. "Can I light it?" she asks.

Father smiles. "Here." He reaches in his pocket and hands her a pair of spark rocks, small but hardly used. Mother manages the cooking and the lighthouse entirely with Song, so Father rarely needs them. Tonight, however, Singers will only Sing during the ceremony.

He kneels and holds the torch out. "Hit the rocks together hard."

Miren nods, feeling the men's gazes behind her. She takes the flint between her fingers and snaps them together. A feeble pinprick of light flashes.

"Harder," Father advises, "and be sure to aim for the torch."

Miren tries again, and again. She does it until a rhythm forms and the sparks flicker each time, many of them landing on the cloth of the torch, but a flame doesn't catch.

"Maybe oil's good for just this once," the carpenter says.

The men chuckle, but Miren's eyes burn. She hums quietly and imagines the wood bursting into flames, though this Song wouldn't work for that. The melody is too slow, the pitch is wrong—

"Hey now," Father says. "Wait until tonight."

She groans. "I can't do it the normal way!"

"You just need practice."

She drops the rocks and stands, her face hot. "Never mind. I'll help with the food."

Perhaps it's in the way he smiles, the way the skin around his eyes tightens, but she imagines that he will finally tell her that she is too old, that her worst fears are true; there is no Fire Song in her breath. For a heartbeat, she silently wills him to do so, dares him to prevent any embarrassment she will endure tonight.

But he says, "All right, then."

Miren brushes grass from her skirt and walks away, not looking at the other men. Perhaps the women will be more understanding.

But there is little to do in the way of preparing food. Most of the meat is sliced, fresh beef and chicken arranged with chopped vegetables on platters. A couple of women glance up at her, but she turns, hoping to appear nonchalant.

"Did you hear of the influx of Avi'ori workers?" says one woman.

"Yes," the other replies. "The last round of traders mentioned a sudden increase in farmers looking for work in Kaleo. Apparently Avi'ori farms are not doing well."

"Hope they don't come here."

"No, it's mostly northern lord territories." The woman leans in and murmurs, "I doubt Darius could afford such help."

"It's strange, though, considering the tensions between the Crown and Avi'or, isn't it?"

"My husband doesn't think there will be war. The king is not so foolish."

Miren wanders away from the group, bored with the conversation, and comes to the edge of the plateau. She gazes out toward the east, the faint ridge of Avi'or's mountains just visible now, and waits for the tension in her throat to ease.

A flicker of light catches her eye. At first she thinks it's a star, but the light undulates orange and yellow. A fire, she realizes, somewhere in the mountains across the bay. In Avi'or.

Miren stares, clinging to the well of delight, of *promise*, that stirs heat in her again. Why has she never seen this before? Do the Avi'ori celebrate Skyflame too? They must, she realizes, because they have Singers. She has seen their trade ships sometimes come to port, their sails full with Air Song.

"Lord Baron!" a man calls over the crowd. Miren turns to see a fisherman holding the lighted torch. "We're ready for you."

The hum of conversation dips as the baron stands and takes the torch. Women call to their children, and everyone finds a seat among the quilts. Kesia sits on Father's crossed legs, and he puts his muscular arms around her small frame, tucking her under his chin until she giggles at his coarse beard. Miren nestles next to Mother, who flashes a distracted smile. It's not the comfort Miren was hoping for; her heart pounds in her chest.

The baron is plumper than most, his stomach protruding over a shiny belt buckle, his clothes made of a shimmering dark fabric without a single patched hole. Amid the grass of the plateau and the villagers with their plain clothes, he seems out of place.

He clears his throat. "Citizens of Crescent Bay," he begins. Miren makes a face at *citizens;* it's such an impersonal word, heavy with thoughts of the richer cities in the north where she has never been. Such a word doesn't belong here.

The baron continues, "Tonight is a special night. Legends of Skyflame's beginnings have drifted beyond our reach, but we still celebrate the beauty of Song that graces our community and all of our great kingdom of Kaleo. Once again, a few of our younger members will be gifted with a Voice. They will join the ranks of our great men and women who now serve our town as fishermen and blacksmiths and farmers and lightkeepers. It is an honor to be given such power, and a greater honor to use it for the good of the community."

Movement catches Miren's eye, and she sees the baron's son shift uncomfortably. His mother slaps his knee, and he stills.

The baron raises his torch. "But before that, we feast!"

He slowly brings the torch down on the nearest beam of the structure, and the stack of wood bursts into bright, oily flames. Everyone cheers and hurries to the platters of food.

So begins Skyflame.

Before the children can spoil the spread, the women assemble food in small pots and place the pots carefully in the fire to cook. Some of the men skewer meat on thin sticks and hold them over the flames. Miren watches, waiting until the adults deem the food ready. Then she grins at Kesia and sprints to the front of the crowd, swiping a pot from the fire. She rushes back to the quilt, smiling wickedly as her family laughs.

Everyone finds food and settles down on their quilts. Mother and Father discuss the garden and the fishing boat, their conversation taking on the familiar rhythm of voice and sign. Miren and Kesia squabble over the last piece of chicken until Father grabs it and pops it into his mouth. Mother laughs silently and hands each girl a skewer. The baker stops by their quilt with a basket full of sweet rolls.

Just as the last light of sunset fades, when the horizon shows but a hint of soft pink, the crowd begins to quiet. Miren scans the circle, taking a quick head count. There will likely be a dozen or so others participating tonight, besides her and Kesia.

Miren watches as Mother stands and goes to the center of the plateau, holding kindling from the basket that the sisters had carried. The three other Singers each present their own elements: the carpenter has a pile of stones; the fisherman, a pail of water; and the seamstress, leaves from an oak tree. The fire silhouettes them as they place their items in a square and wait. The rest of the village forms a lopsided circle around them, with Skyflame at the northern tip.

The Water Singer Elij turns to the circle and raises his hands. *Who would like to go first?* he signs.

It is customary for the boys to begin the ceremony with Songs of Water and Earth, though part of Miren would like to make her attempt now and be done. After years of anticipation, she almost can't bear another minute.

A boy steps from beside the blacksmith: Etham, a leaner, taller version of his older brother, Jonath. The blacksmith pats him on the back as he walks to the center, smiling nervously.

Elij signs, *Which Song would you like to Sing?*

The Song of Earth, Etham signs.

Miren straightens, and a few villagers share looks of excitement. Earth Song is even rarer than Fire; few boys bother to try. But Etham's voice has dropped to a rumbling bass in recent months. If he were to be gifted a Song, it would be Earth.

The carpenter steps forward, lowers his head, and hums a note. Miren feels the ground hum with him. Earth Song is nothing like the other three. While most Singers place the Song in their mouths, the sound reverberating in the Singer's head, Earth Song comes from the stomach, the bones. The sound doesn't drift through the air, but through everything else. Miren shivers as she feels it hum in the ground beneath her.

The piled stones vibrate and lift into the air, swirling around each other in a windless tornado. Etham joins his voice to the carpenter's, but the notes are wrong, and he soon stops. The carpenter grins through his Song, and the rocks slow and settle on the grass. Etham glances at his father and shrugs, but the blacksmith smiles and signs, *It's all right.* It would have been an incredible stroke of luck to have three Earth Singers in Crescent Bay.

The rest of the boys follow suit, all of them asking to Sing the Song of Water with the fisherman. Every child on the cusp of adulthood, even those with non-Singer parents, partakes in the ritual, though they rarely have a Voice. When the boys don't have a Voice, or simply can't sing a single note correctly, they shrug or lower their heads and take their seats. Sometimes they decline before they utter a note, recognizing an absence within themselves. A fisherman's son manages to splash water from the pail, but otherwise the night is silent.

Eventually, the baron shifts uncomfortably in his seat. "Davri," he murmurs.

The hunched blond boy beside him stands. He is nervous; Miren sees it in his trembling hands, his tight lips. His mother, an angular woman with milky skin, watches her son with a sharp frown.

What Song would you like to Sing? Elij signs.

Davri looks at the two elements before him. *Water,* he signs. He quickly corrects himself, *The Song of Water.*

Elij nods and begins to Sing. The water swirls in the pail as though draining from a hole in the bottom.

Davri wipes his hands on his trousers absently, his eyes darting to his father and quickly away. Miren grimaces in disapproval; he should be far more excited about the prospect of earning a Voice.

Elij continues his Song, an expectant look on his face. Davri leans in and sings.

His voice is so strong that Miren gasps. Elij isn't ready for an addition of such power, either; the water sloshes in the pail.

Davri's Song shifts.

His tone, light and crisp like a bell, latches to the swirling water with a sudden chill. The water slows to a stop and gleams in the light of Skyflame, frozen.

The group stares in silent wonder. Turning water to ice is a difficult task, particularly for a younger Singer, when his Voice is still unruly. A few adults in the circle smile widely and sign, *Well done.* The baron does not, and Davri does not look at him as he returns to his seat.

Miren signs congratulations with the other villagers, though the message is clumsy in her hands. She wants to impress, but she can't imagine how she could outshine such an accomplishment.

It is time for the women, the keepers of Air and Fire. The two men step from the circle as Isha and Mother take their places.

Who would like to go first? Isha signs.

Before Miren can decide if being first is a good idea, the seamstress's daughter jumps up and hurries to the circle, signing *Song of Air* without waiting to be prompted. A few villagers laugh quietly. After a quick attempt, however, she slumps and returns to her seat, unable to replicate the Song.

Miren watches the girls enter the circle one by one, each of them attempting to Sing Air. Only two girls leave the circle having joined Isha, who swept the leaves into a whirlwind. The people sign *Well done* eagerly. Air Singers and Water Singers are more common than

Earth and Fire Singers, but they provide great service in fishing, sailing, and irrigating crops.

And then it is Miren's turn.

She stands and enters the circle, her mind suddenly full and empty at once. The flames dance, chasing and stretching shadows across the grass. Isha asks what Song Miren wishes to Sing, and mercifully her hands know what to do: *The Song of Fire.*

Mother, her brown eyes shining, steps forward and parts her lips.

Miren listens intently. Her mother's Voice doesn't draw from the world like the other elements; her Song *is* warmth, a heat that comes from within her. Miren waits, letting the notes set the stage, just as a painter would wet her brush with orange and yellow. She will wait for Mother to provide the colors and warmth. Miren will add shape.

As the notes rise and blend into something tangible, the small pile of wood begins to glow. Miren expects an explosion of heat, but the flames grow slowly, climbing the sticks as if Mother isn't even Singing.

Mother tilts her head in invitation, and Miren nods. She opens her mouth and sings a note.

The syllables are nonsensical, and meaning is illusive—it is not until a Singer finishes her Song that she realizes there were no words—but the melody weaves like a single strand of light through the air, bright and easy to follow. Miren lets her voice rise next to Mother's, willing, begging the fire to grow. She sees the people's eyes pivot to her with excitement, just as in her fantasies of this night, but she suddenly wishes they weren't here. She needs to concentrate, to follow Mother's lead, her tempo and volume.

A breeze drifts through their circle, a cold gust from the bay. The fire flickers dangerously, and Mother's Song shifts to catch it. Miren's heart lurches. She doesn't know this Song—she hasn't practiced it. The string slips from her grip, and her notes are sour.

The faces around her wince at the tone, some with pity. The spell is broken.

She does the only thing left to her: she stops.

Mother lets the Song drift away, like ashes from the small pile of kindling that no longer glows. Mother smiles and signs, *I love you, daughter.* Miren looks away, feeling the future drop from beneath her. She is not a Singer; she is not special. She is not important like her mother, like the young fishermen and sailors who have been made tonight, like Davri, who will never need to use his Voice to work as the other boys do. He has been given his gift for nothing.

She returns to her spot beside her father and sits, the weight of the village's stares burning her skin. Father hugs her, kisses her head, and whispers, "Love you." She will not cry—she *won't.* Her sister, still in Father's lap, frowns. Miren winces as the word *pitiful* spikes in her mind. Kesia offers a smile and signs, *It's all right.*

It is not, but Miren gives a little shrug, her eyes stinging.

Father pats Kesia's shoulder.

The group's attention shifts as Kesia stands, and her knees tremble so much that Miren feels a pang in her chest. Kesia takes her place in front of Mother, who smiles and signs, *Which Song would you like to Sing?*

Kesia raises her shaking hands. *The Song of Fire.*

Isha steps back, and Mother begins to Sing.

As the kindling glows again, Kesia takes a deep, steadying breath, and her own thin voice drifts into the air. It doesn't catch; Miren can hear her reaching for the thread as she tries to align with Mother's Song. Her voice quavers, more breath than sound.

And then it blooms.

Miren inhales. Kesia isn't strong or loud like Miren, but she has whatever Miren lacks—a level of control Miren never mastered, perhaps the occasional trill or slide to another note, or the instinct of knowing when to take a breath. Miren feels the pleasant heat that

Kesia is somehow weaving. The stack of kindling flashes with the additional power.

Kesia's knees give way.

Mother abandons her Song with a gasp, and murmurs of concern from the audience break the rule of silence. Father rushes forward. Miren follows, her heart hammering in her chest. She stares in the direction of her sister's pale face, but she can't see past the imprint of bright flame behind her eyes. She thinks to check the wood this time and sees only ash.

ONE

MIREN

Five years later

MIREN SCRUBBED THE LIGHTHOUSE MIRRORS, THE POLISH smearing in greasy ripples and coating her hands. She was being sloppy, but she couldn't bring herself to focus on the menial task. The merchant ships were likely to come soon; the seasons were warming, the green of the hills reaching its brightest hue. Miren wished she were excited.

She left the inside paneling as it was, frustrated at being saddled with this chore. She capped the bottle of polish and stepped from the lightroom onto the widow's walk, noting that the door to the chicken coop nestled against the other side of their small cabin was closed. Her sister was nowhere to be seen.

"Kesia!" she shouted. "You have to feed the chickens before we go."

An angry clap sounded from the cabin window. Kesia was likely just getting dressed.

Miren groaned. "Well, hurry up."

To the north, Crescent Bay curved around a herd of crooked, creaking docks and well-worn fishing boats. A tilt in the land pushed the collection of homes close to the shore, where villagers busied themselves with booths and fish and crops. Things to sell to travelers who rarely came.

Against her will, Miren's gaze drifted west, up a hill, where a fire had burned once a year, where Voices had bloomed. It had been years since the king had drafted Singers into the war, years since the remaining villagers had agreed to stop celebrating Skyflame.

Miren rounded the widow's walk to face the sea and leaned against the railing, the wind weaving the scent of kelp and brine through her hair. The water glittered in the early morning, the sun rising out of the ocean. She looked as hard as she could, trying to spot the slight ridge of Avi'or across the Tehum Sea. She couldn't decide if the world seemed large or small from up here, but she felt an ache in her chest if she stared too long.

It was so tiny that she nearly missed it: a pinprick of white floated along the horizon, heading for the bay.

"Kesia!" she shouted, nearly dropping the polish as she hurried down the stairs. "Kesia, a ship's coming!"

She flew through the door at the bottom of the lighthouse and saw Kesia stepping from the cabin, a bag of feed under her arm, her long hair tied messily behind her.

"I saw a ship," Miren said. "It looked huge!"

Kesia signed, *Traders?*

"I assume so." Miren closed the lighthouse door and locked it behind her out of habit. Her heart thudded with possibilities. It could be a military ship, a wanderer from the Kaleon fleet. Or the Avi'ori fleet. Or pirates. Or a royal Kaleon messenger looking for Singers to force into the army to fight in the endless, consuming war with Avi'or.

It was most likely traders.

But still.

"I'm coming to town with you," Miren said.

Her sister rolled her eyes. *I'm meeting Davri,* she signed.

Miren groaned. "Not before we sell a few things. And we're out of eggs. And I'd like some bread from Etela."

Kesia sighed voicelessly. *And then I'm meeting Davri.*

"We still have to make those apricot preserves."

Miren.

"And you said you'd help me clean this place."

Stop it, Miren. Kesia glowered, but Miren pretended not to notice.

"I'm just saying that chores come first, before . . ." She couldn't bring herself to say *love,* even in a derisive way. "Whatever you call it."

Kesia narrowed her eyes. *You're afraid I'll tell him.*

Miren instinctively raised her hand to cover Kesia's signs, but there was no one close enough to see—everyone was down in the village. "We agreed you wouldn't, right?"

Kesia pointed at Miren.

"Because it's dangerous and stupid and we don't need to argue about this anymore." Miren's chest tightened in panic. "No one can know. No one. Please, Kesia, you agreed not to."

I hate lying to him.

"It's not lying; it's keeping you safe."

Let me tell him. Please.

Miren clenched her jaw. This conversation became more difficult each time. "Stop asking me that." She headed to the cabin to make her escape. "Please, let's not start this again. It's a beautiful day, we might see traders, and I have some salted meat I've been saving. We can have it tonight, all right? I'm going to package the candles."

Kesia was signing, but Miren closed the cabin door. Hopefully, Kesia would be cooled off by the time they left.

Their square cabin pressed comfortably around her, returning the world to its normal size. A large bunk bed, a table, a desk, and a fireplace left almost no room to walk. The cabin was far too small, despite the fact it only housed two now. With all four of them, it must have been oppressive, though she didn't remember it that way. Of course, running *under* the table had once been an option.

She drifted over to the desk, pitted and smooth with use, where a few precious books were stacked. She lifted the cover of their mother's book of recipes and slid out a letter. The seal of the King's Army, a tower with a sword protruding from the top, was broken and crumbling, the paper soft from being read dozens of times.

It was the last letter their father had sent. They'd received it nearly four months ago.

Father had left at the onset of the war almost five years earlier, with the first draft that had called for all able-bodied men in Kaleo. The goodbyes had been long and tearful, with most of the remaining villagers piled on the docks as they waved at the departing ship. They had been worried but hopeful; surely neither country wanted a long war.

Now she opened the letter more from habit than anything; she had it memorized. Father had warned that he might not be able to write for a while, which was what Miren said every time Kesia expressed worry. But four months without word was concerning. Four months could mean anything.

Their mother hadn't sent any letters. She'd been gone for four years.

After the men from Crescent Bay were drafted, the tide of the war had quickly turned against Kaleo; despite a protected northern coastline, the navy couldn't stand against Avi'or's superior steam-powered ships. So the king had decided that Singers would serve their country in combat and declared a Singer draft. Singers of all ages were called to report to the capital.

The village had been in an uproar. That was not what Singing was intended for. To use it for violence was sacrilegious, dangerous, evil. The Singers were needed in the village, and many of their number were far too young to be thrust into combat. At the time, Kesia had been twelve and sick with cloud fever.

Miren remembered screaming at the uniformed men who came

to their door. They looked at Kesia sick in bed, her Voice likely lost to the illness if she survived, and instead took their mother, one of the most powerful Singers they would likely ever find.

Miren had run after them, still screaming, but Mother had marched willingly to the docks with the rest of the Singers. Miren could still picture her turning back one last time to sign: *Protect your sister.*

In the four years since that day, Crescent Bay had worked in silence. There was no one to Sing the fish into nets, to fill sails with a steady wind, to till fields, or mend horseshoes. There was no one to lead new Singers in the Skyflame ceremony; no new Voices were heard.

Miren tucked the letter back inside her mother's book. She looked around, but the candles were already wrapped in string and paper. She grabbed her pack and slid the candles in, along with some carrots, potatoes, and a few pieces of jewelry, necklaces of seashells and stones, that Kesia had made.

She glanced at the bottom left drawer in the desk, then opened it slowly, as if Kesia might hear.

Inside sat a large, black revolver, one of the few Kaleon-made firearms that had existed before the war. Her father had received it from a friend who had served in the military some ten years ago, though Father had refused to take it with him when he had left for the war. *Just in case,* he had said, his well-used hunting rifle slung over his shoulder, the draft notice peeking out from his shirt pocket as he headed for the docks.

Miren picked up the revolver, the stock cold and heavy in her hand. It was loaded, but she checked and rechecked that the safety was still on. The metallic weapon made the wooden cabin feel brittle around her.

She placed the revolver back in the drawer and instead clipped her father's old fishing knife to her belt. *I won't need it,* she thought. *I've never needed it before.*

From the open window, she heard the chickens squawk happily.

"Kesia," she called. "Let's get going."

By the time they made their way down the rise, the ship was visible to the entire village. Everyone moved with enthusiasm, spurred by the prospect of selling their wares to someone other than one another. Kesia carried the coin purse on her belt, her smile eager. She was always so much happier outside, but Miren noticed how the sun made her skin seem paler, her cheekbones a bit too prominent.

Haro the blacksmith pounded at his furnace, the rhythmic clink of metal ringing through the village. He had burn marks on his arms that had been there all of Miren's life, and a heavy hunch in his back that had not.

Miren arranged her features into a warm smile. It had been difficult to speak with him for the past six months, since his older son, Jonath, had abruptly stopped sending letters home.

Haro looked up as they approached, and his bushy, peppered beard tweaked in a smile. "Morning, ladies. Did you see the ship?"

"We did," Miren said. She sometimes felt like her voice wasn't hers—it was too controlled, too polite to be true. "Kesia wants to spend all of our savings on whatever they're bringing."

Haro chuckled. "I could go for a stronger drink than wine, you know?" he said.

Miren smiled cordially. "Sure."

"At least we know it's not from the army, huh?"

Miren blinked. "How do we know that?"

He nodded at the horizon. "Wrong flag."

"Oh." Of course. Military ships always flew the king's crest: a white star on a deep purple background.

Haro looked at Kesia, and his features softened. "How are you feeling?"

Miren winced. When the villagers had pity to spare, they often saved it for Kesia, the last Singer among them, who, they believed, had lost her Voice to cloud fever years ago. Miren knew how her sister hated their pity.

Kesia smiled and signed, *Thank you. How are you and Raila?*

"Fine, fine." Haro kept grinning. "Raila spent all night working on some pies. I managed to restrain myself and only ate one."

Miren joined in his laugh. "We're going to see if Etela has any bread," she said. "But be sure to save us a slice or two of pie."

"Will do. Take care, Kesia."

Kesia waved as they walked away. She glared at Miren, but Miren put a hand over her signing fingers. "Wait until he can't see," she murmured.

But Kesia discreetly flicked her hands. *I'm going to see Davri. You don't need me to come.*

"Just a few more stops," Miren said, trying not to sound frustrated. "Don't you want bread?"

I don't want pity bread, Kesia signed.

"I'm pretty sure it tastes the same as regular bread."

Kesia glared for a long moment.

Miren sighed. "Don't be angry with me."

You won't give him a chance.

"Let's not do this here."

He's considerate and kind and respectful—

"And he's young, and you're young, and I really don't want to discuss this in public," Miren hissed.

Kesia narrowed her eyes. *We need to find you someone. Then you'll understand.*

"Ah yes," Miren swept a hand around their village. "Will all the eligible young men please line up!"

Kesia rolled her eyes again, but Miren thought her anger was fading. This conversation was so overdone that Kesia could probably argue Miren's side for her.

"Come on," Miren said. "Let's get bread."

Etela's cabin was toward the center of the village, just by the dock. Miren glanced out toward the horizon, where a large brown hull sliced the water only a few hundred paces away. "The ship's almost here."

Kesia looked past her and opened her mouth in surprise. *That ship is fast.*

"It is." Miren swallowed a muted panic. It might be of Avi'ori make. "Maybe we should go back to the cabin."

Kesia grimaced. *I want to see!*

"I know, but—"

A slow-rolling noise of excitement grew from behind them as fishermen and farmers and their eager children hurried past. Miren felt a tug at her chest at the sight. There were so few reasons to be happy these days.

The flag, sporting an odd symbol of a sword parting an ocean wave, flew high on the tallest of three masts. There was no royal seal on the hull, and if the ship had been military, it would've docked closer to the baron's estate at the northern end of the village.

So they were either traders or pirates.

Miren shuddered.

The crew were on the deck now, all male, their clothing rough and weathered, their skin darkened from the sun. Some carried crates between them as though they weighed nothing.

Kesia patted her arm and walked past Miren, signing, *I want to see*, again.

"No." Miren grabbed her arm but kept walking. Curiosity was overriding her fear.

One man dressed more extravagantly than his shipmates stepped down the loading dock. His coat was long and deep blue with angular patterns embroidered in golden thread—Miren had the ridiculous notion that it was somehow real gold. His fingers glinted with jewelry, and glittering threads were woven into his gnarled beard as well. He flashed a gold-toothed grin at the crowd.

"Greetings, Crescent Bay!" the man said grandly. "I am Captain Edom of *Darkcrest,* the most adventurous trading ship on the sea. Please come see our wares, the finest goods from all of Kaleo and Avi'or."

Avi'or. Miren swallowed. "Are they Avi'ori?"

Kesia glanced at her, an eyebrow raised in confusion. *He doesn't have an accent,* she signed.

"Proving nothing," Miren said. "They have wares from Avi'or."

And?

"Well, there's a war, see?"

That's not strange. Must you worry about everything?

Miren shook her head but said nothing. Though the war had officially halted trade between the two countries, there were active trade ships on both sides. Still, ships willing to risk being caught rarely bothered to come this far south.

Captain Edom continued, "We hope, in return, you'll show us your own finest quality goods."

Miren stiffened, not sure why she heard that as a threat, but already her Crescent Bay neighbors were surging forward, inviting the traders to their booths, insisting that theirs were the best hand-sewn gowns or the thickest fleece throw rugs.

Miren's fishing knife nudged her hip, light and useless like a child's toy. She felt she would more likely cut her own finger accidentally than successfully defend against these men.

Kesia made to approach one of the traders, a lumbering man with a sharp jaw, but Miren snatched her arm and held firm. Kesia glared.

"We can come back," Miren said. "I want to visit Etela's first, before the bread gets stale."

Kesia rolled her eyes. *You are cynical,* she signed.

"Come on. We probably can't afford their wares, anyway."

Miren pulled until Kesia relented, and they continued down the main road.

Just as expected, the smell of bread and butter wafted over the warm breeze. Miren smiled as she spotted the baker leaning out of her window. "Good morning, Etela."

Etela's thin face wrinkled with a smile. "Hello, ladies," she called. "I see we have a few new customers today."

"Are they?" Miren asked. "I mean—" She came closer and murmured, "Do you think they mean well?"

Etela frowned. "They seem to. We should assume they're peaceful until they prove otherwise."

Kesia signed, *Do you have bread?*

"Of course I have bread, silly girl!" Etela said cheerily. "This entire village would revolt if I did anything else with my life."

Etela produced two large loaves of bread. Kesia held out four copper coins.

"Oh no, my dear." Etela waved her hand as though offended. "These are gifts for you."

"Etela," Miren said. "That's not necessary—"

"The two of you have done an amazing job keeping that lighthouse going without your parents, and you were always the least troublesome children in the village. I don't think your mother would object to a couple loaves of bread."

Miren glanced at Kesia and suppressed a sigh. "Thank you, Etela."

Miren took the gleaming, paper-wrapped loaves as Kesia started to sign. Miren pulled her around so Etela couldn't see.

I hate that.

"I know," Miren whispered.

I feel like I take advantage of people.

"You don't. They're compassionate."

Because they think I went through something terrible.

"You did go through something terrible." Miren pulled a large chunk off one of the loaves. "Have some bread."

Kesia glowered, took the bread, and shoved it into her mouth.

Miren smirked. "Do you still want to complain now?"

Kesia slapped her arm, fighting a smile. Miren tore off another chunk—warm and soft, with hints of salted butter—for herself. Her stomach clenched. Hunger was an old, stale companion in this village.

"Do you want to go see if Cari will buy our candles? She might have honey, and you can show her your jewelry—"

But Kesia was staring ahead with an excited smile. Miren followed her gaze and groaned.

Just past the gates of the baron's estate stood a young man with a shock of straw-blond hair. He waved shyly as they turned to look at him.

Miren hooked her arm in Kesia's. "Come on, we need to sell these candles."

Kesia tugged, but not hard enough. She twisted in Miren's grip and waved back, her face flushed.

Miren rolled her eyes. "You should be glad I pulled you away. You look like a tomato."

Kesia tried to pout but couldn't hide her smile. Her infatuation with the baron's son had not waned as Miren had hoped. Davri was a Water Singer, but his noble status had exempted him from the draft. He hid on his father's estate most of the time, but Kesia would steal away to meet him.

So much about their relationship seemed reckless to Miren, but little else made Kesia smile like this. And at sixteen, marriage was a real consideration. Miren just didn't believe that Davri was considering it. She wondered what her mother would do if she were here.

"Hey!" a voice rang out. "Stop that!"

Farther down the row of booths, a group of the traders crowded the dirt road. They chuckled as one of their number—a tall, broad-shouldered man with more hair on his chin than on his head—dangled a piece of jewelry just out of Cari's reach. Pistols glinted in men's hands.

Miren froze. These were not traders.

Pirates.

The village men gathered around, looking helpless and uncertain as the pirates leveled their weapons. A few villagers hefted hammers and shovels, but most of the weapons in the village had been taken to war.

Kesia turned to face Miren. *We have to DO something.* Kesia's hands slapped together loudly on the word *do*.

"No." Miren grabbed her hands and held them. "Go to Davri and get inside."

A scream. A crash.

Jewelry spilled from an upturned table and littered the dirt road as Cari stumbled back, terror on her face. Her mother and husband surged forward, shouting, but a pirate grabbed Cari, pulled her toward him, and pressed his knife roughly against her throat.

The villagers froze as one, their feeble excitement shattered.

Then Captain Edom was there, sweeping everyone's attention to him with a grand wave of his hand. "Ladies and gentlemen, we mean no harm," he announced. "Do not interfere, and this lovely young woman will not be hurt."

Cari whimpered in the pirate's grip, flinching from the long, curved knife that he held against her neck.

Edom seemed to find confirmation in the crowd's silence. At his gesture, the crew of *Darkcrest* dispersed among the remaining booths, inspecting the goods, their pistols swinging casually in their hands.

Why, *why* had Miren left the lighthouse without her father's revolver?

"We have to get you out of here. Don't sign!" Miren shoved Kesia's hands down. "They'll see you."

Kesia glanced at the pirates, nodding vehemently in Cari's direction.

"I know." It was too late to seek refuge in the baron's estate now. That would draw attention to Kesia. "Just—stay close to me."

Slowly, subtly, Miren edged Kesia toward the nearest booth, Gilad's collection of handmade fishing hooks. Gilad caught sight of the girls and beckoned them over.

"What do we do?" Miren whispered.

Gilad shook his head, his brow pinched. "I don't know. We can't do anything."

Miren pushed Kesia around the rear of the booth. "Stay behind me," she whispered.

The pirates took their time, plucking items from booths like vultures on a carcass. A few raised their pistols threateningly or lingered over the younger women.

Another pirate, this one with lanky hair and narrowed eyes, sauntered over to Gilad's booth. He glanced at the fishhooks and snickered. "Where's the money?"

Gilad yanked the coin purse off his belt and slid it across the table, his hands shaking. "That—that's most of what I have. I mean —a few silvers in the—the house—"

The man laughed derisively and snatched the purse from the table. He glanced between the girls and eyed Miren up and down. A shiver crawled up her spine, but the pirate snickered again and ambled on. She choked back a sigh of relief, Kesia's hand tight and sweaty in hers.

The captain returned to the middle of the street, sweeping his gaze approvingly over the mess of tables and food, a proud fisherman admiring the day's catch. Behind him, Cari squirmed in her captor's grip. "What a lovely day," Edom said. "And not a single drop of blood to be seen."

Cari's husband hobbled forward on his cane. "Sir, please, let my wife go." His desperation made Miren's stomach churn.

Cari strained against the pirate's grip.

Captain Edom smiled. "I'm sorry, good sir, but she must come with us. Insurance, you see. And she'll sell well in other places."

The pirates chortled.

"*No*," Cari sobbed, struggling as her captor dragged her toward the dock.

Cari's husband waved his cane. "No! Stop!"

"*Cari!*" her mother wailed.

Other villagers shouted at the pirates, surging forward.

"Let her go!"

"We won't attack you!"

"You got what you wanted!"

But the pirates kept their weapons trained on the crowd as they made their way to the docks, and no one dared to follow.

Miren ached for Cari, but she didn't move. She could see their mother in her mind, signing, *Keep her safe, keep her safe.* She squeezed Kesia's fingers; Kesia squeezed back.

And then released.

Miren felt Kesia's hand slip away as her sister bolted down the street, past the villagers, their faces slack in confusion.

Before Miren could shout or go after Kesia, a sound erupted, a ringing Song of Fire.

Kesia's Voice, cracking with disuse, took a moment to catch. Miren felt the familiar notes warm the air, saw her sister's lips curve as she summoned heat, a biting flame, and flung it at Cari's captor.

The pirate shrieked and dropped his knife. Cari staggered away from him as he fell to his knees, slapping at his arm as flames licked his sleeve.

The Song ended, and the silence filled Miren's ears. She knew something terrible had just happened, something that would shatter the life she had constructed for herself and her sister. But her heart throbbed with Song, drowning out thought and fear.

The captain's sharp gaze darted between Kesia and his crewman. And then a smile split his features.

"Well, bless the seas," he said. "A Fire Singer."

TWO

KESIA

JOY WAS SUCH A RARE THING IN CRESCENT BAY.

There were days Kesia was happy, she supposed, days when she and Miren weren't fighting, or she had visited with Davri, or the garden had produced something edible. There were times she felt pleasant, almost content, cleaning the chicken coop and cooking dinner and polishing the lighthouse mirrors. On those days, the ocean winds didn't sting her cheeks or tangle her hair but instead made her think of seagulls and full white sails on boats.

Kesia had always known that to refuse to Sing was to deny a part of herself, to suppress the hum in her bones that her mother had taught her to listen for. She just hadn't realized—or perhaps she had forgotten—how much of herself was Fire, how much she had missed it.

She was *Singing*.

Even after all this time, she could hear it. The power rose from deep within her, living and swirling and pulsing in her chest. The notes were clearer and brighter than she remembered. It was the Song for a fireplace, a Song of home and cooking and her mother. But there was no fireplace here. Instead, she stood in front of a pirate crew, doing the only thing she could think of to save Cari.

She threw the power at the man's sleeve, and he screamed, releasing Cari.

His pain burst her focus. She broke off her Song, and the man crumpled, whimpering as he cradled his sweltering arm.

Pain—she had never thought to use her Voice for destruction. Shaken by the Song's effects, she took a shuddering breath as the bright joy inside her burned and died.

"Incredible," the captain said, his voice soft with admiration. Then he barked to his men, "Take her."

Kesia stumbled back, her throat seizing up in panic. The pirates encircled her like a pack of wolves cornering a deer, their weapons drawn. They eyed her warily, waiting for her to Sing again, ready to shoot.

Sing.

She felt a hand clutch her arm and nearly squealed a note that would've sparked, but it was Miren, her face taut with horror. "Run!" Miren screamed, and yanked Kesia away from the pirates.

Kesia sprinted up the incline toward the baron's estate as the villagers looked on with wide, disbelieving eyes.

They knew.

It was no longer a secret.

Kesia had no attention to spare for the villagers, though. She hadn't really run since she was a child. Her legs burned, her chest tightened. Miren pulled her toward the estate.

Davri—Davri would protect her.

"Open the gates!" Miren shouted.

Kesia wheezed as they ascended the steep incline.

"Someone *help!*" Miren screamed. *"Pirates!"*

Oftentimes the baron had two guards stationed at the gate, but Kesia couldn't see anyone from here. Not even Davri.

Please, Davri, she thought. *Please help me.*

Kesia stumbled and fell to her knees.

"Get up!" Miren yanked at her, but Kesia shook her head. She tried to sign, but her arms were shaking too much.

"Someone help, *please!*" Miren shouted.

But the pirates were upon them, spreading in a loose half-circle, their weapons trained on her.

Miren stepped in front of Kesia and pulled out her knife.

No! Kesia took a breath and exhaled, trying to slow her breathing as her mother had taught her, but her heart hammered against her ribs.

A few of the pirates snickered at Miren's feeble weapon. Panic pushed the air from Kesia's lungs.

"Stay *back*," Miren shouted.

Captain Edom stepped forward. "Ladies," he said gently. "Please don't make this difficult."

"You—" Miren took a breath, shoulders heaving. "You have what you came for. You've taken everything—you can't have my sister!"

"Now, my dear," he said with a smile. "I don't think you understand how much your sister is worth."

"She's sick," Miren said. "She gets winded easily, she can't even run. She's of no use to the military. They already have our mother!"

But the captain was shaking his head. "I run a business, dear," he said with a hint of impatience. "Step out of the way, or we will kill you."

Kesia gulped down air, reaching for the fire in her. She could hear the Song she wanted, but she had no breath to Sing it. *Sing, Sing, Sing.*

The knife shook in Miren's hand, but she didn't lower it. "You can't have her."

Sing, Sing, Sing.

The captain tilted his head and flicked his hand. The pirates surged forward.

Kesia raised her Voice.

The sudden note made everyone flinch away—even Miren.

Kesia cringed against the wrath of her own Song. There was

nothing comforting about this Song. Not warmth and security and *home;* this was a forest fire, a burning ship—unfamiliar to her, and yet the notes came with ease.

A wall of flame erupted between the sisters and the pirates.

Kesia raised a hand, letting the power flow unhindered for the first time in years. The fire within her danced gleefully, like a caged animal that was now free. Kesia altered her Song, and the wall pushed the pirates farther away.

Miren stumbled back from the flames. "Help us, *somebody!*"

Kesia kept Singing. Surely someone would see this, someone would come to help them.

Davri.

But the fire had nothing to cling to, so its life had to come from Kesia herself. She felt it suck the marrow from her bones and fill her head with wool. Her breathing was too shallow—the flames sputtered and died.

For a moment, the men stood gaping. She willed the world to stop tilting, her whole body shivering.

"She's tired," the captain's voice drifted over the crowd. "Take her now."

A few men marched forward, pistols raised.

Miren swung her knife in a flashing arc. The nearest pirate—a bald, portly man—caught her wrist and twisted hard, and the knife slipped from her fingers. She kicked him in the side, but he threw her to the ground and drew his pistol.

"Don't move," he warned in a gravelly voice.

The rest of the crew surged around Kesia.

Kesia gasped for air, but she had no energy left for a Song. She sobbed as hands grabbed her, hoisted her up, slapped her mouth shut, and marched her back toward the village. She tried to dig in her heels, but her captors were far stronger.

She had lost.

Kesia couldn't even turn to glance over her shoulder at Miren. *Miren, I'm so sorry,* she signed, though her hands were behind her and impossible for anyone to see. *I love you. Tell Mother.*

The road flattened as it headed toward the docks. The villagers had hardly moved, watching the scene in terror. The pirates had overpowered a Fire Singer: they could all be slaughtered.

A thump. A gasp. Footsteps pounded against the dirt road behind them, hard and fast.

"Stop!" Miren screeched.

Some of the pirates turned, and Kesia strained to see over her shoulder.

A man lay on the ground, rubbing his head. Miren was thundering down the road, her knife flashing in her hand.

How had she possibly—

"Let her go!" Miren shouted.

One of the pirates marched toward Miren, hefting his pistol.

Kesia thrashed, struggling to keep her sister in view as her captors shoved her toward the docks.

The pirate fired at Miren, but she swerved as the gunshot blasted the air. Before he could fire again, she ducked and swiped at him with her knife. He cried out and staggered back, a line of red blooming on his arm. She aimed her knife at his gut, but he was too fast. He brought the butt of his pistol down with a heavy thud, and she crumpled.

A fresh jolt of terror shot through Kesia.

The pirate standing over Miren pointed his pistol.

Kesia sobbed voicelessly.

A loud *click* drew everyone's attention. The pirate paused and looked up into the barrel of Haro's rifle.

The other pirates immediately pulled out their own weapons, but Haro didn't take his eyes off the man aiming at Miren. "Leave now," Haro said. "Leave us alone."

The sound of the waves filled the tense silence. Kesia tried to struggle again, but her captors' grips were like iron.

The captain shouted, "Let's go, boys! We're done here. No need to waste bullets."

Miren's assailant paused, his eyes trained on Haro while he holstered his own weapon. Blood trickled from the gash in his arm, and he turned away.

The other pirates continued their march toward the ship. Kesia strained to see Haro, who had dropped to a knee over Miren's still form. *Is she all right? Is she alive?*

But the pirates shoved her up the gangplank, and Miren and the village were blocked from Kesia's view.

THREE

MIREN

Pain split Miren's skull, robbed her of her breath, blackened her vision.

Kesia Kesia Kesia.

The world came and went. She blinked, and her eyes burned. Someone was shouting, holding her head. She made to push him away, but her arms weren't her own.

She blinked again, hearing the roar of waves and angry voices. She opened her eyes and looked up at a familiar beard.

"Raila, get some bandages," Haro said. "Gilad, help me get her inside."

Hands moved and scraped her back. Miren's head lolled to the side. Through half-closed eyes, she stared at the sea, where a ship's sail billowed against a bright sky.

Tears flowed before she opened her eyes again.

Kesia is gone.

The pain of it almost overwhelmed the splitting headache. Miren wanted to run into the ocean, chase down the ship that had taken her sister. But she knew the ship was long gone now. There was nothing to do.

Kesia was gone.

She had imagined the royal fleet coming and stealing Kesia, following up on the Singer who might have survived that bout of cloud fever. Or perhaps the Avi'ori fleet would invade, looking for Singers to fill their own armies.

Instead, it had been pirates. Greedy, irrelevant pirates.

Something cool and wet pressed on her forehead. She flinched.

"Lie still, sweet," a woman said. Miren pried her eyes open and saw Raila leaning over her. "You got hit on the head pretty hard."

Miren remembered. The bald pirate that she had attacked.

Attacked—she'd never attacked anyone in her life.

How would she tell her mother?

A sob grated her throat.

"Shhh, hush now," Raila crooned. "It's all right, you're all right. Haro!" she called.

Miren heard footsteps and looked up at the wooden ceiling and walls. Pillows supported her throbbing head. Raila and Haro's cabin was slightly larger than hers, or perhaps it was the carefully arranged wardrobe and the small wooden birds that Jonath used to carve that made the room feel spacious. He had enjoyed using Earth Song to control the knife. She remembered arguing with him about whether that was cheating.

Miren had not been inside this cabin since he had left.

Haro appeared, a steaming bowl of broth cupped in his rough hands. "Hey, girl," he said, his voice low. "How do you feel?"

She felt split open, raw, and bleeding, as though she'd fallen on a bed of rocks from the widow's walk of the lighthouse.

Kesia is gone.

"Fine," she whispered.

Carefully, Raila helped her sit up. Miren took the broth from Haro and brought it to her lips, realizing what a horrid betrayal it was to eat. Tears clogged her throat. She pretended to take a sip and lowered the bowl to her lap.

The couple stared at her, their eyes tight with concern.

"Is Cari all right?" Miren asked.

"Yes," Haro said, as Raila answered, "She's fine."

Miren nodded, and tears spilled from her eyes.

"I'm so sorry, Miren," Raila said, her eyes glistening.

Miren wished she wasn't crying. She wished she had lost a leg rather than her sister. She wished there wasn't so much *pain* everywhere. She wiped her eyes. *Kesia Kesia Kesia*—

A knock at the door startled them.

"Skies," Haro breathed. "Who would that be?"

Miren leaned back and closed her eyes as Haro answered the door. It was probably Cari or Etela or Gilad—someone coming to offer condolences.

The door creaked open, and the murmuring voices of men drifted from the other room.

"How *dare* you!" Haro shouted. Raila jumped in surprise.

Footsteps thudded into the room. A man appeared, dressed in a green uniform, his coat and trousers trimmed with bronze-colored thread.

The baron maintained a few guardsmen—presumably from the king's military—though Miren could not imagine a more inauspicious place to guard. She had seen this man in town on occasion, drinking with some fishermen.

"Hello, Amuel," Miren said.

"Miss Miren the lightkeeper," Amuel said in a deep voice, "the baron has summoned you to the Manor of Crescent Bay."

Miren fought a wild urge to laugh or scream. *Now* the baron would open the gates for her. Her thoughts drifted to Davri with a hiss of fury, like water over coal.

"Tell my lord that his condolences are appreciated," she said, "but I'm currently . . . indisposed."

Amuel shifted uncomfortably. "I'm afraid Lord Baron has insisted."

"She's not well," Haro cut in. "She's injured. She just lost her sister—"

"I'm afraid," the guard said, "that I have orders to take her in by force if necessary."

Haro's eyebrows shot up. "By *force?*"

This was not proper mourning. People should be bringing flowers, food, tears. The loss of Kesia was so great that surely the entire village should rally—even the baron.

"I'm being arrested," Miren guessed.

Raila gasped. "What?"

"This is absurd!" Haro said.

Miren's eyes still burned, but no tears came. "I'll go," she said. "It's fine. I'll go."

She would not fight this. She had already lost the one fight she couldn't bear to lose.

Haro and Raila stared at her. "This shouldn't be happening," Raila said. "Why would the baron do this?"

Miren pushed herself upright, her head throbbing. "I guess I'll find out."

The devastation from the pirate's attack was less than it might have been, Miren thought, as she followed Amuel to the baron's estate.

Cari was bent over her jewelry stand. She caught Miren's gaze and turned toward her. "Miren," she said, eyes brimming with tears. "I'm so sorry."

Miren shook her head, her throat tight. She knew she should say something kind, but she couldn't speak.

The gates to the baron's estate opened with a loud creak as they approached, and Miren saw two pristine guards manning their posts. Most villagers had never been inside. The gate surrounded a wide, simple lawn of grass with a few uneven flower bushes lining the path toward the mansion.

Miren followed Amuel up the steps to the front entrance. The wooden double doors opened to reveal a parlor as tall as a house, its marble walls decked with paintings.

The guard led Miren through the main hall and down a set of hallways. They passed a room with the door ajar, and her gaze drifted inside.

It appeared to be an office. A shelf full of books — *books*, a luxury unto themselves — stood against the wall, just beside a desk. At the desk sat Davri.

He and Kesia had been stealing away to see each other for months now, but Miren hadn't seen Davri up close in ages. Even seated, he was taller than she remembered. Wearing trousers, a dress shirt, and slippers, he sat, head in hands, his hunched shoulders the most defined aspect of his soft bulk.

He looked up at the sound of their approach, but Miren passed the door before their eyes met. Something hot and primal in her wanted to lash out at him, but the marble walls were oppressive, and she remained silent.

Amuel led her to a set of double doors carved with intricate swirls and patterns. He opened one and stepped aside to let her in.

Miren found herself in a heavily furnished office. Shelves lined the walls, and the floor was layered in carpets. At the desk, hands folded neatly and deliberately, sat Baron Darius of Crescent Bay.

His plump waist nudged the edge of his desk. His remaining hair made a thin, dark crown tucked behind his ears. He looked at her with a carefully constructed distance. Or perhaps that was just the rich mahogany desk between them.

The baron glanced past her and nodded to the guard. "That will be all."

The guard closed the door behind Miren with a click. Silence pressed down. Miren remained by the door.

Darius gestured to the chairs in front of his desk. "Please sit, Miss Miren."

She took her time approaching a chair. A piece of her wanted to flip the desk over or shove the papers to the floor — anything to upset the pretentious room.

Darius leaned back slowly, the cushions sighing against his weight. "First, let me give my most sincere condolences for the loss of your sister. Truly, I'm devastated that such barbarians came to our city."

Your condolences mean nothing. You don't know her name. You speak as though she's already dead.

"Thank you, sir," Miren murmured. Her head throbbed.

He leaned forward, his hands folded. "It pains me to tell you that you have been charged with treason against His Majesty for purposefully hiding the identity of a Fire Singer from the Imperial Military recruiters."

She shouldn't be surprised. She had always known the consequences of keeping Kesia's secret. She just had never considered living them. Losing Kesia had always been the end of the narrative.

Darius continued, "I'm afraid I must send a report to His Majesty, explaining what occurred today."

Miren blinked, finally paying attention. "Why?"

"It's considered treason to avoid service to —"

"No." She kept her eyes on him. "Why are you reporting it? Kesia's not here, and they wouldn't dare punish my mother — she's a Fire Singer, she's too valuable. All this does is land me in prison. Or executed." She leaned forward. "Do you want me dead, Lord Baron?"

Her anger was boiling, threatening to overflow, filling her with movement, purpose. It was a fire — insubstantial, fleeting, costly — but she clung to it.

His gaze turned hard. "We have laws for a reason, Miss Miren. Of course today has been tragic for all of us here—"

"Not for you, though." Miren hardly recognized her own voice. "You and your guards were safely locked behind your iron gates."

"These guards are a provision from His Majesty—"

"To protect your people? Or just you? Because you must be a very important man—"

"Miss Miren—"

"—to govern this tiny fishing town so far south from the capital."

"That's enough!" Darius rose to his feet, and so did Miren. "I do not enjoy this, but His Majesty has given strict orders about hiding Singers from the army. I only meant to give you a proper warning so you could set your affairs in order."

"My affairs," she echoed. "Do you mean asking someone to be the new lightkeeper, or do you mean sending letters to my parents, telling them that they have lost one daughter and are now losing the other?"

"Get out." Darius came around from behind his desk. "I won't be insulted by the likes of you."

"By a peasant girl," she corrected.

"I could have you locked up here until the royal fleet comes to take you. I could execute you myself!"

"Then *do it!*" she shouted, and for one sweeping, breathless moment, she meant it. *Do it do it do it.* Her mind echoed the words. *Kesia Kesia Kesia.*

Darius opened the door; Amuel still stood outside.

Miren slipped past the guard, her fury already dulled.

"Davri," Darius shouted. *"Come here.* I must write a letter to the king."

Further down the hall, Davri stood in the doorway of his own study.

His eyes were blue—a stunning blue, like the sky. And swollen red. They caught her gaze.

He looked just like his father, with the same full cheeks and sharp nose. Miren set her jaw and glared, willing him to read her mind, to flinch. He stared back, his gaze too open, his shoulders slumped forward in defeat.

He didn't look away until she passed.

FOUR

KESIA

KESIA OPENED HER EYES, HER HEAD POUNDING.

Pirates taking Cari, Kesia herself Singing—*Singing*—and running, Miren screaming. Miren—crumpled and unmoving on the ground, pirates shoving Kesia up the loading dock onto their ship, stuffing her mouth with a gag until she could hardly breathe, choking on her sobs.

She bolted upright and gasped in pain. Her hands were tied behind her, the rough rope cutting into her wrists. The rancid gag was still in her mouth.

The floor was hard and filthy. The only light came from a slatted door above her. A chorus of men's voices, shouting, laughing, and boots stomping, hovered over the opening. The stench was so strong that her eyes watered.

Kesia fought the urge to vomit. She leaned back and kicked against the walls of her small prison. Voices shouted warnings.

She pulled against her restraints, but they were tied so tightly that she felt the heat of scraped skin, the tingle of restricted blood flow in her fingers. Every movement stretched and twisted her muscles the wrong way.

It had finally happened.

The pirates would turn her in to the army, and she was going to fight in the war.

Nightmares of what military service would demand of her had

haunted her for years—images of burning, dying men and women, the charred wreckage of a ship. Such thoughts were easy to ignore with Miren, with Davri, in the market or the lighthouse in Crescent Bay, but they always lurked in some corner of her mind.

She knew most of the war was fought on the water, toward the northern end of the Tehum Sea. She had never been able to imagine what combat itself would look like, though, or how the Songs she had learned as a child would be useful as a weapon—yet that was exactly how she had used one today. She had aimed a Song normally meant to start a small cooking fire at a man's arm. It was jarringly simple.

And Miren—

Kesia cringed at the memory of her sister falling onto the rough ground. The strike must have been hard—what if it had killed her? No, Miren had to be all right. She was strong; she could withstand a blow to the head. But Kesia ached with uncertainty.

And Davri. Had he heard her Singing? Even if he hadn't, surely he knew by now that she hadn't lost her Voice. She pressed her forehead to her knees. This wasn't how she had wanted him to find out.

Her fear soured to resentment. Why hadn't he come? How could he not have heard Miren's shouting when he had been standing by the gate just a few minutes before? Had he gone indoors? Did he even know she was gone? Perhaps it was better this way. He might have tried to defend her with his own Song, and then they both would've been taken. No, it was better he hadn't been there.

A shadow fell over her. She craned her neck to look up the shaft. Captain Edom.

"Good afternoon, Lady Singer," he greeted her. "Welcome to my ship. I hope you enjoy the accommodations."

A few men chuckled, though Kesia could not see them. It took her a moment to understand his words; his speech pattern had changed. He pronounced certain consonants with an unfamiliar mix of harshness and subtlety, and some of the vowels were drawn out or flattened.

He had an accent.

An *Avi'ori* accent.

A new wave of fear set her heart hammering, though she didn't know what his nationality meant for her. What would the Avi'ori want with a Kaleon Singer? Did the Kaleon Crown offer bounty to anyone who brought in a Singer, even Avi'ori pirates?

"Before you attempt escape," the captain continued, "you should note that while the ship is made of wood, your prison is made of iron."

She realized the surrounding cage was indeed slick, brown grime over coarse metal. Kesia saw dried fluids, including blood, and she heaved again.

"So," the captain said, "if you attempt to Sing at all during our voyage, we will kill you. If you harm any of my crew, we will kill you. And if, miraculously, you set this whole ship on fire—" he grinned, "you drown with us."

Kesia shivered, imagining the churning waters beneath the ship, ready to swallow her.

Captain Edom raised his arms in a grand gesture of welcome. "Enjoy your time on *Darkcrest*, Lady Singer!"

FIVE

MIREN

TIME SKIPPED AND COMPRESSED AROUND MIREN; IT WARPED and shredded and pulled.

She had fled from Darius's estate, through the town, and all the way to the cabin, blinded by unshed tears and the pain splitting her skull. A few people called out to her, but she didn't stop.

She must have unlocked the cabin and stumbled inside. She sank to the floor and stayed there, a pool of misery.

When she looked up again, night had fallen like a heavy curtain. Her stomach knotted with a dull, nauseous hunger, and her throat was ragged. Her skin felt hot and dry.

Miren blinked, wondering why the world was suddenly so *there*. And then she heard it again: a knock at the door. She had always made it a point to answer the door. Another stupid, useless habit formed to shield Kesia.

Perhaps it was someone with pity for her, with condolences or a pie to convince her that they really did care, that they hadn't watched idly while —

Another knock, more insistent.

Miren pulled herself slowly to her feet. Her hand seemed to open the door of its own volition.

A young blond man stood before her.

"You," Miren said.

He winced, his gaze flitting to her and away. She imagined slamming the door, but she didn't move.

Are you all right? Davri signed.

A stupid question from a stupid boy. "Why are you here?"

He flinched again, as if he expected her to strike him. Perhaps she would.

I understand, Davri signed rapidly. *I understand why you lied to everyone. I would have done the same thing for Kesia. I'm not angry.*

His sympathy made her hands curl into fists. "Why are you here?" she asked again.

Davri reached into his bag and handed her a sealed envelope. Absently, Miren took it, the paper rough and foreign in her hands.

"What is this?" she said.

Davri signed, *The report my father wrote to the capital. He thinks I sent it with a messenger.*

Miren stared blankly at him.

The report.

The *report.*

Miren gripped it in both hands and tore it down the center. The wax seal snapped off and fell to the ground between them.

She looked up, and Davri gave a single, conspiratorial nod.

"Why did you do that?" she demanded, dreading his answer.

To protect you, Davri signed. *At least you have time now.*

"Time," she said. The concept felt particularly cruel. Time to sit and grieve. Time to wonder what she'd tell her father in her next letter. "Why?"

To leave, he signed. He looked close to tears. *So we can find Kesia.*

He paused, his eyes wide and pleading.

"Find Kesia," she echoed. "You want to . . . chase after her."

I want to go after her, he signed. *I think we can save her.*

Anger filled her stomach like bile; she felt sick with it. He wanted to *save* her. Was he hoping to be some kind of hero? Miren had been protecting Kesia for years, and yet this—this *boy* thought he somehow had an equal stake in her loss. As though his pain was anything close to Miren's.

I am a baron's son. Davri signed hastily, sensing her fury. *I can say she is exempted from the draft.*

Exempted from the draft, like he was.

The heat of her anger dissipated. "How can you do that?"

He reached into his trouser pocket and produced a ring. It was the baron's crest, a collection of five circles arranged to look like a rose, used to seal his letters in wax. Davri must have stolen it.

He truly intended to go.

Miren's pulse spiked. "Do you have a plan?"

Davri nodded. *I know the duke of the province just north of here. He will likely have connections to find out exactly where she was taken. We may need to cut a deal, but it's our best option.*

"And you can just . . . *ask* him?"

He nodded once, his brow furrowed.

He believed it was possible. He wouldn't be here otherwise.

There were holes, glaring uncertainties, a litany of ways this could go wrong. She didn't know how Kaleon nobility operated, the rules or expectations—they might be set to fail before they began. She had never left Crescent Bay. She had very little money. She might be reduced to begging at some point. She might be arrested for breaking a law she didn't even know. And the only person who was willing to help her was a soft, entitled baron's son.

But how could she stay, knowing that in some way, there was a sliver of possibility that she might see her sister again?

Kesia Kesia Kesia.

Protect your sister.

"I'll need time to pack," she said.

※

A day of mourning had left her exhausted, but now everything was in sharp, pristine focus. She flitted around the cabin in search of supplies while Davri stood at the door, shifting his weight uncomfortably and asking if he could help.

"No, I just need a minute."

The truth was that she didn't want him here, in her house. He was here because Kesia was not.

Miren hated him. But he was the only chance she had.

Can I save you? Miren thought. *Can I bring you home?*

Once she had her largest pack full of essentials—bread, jerky, candles, spark rocks, a change of clothes, money, rope, a topped-off canteen—she reached for her father's revolver, still in the desk drawer. She located bullets and powder and the leather holster that went with it and suddenly found herself thinking of her father supporting her from behind as she practiced her aim, holding her arm, Kesia jumping impatiently for her turn—

Kesia Kesia Kesia.

She looked around the small cabin, trying to consider what else she should bring without letting the barrage of memories overtake her. Her eyes landed on her mother's favorite book of recipes. She let her hand drift over the well-worn leather cover and heard the rustle of her father's last letter underneath, right where she had left it.

What would he say? What would Mother say?

Father might still be alive, but Miren's hope that Mother lived felt stale and poorly kept. Neither would be coming home soon, if ever.

Their crops would die. Their chickens might starve or be eaten by wolves. The lighthouse would never be lit.

"I have to visit someone," she said to Davri. "I'll meet you down at the beach."

It must've been past midnight, the sky thick and dark. Not a single home flickered with light, not even the manor at the top of the northern hill.

She headed to the blacksmith's house and found the bedside window in back. She tapped out the rhythm of an old fishing song her father sometimes hummed, one of her favorites.

Welcome brother, welcome home.
We've missed you these years three.
Welcome brother. Tell us of your
Love across the sea.

The window opened, and she saw Haro blinking sleep from his eyes, the tufts of hair on his head sweeping in all directions. "Miren, what are you doing?" he asked.

"I'm sorry," she said. "I need you to do me a favor. Can you water Kesia's garden? Just once in a while, to keep the plants alive. You can have the fruit, and the carrots have been good lately. Also the chickens, just feed them once a day. Or you can take them—"

"Miren," he repeated slowly, "what are you doing?"

She swallowed. To say it aloud would sound ridiculous.

"I'm going after Kesia."

"Skies and mountains, girl, that's a stupid thing to do! Are you going to leave your mother childless in one day?"

"Don't do that, Haro, I swear—" She took a shuddering breath. "Don't make this harder than it is."

"You idiot girl, how are you expecting to get her back?" he demanded, and Miren found a strange comfort in his anger. "Do you have any idea how dangerous it is? What are you planning to do?"

"You'll know by tomorrow." She didn't think she should mention Davri's involvement. "I shouldn't have woken you, but I didn't know who else—what to do."

Miren couldn't see Haro's features in the dim light. She thought of what Davri had told her: *I understand why you lied.*

"I'm sorry," she murmured again. "About keeping Kesia's Singing a secret. I didn't—I never thought—"

"Don't apologize, Miren," he said, and she thought he suddenly sounded much older. "If I were given the chance, I would've done the exact same thing. Anything to keep my boy alive."

Miren's eyes stung, aching for Jonath. She nodded.

"Perhaps if I were younger," he continued, "I'd be doing the same thing you are."

She leaned forward and placed a kiss on his bristly cheek. "Take care, Haro."

She hurried down the road, quietly humming her father's old song, its lilting melody plucking at the silence.

Welcome brother. Tell us of your
Love across the sea.

Davri stood at the very edge of the surf. He turned at her approach, his blond hair silver in the light of the moon.

He was even taller than she'd thought; she came to his nose. But he was still soft. Little work and more food than most had given him a belly and a bit of extra chin. He would be useless on this trip. She couldn't fathom how Kesia found him attractive.

It was too dark to sign, but Davri motioned for her to follow him.

"Do you have a boat ready?" she asked.

He nodded emphatically. They walked the shoreline in silence, Miren staying just a pace or two behind him.

It was one of those rare times when the sea was brighter than the town. The Southern Hills circled around the village as though herding it toward the surf, where the flat surface of water stretched out of sight.

Miren knew Kesia had dreamed of leaving. She had acted casually with her questions—*What is the capital like? Or Avi'or? Don't you ever wonder?*—but Miren often saw her staring out the window, one hand cupping her chin, the other tracing something on the table.

Miren expected Davri to lead her to a boat at the docks, although she couldn't quite convince herself that it would be right to take one of the villagers' fishing ships. No one could afford such a loss.

But Davri passed the docks and continued on, down a dip in the shore that curved around the rise where the estate sat. The shore was soaked black from the high tide. Miren's boots squelched in the wet sand, just behind Davri's footprints.

"Where are we going?" Miren whispered, the surf loud in her ears. Then she remembered he couldn't respond. "Never mind."

Davri pointed around the turn, where a small cove had come into view. In her eighteen years, Miren had never seen this cove before; it would be impossible to spot from the village. She opened her mouth to comment, but Davri's Water Song hushed her.

Water Song was different than Fire. Where Kesia's Voice would leap and flutter, Davri sang low and constant, with fewer notes and syllables and slower changes in pitch. Miren wasn't as familiar with Water Song, but she thought this one felt like reaching, or welcoming. Bringing something close.

And then she saw the boat.

It was smaller than the fishermen's boats, with a single mast in the center built for a triangular sail, which was now furled.

Set in motion by Davri's Song, the boat drifted close to them and turned to face the ocean. Davri grabbed the stern and pulled it up on the sand. He motioned for Miren to climb aboard.

She hesitated. There were a rudder and paddles—she didn't know why she was so surprised—and even some packs. Davri must have spent the whole afternoon preparing for this.

She realized she hadn't lit the lighthouse. She whirled and stared in shock. Sure enough, the tower was nearly invisible.

She had forgotten.

She had *never* forgotten before. She was occasionally late, but when she was, Kesia would take care of it without comment.

She looked back at Davri and found him staring at the lighthouse too. He turned to her and waited, his expression impossible to read in the dark.

Miren stepped forward and climbed into the boat, thinking it small and brittle against an entire sea. This was so foolish, so reckless. Her mother would set her shirt on fire for this.

It's for Kesia, Mother. I'm going to save Kesia.

Miren found a seat near the bow and tucked her pack underneath it. Davri pushed the boat forward into the surf. Too late, Miren realized that she should've done that. Not out of politeness, but because she didn't want his help.

He jumped into the boat, his trousers sloshing, and began a new Song.

This one was faster, if Water Song could be such a thing. Miren grabbed the side of the boat as she felt the current surge. The boat tipped forward, then back, then steadied. Water churned against the hull as the air brushed past her.

Miren watched the wake, surprised at their speed. The dark line of the town grew small and indiscernible from the mountains. The baron's estate sat still and bloated on its hill. The lighthouse did not glow. Before them, the Tehum Sea filled the horizon.

SIX

KESIA

MIREN, I WANT TO GO HOME.

Kesia breathed the stench of fish and grime. She cringed every time she heard a crew member approach her cage. She had caught a few cautious glances from above, brief and fleeting, but the men otherwise left her alone.

They were afraid of her.

She knew that she should use that fear. She should terrify them somehow, so she could . . . But no second step came to her. She couldn't Sing. She was trapped in a large metal box on a pirate ship, with her arms tied so tightly behind her that her shoulders screamed with pain. Her jaw ached from the gag.

She had no way to escape.

Everything Miren had worked so hard to prevent had come to pass. Her sister would live in the lighthouse, alone, waiting for her and for parents who might never come home.

Davri.

Sweet, loving Davri with the most honest face she had ever known. Even Miren kept secrets from her, but Davri was never patronizing, never lying, never cruel. His honesty was kind. She was surprised at how much she ached for him.

But he hadn't come. How could he not have known what was happening? How could he not have heard Miren's screams or her own Song? The wall of fire she had Sung had been enormous, and she knew his room had a window overlooking the bay. Where had he been?

Her thoughts drifted to her mother. As far as they knew, she was still alive. Fire Singers were rare and valuable. Perhaps Kesia would get stationed somewhere near her.

But with the thought of military service came a twisting anxiety. She had never been healthy. She had trouble breathing when she worked too hard, and her appetite was small. Miren could run and work the whole day through without pause.

She knew Miren's secret too: Miren loved to sing. Kesia remembered her sister sitting by the fire with their mother, practicing the Songs that her voice wasn't quite ready for. When she went fishing with their father, she would come back humming some new sailor's tune that he had taught her. Her voice was beautiful and rich like their mother's, except that it never made flames dance.

Kesia cried until her gag tasted of her own tears. Sleep was impossible. She tried standing once, just to stretch, and found that she could see some of the sailors shouting orders and pulling ropes. One caught her gaze, and she ducked out of sight.

Her stomach felt bitter with hunger, and her throat grated from so much crying, and she needed to relieve herself. How long would they be sailing? Days?

Toward the end of the day, a shadow fell over her cell, and she nearly choked on her gag again.

It was a boy. No older than nine, she thought, with a long, dark face and unwashed rags hanging over his lanky body. He held a block of cheese and a misshapen loaf of bread. His lip trembled as he looked down on her.

"I'm—I—" He swallowed and tried again. "I'm going to take your gag off so you can eat."

He tucked the loaf of bread under his arm and produced a ring of keys. "I'm coming down there, all right?"

Kesia nodded.

He shuddered. "Please don't kill me," he whimpered.

She ducked her head and backed into a corner as best she could to give him room, trying to look submissive and composed. The boy struggled to unlock the latch, until the door swung open with a gritty whine. His bare feet dropped down in front of her. He put the food on the floor, next to a canteen. Her throat itched in anticipation.

"I'm gonna untie your bindings now." The fear in his voice made her heart ache. "Do you promise not to burn me?"

She paused, so she wouldn't look too eager to convince him, and nodded.

"Turn around," he said.

She slowly shifted so that her arms were facing him. She heard the whisper of a knife being drawn and felt cool metal press against the skin of her wrist.

The rope fell away, and her shoulders cried out in painful relief as she brought her arms forward. She hissed a sigh through her gag, and the boy fell back, flinching away from her.

Stiffly, she signed, *I won't hurt you*—

The boy screamed and scrambled away, pressing himself against the far side of the cage. His keys clattered to the ground as he held out his hands in an odd symbol that she didn't recognize. *"Witchcraft! Witchcraft!"*

A shadow fell over her again. She looked up at the barrel of a gun pointing down on her.

"No tricks, girl!" the pirate snarled. "What's wrong?"

The boy was shaking so badly that his elbow smacked the wall of the cell. "She—she did something with her hands—"

The pirate groaned. "Ah, that's just the way they talk, boy. She don't even have the gag off yet."

Kesia nodded, suddenly desperate to win the boy's trust. Slowly, she slipped off the cloth and spit out the gag, the muscles in her jaw throbbing. She carefully reached for the canteen and drank, water streaming off her chin.

The boy handed her the loaf, and she tore into it. He remained rigid and silent until she was finished, then flinched again as soon as she looked at him. "Captain says I don't have to bind your hands, but you have to keep the gag on."

Kesia grimaced, then gave him a reassuring smile and tied the cloth around her mouth.

The boy snatched the keys from the floor and vaulted out of the cage. "I'll pick up your chamber pot later," he called back.

She curled up and buried her head in her hands, but the tears didn't come this time.

SEVEN

MIREN

THE CHILLY SEA AIR SNATCHED AT DAVRI'S VOICE. IN THE bow, Miren could feel the gurgling water shoving them forward, could sense the boat angling over a wave or tilting to skirt a current. Davri had steered them north and was now running parallel to the coast, always keeping the black ridge of land in sight. Crescent Bay was far behind them now.

Miren was almost convinced that she wasn't awake. The day would seem like a bad dream, if it weren't for the painful pounding in her head where the pirate had struck her. It felt impossible that Kesia was really gone, and Miren found herself glancing around for her, as though to ask if she had fed the chickens or heated water for tea.

It was too dark for Davri to sign, so Miren stayed tucked in the bow, angling herself as far from him as possible, even as her hip started to ache from the effort.

The sea bobbed and splashed, but Davri's Song caught most of the current. Singing did not use words, but Miren felt she could almost understand the Song. She heard the rumbling bass melody that pushed the boat up and forward. An occasional rise in tone caught the edge of a wave or halted a splash. At one point, a wave took Davri by surprise, and he had to switch to another Song to keep them from capsizing.

How long had it been since she had heard someone Sing? Four years, at least, since the Singers were drafted. She thought of the village fishermen bringing in the morning catch, the time her father's friend once trapped a seagull on the beach by Singing ice around its feet. She thought of the Air Singers clearing the bay of fog on chilly mornings, or her mother lighting a fire to boil tea. She thought of Jonath, hammering in his father's forge, his clumsy Song trying to shape molten metal into a horseshoe.

Would she have left if Davri hadn't come to her?

She couldn't picture it. She would likely have gotten up the next morning. Maybe she would have eaten, maybe she wouldn't. She would have stepped out of the cabin and heard the chickens squawk and thought of Kesia. She would have looked to the lighthouse, cold and lightless for the first night of her life, and thought of Kesia. She would have cleaned the cabin, the bowl Kesia always left on the table, the mess she made cutting carrots, the spark rocks tossed carelessly by the fireplace.

Miren turned her face into her coat and cried.

Mercifully, she fell asleep. She hadn't meant to, but she opened her eyes to a lilac sky.

Davri's Water Song still carried the boat forward, but his Voice was ragged and breathy. Miren sat upright, her back aching and her arm nearly numb. The cold sea air clung to her, but the wind that brushed past promised a warm morning.

Miren stared out at the passing water until her eyes hurt. Her back pressed to the boat's side, she watched the Kaleon coast drift past on the right, jagged precipices giving way to smooth beaches and towns with wooden buildings and roads and horses and people.

She had never left Crescent Bay before, but she had always had the notion that they were farther removed from the rest of the world than this.

Davri sat hunched in the stern, his arm on the rudder, his mouth still moving in Song. His eyes caught hers only briefly before an oncoming wave demanded his attention. He shoved against it so it lapped harmlessly against the hull.

He had Sung through the night.

Miren almost cried out in surprise but caught herself. She had never heard of such a thing. Singing took much from the Singer; even those who served as fishermen worked no longer than a few hours, and no Singer was expected to use his Voice continuously for that time. Perhaps Davri had taken breaks, although she didn't think so. His tone was low and hoarse with fatigue.

Her memory flew back to that fateful Skyflame, when Davri had first managed to Sing ice.

She did not want to be impressed.

"You can stop," she said, her voice harsh against his Song. "I can sail from here."

Davri shook his head, but the Song faltered anyway. The churning water stilled underneath them, and the boat began to drift.

Give me a moment, Davri signed.

"Fine. I'll get us to shore." She scooted to the next bench and reached to untie the sail.

But Davri was still shaking his head.

"I can get us there," she insisted. "We can stay at an inn or something, right?"

She had to make it a question because she wasn't sure how exactly inns worked, or, more important, how much they cost. The people of Crescent Bay had currency, but they rarely used it among themselves.

Davri held up a hand.

"Why don't we stop?" She gestured at the shore, where there was a town in sight. "We're not going to get all the way to the capital in one day."

He shook his head. *Need to find a lord of Fourth Circle.*

Miren didn't know what that meant. "Where will we find one?"

Davri spelled out a name.

"Isakio," she said aloud.

He nodded.

"I don't know where that is."

Davri pushed himself upright and reached for one of his packs. She noticed that he had brought several, all of them stuffed to the brim and tied shut. She felt unprepared in comparison, but there had been nothing else in the cabin for her to bring.

He pulled out a long scroll of parchment and unrolled it.

It was a map of Kaleo and Avi'or. She only knew because her father had once shown her something similar, but it had been made of crinkled paper and smeared ink. This was artwork: countries and towns were labeled in complex calligraphy, with watery paints casting different areas in greens and browns and grays. It even included the cliffs that surrounded both countries. The Tehum Sea, the long body of water that split the two countries from north to south, featured a caricature of a Kaleon ship sailing across deep blue paint. Faint gold circles were drawn over Kaleo, starting at the capital to the north and spreading from there, each labeled in turn from first to fifth.

Davri pointed at a town toward the southern end of the map. *We go here,* he signed.

A small dot near the coast was labeled: *Isakio.* Instinctively, Miren ran her eye farther south, but there was nothing labeled beyond that. "Where is Crescent Bay on this?"

Davri pointed down the coast, closer to her. She could see now that there was indeed a curved bay that would have been her home. It was in the gold ring labeled *Fifth.*

"So we're likely here now?" She pointed just north of that, along the coast.

He nodded.

"Why isn't Crescent Bay labeled?" she asked.

Fifth Circle city, he signed. *This map was made for Second Circle family.*

Miren didn't understand how that was an explanation, but Davri was blinking rapidly to keep his eyes open.

"All right, fine. Then we keep going." Miren started rolling up the map, being careful with it. "I'll sail. You sleep. We'll trade off later."

Davri nodded and slipped the map back in its pack. He pulled out a small loaf of bread from another pack, broke it in two, and handed a piece to Miren.

"I have to sail." Miren wrapped the line around her hand.

Davri frowned. *Have you eaten?*

Miren didn't answer, but her stomach felt tight and acidic.

Davri signed with both hands, *Stop mourning. We'll find her.*

"Don't you—" Miren caught herself. "Don't act like we're going through the same thing right now."

He narrowed his eyes but didn't reply.

Miren moved on, tugging at a thought that had been nagging at her. "Does it seem odd that the military would be willing to do business with pirates?"

What do you mean? Davri signed.

"The pirates want the Singer's bounty, right? They'll have to strike a deal with some military officials, won't they? Or else where would they go?"

Davri frowned. *I'm not sure.*

"You're not *sure?* I thought you had a plan!" Panic fluttered in her chest.

I do! Davri slapped. *We're going to find the lord of Isakio of the Fourth Circle. He will have the connections to find her.*

Miren groaned, her initial doubts returning full force. This wasn't a plan—it was a desperate gamble. Nothing short of a miracle was going to find Kesia. So why was she here now?

Because I made a promise, she thought. *Because I need a miracle.*

"Fine," she said, untying the lines that held the sail in place. "Go to sleep."

He started to sign, but she refused to look at him as she pulled the sail taut, and soon he settled on the packs and began snoring.

Perhaps two hours later, she heard a faint crack of thunder drift across the water.

The sky was clear, save for a few mountainous clouds floating by, but if she squinted against the morning sun, she could make out a few ships on the horizon.

Miren's heart rate spiked—a naval battle? She thought the war was fought much farther north. She almost kicked Davri awake, but what were the odds the warships would make their way closer?

She reached for her pack and pulled out a carrot. It seemed that she was no longer mourning. Did that mean she thought it was possible to save Kesia? She didn't know.

When Davri finally stirred, the afternoon sun glared angrily above them. Miren yanked on the line with a grunt.

He sat up, rubbed his face, and looked around. The coast hadn't changed much, though the towns had started to appear with greater frequency. *Where are we?* he asked.

"I don't know," Miren said. Her neck had grown stiff from looking over her shoulder. "How far is this city?"

Davri fumbled for the map. Miren gripped the rudder, already annoyed that he hadn't offered to Sing the rest of the way. It was a full two minutes before he lowered the map and signed, *Very close.*

"Wonderful." Miren glanced back over her shoulder, pain biting her neck again.

Without comment, Davri began Singing, and the boat surged toward the shore. Miren dropped the sail.

The familiar cragged green hills continued along the west but stretched farther away as they came north, looking smaller. She and Davri were sailing toward a town set on uneven land. A road ran parallel to the coast, rising and falling.

The boat passed a couple of docks, where fishermen and women tied their own boats and lowered sails and hauled in their nets. A few people glanced at them curiously, and Miren ducked her head, suddenly nervous. How odd they must look, coming into the docks with their sail already down. All Singers should be in the military, shouldn't they? Would someone report them?

But Davri didn't seem worried. Would he have to prove his exemption from the military? She didn't interrupt his Song to ask.

A lilt in the Song, and the boat turned toward one of the few open docks. Fisherfolk stared at them as they approached, but most soon returned to their own work. Davri angled the boat so Miren could jump on the dock and tie them up.

She watched him stumble, exhausted, under the weight of three packs. She thought of reaching to help him, but instead she just waited. He pulled himself clumsily onto the dock and stood, taking an extra step to steady himself.

I must change clothes, he signed. He reached into the boat and dragged out yet another pack, pulling out a crumpled dress shirt and long trousers.

He threw them over what he was wearing. He wasn't undressing, but Miren turned to face the other direction anyway. The rest of the town seemed busy. Past the line of dock houses, people and horses and carts passed one another on a well-worn dirt road. The faint shouts of merchants drifted toward them, unintelligible at this distance.

"I don't see how talking to nobility is going to help," Miren said over her shoulder. "What noble is going to know anything about pirates? We should speak to the people in the town."

Since she was facing away, he wasn't able to answer. Feeling petty, she continued, "Unless it's really considered common for people of rank to make dealings with pirates. If that's the case, I suppose I shouldn't be surprised—"

A hand clapped on her shoulder. She whirled, about to protest, but Davri signed, *This is the way things are done.*

He strode ahead of her, carrying his packs. She clenched her jaw for a moment before following.

The town itself—if this really was what qualified as a town— was, in Miren's estimation, a more crowded, larger village.

The main road she had spotted from the docks was just one of many. Other paths split off from this one, narrowing or turning out of sight. All along the roadside were buildings—wooden structures that shrugged against each other like people in an overcrowded room. Men and women yelled from beside booths of fish and produce and other items, competing for the passing crowd's attention.

Though they were farther north, the people she saw seemed just as shabby as her neighbors in Crescent Bay. They wore hand-stitched trousers and shirts and dresses, dusty boots of faded leather, wide-brim hats that drooped from use.

Miren had never seen so many people in one place before.

She followed Davri hesitantly, not sure how wandering eyes would perceive them. Did nobility often roam the streets with the rest of the common folk? Shouldn't he have servants or guards flank-ing him, not some village girl in trousers?

She realized too late that she had been trusting him to know what to do, and now she regretted her stupidity as well as his. "We shouldn't be doing it this way," she murmured to him.

He glanced at her, then looked away. Perhaps he was nervous to sign around here.

Miren fell back into step behind him. Merchants boasted of their goods as they passed. People jostled them aside without apology. Rau-cous laughter tumbled out of a nearby pub. A horse relieved itself in the middle of the road.

They crossed the street and turned a corner. Miren bumped into Davri, who had paused as a woman carrying a basket of corn passed in front of them. He looked down at Miren, a question in his eyes.

"Where are we going?" she hissed.

Davri gave her a hard look and pointed.

The road they were on wound upward and to the left, farther from the coast. At the crest of a small hill, she saw a gated estate.

"We have to go there?"

Davri shrugged, as though to say, *What did you think we were doing?*

She shook her head, embarrassed and frustrated, and followed Davri.

The crowd thinned as the road grew steeper. The estate was larger and better built than Darius's. A fully gated spread of green surrounded a mansion of off-white walls and dark trim.

A couple of uniformed guards watched them approach, looking impassive. Shouldn't Davri have a carriage of some kind? Should he have sent word of their coming?

The guards conferred, and one came forward. "Can we help you?" he said.

"Excuse me, sir," she blurted, before Davri could sign. "This is Davri, son of Baron Darius of Crescent Bay. We would like an audience with the duke at his earliest convenience."

The guard stared at her for a long moment. She glanced at Davri, wondering if she had somehow offended, but he was looking at the guard with a pleasant, expectant smile on his face.

"The duke is not receiving visitors this evening," the man said.

"This is an emergency," Miren said. "If you could just announce us—"

"The duke will not be able to see you tonight," he said. "You may write him a letter of request explaining your difficulties, and he may respond within the next moon."

Miren took a step. "Sir, this is the son of a baron. We're not—he is of noble blood—"

Before she could stop him, Davri signed, *As the son of Lord Darius of Crescent Bay, I wish to speak with Lord Cheliem. Please announce my arrival.* He then raised his hand to show his father's gold signet ring.

The guard's eyebrows shot up, and Miren's heart pounded. Would they believe him, or could they just arrest Davri now and take him in for avoiding the draft? Should they start running?

"I will announce you," said the guard who had spoken first. He nodded to his comrade and marched up to the mansion.

Miren glared at Davri, but his serene expression didn't shift. The other guard was still staring at them. *This was a bad idea,* she thought, but there was nothing to do but wait.

The minutes ticked by; Miren fought the urge to pace. The sun was already ducking behind the western cliffs, and the wind from the bay carried a chill. She was well into a silent rant about the rudeness of all nobility when the guard returned. He motioned to his counterpart, and the gate opened with a screech of metal.

"The duke will receive you in his parlor," the guard said. "This way, please."

The gate creaked, and they followed him inside.

EIGHT

MIREN

A BRICK PATHWAY LED INTO A LARGE, CIRCULAR COURT-
yard with a stone fountain in the center, a sculpture of a robed woman
pouring a never-ending stream of water. Rose bushes lined the sides
of the path.

The guard led them through the courtyard to the estate itself:
a sprawling building of marble and polished wood. Great pillars
framed the entryway, and windows taller than Miren glimmered
along the walls.

Heavy double doors gave way to an immaculate marble hall, its
simplicity elegant in comparison to Darius's desperate clutter. The
guard opened a door and beckoned them into a room furnished with
green and gold couches and a large matching throw rug. Miren felt
out of place.

She carefully took a seat on one of the couches, its cushion dipping farther than seemed possible. Davri took a chair beside her. He
was straight-backed, his hands folded in his lap as his elbows rested on
the arms of the chair. His posture was clearly practiced. Miren tried
to straighten her own back, but the couch refused to accommodate.

A woman wearing a green-and-white gown entered the room.
Her long blond hair was neatly braided, and she carried a tray laden
with a porcelain teapot and cups. She couldn't be more than ten years
older than Miren. Perhaps she was the lord's wife, but Davri hardly

looked at her as she set down the tray and began pouring tea. She silently handed a cup to each of them.

"Thank you," Miren said.

The woman paused, then ducked her head in acknowledgment and quickly left the room, leaving the tea.

Davri signed with one hand, *Shouldn't talk to servants.*

"At all?" Miren said quietly. "Not even to say 'thank you'?"

Davri nodded. *Only when you are making a request.*

"That is so . . ." Miren searched for a word that properly expressed her distaste. "Entitled."

Davri shrugged noncommittally and sipped his tea.

Miren took her cup from the saucer; it felt so delicate that she thought it might break in her hand. Faint paintings of faded roses surrounded the white porcelain, and a polished yellow rim covered the top. "Is this *gold?*"

Davri winced. *Too loud,* he warned. *Yes, it's most likely gold.*

She turned the cup to see if the gold went all the way around the rim. It did. She put the teacup back in its saucer.

A few minutes later, a door opened.

Davri got to his feet, motioning for Miren to stay seated.

A man strolled into the room, his small eyes set in a serene face, his light reddish hair swept to one side, his short beard neatly trimmed around a square jaw. He wore a sleek coat of deep blue with matching trousers and polished black dress shoes.

Everything about him suggested ease. His gaze flitted between the two of them. Miren felt a flash of shame at her appearance. This must be Lord Cheliem.

He held out his hand. "Davri! How good to see you! I almost didn't recognize you. How is your father doing? Does he still take the boat out?"

The two shook hands, which delayed Davri's response. *Thank* you, *Lord Cheliem*, he signed. *He doesn't take the boat as much these days, but he still fishes when he can.*

Miren had never once seen Darius in a boat.

"Always had far more patience than I did," Cheliem said. "We started after that rail system when you came to my hip, and now look at you!"

Thank you, Davri signed. *Father was quite looking forward to those tracks as well, but it seemed unlikely the Crown would choose to carve through that southern range.*

"Yes, it was a shot in the dark." Cheliem's attention jumped to Miren as though he had just noticed her. "Who have you brought with you, Davri?"

Davri ducked his head and signed an apology. *This is Miss Miren of Crescent Bay, from the family of lightkeepers.*

Cheliem extended a hand. Miren took it, expecting to shake as Davri had, but the lord held it gently and bowed. "A pleasure to meet you, Miss Miren."

"And you, Lord Cheliem," Miren said. "Thank you for seeing us unexpectedly."

"Oh, it's no trouble." Cheliem straightened and released her hand, then took a seat across from Davri. "Though I'm sorry you missed dinner. I take it the journey wasn't terrible?"

"It was about as expected," Miren said, looking to Davri. It likely wasn't wise to tell him they came via sailboat.

Davri signed, *Truthfully, we came as quickly as we could. We have an urgent matter to discuss with you.*

Cheliem's expression didn't change as he poured a cup of tea. Miren worried for a beat that he didn't believe Davri. Had Cheliem missed the word *urgent*?

Davri raised his hands to sign, but Cheliem was intent on stirring his tea. Davri folded his hands in his lap.

"I see," Cheliem finally said, setting the spoon on the saucer.

This is not about my father's estate, Davri signed quickly. *I come with a personal request.*

"Ah," Cheliem said. "What is your request, then?"

"It is on my behalf, I'm afraid," Miren said. Both men's heads swiveled to her, Davri's expression alarmed. "Davri is doing everything he can to help me find my sister. She was taken from home, you see."

Cheliem's eyebrows lifted slightly. "I am sorry to hear that."

"I wasn't sure about bothering someone of your station for this, but Davri insisted that you have the . . . the connections to help."

"Hmm." Cheliem nodded. "Well, I might be able to do something, but I'll need more. Who took your sister?"

Davri jumped in. *Pirates. They have likely taken her for the bounty on those who avoid the draft.*

"Ah. Your sister is a Singer?" Cheliem said to Miren.

"Yes, but she isn't physically fit for service," she said quickly. "She has difficulty breathing, and she can't exert herself too much —"

"Well, that's for the military recruiters to decide, I'm afraid," Cheliem said smoothly. "Has she been exempted from service?"

Of course this man isn't going to help us, Miren thought. These people with their titles and their sprawling estates and their army of servants and field workers would never inconvenience themselves for someone they didn't know. Darius was the same.

Kesia Kesia Kesia.

She was ready to stand and leave right then, but the room had gone quiet because Davri was signing.

She is my betrothed.

Miren didn't immediately understand.

Betrothed.

Betrothed.

It wasn't true — no matter their differences, Miren knew Kesia would never make such a decision without telling her first. And, Miren decided with sudden vitriol, Kesia's betrothed shouldn't be *him*.

"Your betrothed," Cheliem said, and the disbelief in his voice brought Miren back to attention. "Is this true?"

"It is," Miren said, not looking at Davri, and resenting the necessity of supporting his lie. "It's fairly recent, actually." She forced herself to smile. "My sister didn't want to tell me right away."

We hadn't yet sent out the papers, Davri added. He did not look at Miren. *The bounty hunters took her by force.*

"Well, that is their job, isn't it?" Cheliem said.

Davri pressed on. *Do you know anyone who can help us find her? Preferably before the Crown spends money on a bounty.*

Cheliem set his tea down. "Well, this is a bit of a predicament, isn't it?"

There was a pause, as though he genuinely expected an answer. Miren glanced at Davri, who was looking pale.

We would not be here if we could do this ourselves, Davri signed.

"I'm sure that's true," Cheliem said amicably.

Miren looked between the two men, not understanding. Davri shifted uncomfortably in his chair and signed, *Of course, my father would be happy to compensate you.*

"Oh, that's not necessary," Cheliem said. "I'm sure your father and I can work something out. Perhaps direct funds to building that railway we always wanted, huh?"

Davri nodded, still looking a little sick. *I'm sure we can work something out.*

"Wonderful." Cheliem pushed himself to his feet. "Well, why don't I set you each up with a room? I will have some food brought up to you. And maybe hot water for baths?"

He looked at Miren as he spoke; her cheeks flushed with embarrassment.

He rang a small bell, and the blond servant appeared in the doorway. "Please show these two to the guest quarters."

Miren and Davri silently followed the woman back into the entrance hall, up a flight of curved stairs, and down hallways of lush red carpet and dark walls. Oil lamps flickered mutely from their sconces. An occasional window revealed a darkening sky of light purples and blues.

The woman finally stopped in front of two adjacent rooms, each with light blue walls and a large bed overflowing with soft pillows and bedcovers. Windows opened over a field of crops, now little more than an indistinct sea of shadows.

Miren looked at the servant, remembered that she shouldn't speak to her, then decided that was a stupid rule. "Thank you," she said.

The servant blinked at her, then nodded silently.

Miren watched her walk away and tried to remember the way back to the parlor. She wasn't even sure where she was in relation to the front of the estate.

Davri walked into the first room and flopped on the bed. Miren stayed in the doorway, watching him.

"Was that how things were supposed to go?" Miren asked.

Davri threw his hands up in a shrug. *I suppose it could have been worse.*

"Is he really going to help us?"

He'll send letters. That is all he can do.

"But you had to offer to pay him to do it?"

Davri sat up, looking dejected. *I didn't want to pull my father into it, but it was natural that Cheliem would expect some kind of compensation.*

Miren didn't understand his frustration. "Your father has money, doesn't he?"

It will be fine. He leaned down to unlace his boots.

"You called Kesia your betrothed," she blurted.

Davri nodded, but didn't look up from his boots, his hands busy with the laces.

After a few seconds he signed, *In order to get Kesia out, she needs to be exempted from the draft. To say we're betrothed is the best option. Most believable.*

"Most believable," Miren echoed. "And you . . . you didn't tell me."

Davri furrowed his brow. *It was the only way to make her eligible for the exemption.*

"And after this," she said, "after we find Kesia . . . do you . . . intend . . . is that what you're hoping for?"

Davri frowned. *What do you mean?*

"You want to marry my sister."

I do.

"Have you talked to Kesia about it?"

He jutted his jaw out in exasperation or frustration, she wasn't sure which. *No, we haven't discussed it.*

"But you want to? You want to marry her?"

Yes.

"And she wants to marry you?"

I don't know, Davri signed slowly. *We have not discussed it.*

Miren nodded. Kesia had never said anything about marriage. Had she not considered it, or had she been keeping it to herself, knowing that Miren wouldn't like it? Perhaps she had wanted to wait for their parents to return from the war before she made such a decision. Would Davri's family even approve of the union?

Miren took a breath. "So what is your plan, then?" she demanded, more loudly than she'd intended. "Are you going to become a farmer? A fisherman? Or would Kesia come to live at your father's estate?"

Davri looked at her sharply. *I would rather not talk about this now.*

"Why? These are genuine concerns—"

And I would rather talk to Kesia about it first before I discuss it with you.

Miren opened her mouth and shut it. She wished this conversation wasn't happening. She wished she had never left Crescent Bay. She wished Kesia was here to tell her what she wanted.

She retreated to her room and closed the door.

It felt as though she was losing Kesia all over again. Davri wasn't too young, but he was immature. Too soft. Too ignorant.

He did not deserve Kesia. Of that she was certain.

A few minutes later, someone knocked. Miren was about to yell something obscene, but she realized that it might not be Davri. Slowly she opened the door.

The blond servant stood just behind a wheeled cart that held several metallic domes.

"Dinner, miss," the woman said.

"Oh." Miren opened the door wider to let her in.

The cart smelled of unfamiliar spices and butter and freshly grilled fish. Miren's stomach twisted painfully. Since Crescent Bay, she hadn't eaten much more than a half loaf of bread, a carrot, and some jerky.

The servant brought the cart into the room and uncovered each plate: grilled salmon in a light pool of yellow sauce, a medley of cooked vegetables, sliced bread and butter, a tall glass of swirling amber liquid.

Mounds of food—Miren couldn't fathom the amount of time it had taken to prepare so much.

"I'll have the—the fish, please." Hopefully Davri wouldn't complain about getting the vegetables.

The servant woman blinked. "That is your dinner, miss."

"This is *all* for me?"

The woman nodded. "Yes, miss."

Miren stared at the plate. It was enough to feed her and Kesia for a day.

"I won't be able to finish it," Miren said.

"That is fine," the woman said. "Just eat what you like."

Miren hoped that whatever she didn't finish would not be wasted.

"Thank you." Miren picked up the fork—cold and polished and weighty—and held it over the fish.

The woman was still standing by the door.

Miren didn't enjoy the prospect of being watched while she ate. "Um, you don't have to wait there."

The woman raised her hands. *Crown's Guard will come for Singer,* she signed. *Run north tonight.*

Miren blinked, confused. "What?"

"Enjoy your meal, miss." The woman bowed her head and slipped from the room.

NINE

MIREN

MIREN SAT, FROZEN. BY THE TIME SHE THOUGHT TO OPEN the door and ask for an explanation, the hall was empty.

Crown's Guard coming for the Singer? For Davri?

Cheliem had never intended to help, she realized. He had just wanted to keep Davri here long enough to be arrested. The Crown's handsome bounty for a Singer was an impressive sum—even for a lord, apparently.

Miren ran to Davri's room and wrenched open the door.

Davri sat over a cart like hers, laden with more food than any one individual could eat in a single night. Miren felt a pang of jealousy—how many times in her life had she gone to bed hungry? She couldn't imagine knowing that there would always be food available.

Davri looked up, his expression wary.

"Davri, listen," she said, keeping her tone even. "The servant who brought me food said that we should leave tonight."

Davri frowned. *Cheliem sent word?*

"No, she was warning me. She said the Crown's Guard are coming for you."

Davri paused in his chewing. *Crown's Guard are coming here?*

"Yes," Miren said. "She said to escape north."

Why would she say such a thing?

"Why would she lie?" Miren said impatiently. "We need to get out of here."

Davri shook his head as he wiped his mouth. *Cheliem will sort it out.*

"Unless Cheliem invited them. What if he wants to turn you in for the bounty?"

Davri raised an eyebrow. *Is that what the servant said?*

"Why would the Crown's Guard be coming unless Cheliem summoned them?"

Maybe someone saw me signing in town.

"Then why would the servant warn me about it?" Miren couldn't hide her exasperation. "What if Lord Cheliem wants to collect the bounty on you?"

There is no bounty on me. Davri's brow was pinched. *I am exempt.*

"But if he takes your father's ring, you won't be able to prove that. You would just be another Singer avoiding the draft." Miren felt her heart begin to race as she realized how plausible it sounded. "Your father doesn't even know we're here."

Davri tossed his napkin on the cart and stood. *If we sneak out in the middle of the night, we will lose our chance to help Kesia. No other lord is going to help us like Cheliem is.*

"And if you're wrong and you get arrested, how will I find Kesia alone?" But she wondered briefly if she really *did* need Davri's help.

Another part of her mind reminded her that Kesia cared for him.

You are being cynical, Davri signed.

"Why would Cheliem keep his word?" Miren said. "Why would he care to help?"

Because he can. Because that is his duty as a lord.

"Because you promised that your father would pay him. Maybe he knows that a bounty would pay better."

That is not how nobility works.

Miren threw her hands up. "What does that mean? Nobles are surely as greedy as everyone else."

Davri looked away, a muscle twitching in his jaw. *I would like to finish my meal,* he signed.

For some reason, Davri's irritation had curbed Miren's own. "Fine. Good night," she said. She closed the door behind her and returned to her room, where the scent of butter and fresh fish awaited her. The servant had said to leave that night, but she might as well eat.

Miren tore a piece of bread from the loaf and shoved it into her mouth. Had the servant meant for them to leave as soon as it grew dark? Or later, when everyone was asleep?

She ate without tasting, though her stomach protested the rich food. Why had the woman told her this? What did she have to gain? And why specify north? Why not east, toward the docks, where they might find a boat? What did the woman know?

The sky outside her window was nearly black now. Despite Davri's insistence otherwise, Miren found that she didn't trust Cheliem, but she would never convince Davri of that without more details. She needed to speak with the servant again.

She stood, her stomach churning, and a faint light caught her eye.

Outside the window, a fire was burning.

She blinked and rushed to the window. A flicker of firelight was slowly growing around the far end of the cropland. She bolted for the door but paused, spotting her pack on the floor by the bed. Should she bring it? Had the servant told Miren to run north because she knew there would be a fire? Was this part of some larger plan? Nothing about being in this place felt safe. She stared at the pack. If she was wrong and they were caught sneaking from the estate, they would ruin their chance of getting help from Cheliem. But did he actually intend to assist them?

It didn't matter anymore. She threw her pack over her shoulder and ran next door.

Davri was still seated in front of his food, his plates almost cleared.

"Look outside." Miren threw open his curtains. "The crops are on fire."

Davri frowned, as though considering whether she might be lying.

"Look," she repeated, gesturing at the window.

He dabbed his mouth with a napkin and placed it carefully on the table. She held the curtain open and watched his expression fall.

What's happening?

"I don't know."

Do you think that servant set the fire?

"I don't *know*, but we need to leave now." Miren reached for two of Davri's packs and pushed them against his chest. As he fumbled to catch them, she grabbed a third pack and slung it over her other shoulder.

Davri was lingering at the window, a crease in his brow.

"Davri," she snapped. "Are you listening?"

I can put out the fire.

"What? *No.* We need to go now."

I can sing water over it, he signed, not looking at her as he dropped the packs and pulled out a coat. *I'll be back.*

He marched out the door.

Miren bit back a groan. She should let him go. She *wanted* to let him go. He was too naive to be helpful, with or without his noble status. She would be better off alone.

But she could imagine too well Kesia's protest. *Please don't leave him,* she would sign, fighting tears.

Miren groaned. Only for Kesia.

She ripped open Davri's packs. One held dress clothes, folded and rolled carefully. Another was packed with food wrapped in paper. The third held the map, some rope, and a jangling purse of what had to be coins. She stuffed as much food as she could into the third pack and took it with her.

She ran down the hall and caught up with Davri, who was walking brusquely toward the front parlor.

He glanced at her. *Don't bring the packs.*

"Don't go out the front entrance! The servant said north."

What if Lord Cheliem sees you with that? He'll think we're trying to leave.

They turned a corner, and Miren spotted the top of the stairs that led down to the main entrance. "You're not listening to me," she said. "Why would that servant lie?"

Noblemen rely on each other, Davri signed. *It's a delicate power balance between the aristocracy and the Crown. We rely on—*

They came to the stairs and froze.

At least eight Crown's Guard were gathered at the foot of the curved staircase, distinct in their black uniforms with the royal insignia sewn in their shoulders: a four-pointed star set in a single white circle. Each guard wore a pistol at his hip.

In front of them stood Cheliem.

Miren's heart jumped into her throat.

The men fell silent as they noticed Miren and Davri. One guard signaled to Cheliem, who turned and glanced up at them.

"Davri," Cheliem greeted cheerfully. "Is there something I can help you with?"

Davri signed, *Why are there Crown's Guard here?*

Cheliem sighed. "Davri, we live in challenging times. This war has taken much from all of us. Avi'or is a difficult enemy. The only way we can keep up with them is through the service of Singers, and those are growing scarcer every year. Your father confided in me years ago that he would have liked you to join the war effort. Don't you want to serve your country?"

Davri's hands were shaking, but the rest of him was stone-still.

Miren willed him to sign something—anything, but he just stood there.

Every muscle in Miren's body begged her to run.

"Lord Cheliem," she blurted. "Your field is on fire!"

"I beg your pardon?" Cheliem sounded amused.

"We saw it from the windows."

The guards glanced at each other, but Cheliem remained motionless, his eyes trained on Miren. "I'm not sure what you're doing, Miss Miren, but—"

"Sir!" One of Cheliem's own guards burst into the room. "Sir, the crops are burning!"

Cheliem blinked. *"What?"*

"Yes sir, the northern end of the field has caught fire."

Horror rippled across Cheliem's features. He glared at Miren. "That's—what—what did you do?"

"I didn't—" she started.

"You lot!" He gestured to the Crown's Guard. "Get water. My crops are on fire! Get to the well out back. Wake the servants, we have to—we need to—"

Miren shoved Davri's shoulder. "Come on."

He didn't resist, and the two took off, sprinting back the way they had come.

She dashed left, then right, looking for another flight of stairs. A hand grabbed at her, and she tore away. But it was Davri, trying to get her attention. *This way*, he signed, pointing down a hallway they had just passed.

They ran, the lush carpet muffling their footfalls, both packs bouncing on Miren's shoulders. She knew coming here had been a long shot for finding Kesia, but everything had gone wrong so quickly.

A staircase appeared at the end of another hall. They thundered down into a large room with white walls and a huge table in the center —a kitchen. Miren launched herself at the opposite door.

They were outside. The cool night air was heavy with the smell of smoke, with distant shouts of panic and flickers of light. Far to the left, she saw people hurrying between what looked like a well and the field where the fire was. She looked to the right and saw a hint of movement, a flash of something light-colored—hair?

The figures—there were more than one, she thought—darted into a line of trees and disappeared from view.

"There!" Miren ran after the figures in the trees, with Davri on her heels. She was certain now that the fire had something to do with the servant's cryptic warning and that she and Davri were caught up in someone else's plan. She didn't know who they were, or what their plan was, but at least they *had* a plan. And it led away from the estate.

She pushed through the brush under the trees and heard Davri do the same. They were finally out of view of the estate.

"Hello?" Miren called softly.

Two people huddled together in the small, dark clearing in front of them. One of them held a child in his arms. The other was the servant who had warned Miren to escape.

"You—" Miren gasped.

"Don't move," said a voice to their left.

Miren and Davri whirled around. A figure stood about ten paces away, obscured in heavy shadows. A faint gleam of metal flashed as Miren heard the fateful click of a safety catch. A pistol.

TEN

MIREN

RAISE YOUR HANDS."

Miren froze. The voice was a woman's—husky, older perhaps.

"Liviya," the servant said. "You don't need to—"

"These two followed you," the older woman said. The pistol flashed again as she gestured to Miren and Davri. "I told you to raise your hands. Arten, Hana, keep going. Get your hands up!" she barked at Davri. He was trying to sign, but there wasn't enough moonlight to see. He raised his hands over his shoulders.

"We're not chasing you," Miren said. "We're trying to escape too."

The blond woman—Hana, Miren assumed—stepped forward. "Liviya, I told them to leave. Cheliem was going to turn him in for—"

"You *told* them?" Liviya snapped.

"They were going to be arrested—"

"Mother," the man said in a deep voice. "We have to go."

A distant shout from the estate caught their attention.

"Skies," Liviya hissed. She glanced between Miren and Davri and stowed her weapon. "Don't follow us." She ducked into a run and left the clearing, the others close behind.

Miren hesitated, but she and Davri didn't know this area, and it seemed that Liviya did.

"Come on," she muttered to Davri as she bolted after the group. They dove back into the underbrush.

As soon as they caught up, Liviya reached for her gun again. "I said don't follow us."

"Liviya, please," Hana said.

Miren kept her tone level. "Or what, you'll shoot us and draw their attention? We just want to escape."

"Mother, we have to *go*," the man—Liviya had called him Arten—repeated.

"They aren't a threat," Hana said.

Liviya didn't reply, but she took her hand from the weapon and kept running.

Davri caught Miren's arm, but she shrugged it off. "We don't know where we are, and we have nowhere else to go," she said. "These people have a plan and may know a place to hide."

The farther they ran, the thicker the woods became. The ground was rocky and uneven. The man took the lead, weaving through the trees and underbrush. Branches raked at Miren's clothes and face like claws.

They were heading north and perhaps slightly west, she thought, though it was hard to be sure when she couldn't see the stars. She tried to recall Davri's map. Were they moving farther from the coast?

The woods abruptly gave way to sprawling grassland washed in deep blues from the moonlight. The land dipped and fell gradually. Faint flickers of firelight marked a distant town.

A murmuring rose in volume in front of them, and Miren saw a river. Liviya turned left and ran along its bank.

Now Miren hesitated. Heading west felt like running into a corner—even in the darkness, she could see the looming cliffs of the western Kaleon border silhouetted against the night sky. But no one else stopped, and Miren still had no alternative ideas, so she followed.

The land rose as they ran, shielding them from anyone in pursuit from the south. A worn bridge of rope and wood swung high over the river, tethered on a slight rise on each side.

Liviya disappeared behind the rise, just under the bridge. The others followed, Miren and Davri close behind them. Through the mound of brush, Miren saw a small opening, just large enough for someone to squeeze through. Liviya pushed back the brush, and Arten, still carrying the child, climbed through, followed by Hana.

Miren looked at the woman, but Liviya just waved her inside. "Hurry!"

Miren glanced back and saw Davri struggling to catch up. "Come on!"

He lunged painfully up the hill, his chest heaving, and ducked into the alcove. Miren followed.

Liviya entered last and pulled up brush to cover the opening. Miren sat, pressed uncomfortably against Davri's sweaty form.

For a time, all she could hear was the sound of panting as everyone tried to catch their breath. The air quickly grew thick and stale, and the rocky wall dug into Miren's back. Her whole body trembled from fear and exertion, but her instincts were to keep running. Hiding felt like a dangerous gamble.

Liviya whispered, "You didn't take anything, did you?" Her voice seemed loud in the confined space. Miren thought she might be talking to her or Davri, but Arten answered, "No, we left everything."

"I mean *everything*. This has to look like a split-second decision."

"Everything, Mother."

Another, much younger voice said, "Even my favorite spinning top."

"Well done, Ori," Liviya said firmly. "You did a very brave thing."

"What is your plan?" Miren asked.

"Shhh," Liviya hissed. "We wait."

They sat in silence a while longer. The presence of a child made Miren nervous. What would happen to these people if they were caught?

Distant shouting sent a chill through Miren. It was too late to run now.

The voices grew louder.

Ori whimpered.

"Shhh, it's all right," Hana whispered.

Miren pressed against the cavern wall, holding the packs in front of her. Her revolver was still in her pack—she wouldn't be able to dig for it in such a cramped space.

The shouting continued, though it became more scattered. A sudden creak of wood—someone was above them, walking over the bridge. Miren ducked her forehead into her knees. *Please don't look here, don't look here.* If they were found, Cheliem would blame her for starting the fire, he would turn in Davri for the bounty, and Kesia would still be lost.

The men's voices grew faint, and silence again filled the night outside. Miren forced her shoulders to relax.

Arten whispered, "Thank you for coming."

"Always," Liviya whispered.

"Hana told me about Father," Arten said.

"I told her not to," Liviya said.

"I'm sorry," Hana said. "I couldn't keep that a secret from him."

Liviya sighed. "I was careless. I should have planned his escape better."

"It wasn't your fault, Mother," Arten said.

"I won't make that mistake here," Liviya insisted. "I promise you."

"Working for a local fisherman was a very clever idea," Hana said, "though I think some of the kitchen staff grew suspicious when I kept coming back from the market with fish for dinner."

"Did you dig this space out yourself?" Arten asked.

"Most of it was here already."

"You don't think they'll look here?" Hana asked.

"They won't find us," Liviya said. "They'll think we either took the river to the coast or kept going north."

Miren listened in silence and wondered if Liviya—clearly the mastermind behind tonight's plan—was right.

As the night drifted on, it seemed Liviya *was* right. The voices never returned, though no one suggested leaving their hiding place.

"Shouldn't we move on while it's dark?" Miren whispered.

"Not yet," Liviya said.

"What about the ship?" Arten asked. "Did you already pay?"

"Shhh," Liviya said. "Not here."

"You have a *ship?*" Miren said.

"Shhh!" Liviya hissed again. "No, we don't. The Crown's Guard is on alert. That's not an option."

"What options *do* we have?" Arten said.

"Arten," Hana warned.

"Later," Liviya whispered.

Miren wondered if she should press the issue. If they could get on a ship, they could go . . . where? How could they find Kesia now?

"Davri," she said, then realized it was too dark to sign. "Never mind."

She heard him sigh quietly.

The night marched on slowly. Miren's back ached and her knees protested at being cramped for so long. The rushing water of the river was the only noise they heard.

If they managed not to be caught here, where could they go? How would they find Kesia with the Crown's Guard looking for them?

"You," Liviya said, at last. "Girl. What's your name?"

Miren considered not answering, but it seemed pointless—if Hana had known they were going to be arrested, it was likely she already knew their names as well. "Miren. This is Davri."

"He doesn't talk much."

"He's a Singer," Hana said.

Liviya was silent for a moment. "What were you doing at Cheliem's?"

"We were trying to get his help. My sister was taken by pirates for the bounty, but she's too frail to fight."

"Your sister is a Singer?"

"Yes."

Silence. Miren wished for light so she could read the woman's expression. "What about you?" Miren asked. "Why are you all running like this?"

Liviya was silent again.

Hana replied, "We've worked for Cheliem for years under contract—"

"Hana," Liviya growled.

Miren waited, but no one else said anything. She tried again. "Where are you heading?"

"You don't need to know that," Liviya said.

"I'd like to."

More silence.

"You can't stop us from following you," Miren said. "Not without shooting us, at least."

Another pause. "I'm not telling you anything," Liviya said. "If you insist on following, then don't do anything to get us caught."

Miren sat back. That was one problem solved, at least. She closed her eyes, hoping she might get some sleep.

It might have been two hours or five, but eventually Liviya stirred. "I think we're clear. Let's go."

They pushed their way out of the cavern, and Miren gulped in the cool night air. The sky was still dark, with a smattering of stars, the western cliffs silhouetted darkly on their left. The river murmured, and a cold wind bit through Miren's thin coat.

Without a word, the group continued along the river at a jog, ignoring the bridge. The waxing moon had risen; Miren could better see the family in front of her. The boy clung to his father's neck, staring at her. He couldn't be more than five or six years old.

The grassy land rose into low hills as they headed toward the western cliffs, flattening briefly to reveal a small farm beside a field. Liviya led the group around the outskirts toward a barn. Together, she and Arten pushed open the door.

"Arten, light a fire," she said. "A small one."

"Are you sure?"

Liviya nodded. "The window isn't facing the homestead. We shouldn't be spotted."

The barn smelled of hay and dirt and animal. A couple of cows lowed grumpily in their stalls. Miren stepped inside, uncertain.

"We can sleep here for a few hours," Liviya said, "but we need to leave by dawn. Are you hungry, Ori?"

"Uh-huh," the boy moaned, clearly exhausted. Liviya pulled her pack from her shoulder and produced a wedge of cheese. Miren knew better than to ask for food, though she wished she had eaten more of that salmon.

Miren saw a flash as Arten cupped a spark and carefully lighted a rusty oil lantern he'd found by the entrance. The barn filled with a faint, warm light, and Miren could see the family clearly for the first time. The resemblance between Liviya and Arten was striking; they had the same straight nose and prominent jawline. Liviya had a stocky build, though; Arten was rail thin with a hunch in his shoulders as he knelt over the lantern. Ori sat between them, chewing slowly on a piece of cheese. He had his father's dark hair and his mother's bright eyes.

Miren was struck by how desperate they looked, and she wondered if she looked that way too.

"Who are you all?" she asked.

They turned toward her, but it was Davri who answered. In the dim light, he spelled out a word.

"Planters?" Miren said. "I don't understand."

"It's a term used for Avi'ori farmers who come to work on Kaleo farms," Hana said.

It suggests that Avi'ori do not know how to farm, Davri signed. *As though they just plant seeds, though it could also reference how Avi'ori "plant" themselves in Kaleo once they have completed their contract. It was coined by the Fourth and Fifth Circle farmers who resented the competition.*

"You know quite a bit," Liviya said.

Davri shrugged. *I like to read.*

"An expensive hobby. Are you nobility?"

Davri nodded. *My father is a Fifth Circle lord.*

"Explains why you haven't been drafted," Liviya said. "And why you thought Cheliem would help you find your friend."

He and my father have done business in the past, Davri signed.

"And so you thought he would do you a favor?" she said. "Noblemen are not so generous."

Davri grimaced.

Miren felt a spike of anger at him. She had believed he had a plan to find Kesia—or at least knew enough to point them in the right direction. Now they were worse off than they had been in Crescent Bay. At least people arresting her there would have been reluctant about it.

Hana nodded. "Cheliem is a horrible man," she said savagely. "I knew what he would do even before he sent a servant to town to get the Crown's Guard."

"But why did you run away?" Miren asked. "What you did took a lot of planning."

"It was all Liviya's idea—"

"Hana," Liviya cut her off.

"You don't have to tell me how," Miren said to Hana. "But why did you do it?"

"When we came to Kaleo, we signed contracts to work for Cheliem's estate for a set number of years," Hana said. "Once we completed those years of service, we were to receive our pay in a lump sum, enough to start our own small farm. But we realized too late that the contract was written so that a lord can extend a worker's service until he receives a certain amount of profit, and he can deduct from that profit by claiming expenses—food, housing, clothes. There is no recourse, and workers are forced to endure terrible conditions without hope of relief. I didn't know that when I signed on to finish my father's contract of two years after he injured himself," she said. "That was eight years ago. Liviya and her family came here ten years ago with a four-year contract. When she realized the contract was designed to trap her, she escaped. Then she came to find us."

Miren raised her eyebrows. She knew vaguely that Avi'ori farmers often came to work on Kaleon estates before the war began, back when Avi'ori crops were failing and many poor farmers had been bought out by coal mines and expanding railroad companies. She hadn't known they were being exploited and abused.

Hana met Miren's gaze. "Cheliem would have kept us there for the rest of our lives. We had no choice."

"Why do you feel the need to join us?" Liviya cut in.

Miren turned to face her. "Hana warned me that Cheliem was going to have Davri arrested for the Singer bounty. We had to escape."

Liviya gave a wry laugh. "Well, thanks to you two, *our* escape route was cut off before I even started that fire."

Miren blinked. "How is that our fault?"

"Because *that* one's arrival"—she pointed at Davri—"caused

Cheliem to send for the Crown's Guard, and now they'll be looking for all of us." She crossed her arms. "I paid a lot of money to a merchant ship to smuggle us out of here, but with the Crown's Guard searching every ship, they won't take us."

Arten glanced up at his mother. "What's the plan, now?"

Liviya didn't answer him. "You," she said, pointing to Davri again. "You're a Water Singer?"

Davri nodded.

"Your sister is a Singer," Liviya said to Miren. "What kind?"

"Fire."

"Hmm," Liviya said. "So you think the pirates have taken her to military recruiters for the bounty."

"Yes," Miren said.

"Even if you do find her, how do you plan to keep her out of the military?"

Miren glanced at Davri. "We're saying that she is betrothed to Davri. He's a baron's son."

Liviya made a disbelieving *tch* noise. "That won't get you far."

"So we've noticed."

The fire was roaring now. Miren worried that it would be too easy to spot through the high window, but Liviya seemed unconcerned, and Miren found herself trusting the older woman's judgment.

Liviya's dark eyes darted between Miren and Davri.

"What would you be willing to do to help your sister?"

"Anything," Miren said.

Liviya leaned back. "Three years ago, Cheliem sold mine and my husband's contracts to Third Circle lords. My master, Lord Barwick, had a Water Singer son who decided to give up his exemption from military service and become an officer."

Miren raised an eyebrow. "Nobility fight in the war?"

"Some of them. They're given a rank based on which Circle they're from, and they have more choice than other recruits about where they are stationed. And they don't have to pay the exemption tax, of course."

Miren glanced at Davri, but he was staring at the fire, avoiding her gaze. She had never heard of a tax.

Davri avoided the war using his father's money, she realized.

"Do you know this Water Singer?" she asked Liviya.

"No," Liviya answered. "I doubt he would even recognize me. I served on Barwick's kitchen staff, so I was able to eavesdrop whenever his son visited."

Miren narrowed her eyes. "You can't eavesdrop on a Singer."

Liviya waved a hand. "You know what I mean. I served them dinner. The son told them all about his exploits in the navy, his training, his assignments—"

"Why would he just say all of that over dinner?" Miren said.

"To impress his father, I think. Noblemen don't appreciate Singing the way the rest of us do. His son would brag about the ships he sank, the storms he steered them through, all that." She looked at Miren. "He also mentioned what happens to Singers who are caught avoiding the draft."

Miren felt her blood turn cold. "What do you mean?"

"Usually a non-Singer who avoids the draft is tried and thrown in prison, but the navy is desperate for Singers, so they have to serve with worse conditions than Singers who reported willingly—less food, less pay, no chance of advancement—though your chances are slim already unless you have a title." She gave a humorless smirk. "Singers charged with avoiding the draft are essentially treated like us planters."

"But Singers are still valued, right?" Miren said. "They'll still want to keep her alive?" She thought of Jonath, Haro's Earth Singer son, who no longer sent letters to his parents. And of her mother, who had never written in the four years she'd been gone.

"So long as she's useful," Liviya said. "But you can't guarantee a life in war."

Miren's insides were in knots. *Noblemen don't appreciate Singing the way the rest of us do,* Liviya had said. Did they think Singers were expendable?

She glanced at Davri, but he was staring at Liviya with his arms crossed.

Understanding flared in Miren. "Did you *know* this?" she asked him.

I didn't want to worry you.

"You—" Miren clenched her jaw. She could strangle him. She *would* strangle him. Later.

She swallowed her anger. "Where are the Singers taken?" she asked Liviya. "They're put on a navy ship?" Based on her father's letters, she knew that most of the combat occurred in the northern half of the Tehum Sea.

Liviya held up a hand. "I'll make a deal with you. If you help me get my family out of Kaleo, I'll tell you everything I know to help you find your sister."

Arten and Hana exchanged glances.

"What?" Miren said. "What do you mean? You won't tell us now?"

"I'll tell you everything I can," Liviya said. "I'll answer every question you can think of—*after* my family is safe."

Of course, Miren thought: this woman wouldn't just offer information for free.

Arten looked up at Liviya. "Mother—"

"What about Cale?" Hana asked.

"I will get Cale," Liviya said. "Once you three are off Kaleon soil."

"No, Mother," Arten said. "You shouldn't go after him alone."

Miren wondered who Cale was but didn't want to interrupt.

"You'd let Hana and Ori wander around Avi'or on their own?" Liviya countered.

Arten stared at his mother.

Liviya softened. "I got you three out, didn't I? Trust me with this, Arten. Please."

Arten turned away with a sigh.

"What kind of information do you have?" Miren asked Liviya. "What specifically are you offering?"

Liviya smirked. "That's a little difficult to say without revealing the information, isn't it? I can tell you where she'll likely be taken."

"To a navy ship, right?"

"Eventually, yes, but there's often squabbling among navy officers about who gets new Singers for their fleet. She'll be detained for a while until that's decided, especially if she's a Fire Singer."

"How long?" Miren said.

Liviya shrugged. "Weeks, I imagine. I can't guarantee you'll find her, but I can point you in the right direction."

Miren narrowed her eyes. "That isn't much."

"It doesn't seem you have many options. Even if Cheliem doesn't connect you to our escape, he's still interested in the bounty on your friend's head." Liviya gestured to Davri.

He's not my friend, Miren thought instinctively. "What do you want from us?" she asked. "I don't see how we can help you."

"You, no." Liviya jabbed a finger in Davri's direction again. "But that one can."

Startled, Davri sat upright.

Miren said, "You need a Water Singer."

"I don't *need* either of you," Liviya snapped immediately. "I have planned for every way this could go wrong."

Miren paused. She wanted to doubt Liviya's confidence, but it was difficult to argue with her results so far.

Liviya continued, "There is a river north of here in Fisher's Canyon, about three days' travel. It flows eastward toward the coast, but every night a large gate is lowered into the water from a bridge, blocking the boats that might pass. The only way to get past the gate is to go over it." She turned to Davri. "You Sing the current up enough to push us over the top, and then we head straight for the sea. If you get my family safely to the open water, I'll tell you everything I know."

Davri unfolded his arms. *You're asking us to risk our lives, and yet all you're offering to do is tell us where Kesia might be.*

"And?" Liviya said. "Do you expect to find more than that?"

Our goal is to get Kesia out of military service. Finding her is not enough.

Liviya shrugged. "Maybe you bribe some guards. Maybe you fake her death. I don't care. My offer is to help you find her likeliest location."

"You just said you can't guarantee that," Miren said.

"I can tell you where Singers are first detained, and I can even make a few educated guesses as to which fleets will likely get her. You won't find better."

Miren stared at the ground. The problem was that she believed Liviya—they probably wouldn't find a better option. After their experience with Cheliem, they couldn't trust the nobility. And if Miren could at least find out where Kesia was, perhaps a chance to rescue her would present itself.

Miren glanced at Davri. He raised his eyebrows, questioning.

Miren nodded for Davri to follow her. "Give us a moment, please," she told Liviya.

Liviya waved them off, looking uninterested.

Miren stepped into the yard, staying out of sight of the farmhouse. She turned to face Davri. It was just light enough that she could see his hands.

"Are there any other nobles who would be willing to help us?"

Davri signed slowly. *Not many nearby, and none that would know me like Cheliem.*

"Would they turn you in for a bounty?"

He frowned. *It's possible.*

"Is it riskier than going with these people?" she said. "Do you think Liviya made all of that up?"

I know of Lord Barwick, Davri said. *And his son. As far as I can tell, she wasn't lying. It's not uncommon for Singers of nobility to serve as military officers.*

"What do you know of the Kaleon military?" Miren said.

It mostly consists of naval fleets, which are usually stationed along the northern coast near the capital, except for Kilithis Bay, which is the most naturally defensible stretch of coast due to—

"Stop, stop," Miren said. "I don't care about all that. Where would they take Kesia? Is Liviya right about her being detained for a time?"

I don't know, Davri signed.

"Do you think she would be at a military base?" Miren said. "Do you know where those are?"

No.

"Is there anything you *do* know?" she demanded.

A muscle twitched in Davri's jaw. *My meeting with Cheliem wasn't just about finding Kesia. We want her exempt from military service.*

"What difference does that make? We have to find her first."

If we make her exempt, then she'll be released and sent home. We won't need to look for her.

"Will that work? Even if she's already been assigned to a ship by then?"

I don't know.

"If Cheliem won't help us, who will?"

We can go to the capital, Davri signed, though he looked uncertain. *There is an appeals process. If I can convince a court that she is my betrothed, then they won't deploy her. We won't* have *to look for her. But . . .*

"What? But what?"

Given that Kesia is . . . not nobility, it might be difficult to convince them she's my betrothed. I would need . . . confirmation.

"Confirmation? Oh. You would need approval from Darius," she finished. "I doubt you have that."

But we could still try, Davri signed. *Even if we can't get her exempt, we might find out where she is. I know of a few nobles we could ask for help. It could still work.*

"No, it won't." Miren rubbed her forehead, frustration welling in her. Davri was naive—she should have recognized that from the start. He had put faith in the way of nobility and nearly gotten arrested for it. And even if he was right and managed to convince some military officers that Kesia was his betrothed, would they really release a Fire Singer from service? *No.* To find Kesia, they would have to work outside the aristocracy. "It will take us too long to get to the capital. We need to find her before she's assigned to a ship."

I think you're assuming too much—

"Were you not paying attention? We don't have time to wait for an appeals process. Even I know that Avi'or has better ships, better cannons. By the time she's on a ship, she'll—" Miren stopped. "We have to get her out. We'll get this family on a boat, and then we'll go and find Kesia."

Davri shook his head.

"This is what we're doing, Davri. We tried it your way already."

She glared at him. He looked away first.

She marched past him and back into the barn. Four expectant faces turned to look at her.

"Liviya," she said. "We have a deal."

ELEVEN

KESIA

THE SHIP *DARKCREST* WAS A SMALL TRADE VESSEL, TIGHTLY crafted. Kesia could feel the heavy surf pulling and slamming against the hull even from inside her metal cage, while above her, the crew shouted and complained and laughed as they worked.

She would fall asleep a few times throughout the day, but the night was too cold to rest. She shivered horribly, sometimes standing to escape the freezing metal until the sun rose. Once a day, she was given stale bread and dried meat and water. She forced herself to eat despite the churning in her stomach, never looking at the gun barrel that stared at her until she was finished.

Miren's screams for help replayed over and over in her mind. They had fought that morning; Kesia couldn't even remember why, only that it had been petty. The last time she had seen Davri, he had been waving to her through the baron's front gate.

That fateful thud as the pirate had brought his pistol down on Miren's head; Miren's unmoving form lying on the ground.

She might be dead.

Miren was fine, she told herself. Miren was tough. But even if the blow hadn't killed her sister, Kesia was still alone. She was so, so alone.

I'm so sorry.

She tried to think of good memories with Miren or Davri or

her parents, letting them cover her like a blanket. But comfort was fleeting—a jarring comparison to her new reality.

She couldn't think about what was to come. Whenever she considered the military, she wanted to weep.

I don't want to kill anyone.

Singing was a gift—her Mother had always insisted so. It was a beautiful way to assist the village, a way to contribute to something bigger than herself. It was not a weapon; it wasn't meant for destruction. Kesia thought of the man she had burned, how she had thrown fire onto his sleeve, almost feeling the flame bite into his skin. It was devastating, a corruption of Singing. Was that what she would be asked to do in service to the king?

On the morning of the third day, one of the pirates unlocked Kesia's cage.

"No tricks, Singer!" the man shouted. "Or I put a bullet through your head."

Kesia lowered her head and raised her hands to indicate submission. Most of the men, she had learned, could not read signs.

"Climb out," the man said.

Slowly, she pushed herself up. Her arms felt like bags of sand, and her head spun from standing so suddenly. No one came to offer her assistance as she pulled herself out of the cell.

The gag in her mouth was as cumbersome and fishy as ever. Two gun barrels gaped at her, and she cringed. She wanted to collapse and melt into the deck of the ship.

Then she looked up.

We've arrived.

A huge mountain took up most of the sky, dull clouds circling its blue and gray peak. Spread out in front of her was a sight she had never thought she would see.

A city.

Davri had described cities as bustling, crowded places with

huddled, elaborately designed buildings and streets made of stone. The people who lived there were clad in brightly colored gowns, or suits, or well-pressed uniforms, he'd said.

But he hadn't mentioned such tall buildings, or the noise that drifted from them even here at the docks. Or the docks themselves, which were numerous and crowded with ships of every size, some full-masted, others coughing steam from metal columns.

The ridge of mountains was so close that Kesia could see how it curved around and downward toward the coast, as though trying to corral the city closer to the water. She could see buildings along the sheer ridge at the far end of the city. One building even sat on top of the ridge, though she could hardly make it out against the bright sunlight.

And she realized that was why the world seemed skewed, off-color: it was only midmorning, but the sun was hidden behind mountains. Mountains to the east—

"Here we are, little Singer," Edom said, smiling. "Welcome to my homeland!"

Kesia sucked in a breath. A few of the men cried out in alarm at the sound, but she hardly heard them.

They hadn't taken her to the Kaleon Royal Navy.

She was in Avi'or.

The same hazy blue mountains she had once stared at from the lighthouse widow's walk were now jagged and stark before her. Why hadn't she *noticed* that they had been heading east and not north? Had she not once thought to look at the sun's path across her barred cage, or notice the shifting stars at night?

"I must say, Singer," the captain continued, "that it has been an absolute pleasure having you onboard. I haven't had a prisoner so compliant in ages." He slapped a hand on her shoulder. "I have found in recent years, however, that it's best not to tell captured Singers where I'm bringing them. Of course, they assume I'm selling them to their king, but, unfortunately, your king is a bit of a gold-pincher compared to the business we've found here." He flicked his fingers at the crewmen. "Chain and box. Let's get rich, gentlemen!"

The crew roared with approval. Before Kesia could even consider a means of escape, her arms were yanked behind her, and cold, cruel metal pinched her wrists. The pirates produced a crate. Sheer panic made Kesia kick at the men, but they easily wrestled her inside, her knees curled into her chest, and slammed down the lid.

Only faint light came through a few cracks in the crate. Everything hurt—her back ached, her shoulders were aflame, her cheeks were raw from the gag, and her lip had split more than once. Already her wrists were numb against the cold metal.

The crate tilted, and her head slammed painfully against its side. She heard two men grunt as they lifted the crate and started walking.

She listened to the sounds of city life. She tried kicking the side of the crate to attract attention, but she was jostled so violently that her shoulder bounced against the top lid. "None of that," a gruff voice warned.

After a short time, the crate was set down, and she heard Edom's voice. "Oi!" he called. "I'm looking for a witch."

"You're never gonna find better with a tongue like that, Edom," a woman said. "How many this time?"

"Just the one, I'm afraid."

"One Singer, eh?" the woman said. "I guess the waters are getting a bit thin, huh?"

"You could say so," Edom said. "Had to hop across the sea for this one."

"Doesn't mean I'll be paying you more for her."

"Oh, you might," Edom said. "Let's take this deal inside."

More jostling as Kesia heard footsteps thump on wood, and the voices of the crowd began to fade. The crate was plopped on the floor.

"You lot get to trading," Edom said. "I'll take care of this one."

The other men grumbled and ambled out, their footsteps fading. A door closed, and it grew quiet.

Kesia heard more footsteps and the faint clinking of metal.

"You seem to be doing fairly well this season," Edom said.

"High demand," the woman replied. "Let's see what you have for me."

A strain of wood, and the lid was removed. Kesia blinked as two figures loomed over her. The woman was a bit plump, with a long rope of hair hanging across her shoulder. She wore a faded blue dress and apron and stood with her hands on her hips.

"Skies and seas, Edom." The woman waved a hand at Kesia. "This all you've got?"

Edom reached down and pulled Kesia upright, nearly lifting her off her feet as he dragged her from the box. She was in a small wooden room lit only by a single lantern mounted on the wall. Behind the woman, a line of six men and women sat against the wall, gagged and chained. Prisoners?

The captain wrapped his arm around her neck.

"If I hear one wrong note from you," he growled, "I shoot you in the leg. Is that understood?"

Kesia nodded, her eyes watering. *I can't do this, I can't do this.*

He slapped a firm, hot hand on her shoulder like a proud father. "I think this is worth about five of the usual."

The woman arched a brow. "Really?"

"Voice of gold, this one," Edom said.

"Fire Singer? Sweet songs, she is." The woman snorted, but her eyes bored into Kesia.

"Saw it with my own eyes. You really want a demonstration?" the captain challenged. "I thought you liked your pub."

"I'm gonna need proof if you want half of what you're about to ask for her."

Despite the commotion, only a few captives had dared glance in Kesia's direction. They were gagged—were all of them Singers too?

Edom shrugged. "All right, then." He slipped his pistol out and grabbed Kesia's shoulder.

This is it.

Kesia fought back a whimper.

"Girlie, it's time for a little Song, but if you try anything funny, I'll blow a hole through you."

He slipped the gag from her mouth. The air in the room was stuffy and tasted faintly of alcohol.

The woman produced a single stick of kindling.

This was Kesia's chance. She *knew* this was her chance, but she stood rigid between the two Avi'ori. The cold barrel of the pistol at her back seemed to draw all her focus. *He'll kill me, he'll kill me.*

"C'mon, little girl," he growled. "Just give us a tiny sample. You don't want trouble."

Trembling, Kesia opened her mouth and Sang a single note.

The tip of the stick crackled with fire.

Before Kesia could even consider continuing the Song, Edom had his arm around her neck again and shoved the gag back in so hard that she was nearly sick.

"Well, I'll be," the woman held the smoking stick higher, staring at Kesia with wide, hungry eyes. "After all these years. Where'd you find her?"

"You really have to go far and wide for 'em, I tell you," he said, releasing Kesia. "Found this one in Crescent Bay."

"Ah," the woman said. "No wonder I hadn't heard from you, going that far south."

"And look at how compliant she is," Edom said. "You won't find a single charred piece of wood on my ship."

Kesia's eyes burned with shame, her ears going numb as the

two began to haggle. She hadn't once put up a fight. *Coward coward coward*—

If Miren had been taken, things would have been different. Miren would've fought sea serpents to get back home, and there was nothing in Kesia that believed her sister would have lost. *I'm not Miren,* she thought.

Blinded by half-formed tears, Kesia complied numbly as she was led to a seat beside an elderly woman in the corner, while a large sack of gold was passed to the captain. She looked up in time to see Edom pause by the door and give her a mock salute. Then he was gone.

TWELVE

KESIA

Kᴇꜱɪᴀ ꜱᴀᴛ, ʜᴇʀ ʜᴀɴᴅꜱ ꜱᴛɪʟʟ ᴄʜᴀɪɴᴇᴅ ʙᴇʜɪɴᴅ ʜᴇʀ ʙᴜᴛ now linked to the other six captives. After securing her in place at the end of the row, the woman had followed Edom out. The door had opened briefly to reveal a dark hallway and the echoing rumble of voices and clinking glasses. The woman closed and locked the door behind her.

Kesia looked down the line of captives. They were dressed in shabby clothes or even rags, and they were all gagged. Most of them stared at the ground or at the door.

She caught the eye of one of them, an older man with wisps of white clinging to his head. His clothes were stained with black soot, and one of his boots had a hole large enough for his toe to peek through.

She furrowed her eyebrows and nodded, her questions unsigned. *Where are we going? What's happening?*

He just blinked at her, eyes glassy.

A short time later, two men came into the room. One, with a brown beard and shaved head, was so big that his shoulders filled the doorway. The second was taller but lean, his large nose giving him a birdlike appearance.

"Wake up, everyone," the big one said in a deep, booming voice. "Time to go."

The lean one came and unlocked the chain that connected Kesia to the wall. He caught her staring and grinned. "You're a pretty one."

Kesia's stomach churned.

"Not this batch," the big one said, unlocking the other end of the chain from the wall.

The large man led the captives out of the room and down a hall, the lean man holding the end of the chain behind Kesia. They turned and exited through another door.

Kesia blinked in the bright afternoon sunlight. Tall wooden fences surrounded a small dirt yard. The mountains rose directly in front of them, gray in the bright sunlight. They were so close now that Kesia could no longer see the peak. To the right, a wagon stood harnessed to four horses.

The large man motioned for the captives to get in the wagon. The prisoner at the front, a young woman with curly reddish-brown hair and a slight limp, obeyed quickly.

Kesia glanced back as the line moved forward. The woman who had spoken to Edom stood in the doorway, arms crossed. Her dark eyes caught Kesia's.

Kesia shivered and turned away as she climbed into the wagon.

"Don't take long, boys," the woman called. "I'm roasting a bird tonight."

The men hollered and whistled as they covered the wagon entrance, enveloping Kesia and her companions in near darkness. A moment later, a wooden gate creaked open, and the horses began to move.

The captives were jostled against each other for perhaps an hour. At one point, everyone leaned back as the wagon started up a long incline. The cuffs dug and pulled at Kesia's wrists until she felt a warm trickle of blood.

This can't be real. When she had believed that she was headed for the military, she'd had some sense of what to expect. At least she had known she would be valued. But this uncertainty was agonizing — she almost hoped they would just shoot her.

At last the wagon leveled again and stopped, and a sudden clanking of metal made Kesia startle in her seat. The wagon continued forward and then stopped once more.

The back of the wagon opened. "Everyone out," a man shouted.

This time, Kesia led the way out of the wagon, nearly falling onto the ground as she stepped down without the use of her arms. A metal gate stood in front of her, the center decorated with a metallic *A*. Beyond the gate, she saw a wide dirt road that continued downward and out of sight, leading back toward the coast. The gate was flanked by walls of red brick. She looked around and saw at least a dozen large, featureless buildings in rows — she was in a compound.

The leaner man grabbed her end of the chain. "This way," he said.

He led them through a line of warehouses. Some of the buildings coughed up steam or smoke through large chimneys.

They were led to one of the larger buildings. Metal doors screeched open to let them in.

The clang of metal rang around them. Odd machines whirred and whined as metal sheets were pushed through rollers. Molten iron pooled in basins, and steam hissed from pipes. Perhaps twenty people worked busily. No one gave the new arrivals more than a glance.

"Let's collar the Singers!" the lean man called. "The boss wants to get through orientation quickly. Let's go!"

Orientation?

Collar?

From a hall to the right, four men surged forward, their arms ladened with black iron rings larger than dinner plates. They were so thick that Kesia wouldn't have been able to encircle one with her hands.

Most of the captives understood a heartbeat too late. They recoiled, a few waving their hands in refusal. The men slapped them if they resisted and latched the collars on their necks with a heavy click. The Singers clawed at them, eyes wide, as if they couldn't breathe.

A hand grabbed Kesia's hair and yanked. Before she could react, she heard a snip, and all her hair below her chin fell to the ground in light brown clumps.

Kesia shrank back as one man approached her. She shook her head desperately, but he caught her jaw in his hand and forced her head up. Icy metal curled around her neck.

Click.

The collar was so wide that Kesia could barely open her mouth. Her throat felt as though it had shrunk to half its size. Her gag was gone, but she could not catch her breath to draw in the air that would let her run or Sing. She almost didn't notice another man unlock her manacles from behind. She pulled at the collar, feeling around for some kind of lever, but except for a narrow slit at the back, it was cold, coarse metal.

A man stepped forward.

He had sharp, pointed features and a burly build. He wore dark slacks and a long coat, clean and finely pressed. He scanned the lineup of prisoners with a dissatisfied tilt to his mouth.

"Welcome, Singers," he said in a rumbling voice, "to the factory. My name is Parviz. You may call me 'sir' or 'Lord Parviz' if you're ever given the chance to address me." He gestured to a shorter, stockier man next to him. "This is Nadav. If you're lucky, he will never address you at all.

"During your stay here, which will likely be for the rest of your lives, you are my property. My property does what I say. It performs quietly and does not disobey. If it does disobey, it is discarded. Valuable property is only valuable if it functions properly. I advise that none of you overestimates your worth. Understood?"

Kesia shivered. *I'm going to die. I'm going to die here.*

Parviz continued, "Your collars prohibit you from Singing or exerting yourselves too much. When it is time for you to work, your collars will be altered to allow you just enough breathing room." He nodded to Nadav, who opened his mouth and Sang.

Kesia gasped as Earth Song rumbled through the floor. Something clicked inside her collar and she took a breath. The air was cool and metallic. Before she was ready, another note from Nadav slid the collar shut.

"At the same time," Parviz said, "we can kill you with a single note." He glanced at Nadav.

The Song shifted.

Voiceless choking toward the end of the line caught everyone's attention. An elderly man—the one who had met her gaze before—writhed and clawed at his collar, opening his mouth as wide as he could. No sound came from him, not even a breath. His skin began to pale, his eyes wide as he struggled.

Kesia cringed away, her pulse hammering against the collar. *Please stop, please stop.*

The Song ended. The man crumpled to the floor, wheezing and spluttering.

"As you can see," Parviz continued, "you cannot escape, so I suggest you don't try. Any questions?"

Silence, long and chilling. Kesia's bones felt brittle, like glass that was about to shatter under the dull shadow of steel. *When can I go home? I want to go, please let me go.*

Parviz glanced around. "Nice, we got a good haul. All right, take them to their assignments."

Workers surged forward and began herding them farther into the building. Kesia fought not to flinch, no longer fearing these men as much as Nadav, the Earth Singer.

"You," one man addressed her. "You're the Fire Singer?"

Could she lie? Would she get away with it? Would it help her? It didn't matter—she didn't have the courage to try. She nodded as much as her collar allowed.

"Go to the furnace and wait for orders."

The man pointed to the great, gaping furnace in the middle of the room. A number of collared women were already huddled around it, watching as some Avi'ori men poured iron from the second level into the top of the furnace. Kesia joined their circle, looking at each of them in turn, but no one spared her a glance. Only one girl, perhaps thirteen, was staring at Kesia with wide, hollow eyes, her skin ashen.

The men finished pouring, and someone shouted. "All right, light it up!"

An Earth Song hummed around the circle, and each slave's collar clicked open. Kesia felt something at the front of her throat slide out of place, giving her just enough room to Sing.

Most of the women were Air Singers, their Voices tripping and trampling over each other to increase the pressure in the vent below the furnace. Kesia's jaw would have dropped in shock if it could; how did so many Voices compete with each other this way? All this Singing felt twisting and cluttered and wrong, like a crowd of people elbowing each other.

"Hey!" One of the workers waved a hand at her. The Air Singers continued despite the interruption. "Heat the air."

Kesia opened her mouth tentatively and Sang, her Voice discordant against the higher-pitched trills of the Air Singers. She felt like the Song was going to run away with her at any moment, confused by the other Voices in the room, but she also felt the heat in the vents increase and shoot through the furnace. A sweat broke across her brow as the incessant din filled her ears.

She felt the truth of her situation slide through her like cold water. She was not a captive; she was a slave.

THIRTEEN

MIREN

A HAND SHOOK MIREN AWAKE. "UP, GET UP. LET'S GO."

Miren pushed herself upright, her ear aching from using her pack as a pillow. A few paces away, Arten was scraping dirt over the dying embers of the fire while Hana handed Ori a canteen. The boy's eyes were drooping with fatigue. The interior of the barn was still dark, but the faint light of early dawn peeked through a window. It had likely been only a few hours since she had gone to sleep. Since she had made the deal with Liviya.

She glanced at Davri, who lay facing away from her, his pack under his head. He had not spoken to her after making the deal.

Now he sat up slowly, looking ragged. He clearly wasn't used to early mornings.

Miren checked her own pack. The revolver was still there, plus all her bullets and black powder. She checked her meager pouch of coin and counted it out. Everything was there.

She looked up to see Liviya staring at her. "Missing something? Or don't you trust us?"

Miren glared back and began folding her bedroll. "Where are we headed?"

"North." Liviya slung her pack on her shoulder. "Heading west a bit."

"That'll take us farther from the coast."

"So we'll be less likely to be found."

Miren paused. "You think Cheliem will be looking for you?"

"Not just us." Liviya nodded at Davri.

Ori pulled on Liviya's skirt. "Nana, I'm hungry."

"We'll stop to eat in a short while." Liviya rubbed his head gently. "We need to get out of sight first."

The barn they had stayed in overlooked a small town wedged among some hills. Despite the scant light, Miren could see the faint movement of a few figures. Their party would be easy to spot once the sun rose.

She glanced to the south, noting the small woods they had run through last night. Any guards or patrols that Cheliem might have sent must have headed east, as Liviya had said. The farther northwest they traveled, the safer they would be.

Still, Miren couldn't shake the notion that this was the wrong direction. Kesia would be along the coast somewhere. They would soon be farther from Kesia than when they'd started.

Just for a few days, she told herself. *Once they're on a boat, we'll know where to go.*

The group fell into a loose line behind Liviya as she led them back down the rise and onto a narrow dirt road. Arten and Hana stayed close, carrying Ori or holding his hand, while Miren and Davri trailed behind.

Farms were smaller here. The land was too uneven to support a whole field, so many farms had patches of crops—cornstalks, carrots, and beans—on whatever surface was available. Cows and sheep grazed on green slopes, and herders waved amiably in their direction.

The day wore on slowly as they walked. The wind was still cool this time of year, but as the sun rose, Miren soon began to sweat. The group didn't talk much. Perhaps it was nerves, but she wondered if she and Davri were considered liabilities by the rest of the family. A larger party would naturally draw more attention.

A few times, Miren caught Liviya glancing back at them, perhaps checking if they had run off. Did she need Davri more than she had let on? Or was she still suspicious? Maybe she thought Miren and Davri would sneak away and turn them in to Cheliem.

Would that work? Would Cheliem be willing to help them if they returned his missing planters? Would it be enough to convince him to spare Davri *and* find Kesia?

Miren felt a pulse of shame. It wouldn't work, and Miren wasn't sure she had it in her to try even if she thought there was a chance.

Davri didn't sign to her all morning, perhaps still angry with her for making this decision, though he hadn't argued or threatened to leave. Perhaps he knew she was right and was just being stubborn. She considered asking, but she didn't want to be the first to break the silence.

The sun crested overhead, but Liviya insisted that they continue walking. "The bigger our lead, the safer we'll be," she said.

Ori fussed until his father handed him a piece of jerky and picked him up. Miren's feet were aching in her boots, but she didn't complain.

Just past sunhigh, Miren noticed Liviya murmuring something to Hana, who nodded and slowed her pace to match Miren's.

Hana smiled at Miren. "I don't think we've been properly introduced. I'm Hana."

Miren forced a smile. "Miren."

"I'm sorry to hear about your sister."

Miren nodded. "Thank you."

"For what it's worth, I think she'll be all right."

Miren glanced at Hana. "I just mean that she's a Fire Singer," Hana said. "They're very valuable."

Miren wracked her mind for a change of subject. "Is it true that Liviya knows so much about the military?"

Hana blinked in surprise. "Yes," she said. "At least, I think she does. I know her contract was sold to Third Circle Lord Barwick, although I don't know much about how her time was spent until she reached us."

"How did the three of you coordinate the escape?" Miren asked.

"Liviya knew I sometimes would go into town to buy fish and meat. She found a job with a local fish merchant. Later, I did the shopping as an excuse to see her. Apparently she learned that the fish merchant was doing business in Avi'or. She convinced him to smuggle us along with his wares."

"It's legal to do business in Avi'or?"

"No, definitely not, but certain goods fetch a high price there, so some consider it worth the risk. Liviya threatened to report him unless he helped us."

"Mama," Ori called from Arten's shoulders. "Can I have some water?"

"Yes, sweet." Hana took the canteen from her hip and tipped it into Ori's mouth. Some of the water dribbled from his chin and soaked into Arten's shirt.

"Thank you."

"Swallow before you speak, dear," Hana said.

Ori made a show of tipping his head back and making a *gulp* sound.

"You mentioned someone named Cale," Miren said to Arten.

He nodded. "My brother. His contract was sold when our parents' were. The Third Circle lady he works for has a reputation for . . . well, she's not kind to her workers."

Arten glanced away and, for a brief moment, looked much older than he was. How many sleepless nights had he spent worrying?

Miren felt a stab of empathy. Then she realized that they might be playing for her sympathies. Had Liviya told Hana to try to win her over?

"I'm sorry to hear that," she said, her tone brisk. She slowed her pace.

Arten glanced at her in surprise but said nothing. He and Hana continued ahead of her without another word.

If they were trying to manipulate her, it wouldn't work. She couldn't become sidetracked with this family. She couldn't come to care too much. Her first priority had to be Kesia. No matter what. This group might be useful, but if a better opportunity to find her sister presented itself, she would take it.

They didn't stop until sunset, the sky a bright orange as cloud cover rolled in over the western ridge. Liviya led them off the road and around a shelf of rock at the edge of a cornfield, out of sight of a town to the east.

Liviya passed out cured sausages. "We're going to have to share," Liviya said, "if we want to make it through the next two days."

It felt like a trick, but the truth was that Miren was already running low on the rations she carried.

Davri signed *Thank you* and accepted the sausage.

Miren hesitated, then took one. "Thank you," she echoed. She took a small bite. It was bland but fatty, a welcome change from the dried meats she and Kesia ate at home.

Miren looked over at Davri, who was avoiding her gaze.

"Can I see your map, please?" she asked.

He didn't respond. For a moment, she thought he was going to ignore her completely—he had done a splendid job of it all day—but he finished his sausage and reached in his pack for the map.

She unrolled it and spotted Cheliem's town, Isakio, and the forest they had passed through, and deduced that they must be just west of a small town called Sheber. Nothing was labeled as a military base or outpost.

Davri was staring at her grimly. She did not care if he was angry, but it felt foolish to keep him at arm's length if it was going to make him cross. If he left, she would lose her bargaining chip with Liviya.

Miren leaned forward and whispered, "Listen, the deal with Liviya is our best option right now. We have no idea where to go, no one we can ask, and the Crown's Guard is looking for you. If we want to find Kesia, we need to do this."

He stared at her, his expression unreadable. *I'm not convinced Liviya knows what she claims.*

"She knows more than we do," Miren said.

Which means we wouldn't know if she were lying.

Miren's temper flared. "My mother has not sent a single letter to us since she left. We don't know what happens to Fire Singers. Maybe they're put in the thickest combat because the military thinks that's where they'll do the most damage. And what if Kesia—"

Davri motioned for her to stop. *We can disagree on things, but we shouldn't work against each other. We need to make decisions together.*

Miren paused. As irritating as she found him, he was the only one whose motives she trusted.

"Fine," she said.

He nodded, satisfied.

The farther they traveled, the more Miren realized that the rest of Kaleo was nothing like Crescent Bay.

Everything was ragged edges and cliffs. She saw broken shelves of stone and odd chunks missing from hillsides. A miniature canyon was carved by a stream, and small eddies muddied the edges. At one point, the road was suddenly broken in two, as though some great force had split it ages ago; a large ramp had been built to allow for carts to cross.

Their pace was slower today. Liviya couldn't quite hide a limp in her left leg, but she insisted that it wasn't a long enough journey to spend coin on a horse and cart.

Ori did not walk. He was either sprinting ahead of the group, chasing butterflies and the occasional lizard, or he was sitting in the middle of the road wailing until his father scooped him up and put him on his shoulders. When the boy caught Miren staring at him, he would duck under his father's shoulder or hide in his mother's skirts. Miren tried not to let it bother her; Kesia had always been better with children.

"We'll be at the river tomorrow," Liviya said over a lean dinner of freshly caught rabbit. "We'll spend the day looking for a proper boat to take us to the coast."

Davri motioned Miren to step away from the others.

She followed him. "What?" she asked.

He turned her around so that he was facing away from the rest of the group; he didn't want them to read his signs. *I'm not sure I can do what Liviya wants.*

Miren frowned. "What do you mean?"

He looked around, his brow knitted, his shoulders hunched. *I don't really know how to Sing.*

"What?" she said. "Of course you do. You got us to Isakio."

He shook his head. *I was never trained! I can do a few things — like move a boat on the open sea — but I'm not sure how to do more. There was no one to teach me, and I am unpracticed.*

"You — you didn't practice? *Never?*"

Davri winced at her tone. *My father didn't like it when I practiced.*

In Crescent Bay, young people who received a Voice at Skyflame were trained by someone older from the village. Air and Water Singers were shown how to assist the fishermen or irrigate crops; Earth Singers tilled the land or learned blacksmithing; Fire Singers, as they were so rare, were mostly charged with the lighthouse, though no one outside of Miren's family had earned a Voice of Fire in generations.

Miren thought of the days after the Skyflame ceremony where

Kesia had found her Voice. She remembered with embarrassment the hours she had spent sulking, dodging chores until she found that she could avoid pity by doing extra, and she remembered her mother demonstrating the Song to light the lighthouse lamp.

Miren had loved that Song. A simple few notes would have lighted the wick, but this was a true song, the melody longer, the notes carefully shaped. It was not a grand display of Singing; if anything, Miren thought it sounded humble.

Of the other new Singers that year, most were excited to join the adults on the water. Miren couldn't remember Davri among them.

Davri had never learned. He had never even *practiced*.

Miren could not fathom it. *What a waste*, she wanted to say, but she bit back the words. Perhaps it made some sense that nobles like Darius would find Singing less important than the villagers did, or at least less useful. They didn't need to worry about steering ships or fishing or keeping food chilled to preserve it. But surely the training itself would have been worth the time.

Davri glanced at Liviya. *She says I need to steer a boat through difficult waters and over a gate. I don't know how to do it.*

"Well, I grew up with a Fire Singer, and I know some basics. Here, sit." Miren reached for her canteen and poured out a small puddle of water between them. "I don't know Water Singing, but all Songs share some basic principles. The most important thing to do is listen."

Davri looked at the water, then back at her. *Listen to the water?*

Miren shifted in her seat, memories filtering through her mind. "Just listen. Think of what you want the water to do, and then wait for the Song to come."

Davri stared at the water. Miren waited, wondering what Water Singing sounded like to the Singer, how it differed from Fire not just in terms of style, but *feel*. It must be slower, weightier, but less demanding.

A full two minutes later, Davri shook his head. *I don't hear anything.*

"You made the boat move!" she snapped. "How can you not hear anything?"

He winced. *Please stop yelling.*

Miren groaned. "I'm not a Singer, you know. I don't actually know how it's done."

But even as she said it, she knew it wasn't wholly true. She had spent so much of her childhood listening to her mother Sing fire in the hearth, a spark in the lighthouse, a small light over her father's shoulder—she could still recite all of those Songs from memory. She remembered watching Mother heat a pan in the fire and joining in, her childish voice stomping all over her mother's Song. Even hours of practice with the melodies could not properly replicate the tone and timbre of a Singer's Voice. But she still knew the theory.

A complicated mixture of pride and embarrassment heated her temper again. Miren knew she was being unfair, but she couldn't help being irritated with this boy.

She took a deep breath. Snapping at Davri might be satisfying, but it wasn't helpful. "All right. What you need to do isn't difficult. It's just going to be a slightly larger Song than the one you used to get us to Isakio."

Larger? Davri signed. *Do you mean louder?*

"No, not necessarily. I mean . . . more encompassing." Miren tried to remember advice her mother might have given. "It's . . . difficult to explain. It's as though you're addressing a lot of people at once instead of just a few. Sure, you might be louder, but the important thing is to keep everyone's attention when you speak, right? Er, sign."

He nodded, his gaze thoughtful as he stared at the puddle. *So I have to speak to the water?*

Miren considered. "Hmm, no. Not exactly. You are just echoing what you hear."

And what do I hear?

"You have to listen first."

This is very confusing.

"I think it's clearer when you actually do it." She glanced at the puddle. "Don't worry about the water right now. Just listen."

Davri studied the puddle for a moment, then closed his eyes. A breeze combed the grass around them, whispered through the trees. Somewhere beyond a bend in the road, a horse clopped past.

Davri straightened, as though surprised, and looked up. She followed his gaze but saw nothing except a line of trees.

He was looking north.

Miren felt her pulse quicken. How many times had she seen her mother look north when Singing? Miren didn't know what it meant, and she had never asked. She had assumed that she would find out once she earned her Voice.

For the first time in years, Miren felt the sickening ache of that old desire to know what it was like to be a Singer, to hold so much ability and wonder and purpose. What did they hear? Her mother had never been able to explain it.

Davri stared at the puddle, and he Sang.

His high tenor drifted over the shifting wind. The puddle churned and swayed; Miren recognized his tune as a modified version of the Song for the tides, an easy, flowing melody of pushing and pulling. It was a common Song that fishermen used to coax a ship from the shore onto the open water. Miren realized that he might not have ever heard it Sung by another Singer, and yet the notes and syllables were unmistakably similar.

Davri shifted his melody, and the water stilled, then began to swirl. Miren was drawn back to that long-ago Skyflame ceremony and the pail of churning water. His tone was richer and deeper with age, but just as before, his Voice shot up into falsetto, a high-pitched, unsustainable sliding melody that was far too quick and sharp for a normal Water Song.

The water in the puddle spiked upward, cracking faintly as it froze into a glistening sculpture of icy needles.

Davri looked at her, grinning widely. *I had forgotten.*

Miren leaned back, trying to keep her own smile in check.

FOURTEEN
MIREN

THE FOLLOWING DAY, THEY REACHED THE RIVER.

The towns they passed were larger and closer together, with sprawling farmland interrupted by rows of buildings alongside wide dirt roads.

The sudden appearance of bustling carts and an erratic hum announced the next town, Fisher's Point, before it came into view. The hills seemed to level to make room for it, like furniture pushed to the corners of a room. The western mountains felt closer here, though Miren didn't think they had traveled very far toward them. It added to the crowded feeling of the town.

Arten hoisted Ori onto his shoulders. "Remember what we spoke about," he said.

"No talking."

"That's right. We don't want them to know where we're from."

"Because we're the bad people." Ori plucked at his father's collar.

Miren looked up in surprise. "You're not bad people."

Ori glanced at her, then away. "But we're fighting."

Ah, he meant the war.

Davri signed, *Not the bad people. War doesn't have good or bad people. Just people who want different things.*

Ori stared at Davri as he signed. Ori tried to mimic him: *War doesn't have people.*

Davri signed the sentence again but slower, showing the sign for *good.*

"We should practice more with him," Arten said. "Haven't had much reason to."

Miren pushed down Davri's hands. "No signing. Not here."

Davri gave her a hard look but didn't argue.

No one paid them much attention as they walked through town. Though there were plenty of fishermen and farmers, Fisher's Point was an infrequent stop for traders. The river provided a direct eastern route to the coast, but the heavy current made it a one-way trip, and the town was too far from the coast for merchant ships to reach. Davri had explained all this in agonizing detail the night before.

Fisher's Canyon was also known as Jorli's Creek for a time, he had signed animatedly over the fire. *Supposedly, it was a running joke among some farmers. A young Singer couldn't remember the sign for* river *and instead used* creek. *The name was abandoned when cartographers added it to maps, as it created confusion. Its cousin, a river called the Crown's Seam, cuts just along the border of the Second and Third Circle territory. It's much larger.*

Past the houses that seemed to grow smaller and closer together, they finally reached Fisher's Canyon itself.

The river was nothing like what Miren had imagined. She had expected something slightly larger than the scattered creeks of Crescent Bay. Those creeks were cold and occasionally full of small fish that Miren had learned from experience were more trouble to catch than they were worth.

Fisher's Canyon was a large crevasse that split the town in half and was breached by various crooked bridges, some of which swayed dramatically as people walked across them. Miren couldn't see the river itself until she was standing two paces from the edge.

White water roared fifty paces below, the sound amplified by the canyon walls. Rope ladders dangled to the occasional wooden dock or patch of dry land. Mounted at the top on both sides of the canyon were pulley systems, webs of wheels and chains and cranks that lowered boats and pulled up full nets. Miren spotted a couple of women using the pulleys to raise a large basket of fish from the dock below.

Though she was a skilled swimmer, Miren felt a thrill of fear. The fisherfolk seemed unbothered, but she couldn't convince her pulse to slow.

Liviya pointed downstream. Miren followed her gaze to a heavy-looking iron gate that was mounted on the side of a sturdy bridge. The gate was hoisted all the way up, allowing boats to pass underneath.

"They lower that gate at night," Liviya said. "We need to take a boat and get it over the barrier."

Miren stared at her. The river would be impassable once the gate was in place.

Everyone looked at Davri, who was staring down at the water. The roar of the river was loud enough that Miren could whisper without being heard. "Think you can do it?" she murmured.

He glanced at her, his lips pressed in a thin line. *I have to,* he signed.

They camped just outside of town and waited for dusk, the early spring night growing chilly. Miren watched the gate being slowly lowered into the water, dipping below the surface before locking in place.

"The gate explains why no one has issues leaving their boats on the water unattended," she observed.

Hana looked up. "I'm not thrilled at the idea of stealing someone's boat, but there's no other way."

Miren had been struggling with the thought as well. She rationalized it as Liviya and the family were the ones doing the stealing, not her, but she knew this was false comfort.

Hana and Arten had mostly left Miren alone—something she encouraged—but they had taken a liking to Davri. He was well-read and patient and eager to help. Even Ori seemed fascinated with the young man who didn't speak. He imitated Davri's signs, though it was clear the child didn't always know their meanings.

Now, a light hum caught her attention. Davri was Singing water into different shapes to entertain Ori while Arten and Liviya scouted the area.

"No, make the head bigger!" Ori demanded. Davri obliged without missing a note. A small figure made of water attempted to walk across the ground.

Miren listened, surprised that the undulating nature of Water Song could be wielded with such accuracy. She noticed Davri's Voice jump and crack a little with the effort, but the figure retained its shape. It was apparent Davri possessed the same strange knack that other Singers had: Once a Singer understood how to listen, skill and control came rapidly.

What does he hear? she wondered. *What can he hear that I can't?*

It had been a while since she had felt genuine jealousy for Singers, though during the first few days after Kesia received her Voice, envy had been a constant companion.

Miren remembered one particular afternoon: she had crept up the lighthouse stairs and opened the floor hatch just a sliver to spy on Kesia's Singing lessons. Mother's back was turned, and she faced the center of the lightroom. The girls had known how to work and clean the lighthouse for years, but now Mother would show Kesia how to light its lamp with Song.

Miren knew that this Song was special. When Mother explained the importance of listening while Singing, she would refer to this Song. Before Skyflame, Miren had never managed to repeat the Song perfectly, despite all her practice.

Now Kesia stared at the wick, a distant look of concentration pulling her brow together. She looked older and far away, her attention on something the sisters could never share.

"Miren," her father shouted. "Where did you go?"

Miren ducked her head before Kesia could turn. She gently lowered the hatch door and slipped down the stairs. She was supposed to be feeding the chickens.

"Miren!" her father called.

She shut the lighthouse door behind her and found him hammering at the chicken coop.

She wiped sweaty hands on her skirt. "Sorry, I'm doing it."

He gave her a look but said nothing. She unrolled the top of the bag of dried corn and plunged her hand inside. The steady beat of the hammer and the squawking chickens covered up any uncomfortable silence.

The chickens scuttled around her as she tossed the feed. A question hummed at the back of her throat, which was full and bitter. She could never ask her mother or Kesia, of course, but perhaps the other non-Singer in the family would understand.

"Father," she began.

He picked up another nail and set it into the wood. "Yes, dear?"

"Did you ever want to be a Singer?"

He lowered the hammer with a smile, as if he'd expected this conversation. She should have fed the chickens and not said anything. She didn't want to seem jealous of Kesia.

"I think," her father said, "that everyone wants to be a Singer when they're young. I even remember when I first saw someone Sing. It was my uncle, and we were fishing. I thought it was incredible, a very clever, easy way to catch many fish at once, and with only one net."

Miren nodded. *Incredible* was too easy a word, too simple, but she couldn't think of a better one.

"I remember my Skyflame ceremony," he continued. "I remember going up and trying to Sing Water, because I certainly didn't have the low range for Earth. But as I walked into the circle, I thought about how difficult it was for my uncle. He was ignored much of the time. Not on purpose, of course, but people didn't always notice when he was signing. I didn't want to *not* speak for the rest of my life."

Miren blinked. She considered crying because she hadn't yet, but now didn't feel like the right time.

Father shifted his grip on the hammer. "Since then, I've always thought that true Singers were those who realized what they were sacrificing and were willing to give it up. You work harder than anyone, but you don't always get the recognition for it. You gain a Voice, but you lose one too."

Miren nodded absently, turning back to the chickens. She hadn't thought about those things at Skyflame. She remembered being nervous, her head feeling full of air. She had never considered the spells of silence in between Songs.

A young Voice drifted from the lighthouse. A light glimmered in the window.

Since then, Miren's envy had shifted into something closer to resigned disappointment. She hadn't experienced that jealousy for years, and she felt immature for entertaining the emotion now. *I have no reason to be jealous of Davri,* she told herself.

"Do you mind if I join you?"

Miren looked up in surprise at Hana.

"No," Miren said.

Hana took a seat beside her, smiling pleasantly. Perhaps Miren's previous standoffishness had been forgiven.

"Your friend is very talented," Hana observed.

Davri sat about ten paces away, still Singing a puddle of water into different shapes while Ori watched. Davri hadn't asked any more questions about Singing, but Miren had noticed him practicing pulling water from a pump into his canteen, drying his bedroll, encouraging a pot over a fire to boil faster. He was learning quickly.

She realized he was the best Water Singer she had known, and as a nobleman, he would never have to use his gift to survive. The irony of it felt cruel.

"He is," Miren said quietly, in case Davri could hear them.

"Are you two . . ." Hana nodded to Davri. "Romantic?"

"Oh no!" Miren said a little too loudly. "No, definitely not."

Hana grinned. "I didn't think so. But you don't look alike."

"No, we're not related. He . . ." Miren searched for a way to say it that didn't needle her and found none. "He fancies my sister."

Hana nodded again, as if this didn't surprise her either. "And does your sister fancy him?"

"Yes," Miren admitted. "She does."

"You don't sound pleased about that."

Miren paused. She had told herself not to grow close to these people, but if all went well tonight, they would soon be on their separate ways. There was no danger to this conversation.

"When you met Arten," Miren said, "what convinced you both that . . . you should marry?"

Hana raised an eyebrow. "We fell in love, of course."

"But is that all? You have those warm feelings inside and decide to marry?"

"Well, no. Those fade over time. But we grew to know each other, and we realized we could share our lives. And then we realized that we didn't want to live *without* each other."

"I don't understand the difference."

"Oh, I'm sure you will someday." Hana smiled.

Miren felt a spark of irritation at that answer, but she said, "Well, I don't think that Davri and Kesia understand that difference either."

Hana considered for a moment. "I'm not so sure," she said.

"Why?"

She nodded to Davri. "He's here, isn't he?"

Miren said nothing. Yes, he was still here. That counted for something, as much as she hated to admit it.

She scrambled for a different topic. "When did you meet Arten?" she asked.

"He and Cale were brought to Cheliem's estate about a year after I was."

"Cale, his brother?"

"His younger brother, yes. Liviya hopes to rescue him as well."

"Alone?"

Hana shrugged. "Arten so badly wants to rescue his brother," Hana said.

Miren pulled at the grass near her heel. "I understand," she said.

Hana nodded. "Not all siblings are close, but those who are have an unshakeable bond. I worry I'm going to wake up one morning and find Arten gone, chasing after Cale."

Miren stilled. "Really?"

"Sometimes." Hana waved a hand. "But I shouldn't. I just worry. Truthfully, if Liviya says she would do better alone, I believe her. She came up with that plan to escape Cheliem's estate. It didn't go as we hoped"—she gave Miren a wry look—"but the idea was to make Cheliem think we had escaped toward the coast and jumped the first ship we saw."

Miren felt a small beat of guilt but quickly smothered it. "But she had a second plan, just in case?"

Hana nodded. "She always comes prepared."

Miren leaned forward on her knees. "Helping us wasn't part of the plan," she said. "What made you decide to warn me?"

Hana's gaze slid down. "Truthfully, when I first saw you, I thought you both were pretending to be nobility. You certainly weren't dressed like it, and Davri being a Singer made you look even more odd. When I heard Cheliem send word to the Crown's Guard,

I thought . . ." Hana bit her lip. "I—I thought having you two try to escape would improve our chances, that maybe Cheliem would think the fire was your fault and focus on you."

Miren blinked. "Oh."

Hana looked abashed. "I'm sorry, truly. I was terrified of what we were about to do, and I believed I had to improve our chances in every way I could. I felt awful about it as soon as I suggested it. When you managed to find us in the chaos, I thought letting you come was the least I could do."

Miren considered Hana's words. "I understand," she said. "It makes sense." Miren thought she might have done the same thing in Hana's position.

They both looked up as Davri's Song leaped into falsetto: the sphere of water he held aloft hardened into ice with a faint cracking noise. Ori plucked it from the air and turned it over in his hand. "It's cold!"

It is *cold*, Davri signed, grinning.

"What about your sister?" Hana asked Miren. "She's a Fire Singer?"

"Yes."

"When was she taken?"

"Eight days ago."

Hana looked sympathetic. "How did she avoid the draft for so long?"

"She grew sick." Miren pulled at a loose thread poking from the knee of her trousers. "Cloud fever."

Hana said, "I may have heard of that."

"It's an illness that goes for the throat and often damages the voice, sometimes destroying it completely." Miren remembered her sister's gaunt cheeks, her small frame wrapped in blankets. "Kesia was always a bit frail. She was often sick. We thought cloud fever was going to take her." Miren remembered lying in bed those nights, weeping as she imagined Kesia not breathing, practicing her good-byes in her mind: *Kesia, I love you, you were a wonderful sister, please don't go, I love you—*

"And so she was excused from the draft?" Hana asked.

Miren took a breath. "The recruiters removed her name from the roster." She remembered their mother standing in the doorway between uniformed soldiers and a shuddering Kesia, signing a warning: *I am the strongest Singer in this village. If you do not take my daughter, I will come quietly.* "I think they were just happy to get our mother."

Hana nodded. "The war has taken so much."

"The Singer draft was the worst thing our king ever did to us," Miren said.

Ori jumped to his feet to chase a dragonfly. Miren glanced up and saw Davri staring at her, his expression looking too much like pity. She glanced away before he could sign anything.

They ate a meal of stale bread and cheese and watched the sun set, fighting sleep and cold until Liviya and Arten returned from scouting the river. "Time to go," Liviya said.

They followed Arten back into town, keeping to the edge of the ravine until he led them down a rope ladder. Davri hoisted Ori onto his back and went next.

Miren landed on the short dock and nearly lost her balance. When she recovered, she saw Liviya pointing to a small fishing boat at the farthest end of the dock. Arten hurried to it and started untying the mooring ropes.

Davri hopped into the boat, then helped Hana and Ori climb in. Miren glanced up at the top of the ravine, but no one was in sight. She climbed aboard with Arten close behind, the boat now dangerously crowded.

Arten shoved against the dock so the bow was facing downstream. Miren braced herself, her pack strapped tightly across her chest. Davri positioned himself at the bow, his knuckles white as he clung to the side. He exhaled, then inhaled and Sang a note.

She felt the Song catch immediately. The water beneath them rose and pushed against the bottom of the boat with surprising force, as though Davri had startled it from its sleep.

Miren had never fully understood where the power of Song came from. She knew some energy had to come from the Singer, but there was a strange singularity to it. How could Singers who had never met other Singers perform a particular Song the exact same way? There was a source to their power, even as each Singer had his or her own strengths.

The boats around them swayed slightly as the water level dipped to support their surge. The boat rose higher and higher, until it almost felt that they would keep going straight into the sky.

The mountain of water passed over the gate, then dropped.

The boat splashed down on the other side, harder than they expected; Miren bit her tongue painfully. Ori squealed with either fear or delight as Arten hunched over him. Davri clutched the bow with both hands, his shoulders sagging.

"Go, go, go!" Liviya hissed.

Davri gulped down more air and Sang, and the boat surged forward. He knew this Song well enough.

Miren looked back up at the town, which was already behind them. It seemed unlikely that no one had seen or heard them leave, but there was no sign of pursuit. All that was left was to reach the coast.

Davri's Song leaped and fumbled, and he seemed to be struggling for breath. Miren looked up to see another gate.

There was no time to correct course. The boat swooped up slightly at the last moment as Davri tried to protect them from the impact, but the craft's momentum flipped it all the way over as it slammed into the new gate, dumping all six of them into the black water.

The icy water shut over Miren like jaws. She felt the cold bars of the gate against her back as her nostrils filled with water. She fumbled for the bars and pushed herself up, suppressing the urge to inhale. Churning water roared in her ears. She opened her eyes but saw only blackness.

She clawed her way up the gate, fighting the current, until her head broke the surface.

She gasped the cool night air as the water rushed past her ears. Next to her, the boat bobbed upside-down against the gate. Gripping the bars, she started pushing her way toward the bank.

A blond head in the water caught her attention. She reached down and felt an arm and pulled.

Hana gasped as her head broke the surface. "Ori! Where's Ori?"

"I don't know!" Miren looked around, but she saw nothing in the dark. "Can he swim?"

Before Hana could answer, the water swirled around them, plunging them under again. The gate was wrenched from Miren's grip as the water shoved her upstream — against the current.

Her hip and shoulder slammed into something hard and dry. The water had spit her out onto the bank on the opposite side of the river. Water Singing filled the small canyon. Davri stood poised on the rocks, a sodden Liviya lying beside him.

A few moments later, the water surged and spat out Arten, his arms wrapped around Ori. Hana cried out in relief.

"Come on," Liviya said, breathing heavily and pushing herself upright. "Climb. We have to go."

Miren followed, her hands slick as she clawed her way up the ravine. She thought she heard someone shout over the roar of the river, but she dared not take the time to look.

Arten hopped over the ridge, then knelt to help Liviya. Davri pushed Ori up over a bulge in the precipice too big for him to climb. Every second felt too long; the rocks were slippery under Miren's wet hands; her pack streamed water. She heard another shout—she knew she hadn't imagined that one.

Someone grabbed her and hoisted her onto flat ground. "We have to go," Arten said. "They can see us."

Miren glanced over her shoulder. Torchlight flickered from the other side, and more fires moved along the ravine—local men on watch maybe, or some kind of patrol readying to cross a bridge.

Miren looked around. They were no longer in the town—flat, open farmland stretched in every direction.

"Go, let's go!" Liviya led the way, and the group dove into the nearest cornfield.

FIFTEEN

MIREN

THEY RAN NORTH. EVEN AFTER IT BECAME CLEAR THAT NO one was following them, they didn't stop wading through stalks of corn from one farm to the next until the sky began to lighten. Ori cried quietly until Hana soothed him and Arten scooped him up. Davri continued to hum, slowly drying everyone's clothes, starting with Ori. Eventually, fatigue won over caution, and they sat on the far side of a small hill, out of sight from the nearest farm.

Davri was the first to slump to his knees, exhausted from so much Singing. Arten began gathering kindling. Hana looked through her pack for items that hadn't been damaged by the water. Ori sprawled on the ground next to Davri, looking tired and miserable.

Miren lowered her pack but remained standing. "What happened?" she asked.

No one answered immediately, but in the growing silence, everyone paused to look at Liviya, who was busy wringing out the hem of her shirt, though it was mostly dry now, thanks to Davri. Miren waited, her anger mounting.

Davri sat up. *My fault. I didn't see the gate in time.*

"This isn't your fault," Miren said. "Is it, Liviya?"

Liviya straightened her shirt. "It seems," she said with a sigh, "that Fisher's Canyon has a second gate."

"Oh, does it now?" Miren asked acidly.

"How did we miss that?" Hana asked.

"It must be a new structure," Liviya said. "It wasn't labeled on my map."

"How old is your map?" Hana asked.

Liviya carefully pulled the rolled-up map from her pack and laid it on the ground. It was still damp from the river, and much of the ink had bled in illegible streaks. "I purchased it about eight months ago."

While Liviya pored over the sodden map, Arten knelt, rubbing wood together for a fire, his expression grim. Davri was rummaging through his pack and trying to Sing some crackers dry.

"We'll have to try another river," Liviya said. "I think the Crown's Seam might be doable, though we'll have to pay off a few fishermen. Davri, can you Sing two smaller boats at once?"

Davri paused in his Song, obviously exhausted.

Miren's anger boiled over.

"No."

Everyone but Liviya looked up at her.

"Care to sit down?" Liviya said.

Miren faced the older woman. "Davri and I agreed to help you get your family on open water."

"That's still the deal."

"The second gate was your error. We held up our end of the deal."

"Then I'll rephrase the deal," Liviya said. "You are not getting a word of information until my family is no longer touching Kaleon ground."

"Well, you had better give us something, because otherwise we walk."

"Oh really? You're going to search the entire coast of Kaleo for your sis—"

"If I have to! It would be better than wandering around waiting to get arrested with you all. Or worse."

Ori whimpered and huddled close to his mother. Miren felt a pang of regret for scaring the child.

"We're still the best option you have," Liviya replied, looking unconcerned.

"I'm not sure that's true."

"Oh, you're not, are you?"

Miren swallowed. "I don't trust that you know what you're doing, not after that surprise second gate. And I'm not even sure that you have the information we need."

Liviya raised an eyebrow. "Meaning?"

"We're not going any farther with you until we get some answers."

"We had a deal," Liviya said darkly.

"We fulfilled our part of that deal!" Miren snapped.

"I won't give you anything until my family is safe."

"That wasn't the deal, Liviya!"

"Yes, it was."

A handclap. Everyone glanced at Davri.

We need something from you Liviya, Davri signed. *We want to help you, but not at Kesia's expense.*

Liviya considered him for a long moment, her dark eyes hard. "What would you suggest, Davri?"

All the naval officers you think Kesia might be assigned to, he signed without hesitation. *If you truly know what you claim to know, you must have some idea, and I will be able to recognize some of the names. When your family is safe, you can tell us where to start looking.*

Liviya narrowed her eyes and leaned forward, but Davri didn't flinch. "What if I refuse? You plan to leave us?" she asked.

This is a gesture of goodwill. We did a lot for you tonight. We need some kind of proof that you really intend to help us. This information won't help us on its own, but it will prove you know what you claim to know.

Liviya leaned back slightly, still staring at Davri. Miren was struck by the notion that Davri had essentially just asked for the very same thing she had, but he had a far better effect on the group.

Liviya said, "I will give you names only, not fleets. I need to be sure you won't leave us in the middle of the night."

"You said yourself that would be foolish," Miren said.

"That doesn't mean I think you won't try."

Davri glanced at Miren, waiting for her approval. Making the decision together, just like he had said. She gave him a small nod.

Deal, he signed.

SIXTEEN

KESIA

KESIA SANG HEAT INTO THE AIR, TRYING TO KEEP HER balance against the Air Songs all around her. The heat from the furnace had dried her skin. The collar chafed her neck and chin. Her hair, matted with sweat and soot, clung to her cheeks and snagged on it.

Life as a slave for Amos Steel held a rigid pattern.

At night, the female Singers were shoved into a heavily fortified closet with nothing but a few mats and tattered blankets. A blaring horn and the clank of a metal lock woke them in the morning, followed by the silent commands of the Earth Singer, Nadav. The slaves followed him down a metallic hallway and set of stairs to the large, clamorous workplace.

Avi'ori men, none of them wearing collars, worked on contraptions scattered throughout a series of rooms filled with conveyor belts, metal rollers, and water basins. Fiery liquid poured into iron basins from a great furnace. Kesia still didn't fully understand the process, but this was clearly some kind of metal refinery.

The Avi'ori workers took turns giving her orders throughout the day. *Make the furnace hotter. Warm up this sheet of metal here. Heat the rollers.* All day she Sang, her Voice struggling to remain true against the Water and Air Singers who worked around her.

She had never kept a Song going for longer than a few minutes before, and even that would leave her head filmy and her knees weak. Flames ate at her from the inside for hours. She could almost feel her cheeks sink and her gaze turn hollow as time passed.

She remembered hearing Davri Sing, his low tenor floating over a puddle as it swirled and waved within itself. All Song took something from the Singer, but water was easy to continue once it was prompted. Fire demanded everything.

Breathing was the worst chore. The unyielding pressure of the collar held her on the edge of panic all throughout the day. She focused on remaining calm, on the steady rhythm of her heart, the air cooling her lungs. *In. Out. In. Out.* She stumbled a few times, her mind swimming, her throat raw. A short note of Earth Song yanked her upright each time.

She glanced often at the only other Fire Singer, the small, frail girl with stringy hair. She was easily the youngest slave, so starved that her shoulders poked against her rags, but she flew from task to task with an impossible energy. Their first night in the barracks, Kesia had asked her name, but the girl had shaken her head. None of the Singers communicated much during the day, and after work hours the barracks were too dark to sign.

Kesia's heart throbbed. They needed to escape.

The trouble was that she couldn't fathom a way to do it. Every open door drew her gaze outside, giving her glimpses of warehouses and what might be a wall. But she saw no gate.

When she wasn't staring out the window, she watched her fellow Singers. The new slaves, those who had arrived with Kesia, winced at every command. Most of the others kept their gazes down, their backs hunched under the weight of their collars. They moved slowly, taking long and measured breaths in between Songs.

A few hours into her first day, she learned why.

She Sang a small fire under a piece of pounded sheet metal. The Avi'ori pointed with his hammer where to heat, never looking at her.

Someone shouted just as a sudden grating of metal shook the room. Kesia whirled, her Song dying on her lips.

A Water Singer, a middle-aged man with a long nose and a mess of facial hair, stumbled away from an overflowing basin, where molten metal had splashed onto the floor. The Singer cradled his hands, his breath coming in short gasps. He must have attempted to catch the metal as it fell.

"Hey!" an Avi'ori man shouted. "What are you doing? It's ruined now!"

The Singer waved his trembling hands as though trying to sign.

Kesia didn't understand at first why he shook so violently, until she followed his gaze to the front of the room and saw Parviz, the slave master, at the door.

Kesia's stomach lurched. She ducked her head as he entered but didn't look away. Parviz glanced between the Singer and the basin. The Avi'ori workers remained silent. The Water Singer fumbled, apologizing, his signs a garbled mess.

Parviz glanced at Nadav and nodded.

Kesia felt her heart drop through her stomach.

The Water Singer wheezed as something in his collar clicked. Nadav's deep voice shifted, throwing the slave to the ground, dangerously close to the puddle of molten metal. A feral choking came from the man as the collar dragged him toward the door, past Parviz's impassive form, Nadav walking beside him. The Water Singer stopped struggling just as the door closed behind him.

Parviz glanced around, as if just noticing his audience. Kesia couldn't help but think that he had enjoyed it. She shivered.

"Back to work," he said.

Kesia turned, convinced she would be sick all over the machine. She found the Avi'ori worker with the hammer watching her.

He shrugged. "Consider that a warning, Singer," he said. "Parviz doesn't put up with much."

The factory workers rarely spoke to the Singers unless to give an order. They talked and laughed over the roar of machinery, never looking at Singers, treating them like part of the factory. What kind of men could work so casually alongside slaves?

"Hey, Fire Singer!" a man shouted. Kesia hurried over.

"We're almost out of coal, and we've still got a load of metal in there. Keep this hot until we get more loaded in."

Kesia nodded and Sang, bracing against the fatigue that pulled at her shoulders. She stared at the fire, watching the flames twirl and flicker. Miren had said that staring at fire too long hurt her eyes, but Kesia had never felt that. She let the fire guide her vision across the furnace, imagining that she could make out shapes.

On a whim, she altered her Song.

The flames ballooned and shifted, bumping gently against their new constraints. She added notes and syllables, and the fire formed into a horse. She thought the head was too small, or the tail too long, so she evened out the proportions, then practiced lowering and raising its head. The hair would fall with it—

"Hey!" a man shouted.

Kesia lost a note, and the fire flickered out.

"What are you doing?" the man said, a bag of coal over his shoulder.

Kesia shook her head and signed, *Sorry, sorry, sorry!* She threw herself into a new Song, and the fire flickered back to life, formless and normal.

The man shoved coal into the furnace, and the fire devoured it. Kesia stopped Singing with a gasp and collapsed to her knees.

"Get up," the man said without concern in his voice. "Before Parviz gets back. And don't let him see you do those stupid tricks again."

She nodded, struggling to find enough balance to stand. Breathing took all of her focus. *In. Out. In. Out.*

A set of hands pulled her up. The other Fire Singer stared at her, her grip firm until Kesia could steady herself. The girl wasn't smiling, but there was softness in her eyes. She flitted away before Kesia could thank her.

The day was unbearably slow. The only measure of time was the light streaming through the windows. When it turned a faded orange, the Avi'ori workers headed for the door, chatting about dinner plans and the bar a few streets over.

Nadav escorted the women back to the barracks on the second floor. Kesia measured her breaths with each step, trying to stave off the wave of panic that always threatened to choke her. *In. Out. In. Out.*

A rumbling note, and the metal door swung open. The women filed in without comment. Kesia stayed close to the other Fire Singer and waited until the door shut with a loud *thump.*

The room had no light, so signing was nearly impossible, and it was quiet except for shuffling feet and labored breathing. Kesia bumped into someone short and thought it was the Fire Singer. She caught her wrist and pressed into her hand the signs for *K* and *EH* and *S* and *EE* and *UH.*

The girl went unnaturally still. Kesia braced for her to pull away, but a small, warm hand pressed against hers and spelled: *AY-L-UH.* Ayla.

Kesia smiled, and the cold lump in her chest thawed a bit. If they worked together, they could find a way out. Quickly, she spelled another word, her heart thumping: *EH* and *S* and *K* and *AY* and *P*—

Ayla wrenched her hand out of Kesia's and backed away, slipping into the crowd of women claiming their mats. Kesia felt a pang in her chest and remembered to breathe. *In. Out. In. Out.*

⁕

The next day, Kesia was brought to another part of the large building, a huge space full of enormous metal cylinders. The rollers stood upright as blindingly hot sheets of metal were pushed between them. Singers pelted the finished sheets with water before loading them onto carts and wheeling them outside.

"Over here, Fire Singer," a worker shouted. She shuffled over to a set of rollers. "Heat these up."

This room seemed more bearable, though Kesia couldn't think why. She Sang until her throat grew sore and her legs unsteady. Sparks left biting burn marks on her arms. Perhaps she preferred this room because the enormous furnace didn't loom over her. Perhaps it was because Parviz never appeared in the doorway.

But she didn't waver in her work, because fear was a solid weight in her chest. There were times she forgot it, lost in the task at hand, in the steam and grinding of gears. The workers sometimes shouted over the din, reminding her of summer nights, fishermen gathered around a fire playing rocks for the last swig of wine.

"Hey, we have a problem!" someone shouted.

"You!" a man pointed at her from the doorway. "Get over here! Sing this furnace hot!"

Kesia nearly tripped again in her haste to obey. She quickly returned to the room with the furnace, throwing her Voice at it. A leak near the top was spitting steam and bright orange and blue sparks. She could feel the heat escaping the furnace, pushing against the hole like a desperate animal. Kesia fought to replace it, but she wasn't fast enough. Her legs shook with the strain; her vision tunneled. She fell to one knee, and rough hands yanked her back up.

"Where's the other one?" a man shouted.

Another worker shoved Ayla forward, and she leaped in with her own Voice. The two Voices weren't complementary—Ayla's tone was thin and reedy, and her notes sometimes bent in the wrong places—but the furnace grew warmer.

Air Singers swirled current around the bottom vent, increasing the pressure inside the furnace. Kesia knew it must be helping, but the strain of their Voices on top of hers threatened to topple her, until she felt only the air thrumming from her throat.

She didn't know how long it took the workers to fix the leak; she opened her eyes as hands dragged her limp body out of the way of a sheet metal cart. Ayla sat against a far wall, her eyes fluttering, and many of the Air Singers were on their knees. Kesia noticed that most of the workers were not trying to hurry the Singers back to the job.

She winced as a shadow fell over her, but no hand touched her. A smooth, deep Song wrapped her in a cool mist, pressing lightly on her forehead and the back of her neck. She had heard this Song before, one afternoon months earlier.

She and Miren had fought. She couldn't remember why—maybe it had been about chores, or their parents, or Singing—but cutting words had driven her to the beach, kicking sand and wiping tears on her sleeve and wishing things were different. She often wandered down here, when she needed to leave that small cabin or take a break from talking and just *listen*. Sometimes she could feel her sister staring from the lighthouse, but even ever-protective Miren did not bother her here.

Usually she turned back once she reached the docks, reluctant to run into anyone or interrupt the fishermen, but on this day, she gave the docks a wide berth and kept going, not ready to return home. At the base of the small hill where the baron's estate rested, she turned right, still keeping toward the water, where the beach curled around a sharp bend.

She had never been this far up the shoreline. The rocks were tricky here and often half-submerged in surf, but she accepted the challenge and began to climb.

It took only about two minutes to regret her decision. The rocks were slippery and uneven and sharp in places, and the encroaching surf had soaked most of her skirt. She clung to the rocks, winded already, the way back far steeper going down than it had looked on the way up.

A voice rose against the roar of the current.

A Song.

Startled, Kesia nearly lost her footing.

Perhaps ten paces above her, a blond head poked from above the rise. It was a moment before she remembered his name. Davri, the baron's son. The Water Singer.

She rarely saw him. He occasionally came to the village and bought bread or a trinket, but he and his family spent most of their days at their estate, receiving letters from the messengers or sending one of their servants to buy produce. They were generous with their spending but little else.

She looked at him quizzically, too busy holding onto the rocks to ask a proper question, but he continued his Song. She watched as the rocks between them dried from top to bottom, a spreading puddle in reverse. He gestured for her to climb.

It was still agonizing, her clothes freezing and clinging to her, but she slowly made her way up.

He was seated on a flat shelf of rock that faced the water, his legs dangling over the side. He wore a pressed white shirt, dark trousers, and boots polished to a high gloss. He looked wholly out of place.

He smiled. *Hello,* he signed.

Hello, she replied. *What are you doing up here?*

He shrugged, looking sheepish. *I like to watch the sunset from here.* He gestured to the great expanse of the sea, the afternoon sun gleaming brightly off the water.

She nodded in agreement and sat down.

Do you climb that too? she asked.

He shook his head and pointed up. *I come from the estate.*

She followed his gaze and saw a path winding up in the cliff face.

He looked at her. *I can dry your clothes if you like.*

You mean with Singing?

He nodded.

That would be very nice.

He stared at her skirt, his brow furrowing. He opened and closed his mouth a few times. It was nearly a full minute before he started to Sing.

She watched him quizzically. He seemed oddly unsure, sometimes pausing in his Song to find the proper note. She had never seen a Singer struggle like that.

He glanced at her and frowned. *Do you miss Singing?* he asked.

He must have misread her expression. Like the rest of the village, he believed that she had lost her Voice to cloud fever. She felt a pang of guilt at the lie, magnified because he was a Singer. She nodded.

Do you Sing often? she asked.

He shook his head. *Not much reason to.*

Kesia nodded, feeling sympathy for him. She didn't know much about Water Singing, but perhaps she should explain some of the basics.

But they didn't discuss Singing that day. They shared stories of parents and expectations and frustrations born from the loneliness they felt as the last two Singers in the village.

Kesia worried that she was boring him, but he was attentive and patient, his eyes—deep blue, she noticed—never wavering from her as she signed. Perhaps it was just politeness, she thought, but he would consider her words and respond and ask questions in a way that suggested genuine interest.

The sun was setting when they finally climbed down that day. Though she hadn't Sung at all that afternoon, a warmth had begun to unspool in her heart.

She looked up into eyes blue like the sea.

Davri—

Dark hair, though, and a gnarled beard that spilled over the collar. His face was full of crevices. His eyes were old. A fellow slave.

The clink and hiss of molten metal filled her ears again. She was not in Crescent Bay.

The slave's hands moved. He was asking if she was all right. Nodding was impossible, so she closed her eyes, her head pounding, her chest aching for air. *In. Out. In. Out.*

SEVENTEEN

KESIA

KESIA HAD LOST TRACK OF THE DAYS. IT WAS EASIER TO sink, to let time wash over and drown her. Sometimes her conscious mind would sleep for hours at a stretch; she would wake suddenly to find herself carrying tools or pushing carts of iron ore or Singing, Singing, Singing, burning, burning, burning, the collar tight around her neck.

Her Voice rasped when she Sang, something her mother had always warned about, but there was rarely a pause during the day.

Sometime after the midday meal on what might have been her fifth day at the factory, she sat and stoked the fire while the Avi'ori workers shoveled in more coke. Air Singers blasted currents through the bottom of the furnace, and blue flames shot out the top as impurities were burned off. Kesia could feel the competing Songs increase the pressure and heat the furnace.

The sound of voices pulled her attention from her Song: two Avi'ori stood ten paces away, arguing with a third man who was dressed differently than any worker Kesia had seen. He wore a tool belt and harness around his torso, and weird, green-lensed goggles were propped above his brow. Unlike the others, his arms were bare.

"Hey! Quit Singing," someone shouted. "The ore's out!"

Kesia cut off her Song and turned away. Every time she apologized for a mistake, the workers would either ignore her or grow frustrated.

She glanced at the three newcomers. The man with the goggles glanced back at her, but she looked down.

"Hey you!" he called. "Fire Singer. Come here."

The other two men crossed their arms, their expressions sullen. She glanced at Ayla, who was pushing a crate of coke up the ramp to the furnace opening. There were still rollers to be heated, and the back conveyor belt kept jamming—

"Now, Singer!"

Kesia hurried over to the men, feeling the lack of air in her lungs. *Don't panic,* she told herself.

"Parviz's not going to be pleased, Katzil," one of the workers muttered.

The newcomer, Katzil, rolled his eyes. "He can take it up with me, then. Amos wants this tested before the Council sends someone to inspect it."

Amos. The name she had seen on the building, on the machinery throughout the warehouse. Her *owner.* Perhaps she should fear him more than Parviz, but she didn't.

"You'll need an Earth Singer too." The man glanced at her dubiously. "How's Nadav going to be in two places at once?"

Katzil shrugged his broad shoulders. "If this little girl grows to be too much trouble, then one of the men'll shoot her in the leg."

Before the workers could make another offer, the newcomer turned and motioned for Kesia to follow. She glanced at the others, waiting for clear instructions, but the men left without looking at her.

She followed Katzil out of the workshop and through the double doors. Nadav, the Earth Singer, glared at her with a silent threat, but her collar remained open, allowing a little more air.

The day was muted gray; featureless clouds hovered over the walled factory compound. Kesia hurried to keep up, trying to spot something, anything, that might hint at how she could escape. But the buildings were monotonous, and she saw no opening in the wall.

Katzil paused midstride and turned to her. "I meant what I said, girl," he muttered. "If you hurt any of my men, I will shoot you. Are we clear?"

Kesia swallowed, wincing as the collar grated her throat, and signed assent.

Katzil led her past a half-dozen identical factory buildings, each humming with machinery and coughing smoke. She looked between them but saw nothing in the distance except an enormous brick wall, perhaps three men high. Angry metal spikes protruded from the top.

Around a corner, they came to a gate.

Kesia startled, but this was not the gate she had come through five days earlier. They were on the southern end of the property now, facing away from the city. The heavy, two-door gate made of solid metal stood on wheels. A couple of workers rolled it open to let Katzil and Kesia through.

The back of the factory stood in stark contrast to the bustling city. Kesia saw a path from the gate to a cliff, with switchbacks that led down into a small, cragged valley, where tufts of green and gnarled trees clung to the harsh stone. To the right of the valley lay the sea. She dared a few extra steps toward the edge of the cliff to see the surf roar against the rocky cliffside. If she were to go far enough around the western wall of the compound, she would likely be able to see the docks.

"Hey!" Katzil called. "This way."

Kesia hurried over to join him, and the two began the trek down the cliffside. As the incline steepened, Kesia found it difficult to watch her step. Because of the iron collar, she couldn't angle her head to see her feet. She stumbled often and at one point fell to her knees. Katzil merely waited as she struggled to stand.

She knew this was the opportunity she needed. She was out of the compound, away from Nadav. But where could she go? She wouldn't be able to outrun anyone going downhill, especially in the collar. Even if she managed to get around the compound to the other side, they would be able to see her well enough to shoot her.

The path flattened out as they reached the bottom and curved left, winding around the uneven valley to the east. Soon after, they turned into a wide, flat clearing.

Kesia nearly stopped in her tracks. In front of her was a building larger than any she had ever seen. She almost didn't understand the scope of it until she spotted figures walking around its base. It looked like a hill made of metal, the curved roof standing at least four times higher than the lighthouse in Crescent Bay, perhaps more.

Katzil led her into the building without stopping. Inside, the walls were ringed with metal walkways that led to hallways, as though someone had hollowed out this part of the building just to make room. Workers buzzed around, sharing tools and hanging from the ceiling in harnesses, all intent on the project in the center, which was . . . difficult to understand.

It was an enormous oval structure that easily filled most of the space. Kesia thought it looked like an enormous balloon, stretched lengthwise, its outside covered in crisscrossed metal beams. Beneath it was a smaller structure that looked like a boat made of metal.

The entire thing was floating, the metal boat knee-high off the ground, heavy tethers connecting the balloon's metal frame to thick anchors on the ground.

It was *floating*.

She had heard of hot-air balloons. Davri had once explained to her how they worked: a fire heated the inside of the balloon, which somehow made everything float. She hadn't understood how hot air made anything float, but he had seemed excited about it.

Though she had never seen such a balloon, she believed they were far smaller than this structure. A balloon this size didn't seem possible.

Katzil waved for attention. "We got a Singer!" he shouted over the din.

Nearby, a few men huddled around a desk. Two of them smiled in response but gave Kesia only brief glances before turning back to the papers that littered the surface in front of them.

"The furnaces are ready," one man said. "We've got as much coal in there as the thing can handle."

"It'll have to do," Katzil said. "You ready?"

Kesia nodded, but he was talking to the workers.

She followed Katzil to the boat-like compartment under the balloon and stepped inside at his prompting. It was a small, cramped space. To the left was a long, circular dashboard covered with dials and levelers and buttons. Handles and gauges hung from above what could only be a steering wheel, set in front of a curved window. To the right, a small metal door led to a room filled with four huge furnaces, with bins of coal right beside them.

Dozens of pipes lined the ceiling and walls. This machine was more complex than anything Kesia had ever seen, but what did it do?

"This way," Katzil said, motioning her to the furnaces. She thought he might be smiling, but she was afraid to look at him.

"Here's what you'll do," he said. "When I give you the signal, you must light all four of these furnaces at the same time. They heat the boilers that power the propellers. These dials here measure the pressure and heat. They all have to be consistent, especially on each side. These two can't be too much hotter than those. The boys will shovel coal if needed. You understand?"

Kesia nodded, scrambling to comprehend this impossible contraption. *What does it do?* she signed.

He stared at her, and she looked away, her heart thumping at her own daring.

"It flies."

She looked up, baffled. *This? This whole thing?*

"This is an airship." He pointed up at the huge, bulbous structure. "The ballonet is filled with a special kind of air that's lighter than the outside, so it wants to float. The fire powers the engines to the propellers so we can steer and regulate altitude. Stay here and wait for me."

Kesia watched him go, her mind tripping over *engine* and *propellers* and *ballonet*. A few men milled about, bringing in coal or checking gauges or tightening screws. Her escort seemed to be the leader, and though he was quiet, the other men's quick movements and focus suggested a shared excitement.

And why shouldn't they be excited? If what Katzil said was true, they had created something incredible.

A younger man, perhaps in his early twenties, climbed into the craft. "Excuse me," he muttered, not looking up. She pressed against the door to let him pass.

He ambled to each furnace in turn, checking the gauges and sometimes hitting the pipes with a wrench. He seemed to be listening for something.

He caught her staring. "What?" he barked.

She looked away and shook her head.

"I'm not going to hurt you," he said, sounding irritated, then continued his work without explanation.

Katzil returned. "All right, engines are ready, pulley system looks good, and the hatch is open. Where's our pilot? Gauge-watcher, are you ready?"

There was a scramble as everyone found their places. Kesia stayed near the door as two young men filed in with shovels.

"We're ready for launch." Katzil pointed at Kesia. "Start the fires!"

She took a breath and Sang.

The furnaces were enormous. She could feel the cool space inside eat at her Song, resisting the heat she created.

"Keep it even!" the captain shouted.

She nodded and added more breath to her Voice. Without being able to focus on one at a time, bringing the heat high enough was slow, arduous work. But it was rising, if she could just maintain her Song.

"Engines are at thirty-six percent heat," called another worker, the one standing beside the pilot. "Forty, forty-five, fifty—"

"Release tethers!" the captain shouted.

Beyond her Song, Kesia heard the clacking and snapping of metallic cables outside. She stumbled for a moment as the floor tilted.

"Keep Singing!" the captain yelled. "Don't slow down."

She poured more of herself into the Song until the furnaces roared with fire. The two young men fidgeted with their shovels, waiting for orders. Though Singing took nearly all of her focus, her gaze kept drifting to the window. Outside, she could see the jagged, cavernous valley and the path she and Katzil had taken down from the factory. They must have opened the roof of the building.

They were flying. They were *in the air.*

Something metallic snapped and clanged above her head. She sensed a sudden shift in the heat flowing from the furnaces on her right.

"We lost the port boiler!" the gauge-watcher shouted.

"Skies," the captain hissed. "Lower her down."

The pilot pulled levers. The gauge-watcher turned dials. The view shifted.

She continued Singing because no one had told her not to. The captain glanced at her. "Stop the fires!" he shouted. "Put them out!"

She did, a final, relieved note that choked all heat from the furnaces at once. Suddenly dizzy, she grabbed the doorframe to steady herself, noticing that the airship was back on the ground.

Sit, she signed, seeing the captain's eye on her. *I need to sit.*

Katzil ignored her signs. "I have to take you back now," he said.

She nodded and followed him out of the airship, her legs trembling.

She returned just as the Avi'ori workers were filing out of the warehouse, though the Singers had not yet been escorted to the barracks. Nadav saw her and gestured to a pile of pails and rags and mops.

Clean, he signed.

Kesia took a broom and began wandering around the room in a haze of fatigue. She was completely worn out from the demanding Singing and the climb back up to the factory.

Her mind drifted to the airship. Today, she had *flown.* In spite of her exhaustion, she found herself hoping they would call on her again soon.

When the Singers had finished washing the furnace and organizing carts, the Earth Singer finally escorted them to their rooms. Kesia fell into step next to Ayla, who glanced up with a timid question in her eyes.

Flying ship, Kesia signed, taking her time with each word. *I flew.*

Ayla's eyes widened, but she didn't sign. Nadav had just opened the door to the room where the women slept. Kesia fought the urge to look at him as she passed.

The door closed, leaving them in darkness. Kesia wanted to tell Ayla more about the airship, but she lost track of the girl in the shuffle. She curled up on a tattered rug and thought about flying, about large balloons and pulleys and coal and propellers and altitude. She imagined herself holding the wheel, giving orders to others as the craft glided over waters, boats, between mountains, arriving at Crescent Bay—

Her chest tightened: she hadn't once considered escaping on the way back.

Miren Davri Miren Davri—how could she have become so distracted?

Tomorrow. *Tomorrow* she would look for a way to escape.

EIGHTEEN

KESIA

THE FOLLOWING DAY, KESIA RETURNED TO THE FACTORY floor, though she couldn't help looking for Katzil. The *captain*. Of a *ship*. That *flew*.

She gritted her teeth and focused on thoughts of home. If there was a chance that Miren was alive, then Kesia owed it to her to plan an escape. She pretended that Miren was beside her, discussing her options.

You need to pay attention next time the captain takes you, Miren would say. *Look outside, see where the gate is, where people are. Even finding a warehouse to hide in might be helpful.*

But I don't even know if the captain will come again, Kesia thought, feeling guilty at the twinge of disappointment.

He will. Miren's voice was firm. *They just need to fix something, and then they'll want to test again. They'll want you, because you're a Fire Singer.*

Ayla is a stronger Singer. Kesia glanced at the other girl.

They don't know that. Besides, the fewer people who know about the airship, the better. They built it behind that hill for a reason.

Kesia shoved the cart by the door. Some men were pouring iron ore into the furnace; they would need her soon. She set herself between a pair of Air Singers, waiting for orders.

You won't have an Earth Singer watching you, Kesia, the imaginary Miren reminded her. *It will be your best chance.*

Kesia shivered. It was her best chance, but she was frightened. She could fall, be shot by guards —

They won't kill you. You're too valuable.

But even the Miren in Kesia's mind didn't say what they both knew: there were worse things than death.

Kesia imagined Miren smirking, covering concern with humor. *You could steal the airship. They'd never catch you that way.*

A silent laugh pushed against Kesia's collar. Would Miren be as amazed at the craft as she was?

I would, Kesia, but I'd be terrified.

Kesia nodded. She was terrified too.

At noon, the Avi'ori workers passed around glass water jugs and stale bread and cheese to the Singers. Kesia was surprised at the size of her portion of bread, almost half a loaf.

"Captain wants you better fed. You're joining him today."

Kesia nodded and shoved the food in her mouth. The *captain.* Were they ready for another flight?

Focus, Miren's voice sounded in her mind again. *You're looking for escape.*

A few minutes later, her belly aching with so much food, Kesia saw Katzil saunter in. The men didn't intercept him this time as he called to her. "Let's go, Fire Singer."

She hurried after him, daring a glance at Nadav, who gave a nod of permission.

The captain led her out the double doors, toward the southern gate. She walked a few paces behind him so he wouldn't see her wandering gaze. She counted three other buildings in sight, all of them similar in size to the refinery where the Singers worked.

Another gate, Miren urged. *Look for an opening.*

Kesia glanced between the buildings, seeing the brick wall adorned with metal spikes. If there was a door, it must be on the other side of the compound, and guarded, and locked, and—

Then look for something else! Miren snapped. *Don't give up so easily.*

Kesia glanced to the right. The faint roar of waves tumbled over the western wall of the compound. Even if Kesia could get beyond the wall, they were on top of a cliff. Jumping wasn't an option.

There must be something, Miren insisted.

Kesia followed the captain through the gate and down the same path as yesterday. *Sorry, Miren, I'm sorry, I'm trying—*

I know, Kesia. I know.

The Miren in Kesia's mind stayed silent after that. Soon the hangar came into view, and the airship distracted her from thoughts of escape.

Kesia followed the captain onboard and took her spot by the furnace room door. The same two Avi'ori boys stood beside bins of fresh coal, their dark faces smudged with dust and grime. No one spared her a second glance.

She didn't understand half of the words that the crewmen shouted, but she sensed the quiet excitement as more men came aboard and found their places.

Captain Katzil was last to take his position. He looked around, his expression serious. "Don't get too hopeful, men. Every endeavor will have problems. That's just the way of the skies."

Kesia recognized it as a play on a sailor's idiom, *the way of the seas,* and she found herself smiling too.

"All right, let's start the fire!"

Kesia Sang a note, strong and clear. She felt it reverberate through each furnace at once, felt the faint hum as the heat crawled upward through the pipes. The coal burst into flame, startling the shovel boys.

She didn't let herself get distracted by the captain's commands and the bustle around her. The power that the fire demanded was consuming. She glanced at the gauges, seeing the needles slowly climbing.

"Boilers at fifty percent!" the gauge-watcher called.

"Release the tethers!"

The same snapping noise. Outside the pilot's window, the hangar walls began to sink.

Kesia focused on heating the furnaces. *Flying, flying.* Out the window, she saw a glimpse of blue.

"Skies," one of the shovel boys breathed.

The pilot pulled a lever, keeping a firm hand on the wheel. "Clear of the hangar in three, two, one."

"Initiate propellers."

The whirring of the engines grew louder. Kesia shifted her Song as the gauges reached their desired heats almost simultaneously. She let her Song soften and leaned against the wall. The four fires were white hot, and her Song drifted over each one, keeping them stable.

"Keep us in a starboard turn," Katzil said. "This is just a test."

"Yes, captain."

A *flying* ship. Kesia couldn't help a faint smile.

The furnace on the starboard side dropped in temperature, and she noticed that her Song wasn't catching on the coal. She motioned for the boys' attention and pointed. *More coal,* she signed.

The boys glared. "We don't take orders from you," said one.

Kesia turned to the captain, but he was faced away from her, speaking with the gauge-watcher and gesturing out the window. Her heart fluttered with panic. She gasped under the weight of her Song. If she did this much longer, she would collapse, and the craft would suffer.

The ship started tilting.

"We're losing power on the port side boiler!" the gauge-watcher shouted.

She marched forward and reached for one of the boys' shovels.

"Hey!" he snapped and pulled it from her hands.

She swiveled and wrenched the other boy's shovel from him. Her arms trembled as she worked to pour more coal in the hot furnace. She could feel her Song leap hungrily onto the new fuel, but it wasn't enough, not nearly enough.

"Great skies!" Katzil shouted.

Kesia took a deep breath, feeling the constraint of her collar. *More coal,* she signed, pointing at the furnace.

"You two! What are you doing?" Katzil looked furious.

The boys blanched. "We were waiting for orders—"

"If the girl says it needs coal, put it in! She's working harder than the two of you put together, and she ain't even getting paid. Get to *work.*"

"Yes, sir," they mumbled. They huddled around the furnace and shoveled frantically. Kesia stumbled back and fell to the floor.

The captain looked to Kesia. "You all right?"

She nodded, breathing heavily. *Ship all right?* she asked.

He blinked. "Yes, girlie. Ship is fine. Get to work when you're ready."

She nodded again as he passed. It was easy to believe that he was genuinely concerned, that he trusted her to keep the ship flying.

He is not your friend, Kesia, Miren would say. *To him, you are no more than property.*

The day ended in celebration, the men clapping one another on the back and insisting they go out for drinks. A few even looked in her direction, perhaps seeing her through the lens of the captain's approval, but their elation had nothing to do with Kesia. How could one feel so free and so trapped at the same time?

Katzil assigned one of the crew to escort Kesia back to the factory. She glanced around as they walked, but night had fallen like a blanket, and the compound was only lit by a few oil lanterns. Miren would urge her to try again tomorrow, she thought.

As the Earth Singer led them to the barracks and closed the door, Kesia was careful to stay by Ayla. She caught the girl's hand and signed, *Escape*, against her palm, strong and firm and fast.

She waited for Ayla to pull away, to scamper to the farthest corner, but the girl only paused. Slowly she took Kesia's hand and signed, *No home.*

Kesia's heart throbbed, and Ayla slipped from her grasp before she could spell *sorry.*

NINETEEN

MIREN

MIREN HANDED OVER THE TWO GOLD PIECES, AND THE MAN behind the counter gave her the bundle without so much as a smile. It was a ridiculous amount for dried meats and cheese, but Miren knew prices would increase as they traveled north. Besides, it was Davri's money.

Miren made her way through a steady stream of people, trying to study them without being caught staring. Most of them wore work clothes like hers, but the cloth seemed cleaner and more colorful. She saw shirts of blues and greens and reds, rather than the faded yellows and browns and off-whites she knew.

The city itself was larger than any she'd been in yet, and the buildings were taller here than at home. Miren spotted Liviya inside a shop whose sign read BEULAH'S MAPS AND CHARTS. She was likely buying maps to replace those that had been ruined in the river.

Miren turned a corner and in the intersection saw a large, ornate fountain: a statue of several men and women standing in a circle, mouths open as though they were Singing. Behind the Singers was a small mountain with a perfectly symmetrical peak.

At the base of the fountain, a crowd was forming, facing a few men and women who wore the uniform of the Crown's Guard. One guard, whose decorations proclaimed him the most senior, was addressing the crowd in a deep, thundering voice.

" . . . fought to defend the king's land just off the coast of Kilithis

Bay, where our battlements lay waiting, cannons loaded and ready. The Avi'ori ships realized the trap too late. Before they could turn around, the cannons fired on them and drowned their ships."

He paused, waiting for applause, and the group slowly obliged.

"The Kaleon fleets are in need of more brave men and women who are willing to risk themselves at sea for the good of us all. Today, we accept volunteers to join our ranks. Who has the same courage as those sailors?"

Miren's eyes widened as a few stepped forward from the crowd. Volunteers? Weren't all able-bodied men already drafted?

Beside her, an older woman clutched the shoulders of a boy who seemed well into his teen years. The woman looked pained, almost angry.

"Isn't there a draft?" Miren said. "Why are they asking for volunteers?"

The woman glanced at Miren. "Not from around here I take it."

"Fifth Circle."

"Hmm. Didn't know there was anyone still alive that far south."

Miren shrugged. Was that how the rest of the kingdom regarded Fifth Circle territories? "We're small. No cities like this."

"This ain't no city," the boy said.

His mother nodded toward the Crown's Guard. "They pretend to look for volunteers, but if they don't get the number they want, they'll pull names from the town census. This is just for show."

Miren nodded, though she didn't quite understand. Why not just draft the people and be done with it?

She noticed two of the officers signing to one another. "Are those officers Singers?"

The woman nodded. "Singers of the King's Navy come here to lead the Skyflame ceremony."

"Skyflame? Now?" Miren asked, confused. Skyflame was always celebrated at the end of harvest season.

"Tomorrow," the woman said, sounding grim. "They come by a few times a year to host it and draft those who earn a Voice."

Miren stood aghast. She had never heard of such a thing. Crescent Bay hadn't held Skyflame in years. Part of the reason was that they no longer had Singers to guide the ceremony, but there was also the unspoken fear of one's young son or daughter becoming a Singer. With the Singer draft still in effect, the gift of Song had very quickly become a curse.

The crowd was dispersing now that the speech was over. Miren was supposed to meet Liviya at the stables, where they were to purchase a cart and horse together, but she decided that could wait. She made her way toward one of the women guards, whose dark hair was tied back in a bun.

"Excuse me," Miren said. "I had some questions about recruitment."

The officer pointed to the lead officer and signed, *All questions should be directed to Officer Arvek.*

The Singer's signs were so sharp that Miren almost missed their meaning. "No, I mean about Singers."

The Singer nodded, motioning for her to continue.

Miren's heart thudded. Could it really be this easy? "My s— cousin will be participating in Skyflame tomorrow, and I was wondering about what would happen if she becomes a Singer."

Singers who demonstrate a Voice are immediately sent to the capital, the woman replied dutifully. *Air Singers have the great privilege of helping ships sail and maneuver northern waters.*

"Actually, I wonder if she'll become a Fire Singer." Miren scrambled for a story. "You see, our grandmother was a Fire Singer, and my cousin has the same lower pitch in her voice."

The woman nodded placidly, as though she had heard such things before. *That would be a great honor.*

"Where would a Fire Singer most likely serve?"

Those decisions are made by generals and fleet commanders. Your cousin would be assigned where needed.

"But where are some of your Fire Singers stationed?" Could Miren find out where her mother was? "Some examples?"

The Air Singer paused.

"I don't mean to be rude, ma'am," Miren added quickly. "My aunt and uncle are just worried. Hopefully there's somewhere other than combat you would send a young girl."

The woman's eyes flashed. *It is an honor to serve one's country against the Avi'ori.*

Miren blinked, stunned. "Of course," she said. "I didn't mean to suggest otherwise." She had never met someone who seemed eager to serve in the war.

A hand gripped Miren's arm like a vise. She whirled and found Liviya standing there, her expression stormy.

"Mila," Liviya said. "I've been waiting for you. We should get going."

Miren was more startled by Liviya's nearly perfect Kaleon accent than by being addressed by a false name. "I know," she said. "I was just—"

But the Air Singer officer had wandered off and was now in discussion with a couple and their young daughter.

Liviya pulled Miren away from the crowd. "What are you doing?" Liviya demanded, her voice low.

"I'm just asking questions."

"You won't find the information you need from the guard," Liviya warned her.

"Then it shouldn't be a problem that I spoke with them." Miren wouldn't be made to feel embarrassed for wanting to learn more.

"You're trying to back out of our deal."

"And you're stalling in fulfilling your end of it."

"I will give you the names I promised as soon as we get back to camp," Liviya said.

Miren glanced back at the crowd, but the officers were gone. She hadn't had the chance to ask if they'd had a new Fire Singer recruit in the past week, but she supposed that would have been too unusual of a question.

She followed Liviya to the stables, where the older woman and a thin, hunched man with a long gray beard bartered for a full quarter hour. Horses in Crescent Bay were scarce, expensive, and not very useful for farming or fishing, but when she was younger, Miren had often wondered what it would be like to ride one.

Liviya managed to wrestle the price down to twenty-eight gold and six silver. Miren felt the number like a physical wound as she handed over her half of the coin—well, Davri's coin mostly—and the two women led a horse and cart out of the stables.

Davri and the others were waiting near a cotton farm just at the edge of town. Liviya had insisted on keeping the others outside of town, but Miren feared that having them wait along the road would call attention to the group.

Ori had draped himself over a wooden fence lining the road, leaning forward to stare upside down through his legs at passersby. Davri stood near, ready to catch him. A few people glanced at the boy and smiled.

As Miren and Liviya approached with the horse and cart, Arten looked up with a nervous question in his eyes.

"Let's get on the road," Liviya said.

"Wait," Miren said. "What about our—"

"When we make camp, Miren," Liviya said.

Miren glanced at Davri, but he just shrugged, hesitant to sign with so many people around.

Hana and Ori climbed into the cart, and Liviya led the horse to an adjacent road. It seemed she intended to go around the town rather than back through it.

When they were alone, Arten told Liviya, "Maybe we should wait farther from town next time we stop for supplies."

"A few people asked us for directions," Hana said. "We had to ignore them."

Liviya nodded. "We'll try to keep supply trips brief from now on."

Miren stepped up beside her. "Is it really such a concern if anyone knows you're from Avi'or?" she asked.

"It catches attention," Liviya said. "We don't need anyone remembering us."

Miren frowned. "Do you think Cheliem is sending his guards to look this far north?"

"I doubt it, but it's good to be cautious."

Miren glanced around. The near constant stream of people forced the group to remain quiet, and so Miren was left at the back of the party, watching Ori search for creative ways to entertain himself: trying to balance on the side of the cart despite his mother's protests, asking Arten and Davri to let him sit on their shoulders, and throwing stones at signposts until he was relieved of stone privileges.

The landscape seemed to warp and expand the farther north they traveled, leaving room for larger farms and towns. The ridge of mountains to the west looked more cragged and broken, as though a cliff face had been smashed in and toppled on itself. One enormous gash in the side of a cliff was visible for hours as they slowly passed it from miles away.

The towns of Kaleo were beginning to look more like the cities that Miren had heard about. The buildings were larger and more closely packed together; wooden paneling was replaced with marble and brick and mortar. Dirt roads were superseded by cobblestone. Horse-drawn carriages became more common and more ornate.

They stopped by a creek after midday to eat and to water the horse. As soon as Liviya sat, Miren plopped down right in front of her and handed her a slip of parchment and a pencil she had procured in town.

Liviya paused with an apple halfway to her mouth.

"We had a deal," Miren said.

Liviya put down her apple and took the parchment. Miren willed herself to be patient.

About a minute later, Liviya handed the pencil and parchment back to her. Miren looked over the list and felt her insides wilt. She counted the names.

"Six?" Miren said. "That seems like a lot."

"Well, what did you expect?" Liviya said. "Everyone with any military rank is going to want a Fire Singer."

"But who's going to get her? Wouldn't it just be the highest-ranking officer who wants her?"

"Oh, not necessarily. People call in favors or even bribes."

Davri came to read the names over Miren's shoulder.

"Do you recognize any of them?" she asked.

He took a moment, then pointed at four names in turn. *These are related to lords.*

"Lords?" Miren reached for the replacement map that Liviya had bought and rolled it out. "Do you know where their estates are?"

Davri nodded and took the pencil. This map didn't feature the artistry that Davri's had, but it held far more detail. Many smaller towns were labeled, along with variously colored lines that marked different routes and trading outposts. The Circles were outlined in faint green lines. Davri marked off the four estates and handed the map back to Miren.

"Do you think the fact that these are nobles means they're more likely to get Kesia assigned to their ship?"

Davri shrugged and looked at Liviya, who was chomping on her apple.

Miren held her tongue. Arten watched the conversation silently while Hana busied herself with Ori. A pang of guilt caught Miren by surprise; she didn't want the others to think she was trying to abandon them.

But if there was an opportunity to find Kesia, she would have to take it, right?

She fulfilled the deal, Davri signed, though he looked disappointed as well. *For now.*

"Fine," Miren said. Grudgingly, she added, "Thank you."

"Pleasure." Liviya took another bite from her apple.

Miren stared at the list, trying to commit the names to memory.

"So, what's the plan exactly?" Hana asked, handing Ori a slice of apple. "You mentioned another river?"

"The Crown's Seam," Liviya said. She picked up the map. "The largest river in Kaleo. It cuts through Third Circle territory here. It's . . . not for sailing, usually. There are a number of small waterfalls and rapids—"

"Waterfalls?" Miren said.

"Which is why I would have never considered it without a Water Singer," Liviya said.

"Why don't we just go straight toward the coast?" Hana asked. "Couldn't we find another ship willing to smuggle us to Avi'or?"

"Ships this far north would not be traveling to Avi'or," Liviya said. "We're too close to the warfront, which is usually around here." She pointed to the northern end of the Tehum Sea, not far from the Kaleon capital. "Even if they were willing to smuggle us, we wouldn't be able to afford the asking price. And it would be far too risky to try to steal a ship from the docks there. Riding a river all the way to the coast is still our best option."

"What about here?" Miren pointed to a collection of islets surrounding the bay like shards. "Will that be a problem?"

"Another reason we can only do this with a Water Singer. We'll need to navigate between these little islands in order to remain far enough from shore not to be spotted, but not so far that we wander too close to combat."

Miren glanced up and caught Davri's look of surprise. For all that they knew about the war, they had never been so close to it.

Liviya continued, "From there, we will angle south until we clear the islets here, and then we'll go our separate ways. You three"—she gestured to Arten, Hana, and Ori—"will head directly east across the sea. I'll come back with these two to retrieve Cale."

"Uncle Cale!" Ori said happily. He still had crumbs of cheese stuck to his face.

Miren held up a hand. "We didn't agree to help you—"

"I know," Liviya said. "I'll tell you everything once these three are safe, and then we'll part ways. I'll get Cale myself."

"Isn't Lady Rion's estate close to the Seam?" Arten said. He pointed to an area just south of the river. "It's around here, isn't it?"

"You don't need to worry about that," Liviya said.

"But Mother, if we're going that way already—"

"It's going to be difficult enough getting a boat to the Crown's Seam in the first place, and if we try to get Cale first, we risk alerting Lady Rion's guards, and we won't make it to the coast."

Arten looked severe. "You'd rather walk right past and do it by yourself later?"

"The other option is to have Hana and Ori sail across the Tehum Sea by themselves. Would you find that acceptable?"

A muscle twitched in Arten's jaw. "No."

"Good." Liviya rolled up her map. "Let's get going."

As everyone settled into the cart, Ori cuddled between his parents while Davri took a seat by Liviya in the front, Miren sat at the far end and spread out the map. She stared at the four names Davri had scrawled on various cities. One from the Second Circle, one from the Third, and two in the Fourth.

Miren estimated that they were nearing the border of Third Circle territory, if they hadn't already passed it. Liviya's path had them going in a relatively straight line, despite the detours around various towns. They were making good time.

But was that enough? Miren considered her guilt at the idea of leaving Liviya and her family. They had put their trust in Miren and Davri; if they didn't have a Water Singer to navigate the rapids, how else would they escape Kaleo?

Since leaving Cheliem's estate, Miren and Davri had spent eight days traveling with the family, putting all their hope in Liviya's information, but without making any real progress in finding Kesia. It wasn't enough. What more could Miren do?

Kesia, Miren thought as her eyes blurred with unshed tears. *Where are you?*

She rubbed her eyes, composing herself, and studied the map. When she felt confident she had memorized the locations, she rolled up the map and leaned back, hoping to doze.

She heard Arten murmur something to Hana, who stood, holding the back of the front bench. "Liviya, do you mind if I take the reins for a while? Arten would like a word with you."

Liviya pulled the horses to a stop. "I'm sure he does."

Hana took the reins, sitting next to Davri, while Arten and Liviya walked alongside the cart. Miren remained still, pretending to sleep as Hana spurred the horse into motion again.

"I think we should get Cale," Arten said. Despite his low tone, Miren heard every word.

"It's not worth the risk," said Liviya.

"*Cale* isn't worth the risk?"

"Don't change my meaning, Arten," Liviya retorted. "I can get Cale. It isn't worth the risk to your family."

"Suppose we get a boat prepared before we go. You and I can break him out, and we'll be ready to leave."

Miren felt her apprehension rising. Liviya still had information they needed—would she try to make them rescue Cale before giving it to them?

Liviya sighed. "It's not as simple as you think. You know it took weeks to coordinate your escape from Cheliem's estate."

"We can hide out for a few days."

"Rion is going to have much tighter security than Cheliem."

"Then you should have more help."

"This could take weeks as well, Arten. I have to make note of guard shifts and the layout of the estate and figure out multiple escape routes, maybe pay off certain guards in advance. Are you going to risk your wife and child's freedom waiting for all that? Have you asked Hana what she thinks?"

A pause. Miren barely caught Arten's whisper, "I don't want to leave you behind, Mama."

"Arten," Liviya said. "I have spent so long planning, thinking of every way this trip could go wrong, of all the horrible things that could happen to you and Cale. I believe I can do this alone, but if I fail, I don't want to take you and your family with me. I want you *safe*. Please."

Another long beat of silence.

Finally, Arten spoke. "All right, Mama. You win."

"Of course I do," Liviya said.

The rest of the day wore on in relative silence, the road rising and falling and curving around hills. With farms and towns becoming more numerous, Liviya decided to take the risk of sleeping in a barn on the edge of a cornfield.

"I'd rather have to explain myself to one farmer than be spotted by every farmer around," Liviya said. No one argued.

Just east of their position, the land dipped into a shallow valley, where lights from a town flickered sleepily. They were miles away from the coast, but the land continued at a steady enough slope that they could see the faint shimmer of water as the waning moon began to rise.

After a meal of more cured sausage and cheese, Miren stood by the entrance of the barn, and Davri came to stand beside her. "What town do you suppose that is?" she asked.

He shrugged. In the dim light of the lantern they had purchased, he exaggerated his signs so she could see them. *Are we in the Third Circle?*

"I don't know. Does it look like the Third Circle?"

He raised an eyebrow. *What should it look like?*

"I don't know. I assumed it would be drastically different, like Isakio is from Crescent Bay."

"That town is Madafim," Liviya said from her seat on a bale of hay. "We passed the boundary into the Third Circle a few hours ago."

Miren felt a jolt of surprise. Madafim was near one of the estates that Davri had labeled on the map: Lord Eitan's. His relative—brother, she thought—was a name on Liviya's list, a naval fleet commander or captain. She took measure of where they were and could see in her memory where the estate was in comparison. It wasn't far.

Miren's pulse quickened, but what could she do? Break into Lord Eitan's estate? A Third Circle lord, no less. What were the odds that Kesia was with his brother's fleet? Or that Miren could find out anything about her sister's whereabouts by breaking into his estate?

The chances were slim—certainly too slim given the risk.

But still.

It was *possible*.

Was that enough of a reason?

Miren was only half-aware of the others as they made themselves comfortable in the hay. She thought Davri was staring at her, but she avoided his gaze as she lay down, her mind buzzing.

TWENTY

MIREN

Miren waited until the moon was just high enough to peek through the front window of the barn. She remained still, listening, but she only heard the murmur of crickets and soft snoring drifting from various corners of the room.

She sat up, easing herself off the hay. It crinkled underneath her, but no one stirred. Her revolver was loaded and ready; she'd cleaned it carefully and replaced the powder after their plunge into Fisher's Canyon. She strapped the holster around her waist and decided to leave the rest of her belongings.

She crept toward the barn door and opened it slowly, wincing as it creaked and whined. The night was cool and heavy with dew. She started along the edge of the property at a jog, keeping an eye out for any movement. The farmhouse was dark, as was most of the town. She could hardly make out the edge of Madafim, which was marked by a thin line of trees. Miren ducked under cover as soon as she was close and crept along.

Davri had marked the area belonging to Lord Eitan, and even in the dark, she could spot a glittering estate wedged into a hillside just north of the town.

Something rustled behind her.

She slipped her revolver from the holster. "Who's there?" she demanded.

More rustling, a sudden snap of a twig. She realized who it was just before he stepped into view, his hands up.

"Davri," she said, returning her gun to its holster. "How did you find me?"

He stood in the moonlight so she could see as he signed. *I thought you were up to something. Also, you left the barn door open.*

"Oh." A small part of her was relieved to see him; another part resented the relief. "You shouldn't be here."

He raised an eyebrow. *Neither should you. Why are you here?*

"Go back, Davri."

He frowned at her, waiting.

She knew she wasn't going to shake him, but the thought of saying her plan out loud made her feel foolish. "Lord Eitan's estate is just north of Madafim."

He frowned. *And?*

"And I wanted to . . . I wanted to see if I could find something on Kesia."

You want to break into a Third Circle lord's estate? Alone?

"I can try, at least."

His jaw dropped. *That is very foolish!*

"I have to do something," she snarled. "We've been traveling for nearly two weeks now, and we're no closer to finding Kesia than we were when we started. I don't trust that Liviya is going to give us what we need."

We don't have other options.

"I know."

You said so yourself.

"I know!" she cried. "But we—we don't have time. And what if we fail at this other river like we did at Fisher's Canyon? Liviya is still going to string us along, or even get us arrested."

If you don't trust Liviya, then why break into Eitan's estate? We can't be sure his brother is part of the military at all.

Miren wavered. She hadn't considered that.

Davri looked uncertain. *What do you expect to find at the estate?*

"He might have sent letters," Miren answered, but even that seemed thin. "Maybe Eitan's brother asked him to pull some favors, so he would get the Fire Singer for his crew. If his brother is a captain—we don't know. Maybe he asked for bribe money, or . . . something."

Miren rubbed her eyes. She felt like a child trying to explain why she should be allowed to go hunting alone.

Davri signed slowly, *Eitan might have records in his study.*

Miren's heart thumped. "Really?" She felt hope bearing down on her like an approaching avalanche. "What kind of records? About the military?"

Davri eyed her. *Would it matter if I said no?*

Miren paused. It should matter, but she couldn't imagine herself going back to the barn now, having done nothing. Turning back would be like betraying Kesia. If there was even the slimmest chance, how could she not take it? "No."

Davri nodded. *Let's go.*

"Not both of us. You should—"

I'm not letting you do this alone.

"If something happens to you, we won't be able to keep our deal with Liviya."

Then I recommend we don't get caught.

"Davri—"

We discussed this already, he signed, his gestures impatient. *We do this together.*

She fought the urge to roll her eyes at the sentiment. "Fine."

They continued around the edge of town toward the estate, keeping out of sight. The town ended at the base of the hill, but the main road continued, zigzagging up toward the estate. Along the western side of the hill, however, Miren noticed a line of trees.

"That way," she murmured.

They kept under cover as much as they could. The moon was bright, and even from this distance Miren saw figures walking along the outskirts of the estate. Still, they were far enough away that Miren thought it safe to speak.

"What do you know of Eitan and his brother?" she asked.

Eitan and Elul are twin brothers, Davri signed, his hands visible in the moonlight. *Eitan is older, so the estate is his. Elul wanted to start his own farms, but Eitan wouldn't spare him the land. Elul hoped to marry into a Second Circle family, but the engagement fell through. It makes sense that he would join the army. There aren't many options for those who aren't heirs to estates.*

"How do you know so much about this?" Miren still hadn't fully memorized the list of names Liviya had given them.

It was part of my training.

"Training? You had training?"

As a nobleman. Father hired tutors to teach me about the kingdom, mathematics, history, manners—

"You had a tutor for manners?"

A very important subject, mind you, Davri signed. *And I was very good at it. I was good at almost all areas of study. My father had high hopes for me.*

"What changed?"

He shrugged. *I became a Singer.*

"What?"

Davri winced. *Quiet!*

"He stopped training you just because you earned a Voice?"

Singers do not make good aristocrats, Davri signed. *We can't speak, so we can be ignored.*

"That's ridiculous."

Davri shrugged. *It's true, though.*

They continued weaving through the trees, keeping to the shadows as much as possible. Fear rose in Miren as the estate grew closer; she wondered if they should turn back, but the question never made it past her lips.

The moon shone brightly overhead by the time they crested the hill, finding themselves behind trees that were still at least forty paces from a fence surrounding the property. Even from here, Miren could tell that this estate was far larger than Cheliem's. Multiple windows stared out from a sprawling mansion with a marble facade and pillars on both sides of a grand entrance. A pristinely cut lawn surrounded the estate and spread toward the western side, where dark shapes resolved into evenly spaced rosebushes and trees.

Guards armed with rifles circled the grounds every few minutes.

Miren and Davri crouched behind a tree for perhaps a half-hour, watching the guards. Miren thought she had time to climb over the fence without being spotted; she just wasn't sure how to do it. The fence itself was comprised of thin, upright iron rods, with a single rail at the very top, nearly twice her height.

Miren whispered, "How long would it take you to Sing a block of ice so we could climb over?"

Davri signed something.

"I can't see what you're signing."

He took her hand. She instinctively pulled away, but he pressed his hand into her palm, signing letters. *T* and *OO* and *L* and *AU* and *NG*.

"Too long," Miren repeated. "I guess it would be." Davri would have to build and melt the ice in the time between the guards' patrols, assuming they wouldn't hear him first. "Well then, you'll have to lift me over and wait for me to come back this way."

Davri shifted and reached for her hand again.

"Don't argue with me," Miren said, pulling out of reach, "unless you have a better idea."

He paused for a moment. She offered her hand, and he spelled another word: *D* and *AY* and *N* and *J* and *R* and *UH* and *S*.

"I know it's dangerous," she hissed, wrenching her hand away. "I'm not an idiot, I—"

She stopped as another guard ambled into view, gritting her teeth as he passed. They just needed to get over the fence, then they could use the garden as cover. There were likely several entrances around the sides of the estate, though they would probably be locked. Would estates this large have night staff? She would need to hide somewhere inside, or wait in the garden . . .

It wasn't possible.

Miren turned and leaned against the tree, her jaw clenched.

Then she started back down the hill without a word. A moment later, she heard Davri follow.

She focused on her path, struggling to avoid tree roots in the dim light. She didn't realize she had hit the bottom of the hill until the tree canopy above her gave way to moonlight. She stopped in the grass, suddenly too tired to walk all the way back to the barn. She looked up at the deep, clear sky, the moon staring down at her like a blinking eye.

Nothing. There was nothing she could do.

She could try to reach the coast of Kaleo, she could hide from the Crown's Guard, she could make deals. But the truth was that Kesia's fate was in someone else's hands now.

The truth was that she had failed.

She had not protected Kesia. She had not done enough. And for that, Miren had lost her sister. After tonight, it felt less likely than ever that Liviya would help them—if only because finding Kesia felt so improbable. It was as though the world had swallowed up all memory of her.

She heard footsteps, a pair of boots. She looked up and saw Davri, his face contorted in grief and sympathy. This trip had been pointless. They hadn't even made it past the gate, and she realized Davri hadn't expected them to.

But he had gone anyway.

"Why are you doing this?" She almost regretted the words as she said them, but now that she had asked, she wanted an answer. "Why are you doing so much to find her?"

He paused, looking wary. *My father told me to come inside when the ship was spotted. I thought he was being overly cautious, but I didn't argue. I was reading in the study when a guard told my father what had happened.*

Miren watched his face as he continued. *If I had known, I would have brought her into the estate, or hidden her, or*— He threw his hands up, not looking at her. *I'm very, very sorry.*

An owl hooted overhead. The grass whispered as a breeze swept through the field. They listened in silence.

Miren should thank him for being here, for indulging her stupid decisions, for standing up to Liviya. She could imagine Kesia's disgruntled look. *He's a good person,* her sister would have said.

That's not the issue, Miren would have replied. But then Kesia would have asked what the issue was, and Miren would have dodged the question. Sometimes Miren suspected Kesia knew the real answer.

I don't want to lose you, Kesia.

Miren buried her face in her hands and cried.

Once the tears began, she couldn't stop. Sobs shook her shoulders and grated her throat. She heard Davri's footsteps as he approached and felt his arms wrap around her slowly, as if asking for permission. This time, she didn't resist him, feeling his own voiceless crying shake his shoulders.

TWENTY-ONE

KESIA

KESIA AWOKE TO THE WHINE OF GRATING METAL.

Her body insisted it was too early to rise, but everyone else sat up on their mats and blinked against the light spilling from the hallway.

"Where's the Fire Singer?" asked a familiar voice.

Kesia hobbled to the door, still dizzy with sleep. Nadav, looking more irritable than usual, stood beside the airship captain.

"There she is." Katzil gestured for her to hurry. "Let's go, let's go." To Nadav, "I'll have her back to you in time for factory work."

Nadav nodded as he Sang Kesia's collar open and waved her away, closing the door to the barracks.

Kesia followed Katzil, blinking against fatigue and struggling to keep up. The captain's gait was brisk as he hurried down the stairs.

"A representative of the Council is coming today," he explained. "He wants a demonstration before sunrise."

He gave her an excited look, then glanced away quickly.

Kesia's mind struggled to understand. A council representative? Council of what? But the captain was walking too quickly for her to ask, even if she had had the nerve to do so.

Outside, the world was chilly and dark. Stars blinked from a deep blue canvas. The compound was quieter than she had ever heard it; Kesia could hear the dull roar of the surf somewhere to her right.

Miren's voice leaped into her mind. *You're near the coast! What if you could find a boat?*

Kesia glanced west, but she only saw the hazy shape of buildings and a wall. It was too dark to make out more. She knew they were on a cliffside; it didn't make sense for there to be an entrance on the western side of the compound when they were so high above the shore.

The captain nearly jogged down the path to the hangar, where the clang and murmur of work broke the dawn quiet. Despite the early hour, it seemed nearly the entire crew was here.

"Go on to the furnaces and wait for my order," Katzil said.

Kesia nodded. As she headed for her station in the metal boat —the gondola, someone had called it—a few men looked up from their work. She smiled, and one or two smiled back.

Behind her, Katzil shouted, "Those furnaces better be full to the brim with coal! And check the water turrets again."

Kesia hurried up the stairs and into the furnace room. The same two boys who'd been there before were shoveling coal into the furnaces. They looked at her; she waved a greeting.

"You look way too happy for this hour," one muttered.

"She looks too happy for a slave," the other said.

Kesia lowered her hand, feeling sick at the word *slave*. She stood by the door and waited, trying to make herself shrink, focusing on her breathing. *In. Out. In. Out.*

The pilot and gauge-watcher soon boarded, looking jittery but focused.

"Start the fires," Katzil called, coming aboard. "He's here. And close the door. We don't want him to see . . ." His gaze caught Kesia's as she started her Song. The gauge-watcher closed and latched the furnace room door. They didn't want the representative to see the room?

That's important! Miren's voice was saying. *It must be!*

But Kesia turned her attention to the furnaces, her Song still too weak to keep them all going. She took a breath and pushed more power into her Voice.

A minute later, the engine rumbled to life — the propellers whirred. Kesia Sang harder to fill the sudden drop in heat.

One of the boys flinched at the flame. "Hey, watch it, Singer!" he barked.

She felt the floor shift.

We're flying!

The flight was longer than she expected. Perhaps a quarter hour in, she sat down, her Song pulling at her insides as it always did, her stomach tight with hunger and fatigue.

Her mind drifted to the captain's words. Why wouldn't Katzil want the representative to look in here? It was dirty, of course — a cloud of soot hovered over the room, and she and the boys were smeared with it. But there was grime everywhere.

He didn't want the representative to see *her*.

She had never heard of Avi'or having slavery. They had outlawed the form of indentured servitude that Kaleo still practiced, which rumor had it wasn't much better than slavery. Was slavery illegal in Avi'or? If so, perhaps Amos Steel would get in trouble if the Avi'ori government knew of all the Singers being held there.

If she revealed herself to the representative of their Council, would he be appalled? Would he help her?

Kesia's heart leaped, her breath coming short as she Sang. She could be free. She could free *everyone*. She just needed to get the representative's attention.

She glanced at the boys, then pulled herself to her feet, willing the dizziness to pass. The boys were staring mindlessly into the fires and didn't seem to notice her. She inched her way to the door, all the while continuing her Song.

She tried the latch. Locked. She would have to wait for the men to open the door from the outside. She leaned against the wall but stayed on her feet, Singing, her knees feeling like twigs.

Eventually, the faint tilting sensation stopped. The whir of the propellers faded into silence.

We've landed. Kesia halted her Song, feeling the engines already begin to cool. *Run,* Miren told her. *As soon as the door opens, run.*

I don't know if I can.

Yes, you can. Do it! For me, Kesia.

The latch clicked and creaked open.

Now, now, now, it has to be now!

She bolted.

"Hey!" someone shouted, but no one was ready for her. She launched herself through the airship's hatch and looked around.

There—by the large doors of the hangar stood a man in a dark coat and trousers, untouched by the grime around him. He turned a corner out of the warehouse, tipping his hat at the workers.

Kesia sprinted after him, her legs and chest protesting immediately. *Go, just go!* she told herself.

When she neared him, she clapped hard for his attention. He turned, and Kesia saw his pinched brow and pointed lips. His eyes widened at the sight of her.

Slaves, she signed, her hands shivering. *Slaves, many slaves.* She pointed to the refinery. *Help us, we're slaves, we're trapped!*

She heard running footsteps behind her. The man was still staring at her blankly. *Slaves!* she repeated. *We're trapped, forced to work!*

"You!" Katzil shouted, running over.

She cowered, looking at the representative, pleading with her eyes. *Please, please help!* she signed.

The man stared at her, seeing her filthy rags and her iron collar.

"You need a Fire Singer?" he said, "to power the ship?"

"Uh, no, no," Katzil stammered. "It just makes things easier. She lights the furnaces all at once, we don't need—"

"That's quite a cost, you know," the representative said. "I don't know how to cover that in the budget reports."

Katzil's gaze flitted between the representative and Kesia. "Well, the ballistics you requested will be expensive. We'll have to make adjustments in the design to account for the weight. I'm sure this extra expense"—he glanced at Kesia—"can be considered part of it."

"Fine." The representative stared at Kesia. She pleaded with her gaze. "Either way, my benefactor will not be pleased."

Katzil blinked. "Y—yes, sir. I understand."

The representative glanced at Kesia, a sneer of disgust pulling at his lips. "And next time, chain her to the furnace."

He walked away, heading toward the gate.

Kesia's spirits sank. *He didn't help me. He didn't care. He knew. He* knew.

Something slammed into Kesia's back and sent her sprawling. Her iron collar smacked onto the ground, shooting pain down her spine. She pushed herself upright. Katzil aimed a pistol at her.

"Don't move," he said. "Don't—I can't believe you just—you're a fool, girl."

A rumbling note, a snap in her collar. She turned to see Nadav standing over her. When had he arrived?

The Earth Singer hummed a note, and the collar yanked her upright, choking her as he dragged her toward the refinery.

They'll kill me. She was no longer useful. She pulled at the collar, but there was no relief, the metal clamped around her throat, refusing her air. She should give up—it was over—her lungs were burning.

The Earth Song stopped. She collapsed on the cement, gasping for air.

She wasn't in the refinery. There was no noise here, no clattering or shouting. She opened her eyes to an empty warehouse, lit only by an open door. The Earth Singer stood a few paces away. Above her, Parviz loomed.

Kesia wheezed.

"I don't think you know what you've done."

Parviz kicked her, and pain exploded through her abdomen. She curled into herself, her vision lighting with stars, her breath gone. *Breathe, breathe.*

He yanked her up by her hair, pain ripping her skull. "You've cost this entire business a lot of money."

He slammed her onto the ground again, her shoulder screaming. Everything hurt. Her lungs ached for freedom; her head was swimming. *I'm going to die, I'm going to die—*

"We built that prototype for the army. Some people on the Council wanted to see if we could rule the skies. We'd certainly end the war earlier than Kaleo expects, wouldn't we?"

Through a haze of pain, Kesia could imagine bullets raining down from the airship onto navy ships, armies, towns, the capital. Onto Crescent Bay.

"Of course, this is all a very big, expensive secret," he said. "Only a handful of people know about it." He grabbed her by the hair again. His sneer, his hateful eyes filled her vision. "The only reason I'm telling you is because you'll never get to tell anyone. You'll never leave here, do you understand? Do you *understand?*"

He shook her fiercely. Kesia wished she could scream, shriek a note and burn everything, send fire in every direction.

"The only reason I haven't let you choke to death is because of that pretty little Voice of yours." He leaned close, his voice barely a whisper. "You are here forever, girl. You'll be here on the day you die. I swear it to you."

He shoved her away from him, her head smacked the ground again, and once more she saw stars.

Parviz stood, straightened his shirt, and ran a hand through his hair. "Lock her in the barracks for the rest of the day," he said to Nadav. "Give her nothing to eat."

I failed, Miren. I failed.

The Miren in Kesia's mind had nothing to say to this. Miren was gone.

Kesia lay in the pitch-black barracks, stiff, uncomfortable, and alone. Everything throbbed. The muscles in her neck screamed each time she moved. Her stomach churned with a sickly hunger. She should welcome the time alone, more time to sleep, but there was no way to know how many hours had passed, how soon she would have to get up and work again.

Her mind sank into more pleasant memories. She remembered fishing with her father, complaining as the line tangled, laughing when Miren's fish slapped her cheek. She remembered her mother cooking freshly caught fish or rabbit over the fire. She remembered Miren telling a grand story, gesturing to shapes of fire that Kesia summoned in the air.

Pain was everywhere. There was no relief from the Song leeching from her, the fire heating her skin, the clang of metal shattering in her ears. To escape into her memories was like trying to swim in a puddle. Everything was slipping from her.

This was worse than death. Burning up her bones, her heart, her blood . . . Miren, Davri, Mother—they wouldn't wish this. They wouldn't want this for her . . .

Kesia lay on the floor in the dark, silently screaming.

TWENTY-TWO
MIREN

MIREN," HANA SAID, "WOULD YOU SWITCH WITH ME?"

Miren looked up, startled from her thoughts. Arten, Hana, and Davri were gathered around the back corner of the wagon, holding it just high enough for Liviya to slip off the broken wheel and replace it with the new one she had bought from a local farmer.

Miren leaned against the fence that lined an apple orchard, her attention drifting to unhelpful memories: the time they had fought after Kesia had come home late from a day with Davri; the day they had received the letter drafting Singers; the day her father had left, his gaze tight as he handed her his revolver and said, "Protect your mother and sister."

She hurried over to take Hana's place next to Davri. Hana sighed in relief and stood up straight. "Thank you."

"Almost done." Liviya set the new wheel on the axel, then used a mallet to hammer it in place. Although she had refused to take the blame for steering the cart into a large pothole, she had made the mile-long walk to the nearest farmhouse and bought a replacement from the farmer with her own coin.

Miren stared out, trying to distract herself from the discomfort of holding the cart. The heavy clouds to the west and a thick scent of soil suggested they had just missed a rainfall. They were well within the Third Circle now. Towns were close together. The land here was brimming with farms, which blanketed most of the territory to the west, wedging itself between the cragged mountains.

Miren had felt a gnawing sense of dread since returning to the barn after her and Davri's visit to Eitan's estate. Or perhaps it wasn't dread. Sadness? Resignation? She thought again of the days just after Kesia had earned her Voice. Miren had been jealous and bitter, and though Kesia hadn't deserved it, Miren had been unkind to her for a time.

But her father had been right—there was a cost to having a Voice, which the war and Davri's experiences made all the more apparent. She didn't believe she craved a Voice anymore—so why was she thinking of it now?

She wanted to *do* something.

The truth felt like a weight on her shoulders. This horrible feeling of doing nothing stirred up those old, painful yearnings of wanting to be like her mother—being needed and capable of filling that need.

What she was experiencing was the feeling of defeat.

Another few minutes, and Liviya finally said, "Got it!"

Miren, Arten, and Davri lowered the cart to the ground. Miren's shoulders ached, and her hands stung from the rough wood. A patch of red on Arten's shoulder caught her eye.

"Arten," she said, "you're bleeding."

He paused and turned. "Really?" He pulled up his sleeve over his shoulder. "Oh."

"Here," Hana said. She led him to the side of the cart and helped him ease off his shirt.

Miren stifled a gasp.

Arten's back was a patchwork of scars—long, deep slashes in every direction. Many of them were white and purple, scarred over, but a few were red and swollen.

Liviya wordlessly handed Hana a small, circular container. Hana opened it and scooped up some pale green paste and covered the bleeding scars. Miren dug at a splinter that had lodged at the base of her palm, understanding the peril of being a planter more clearly than ever before.

The group was quiet for a few minutes as Hana tended to Arten with practiced deftness. Miren glanced at Davri, but he had taken it upon himself to distract Ori. The boy laughed in delight as Davri held him upside down by the ankles.

"Should we really go through the town?" Hana asked Liviya.

The next town, Gorrish, was the largest yet. Though it was still a half-day's travel away, Liviya had announced that they wouldn't avoid it as they had the others.

It was also just within Lady Rion's territory. Miren could sense the mounting tension between mother and son as they neared the estate where Cale was.

"It will take too much time otherwise," Liviya said. "Besides, we need to find a boat."

"It will be difficult this far from the coast," Arten said.

"We're still not too far from Fisher's Canyon. We should be fine."

"We'll need to pass Rion's estate to get to the Crown's Seam," Arten said.

"Arten," Hana murmured.

"Then we had best do it quickly, hadn't we?" Liviya said.

"You think it's safe for us to speak?" Hana asked. "In case anyone in town talks to us?"

"Planters are fairly common up here. Try to avoid speaking, but if you have to, yes, it should be all right." Liviya took the container of paste from Hana and fastened the lid on. "No signing, though."

Davri nodded, not looking up from Ori, who was standing on Davri's feet. Davri held the boy up by his hands, and the two swayed while Ori giggled.

Liviya added, "We'll ask around about boats and see what people say. If we have to, we'll hedge east a bit. Does that sound acceptable? Miren?"

Miren looked up. "Yes. Fine."

They piled into the cart, and Liviya took the reins. Miren sat next to her.

"You've been quiet," Liviya said. She was staring ahead, back straight.

Miren slumped in her seat. She had come to the front to avoid conversation. "Just . . . worried. Tired."

"From sneaking away with Davri two nights ago?"

Miren flinched, then relaxed. It wasn't as though she could be in trouble. "That barn door needs to be oiled."

"Where did you go?"

"Out."

Liviya glanced at her. "Hana says the two of you aren't romantic."

"No," Miren said, trying not to appear offended. "He has feelings for my sister."

"Hmm," Liviya said, sounding unconvinced.

Miren grimaced. What did it hurt to tell Liviya, anyway? "We went to go break into Eitan's estate for information on my sister."

Liviya's gaze shot to her. "What? Why?"

"His brother is on the list of names you gave us."

"And so you thought—"

"We didn't do it," Miren said. "We couldn't get past the fence."

Liviya didn't respond, and Miren wilted as shame washed over her like a cold tide. She felt even more foolish now that Liviya knew.

Liviya held the reins out to Miren.

"No, thank you," Miren said stiffly.

"I wasn't asking."

"I don't know anything about horses."

"Only one way to learn."

Miren sighed and took the reins. They were heavier than she expected.

For all of Liviya's sharp words, she was a patient teacher. She would let Miren try a command a few times before giving more instruction, and she kindly cursed out a passing carriage driver for complaining that Miren was blocking the road.

Miren's hands felt raw from helping to hold up the cart, but she didn't offer up the reins when Liviya declared the lesson over. It felt good to do something other than sit or walk.

Liviya said, "Did you ever hear how I managed to break them out?"

"Um, I think Hana mentioned that you planned the escape."

"Over months," Liviya said. "It took us nearly three months to enact that plan."

Miren nodded, not sure how to respond.

"Did you ever hear how I tried to rescue my husband?" Liviya asked.

Miren startled. "No."

"Watch your grip there," Liviya said, pointing to the horse as it turned toward the middle of the road. Miren straightened the reins.

It was nearly a minute before Liviya spoke again.

"I escaped the lord I was contracted to two years ago."

Miren turned. "Two *years?*"

Liviya grimaced and waved a hand. "No need to shout."

"Sorry."

Another long pause, but Miren knew better than to pelt Liviya with questions.

"I was a fool. I thought it was obvious that I was going to try to find my family, so I hurried to where my husband was, since it was closest. I thought the two of us could continue to Cheliem's together.

I didn't know Cale had been sold to Rion by then. As long as I arrived before any messenger from my lord's estate, I figured I would have the advantage."

Liviya's gaze grew unfocused as she stared out at the road. "I broke into the servants' quarters in the middle of the night, woke him, and we ran. It was a foolish strategy. I thought some of the servants might want to escape with us, but one sounded the alarm, and the guards shot at us."

Liviya pulled up her sleeve and showed a gnarled scar on her upper arm. "My husband was shot in the head," she said. "The guards thought it was better to shoot a servant than let him get away.

"Now that a lord's guards had seen my face, I couldn't risk my sons' lives. I fled back to Avi'or on a smuggler's ship and waited a full year before returning."

"A whole year," Miren whispered. A year was plenty of time for Kesia to be assigned to a ship, to sail directly into cannon fire.

"I knew it was the only way to help them. Let the lord's guards assume that I had died from starvation or drowned at sea. An old woman isn't worth enough to stew over.

"It was the worst year of my life. Every day I went to work in a cotton mill, thinking about those boys, knowing what kind of woman Rion is, knowing Arten was trying to raise a child. I can't tell you how many times I went to the docks searching for a ship to take me back to Kaleo. But in the end, I knew I had to wait. I knew I wouldn't be of any help to them until enough time had passed."

Liviya's voice was barely above a whisper. "The only thing that kept me going was the belief that my boys were strong. That they would survive long enough for me to come and get them. I can't even be sure if Cale is still alive. At least, I haven't seen him for myself. But I know he is strong." Her dark eyes glittered.

Miren felt it would be rude to look away, so she held the older woman's gaze, searching for something to say. "Then he must be."

Liviya placed a hand on Miren's shoulder. "Sometimes," Liviya murmured, "we can't protect the people we love. Sometimes that's our fault, but sometimes it's not. Sometimes we need to trust that they're strong enough to hold out for us."

Miren was horrified to feel her eyes brimming with tears. "But what if she's not?" she whispered.

"If you're doing your best to get to her, what makes you think she's not doing her best to get to you?"

Miren didn't reply. She had spent years wondering what her mother was going through, too hopeful or too cowardly — she wasn't sure if there was a difference — to truly consider her dead. Now her sister existed in that same dark, unknown space in Miren's mind. She didn't know what Kesia would do.

Perhaps, she reasoned, she didn't know what Kesia *could* do.

Wait for me, Kesia, she thought. *Please. I'm coming.*

"We should stop to water the horse," Liviya said. "You know how?"

Miren nodded and steered the horse to the side of the road. She pulled sharply on the reins and said, "Whoa." The horse stopped.

Everyone climbed out. Miren wiped the tears from her face before anyone else could see.

After a brief rest, Hana asked, "Miren, could you keep an eye on Ori? I'd like to walk and stretch my legs."

"You should ride in the back, too, Mother," Arten said. "I can drive the cart."

Busy with the horse's bridle, Liviya didn't look up. "I'll take a break when I need to, Arten."

Arten sighed and joined Hana. Davri glanced at Miren, but she looked away. "Fine," Miren said. "I'll ride in the cart."

Liviya climbed into the front and took the reins as Miren, Davri, and Ori took seats in the back. Miren angled herself to avoid catching Davri's gaze by mistake; they hadn't really spoken since their foray into Madafim to break into Eitan's estate. She still felt embarrassed about the whole thing, and she resented it.

Across from Miren, beside Davri, Ori held two stones and occasionally smacked them together, playing a game she didn't recognize. He solemnly handed her a stone.

"No, thank you," she said. She had never been comfortable around children.

Ori continued to hold out the stone, his eyes boring into her.

She suppressed a sigh and took the stone. It was dark and weighty and smooth. "What is this for?"

"It's for this." Ori held up his stone and slammed it into the floor of the cart with a dull thud.

Miren looked to Hana for help, but only Davri was paying attention. He grinned at her. *Play along,* he signed subtly.

She shot him a look, feeling that he was setting her up to look foolish, but she held up the stone and tapped it against the cart.

"No, like this." Ori lifted the stone over his head and smashed it into the wood.

"Ori, be gentle," Hana called. She caught Miren's eye and grinned.

"All right." Ori slammed the stone down even harder.

Miren was forming a newfound respect for parents. "Have you ever met your uncle?" she asked, hoping to distract the child.

"Yes!" Ori placed the stone on his head, but it slid off and flipped into his lap. "Papa told me stories about him. One time, he stole a whole cow from a neighbor!"

"It was a chicken, Ori," Hana corrected gently.

"A whole chicken." Ori lurched, and the stone rolled off his head once more. Miren leaned over to grab it and handed it back to him. "Thank you," he said. "A whole chicken!"

"That's . . . a lot of chicken."

"Yes. We're going to rescue him."

Miren frowned and glanced at Hana, but now she was deep in conversation with Arten.

"How are you going to do that?" Miren said.

"We go to Rion's 'state," he said firmly.

Miren looked at him in surprise. "How do you know that's where your uncle is?"

"I heard Nana say so. It's that way." He pointed straight ahead.

Perhaps children were more observant than Miren had thought. "Ori, you can't go rescue your uncle," she said. "It's too dangerous."

"No," he insisted. "Papa wants to rescue Uncle Cale."

"You and Papa and Mama are going to Avi'or." Did it make sense to call Avi'or *home* when Ori had never been there?

"No!" Ori slammed both rocks down at the same time.

"Yes, you are," Miren said firmly. "Liv—Nana will help Cale."

"No, no, no!" He slammed the rocks so hard that one bounced out of his grip. Miren caught it once more.

Davri snapped his fingers for her attention and shook his head.

Miren shrugged helplessly. She knew she was doing something wrong, but she didn't know what. She wracked her brain for a way to change the subject. "Do you . . . like to play with rocks?"

Ori ignored her, holding a rock in each hand. She sighed and leaned against the edge of the cart, feeling guilty and frustrated.

Just before sunset, they rounded a sharp cliff and found themselves on the outskirts of Gorrish. They saw buildings that might be homes on roads that led to a bustling city center.

The closer they got to the center of town, the more crowded the road became. Miren caught more than one person staring as they passed, their gazes circling between Liviya and Arten, who was now seated at the front of the cart.

"No one speak," Liviya said suddenly. "Davri, don't sign."

Davri nodded, and even Ori sat quietly, thumping his stones together until Hana gently threatened to take them away.

Miren was just about to ask Liviya what she thought was going on when the crowd in front of them parted, revealing a large board in the center of a plaza. Three papers had been tacked to the board, each with a sketched portrait: Miren looked closer and saw the faces of Arten, Hana, and Ori, just above the word WANTED.

TWENTY-THREE

MIREN

MIREN AND LIVIYA LOOKED AT EACH OTHER.

"What do we do?" Miren said.

"Get us out of here." Liviya tossed the reins to Miren as she hopped into the back of the cart. "Hana, put something over your hair."

"What's wrong?" Hana asked.

"Don't speak," Liviya said in her Kaleon accent. "Cover Ori with a cloak."

As soon as Liviya was settled, Miren flicked the reins, and the horse started forward. She kept pace with the carriage in front of them, fighting the urge to slap the horse into a trot.

As they passed the posters, Miren squinted to read the print. Each poster promised a reward for information on the fugitives, and as much as a hundred gold for their return alive to Her Ladyship Rion.

Lady Rion? Cale's master? Why would she be looking for them?

Miren's heart thumped. She didn't know where Liviya had planned to go, and she didn't want to slow down to ask. She watched people's faces as she passed, but the cart itself didn't draw much attention. She glanced back briefly and saw everyone huddled just behind her, their heads down, Hana's covered in a blanket.

Guards patrolled the streets in pairs, wearing sky-blue and gold uniforms—the colors of the Third Circle. They would be Rion's guards, then, not the Crown's, who wore black uniforms. Why would Rion station so many guards in a town like this?

Had Rion somehow *expected* them to come here?

Miren tried to control her expression as the passing guards glanced at her, tried to contain her panic. She struggled to look bored, tired — a farmhand traveling a long distance.

She squeaked in surprise when Liviya grabbed the back of the seat and whispered in her ear. "I'm going to create a distraction. Get them out of here. As soon as you get out of town, go west. Don't wait for me."

Before Miren could protest, Liviya hopped over the side of the cart and crossed the street.

Miren fought the instinct to pull the horse to a stop. Splitting up seemed like a terrible idea, but halting traffic would be worse. They had to get out of the city, then figure out what to do.

The cart came to another intersection of cobbled streets. Miren badly wanted to urge the horse forward, but she waited, forcing her shoulders to relax and smiling at the pedestrians.

She kept herself from looking back at the rest of the group again. They all must be obscured well enough — but then why had Liviya run off to create a distraction? She wouldn't be of any help to them if she got arrested.

The town center stretched on for another two blocks before the line of buildings gave way to more spacious plots. Miren flicked the horse into a trot.

She glanced behind her. Everyone was still huddled in back, Ori bundled in a blanket and tucked by Arten's side, his face buried in his father's chest.

Miren turned back toward the front and saw another cart parked on the side of the road. She steered the horse away, but too late — the corner of her cart nicked the back end of the other. Wood splintered with a loud crunch.

"Hey!" A man stood just a few paces away, speaking with an older woman. He was portly with black trousers and a light blue coat. He had thin, brown sideburns and a dark hat with a wide brim.

Miren yanked on the reins. If she tried to run now, she would create a scene. "Sorry!" she called.

The man's face flushed red as he assessed the damage, his companion watching with alarm. Miren jumped off the cart and joined him. A board hung crookedly off the side of his cart, but the crates in the back were untouched.

"Skies and seas, woman!" he cried. "What have you done?"

"What?" Miren said. "It's not so bad."

"Not so bad!" he shouted. "I run a business. This is unsightly! You're paying for repairs!"

Miren hunched as his yelling drew more eyes. "Sir, I—I will, of course," she stammered. "Please, sir, there's no need to—"

"I think twenty gold should suffice," he said, holding out his hand.

"Twenty *gold*," she cried. "I don't have that much coin."

"Then you'll spend a week in the stockade." He called, "Guard! Guard, here please."

"No, no, please!" she said. "I can pay, I can pay—I just don't have the money with me today. I need to go home to get it."

"Oh, do you?" he sneered. "You think I'd just let you skip away without paying me?"

"But I don't have the money!"

"Then you can stay in the stockade until you've paid me. Guard! Here!"

Miren turned as a pair of uniformed guards waded their way through the crowd toward them. One had long, dark hair tied back, and another had a thick beard. She recognized them; they had been patrolling the plaza where she'd seen the wanted posters.

Had the guards followed the cart?

Miren's heart was pounding now. Arten still had his head down, hunched as though he were trying to shield Ori with his body. Hana sat facing away, head covered. Davri, however, sat straight, watching the exchange, one hand on the edge of the cart as though he were about to jump out and intervene.

Miren clenched her hands into fists. What would Liviya do?

Where *was* she?

A couple of women walking along the road paused and pointed. Miren followed their gaze and spotted a column of dark smoke rising a few blocks away.

A fire.

Had Liviya set a building on *fire?*

Miren stepped in front of the other cart's owner as the guards approached. "Sirs," she said. "Is that a fire over there?"

"What?" the cart owner said, looking up.

People around them began to notice.

The guards bolted in the direction of the smoke. The other cart's owner was distracted by the sight, pressing forward and peering over the crowd.

Miren darted back onto the cart, grabbed the reins, and flicked them hard. The horse surged into motion and out of town.

They kept going until it became too dark to see the road.

Miren finally pulled the horse to a stop behind a small shelf of land that was just about her height. It wasn't as hidden as she liked —she could spot three farmsteads from here—but it was far enough away that the town was now a collection of silhouetted buildings and faint lights from the streetlamps.

The group climbed out of the cart, slow and exhausted.

Hana finally broke the silence. "Should we build a fire?" she asked.

"We don't need to cook anything," Arten said.

"But it will be too cold to sleep without one," Hana said.

If they built a fire, they would be easily spotted. But if they didn't build a fire and were still spotted, they would look suspicious. Miren rubbed her forehead. What should they do?

"Keep the fire behind here." She pointed to the outcropping. "At least it won't be seen from town."

No one responded, but she saw Arten's silhouette leave to look for wood and dried grass. Ori complained about being hungry, and Hana pulled something from a bag. Miren wanted to talk to Davri, but of course he wouldn't be able to answer her questions in the dark.

A half-hour later, the party sat around a small fire.

"How did he know?" Arten said. "How could Cheliem possibly have known we'd come this way?"

"How do you know it's Cheliem?" Miren asked. "The poster said that Lady Rion was looking for you."

"This is her territory," Arten said. "Cheliem would have needed to get her permission to put those posters up. Why else would she be looking for us?"

Miren glanced at Davri. He nodded. *That makes sense.*

"So Cheliem is still looking," she said.

No one answered. Arten paced, rubbing the back of his head. Hana held Ori, watching her husband worriedly.

Liviya had seemed confident that Cheliem wouldn't look for them beyond Fourth Circle, and he would have focused his attention on the coast. The fact that he not only was looking for them this far north, but had managed to send word before their arrival, was concerning.

Miren didn't think going north had been too obvious. Who would travel closer to the capital to escape the government? "Cheliem must have thought you'd come here to save your brother," she said.

"Or he guessed our plan to take the Crown's Seam to the coast," Hana said.

Taking the Seam to the coast is not something a reasonable person would think of, Davri signed, his fingers barely visible in the firelight. *I think Miren is right. He thinks we're here to find Cale.*

The group fell silent. If Cheliem was behind this, then it meant that none of them were safe. Although—

"Davri's face wasn't posted," Miren said. "Wouldn't Cheliem be looking for you as well?"

Davri shrugged.

"Maybe Cheliem doesn't want the competition," Arten said. "If there's word of a Singer avoiding the draft, then bounty hunters might start looking for you."

"Would that really happen?" Miren asked.

If the bounty is large enough for a nobleman to be tempted, Davri signed, *then it would attract attention.*

"But the wanted posters—why would Rion do such a favor for Cheliem?" Hana said. "She ranks higher than he does."

Davri signed, *If Cheliem sold Cale's contract to Rion, then it's likely they have some connection.*

"What do we do now?" Hana asked.

"I'm not leaving without my mother," Arten said.

Miren glanced at Davri. Should they stay and wait, or should they press on? Each choice felt riddled with unacceptable consequences. Skies, how had they managed to get this far?

"Maybe . . . someone can wait here for Liviya," Hana said, looking at Miren uncertainly, "while the rest of us try to find a boat?"

"She said we shouldn't wait for her," Miren replied. "We can't risk anyone seeing you all."

"We need to find her," Arten said. "Miren, you're the only one who can safely go to town. You can go look for her!"

"And what if someone finds you while I'm gone?" she countered. "How are you going to talk your way out of anything when your faces are plastered all over town? Have Davri do it?"

A cold, pragmatic corner of Miren's mind reminded her that she didn't need the whole family—Liviya was the only one who could help her find Kesia. The rest of her mind was telling her that deserting Arten, Hana, and Ori would be a heartless thing to do. She wasn't sure which side would win.

"Mother had a plan," Arten said. "Let's find her and carry it out."

Liviya's plan was based on the assumption that no one would follow us this far north, Davri signed. *We need a different plan.*

"The river is still our only option," Arten said. "If the coast wasn't dangerous for us before, it certainly is now."

"Do we even need a boat?" Hana said, looking to Davri. "What about when you Sang us out of Fisher's Canyon?"

Miren and Davri both shook their heads. *That was an emergency,* Davri signed. *I can't keep us all together.*

"And it would take too long," Miren said. "With a boat, he just needs to direct the current underneath us. Without one, he would need to Sing to keep us above water and propel us forward at the same time."

That too, Davri signed.

"We still need something to get us across the sea," Arten said. "A sailboat was always the hope."

"How was Liviya planning to get a sailboat to the Crown's Seam?" Miren said. "I thought it was a canyon."

"I don't know," Arten said. "That's why we need her."

Miren took a long breath. "We wait, then," she said. "We'll sleep in shifts, and when it's light again, I'll go back to town to look for her, all right?"

Davri nodded. Arten and Hana shared a look.

"Fine," Arten said.

"Fine," Miren echoed.

"What about Uncle Cale?" Ori asked loudly.

Hana shushed him gently. "Ori, we can't right now."

"Nana will get him," Arten said. "We need to go to Avi'or and wait for him."

"No!"

"Ori—" Hana began.

"You're just scared!" he yelled.

"Ori," Arten said sternly. "Don't talk to your mother that way."

"No!" Ori began to cry. Hana leaned over and murmured to him, but the little boy wailed inconsolably.

Miren suddenly felt very tired. "We should take turns keeping watch," she said to Davri.

He nodded. *I'll go first.*

TWENTY-FOUR

KESIA

KESIA REMAINED UNMOVING IN THE LIGHTLESS BARRACKS
until the door opened and the other Singers filed in. In the brief light
from the hall, no one met her gaze.

The next day of work began with the same note of Earth Song
that always unlocked the door, the same creaking sound as it opened,
the same shuffle downstairs. Kesia felt bruises along her jaw and hip.
Her ear throbbed, and her knee twisted painfully with each step. She
ate the dry bread and soggy vegetables, sitting numbly among the
other Singers.

The Avi'ori workers arrived, and the day began as usual. Everyone gave her glances. They didn't help her walk, or lift things, or push
the crates. The same rhythm as before. It was like they had all been
waiting for her to realize what they had already accepted.

This was their lives. This was all they would ever know.

Then why? she thought. *Why am I working? Why am I trying? Why
am I still going?* For hours, the word echoed in her mind until it ceased
to mean anything. *Why why why why why.* The question never left as
she Sang the furnace hot, warmed the rollers, pushed crates of slag to
the back.

A shout. Someone had said *Fire Singer.* She turned. Katzil spoke
with Nadav at the door, beckoning her with a hand. How long had he
been standing there?

She hobbled over, the world moving slowly past her. Katzil stared at her, taking in her injuries, her bruised cheek, her collar, her limp. He motioned for her to follow him. She thought of Singing, of bursting out with fire until everything around her was burning.

Outside was the same. A thick fog had rolled in from the bay, seeping into the air with a wet chill that clung to her clothes. She limped after Katzil, who slowed his pace for her. *Why why why why—*

In the hangar, the men worked as usual. They shouted and argued and even laughed, because they would see their homes in a few hours. They would *leave*.

She climbed into the airship and took her spot in the furnace room, not remembering if she had been given orders to do so. The boys stood there, shoveling coal as they had yesterday. They did not look at her. She wondered at the Song she would need to set their clothes on fire. She could hear it, past the din of work. High and fast, fierce and precise. She watched the scene in her mind with utter detachment.

She heard someone shout *fire*. She Sang the furnaces alight, and the room bloomed with sudden heat. Her Voice didn't hint at the change within her; it burned and consumed her just as it always did.

Hours dragged on. Memories tumbled over her like waves. The morning the chickens got out because she hadn't latched the coop. The day she caught Davri sneaking around the village, staring at Haro as he worked over the forge. The day her father left. The day her mother left. The first time Davri took her to his favorite place, the secret cove under his father's estate. The way his hand felt warm and dry in hers. That fateful night atop the plateau, Skyflame, her Voice bursting forth. The day she was taken, Miren screaming for help, crumpling from a blow to the head.

Kesia choked on her Song. *I tried, Miren, I really did.*

The Miren in her mind was silent.

The day passed at a crawl, but eventually the craft landed back in the hangar. She stepped off the airship and waited. Katzil approached her, and she followed him out of the hangar and up the path to the refinery. A bright orange sunset shone against the jagged cloud cover to the west, silhouetting the sharp cliffs and mountains along Kaleo's western border.

They came to the plateau, just steps from the refinery. To her left, the plateau cut to a cliff overlooking the coast. Even from such a height, she could hear the distant echo of waves on the rocks. The same sound she would hear from the lighthouse in Crescent Bay.

No, Miren said. *It's too high up. There are likely rocks at the bottom.*

Yes, there were likely rocks at the bottom.

Kesia turned and started walking.

Her heart pounded. She was not supposed to go this way. She would be caught, beaten, starved, shot.

She kept walking.

"Hey!" Katzil shouted.

Kesia quickened her pace. Her twisted knee ached in protest, but she burst into a run. Her chest heaved uselessly, and the collar threatened to strangle her, but she kept running.

Somewhere over the water, Miren was shouting.

Kesia, don't!

Kesia pushed herself to go faster. The ground to her left erupted with a gunshot. She didn't slow; the cliff drew nearer, the collar grinding into her neck as she pumped her arms, her lungs aching. She waited for more shouting, more gunshots, more footsteps, but there was nothing. She imagined that the captain was giving her time, wondering if he missed her on purpose, but that couldn't be right.

Kesia, please! Miren cried. *This won't work.*

But Miren had always been protective. Always cautious, untrusting. Kesia knew her sister's intentions were good, but she had never admitted to herself how stifling Miren could be.

Perhaps Miren was wrong this time. Perhaps this would work.

It almost didn't matter—Kesia wasn't going to stop running. Her knee threatened to bend the wrong way and send her sprawling. Her vision grew hazy around the corners, but she kept running.

The edge approached—ten paces away, five paces—

Kesia! Miren cried.

"*Stop!*" Katzil shouted behind her.

She leaped from the edge.

Time seemed to slow. There, suspended in the air, she could hear the roar of waves echo off the cliff face below her. To her right, past the curve of the cliff, she could see the port, a huddled collection of docks crowded with ships. The same port she had arrived at. She wondered if Edom was still docked there or if he had continued on in search of more victims.

The dark expanse of water swept out beneath her. The cliffside continued downward at an inward angle, away from her. Directly below her, the foaming surf swirled around shards of rock poking from the water like teeth.

Air screamed past her. There was plenty of time to regret her actions—to call herself a raving idiot, to regret the pain she would cause Miren and Davri and her parents, to remember that the best way to avoid breaking a bone was to cross her arms and point her toes—before the ocean, dark and jagged and biting, slammed into her.

Her collar pulled her under before the current could grip her, down, down. She clawed at the icy water, salt stinging her eyes. Her chest threatened to burst. She pushed for the surface, but the water crashed and choked her. She was drowning, her body slowing, punishing her for the lack of air.

Miren Davri Mother Father Miren Miren.

Her hands caught rock and she pulled up, up, up. Cold air slapped her face.

Kesia coughed, fighting panic as her collar pushed against her throat. There wasn't enough room to cough. She heard no sounds of pursuit over the roll of waves, but her body jittered with anxiety. She grabbed a rock and inched her way along the cliff face, toward the city.

Farther down, the cliff wasn't as high, but Kesia couldn't seem to climb its face. Her muscles were seizing up with cold and fatigue, and her fingers cramped as they clung to divots and protrusions in the rocks.

She climbed for what felt like hours, agonizingly making her way up and to the left, inch by inch. The sky darkened, and the clouds were an odd yellow color, reflecting the lights of the city.

Before she realized it, the cliff gave way to flat ground, and her stinging, bleeding hands dug into sand. She crawled up the shore a step at a time, too tired to shiver, her collar still stiff against her neck. Fatigue pushed against her eyes, begging her to sleep.

Not yet, she thought, shoving herself upright once more. She continued forward, and a collection of buildings trickled into view.

Tools. She needed tools.

A small, wooden shed sat by a large building. She stumbled over and shoved the door open, greeted by the musty scent of sawdust. Shovels and trowels and brooms lined the walls, but she needed something smaller.

She rummaged through the shed until her fingers found a cool, thin piece of metal set in a wooden handle. A file. She picked it up and dug it into a crevice in the collar. She had only seen the collar on others, but she thought there was a panel she could open. She worked blindly, her shoulders and arms aching and then growing numb.

The tool rasped the edge of something that might be the panel. She pulled harder, harder—*ping*. The panel popped open slightly.

She jammed the tool in and wiggled it around. She didn't know what she was doing—a part of her feared that she was making it worse, possibly breaking something vital, but she couldn't stop.

Something caught.

Click.

The collar sagged opened and fell into her lap.

Kesia *inhaled*. Air filled her chest, cool and fresh and *there*.

She breathed fully, exhale, *inhale*, exhale. Sobs formed, but she forced them down. She wanted to *breathe*.

Would they come looking for her? Would they just assume that she had drowned? She hoped so. This might bring trouble on them from their Council. Good.

She thought of Ayla, who would have to do twice as much work now. She was so young, little more than bones and rags, but her Voice could hold out longer than Kesia's. She thought of the Water Singer who had helped her, the Air Singers who had stood close as they heated the furnace together, and she felt a deep sense of regret. She recognized the same feeling she had for the villagers in Crescent Bay, those she had lied to, had refused to help, in order to protect herself.

What would they think when they found her gone? What would Parviz tell them? *She died trying to escape, shot to death on sight. Don't forget that you belong here, you will never leave.*

Kesia trembled. She should keep moving. It seemed unlikely that anyone from the factory would look for her here, though she probably shouldn't take the chance.

But this space was warm and dark, and her wet clothes felt so heavy. She lay down. *Just for a moment,* she told herself. *Just one moment's rest.*

TWENTY-FIVE

KESIA

Kesia awoke to banging.

She shivered in her damp clothes, her side throbbing after sleeping on a hard floor. She remembered—the cliff, the beach, the shed, the *collar*. She could still feel it pressing against her neck, even as she saw it on the ground a few paces away. She pushed it behind a dusty crate, out of sight.

Another *bang*.

Kesia pushed herself up but nearly collapsed again. Her fingers found the file she'd use to remove the collar. She clutched it like a knife and raised it, her arm shaking.

A man wrenched the door open, gold afternoon light pouring in. "No, I didn't break the fence, Gemma! Some idiot scarffer rat must've—" He froze. "Who're you?"

He was old, skin hanging from his cheeks and chin, his shoulders gnarled, and his arms bent at odd angles. His shirt was too small and poorly patched, and his oversized trousers sagged. The brim of his hat shadowed his features.

"Where'd you come from?" he asked.

Kesia raised her hands to answer him but froze. If she signed, he would know she was a Singer. How much should she tell him? Could she trust anyone? She imagined pushing past him and running, but she wasn't sure she could stand.

A woman shouted something. The man leaned out the door to holler, "Hey, Gemma, we got a visitor!"

Kesia heard footsteps. "What the skies you talking about?"

The man stepped aside for a woman who was made of the same gnarled clay as the man. She stared at Kesia, her dark eyes glittering.

"This is the one that broke the fence, I bet," the man said. "She don't talk much, though."

Kesia blinked. When had she broken the fence?

"Oh, shush, Axel," Gemma muttered. To Kesia, she said, "Well, you're soaking wet and probably hungry? Come on in."

"You're quite lucky, little one," Gemma said, stirring a pot of something that smelled like spiced grass. "This home's usually rented out by richer folk at this time of year."

Kesia sat at a spindly table in their nook of a kitchen, wearing a threadbare dress and coat. Although the house was four times larger than their cabin in Crescent Bay, she had difficulty believing that anyone with money would want to spend time here. Grime crept up the corners of the white walls, and the parlor furniture was torn and lopsided.

Axel stared at her from across the table. Kesia wasn't sure if he was suspicious or just curious. She still hadn't tried to sign at them.

"All right." Gemma brought three bowls to the table and sat down. "You'd better tell us about yourself before my husband decides to shoot you."

Kesia was shocked, but apparently this was meant as a joke. Axel waved a hand. "I'm not shooting any little girls."

Kesia nodded and raised her hands. *My name is Kesia*, she signed.

"Hey," the man growled, intrigued. "Are you a Singer?"

Kesia shook her head. *I was*, she signed. *But I lost my Voice to cloud fever when I was young.*

"Ah, I've heard of that," Gemma said. "It's not so common here, but it ravages the Kaleons something fierce." Her eyes narrowed. "You're Kaleon, then?"

Kesia swallowed, her heart thumping. Miren was so much better at this. She nodded.

"Hmm." Gemma exchanged a look with her husband. "But you're not a Singer?"

Kesia shook her head.

"What are you doing here?"

Kesia scrambled for some answer. Was there a chance they knew what Amos Steel was doing? Would they turn her in? How else could she explain her presence here? Her hands shaking, she signed, *Ship sank.*

Gemma waited for more, but Kesia couldn't think of more to say. Should she have admitted that she was from Kaleo? In the growing silence, she became more convinced that had been a foolish thing to do.

"I see," the man said.

Gemma nodded. "That's unfortunate."

They ate in silence. Kesia swallowed without tasting.

When the bowls were empty, she stood.

I can clean, she signed, reaching for the plates.

"Well," Gemma said, handing over her bowl. "About time I had some help around here."

Kesia carried the dishes to the basin and began scrubbing. The silence behind her felt tense; when she turned to look, the couple sat stiff, staring at each other without speaking.

Did they think she was dangerous? Did they believe her story?

She needed to see if they trusted her. *I'd like to sleep here,* she signed. *If you don't mind. Only one night.*

Gemma glanced at her husband. "Well, I think sleeping here one night is acceptable, don't you, Axel?"

Axel nodded vigorously "Sure, sure," he said jovially.

Gemma gave her a blanket and motioned to the lopsided couch in the parlor. "This is all we've got, I'm afraid, but I'm sure you don't mind."

Kesia nodded, and the couple went to their room. She lay on the couch, irked by something, but sleep pulled her under before she understood what it was.

She dreamed of the refinery, of metal clattering in a slow, dirge-like rhythm. Hunched, mindless Singers pushed crates that didn't need pushing and heated rollers that weren't being used. The furnace screamed with blue fire. White-hot liquid overflowed and splashed onto the floor, but the Singers didn't care. Kesia opened her mouth to scream, but the Earth Singer was there, humming a note. A collar clicked.

She blinked awake and saw a figure silhouetted against a window, approaching her, a collar in hand.

She vaulted off the couch and Sang.

Fire erupted and latched onto the couch, flooding the room with intense light. Axel stumbled back, screaming as flames crawled up his sleeve. The collar fell from his grip and thudded on the floor. Gemma bolted into the room, yelling and waving her arms. Kesia's Song scaled the walls, bit into the furniture. Axel was shrieking in pain, begging her to stop.

Kesia's chest hummed as she Sang, her stomach tense with fury. *Out,* she needed to get out. She pushed past Gemma to the kitchen and grabbed rolls, dried meats, celery, and put them in a bag she found hanging by the door. Gemma was standing over her husband, trying to put out the fire with the blanket. Kesia barely heard their screams as she gathered supplies.

The glint of iron caught her eye. The collar. Against every instinct, she picked it up and shoved it in her bag.

She didn't stop Singing until she was out of the house and the sound of a frantic bell pierced the night. Behind her, fire stabbed the dark sky.

Kesia staggered into an alley and collapsed behind piles of garbage, breathing heavily, fatigue stuffing her head with cotton. Despite the noise, she succumbed to sleep.

TWENTY-SIX

MIREN

Ori? Ori!"

Miren shot upright from her bedroll. The landscape was still dark with early dawn, and a light dew covered the ground. In the faint light, their camp looked small and inconspicuous.

Hana had moved some twenty paces past the wall of rock and was calling Ori's name.

Miren scrambled to her feet. "Stop, stop! What's wrong?"

But she knew already, before Hana answered. "Ori's gone, he's missing."

"What?" Arten was on his feet, his deep voice loud with panic.

"Ori's gone," Hana said, again, her voice thick with tears. "I dozed off on my watch, and when I woke up he was gone."

"All right," Arten said. "We'll find him."

Davri's signing was just visible in the dawn light. Miren could make out Liviya's name.

"Did Liviya come back?" Miren asked.

"No, I didn't see her," Hana said. "Do you think Ori is with her?"

"Why would she take him without telling us?" Miren said, but Hana had already turned away.

"*Ori!*" Hana shouted.

"Hana, stop!" Miren put a hand on her arm. "This won't help."

"What if he's lost? What if someone from town sees him?"

But Miren didn't think he was lost, and she remembered their conversation in the cart yesterday.

A shiver ran through her.

Ori had wanted to rescue his uncle.

He knew where his uncle was.

It was a foolish thing to do, but Ori was six years old. Children did foolish things. She remembered trying to take her father's fishing boat out on her own when she was eight, believing nothing terrible would happen to her.

Ori had gone to Rion's, Miren thought. They had to find him. But the others had to stay hidden. Even Davri couldn't risk being forced to sign.

Miren would have to go by herself.

If she were caught, she would be arrested. She might be hanged or thrown in prison.

What would happen to Kesia?

Miren groaned. She couldn't abandon Ori, couldn't ignore the cold knot of terror in her stomach.

Hana and Arten were still calling for Ori, oblivious to Davri's signed protests to keep quiet. If they were found, then it was over. No amount of waiting for Liviya would free them then.

"I have to go," Miren said.

Davri looked at her sharply. *Go where?*

"To Rion's estate. To look for Ori."

"What?" Hana's voice pierced the air.

"Why would Ori be there?" Arten said.

Miren paused and looked at the group. "He wanted to go after Cale."

Hana froze. "Oh, skies. We have to go get him."

Miren shook her head.

"We have to!" Hana said. "They'll hurt him, they'll—" She broke off, hands to her mouth.

"I'll go," Miren said.

Hana sobbed. Arten pulled her close.

Miren felt like a cursed idiot, but she would do it. With the same reckless resolve she had summoned after Kesia was taken, she would try to find Ori.

A hand caught her shoulder.

"You can't come with me, Davri," she said, without looking.

His grip tightened.

"I'll be back," she said. She turned to look at him. "Wait here for Liviya. I'll find Ori."

Miren headed around the edge of town at a jog. As the sky lightened, she could see the estate to the north of the town: even from this distance, she could appreciate its size. If she remembered the map correctly, the Crown's Seam, the river that would take them to the coast, wasn't far beyond it.

The horizon was glowing orange as she hurried toward the estate. At the base of the rise between the mansion and the town was sprawling farmland, a short wooden fence marking what must be part of Lady Rion's estate. Evenly spaced cornstalks were just beginning to unfurl their leaves. Dark silhouettes were slowly moving through the crops, hoes in hand. At the edges of the property, guards with rifles over their shoulders watched the workers.

Miren ducked behind some brush so the guards wouldn't notice her. If she were Ori, and looking for someone, what would she do?

I would sneak through the corn.

Ori was small enough, and he probably didn't understand the danger he was in.

She glanced at the corn, hoping to see movement that would indicate his presence, but nothing stood out as more than the nudge of a passing breeze. Not far from the main estate, she spotted a barn and stable. Miren started around the edge of the property.

She scurried behind a gnarled tree and pressed her back against it, out of sight, then looked up into the branches. What child didn't love climbing trees? The line of trees surrounding the property would serve as an excellent vantage point, as well as a place to hide. Would Ori think of it?

Miren moved from tree to tree, growing less certain that she would remain unseen, scanning the branches above her. At the sixth one, she stopped. A small, boy-shaped silhouette sat on a branch hugging the trunk.

She whispered loudly, "Ori. Ori?"

He didn't move.

"Ori, I know that's you."

No response.

"Ori, you need to come down right now."

He shook his head.

"If you don't, I'm going to have to come up and get you."

Ori didn't move.

Miren sighed. "All right, then."

She hoisted herself up to the first branch and started climbing. The tree was tall but not very wide; the weight-bearing branches bent and swayed dangerously. She kept close to the trunk, hoping not to be spotted by the guards. She settled on the branch just below Ori, who looked at the field, his bottom lip jutted out stubbornly.

Miren struggled to get comfortable. "What are you doing up here?"

"Looking for my uncle."

Miren peered around the trunk. Most of the estate was in view from here, including the farmland. Perhaps two dozen workers were scattered about the crops; it would be easy enough to spot Cale from here.

"Do you see him?" she asked.

Ori hugged the tree tighter and shook his head.

"How old were you when you last saw him?"

Ori paused, then held up three fingers.

Miren sighed. "Ori, it was really, really stupid to leave like that."

Ori's face contorted as he started to sniffle.

"Oh no." Miren waved her arm. "Don't cry. Please don't cry. You're not stupid, all right? You're really smart for climbing the tree and waiting; that was very clever. If you cry, they'll find us. Ori," she said softly, "it was very brave of you to come here, but we need to get going."

"But what about Uncle Cale?" he said.

"Uncle Cale is going to be fine."

"But it's bad. I heard Nana say she is a mean lady."

"Nana is a mean . . . oh, you mean Lady Rion. I'm sure she is." Liviya had said as much. "But your uncle is very strong. He will be all right."

"You don't know that. You don't know Uncle Cale."

"You're right," Miren admitted. "I've never met your uncle. But you know what? I bet that he wouldn't want you to be in danger. I bet that if we could ask him, he would tell you to stay with your parents and not run off. He wouldn't want you to get hurt trying to help him. Does that make sense?"

Ori didn't respond. He shifted on the branch and swung one leg over.

"Whoa, careful!" Miren held out a hand to steady him, but he didn't need it. He swung down to the lower branch with practiced ease.

"Wait, wait, wait. Ori, we need to be careful, all right?" Miren struggled to follow, the branches swaying sharply as she moved. "We can't be seen by the men over there."

"I *know*," he said.

She dropped down next to Ori. "All right. We need to get back to the barn." She looked around, but there was no other cover by the sparse tree line. "How did you get here without being seen?"

"It was still dark out," Ori said.

"Excuse me."

Miren whirled around. A man in a sky-blue and gold uniform stood a few paces away, a rifle in his hands.

"You are trespassing on the property of Lady Rion," he said. "State your business."

Miren scrambled for an answer. "I—I'm sorry to bother you," she said. "I was hoping Lady Rion could help us. We've been looking—"

But the guard's eyes flitted to Ori's face. He leveled his gun at Miren. "That boy is wanted."

Miren pushed Ori behind her. "He's just a child."

"We have orders to arrest him and his family. Where are his parents?"

Miren swallowed. "You can't—that's what I was trying to tell you," she said. "I—I found him wandering the streets alone, and I was worried for him. I didn't know he was wanted."

The guard's eyes narrowed. "I need you both to come with me," he said. "The Lady will want to see you."

Miren looked around, hoping to see a direction she and Ori could run, but the man clicked the gun's safety off as if he knew her thoughts. "Now, miss."

TWENTY-SEVEN

MIREN

Miren kept her hands up as she and Ori walked. Not far from the field, the green gave way to a cobblestone road that led to the mansion. She kept Ori in front of her so that she was between him and the rifle.

A few workers in the field seemed to notice the new arrivals, but they hardly gave Miren and Ori more than a glance. A couple of guards nodded to their escort. Ori stared out at the field as he walked, as if still looking for his uncle. Miren could only assume the boy didn't understand how much trouble they were in.

"Sir," Miren said. "I don't know what you're talking about, but I'm certain this boy isn't the one you're looking for."

"I thought you said you just found him alone on the streets."

"I said he wasn't with his parents. I just thought they had—come to work for Lady Rion."

The guard gave a disbelieving *tch*. "Walk faster." He nudged Miren in the back with the tip of his rifle.

"Really, sir, this isn't necessary. I know his parents—"

"Lady Rion will want to hear about that too."

Two guards flanked the front doors. One came over and wordlessly unclipped Miren's holster. The three guards pushed Miren and Ori through the front doors and into the mansion.

It was a sprawling space furnished in rich blues and deep purples.

Portraits of stoic-looking dark-haired figures in intricately carved frames lined the hall. Servants clad in fine clothes of yellow and light blue walked past without a glance at the odd party.

They came to a parlor furnished in maroon upholstery and a lightly carpeted floor. Two figures reclined on lush couches.

One was a woman: angular, with a long curtain of dark hair. She wore a green dress with an embroidered skirt that contrasted with the room's darker hues.

The other figure was Cheliem.

"Ah, and here we are," the woman said.

Lord Cheliem leaped to his feet, his eyes on Miren. "Wonderful! Oh, this is stunning. Do you have the others?"

"No, sir," a guard said. "She is the only one I found."

Miren said, "Hello, Cheliem."

Cheliem glared at her. "Lord Cheliem, if you don't mind."

The woman laughed. "Isn't she plucky. Is she yours, Cheliem?"

"No, she isn't. But she knows where mine are." He turned to the woman. "I can't thank you enough, Lady Rion."

"Of course. Although next time, check with me before you insist on wanted posters. It doesn't serve morale well when servants hear that someone's hands have successfully escaped. I've had more discipline issues than usual this week."

"I do apologize for the inconvenience." Lord Cheliem put a hand to his chest and bowed. "If you'll excuse me."

Lady Rion nodded and waved a hand, dismissing everyone. Lord Cheliem stepped from the room with a beckoning motion, and the guards prodded Miren and Ori to follow.

They went down a dark, uncarpeted stairway. The light from the hallway sconces faded after only a few steps.

At the bottom was what could only be called a dungeon: rows of barred cells on the left, faint lantern light to the right.

"Put the boy in that one." Cheliem pointed to the nearest cell on the left. "Ready the girl in the far chamber."

One guard began to pry Ori from Miren's leg. She suppressed the urge to try to fight the man off. "It'll be all right," she said to Ori as the cell door opened with a heavy squeal of metal. "I'll see you soon."

Ori's face was blank with terror as he was shoved out of sight. The barrel of a rifle dug into Miren's back while she was herded to the room at the very end of the hall.

In the center of the room was a chair with chains and cuffs on the arms. To the right hung strange instruments of metal, some of them stained dark red.

Miren flailed out, true panic taking over, but the men caught her easily and forced her into the chair. Cold metal snapped over her wrists, ankles, and chest.

The guards filed out of the room, and the door clicked shut behind them, leaving her alone with Lord Cheliem.

"Miss Miren," he said. "Truthfully, I'm not convinced that is your real name, but I'll call you that anyway. How are you today?"

"You can't do this," she said, her voice shaking. "I'm not—I haven't done anything wrong."

"Oh, well, that's certainly not true. You helped my servants escape."

"I didn't."

"Oh, is that so?" Cheliem paced leisurely in front of her, hands in his pockets. "You and your Singer friend just decided to come unannounced to my estate with a wild story about a sister who managed to avoid the Singer draft, and then wandered around my mansion and spotted that my crops were on fire. That very night, my servants escaped. You see how it would be quite easy to assume that you orchestrated that entire thing."

"I didn't," Miren said again. "I really am looking for my sister."

"And yet here you are, milling about Lady Rion's property with the very boy I'm looking for. Tell me where the rest of my servants are."

"Ori isn't your servant," she said.

"Both of his parents now owe me more money than they will be able to pay in their lifetime. Their debt will transfer to their son."

"You can't do that," she said. "He hasn't signed anything."

"Sounds like you know plenty about their situation," he said. "Are you friends?"

Miren didn't reply.

Cheliem continued his pacing. "You know what would happen to that family if the Crown's Guard caught them first?" Cheliem said. "They would be tried in court, all three of them, and then turned over to me to be punished as I see fit. Given the public nature of a trial, I would have to make an example of them. Nothing that would decrease their monetary value, of course, but something people would remember. Perhaps I would sear my crest into their cheeks with a hot iron. All three of them."

Miren imagined Ori held down while a red-hot iron hovered. "Don't," she said.

"Tell me where they are."

"I don't know."

Cheliem stood over her, leaning on the arms of the chair. This close, she could see the fury that simmered just beneath his surface. "I will be plainer. You have no leverage. You are no one. I could have you shot and buried in a flower bed anytime I like."

Miren looked away, her blood feeling like ice in her veins.

"You know"—Cheliem resumed his pacing—"I did some research into your story. The one you spun at my estate about a sister being snatched by bounty hunters. Despite your rude exit from my estate, I did keep my end of our bargain. It turns out there is not a single record of a Fire Singer being recruited to the navy in the last two months."

Miren stared at him, struggling to understand. "No—no bounty hunters have—"

"Have turned in a Fire Singer, correct. I did quite a bit of digging, as a Fire Singer would incite quite a stir. There are only four others in the entire army. Did you know that?"

Only four—was her mother one of them? Miren shook her head. "You're lying."

"I can only assume that if your story *is* true—which again, I highly doubt—then your sister is working in some factory in Avi'or right now."

"What? Why would she be in Avi'or?"

Cheliem paused. "There are a few Avi'ori businesses who rely on Singers to work but can't pay them what the market demands—rumor has it they use Singers like slaves. Oftentimes Avi'ori prey on their own, but occasionally a rogue pirate ship will wander to our southern coast and find a village worth terrorizing. To find a Fire Singer in such a way would be an incredible stroke of luck, though, so I can't help but be skeptical."

Miren's mind reeled back to the day Kesia had been taken. The ship had been Avi'ori, hadn't it? The pirates had spoken with Kaleon accents—but an accent could be faked. Liviya had a decent Kaleon accent. She had never even considered—

Kesia Kesia Kesia.

"No," Miren said. "You're lying."

He looked at her curiously. "Only people without power feel a need to lie, Miss Miren."

She shook her head. She had to focus. Ori was still in danger.

"You do anything to me," she said, "and the house of Darius will come down on you with full force."

"You're referring to your Water Singer friend?" Cheliem said. "A Fifth Circle house can't do much this far north. Try again."

Miren twisted against her bindings. Her fear was mounting, she couldn't think. "Please," she said. "Please let me go."

"As I said, I have no business with you," he said. "Just tell me where my servants are."

Miren swallowed.

Cheliem sighed. "Fine." He called through the door, "Bring the boy here."

"No!" Miren's scream echoed in the small space. "I . . . I know where they are."

Cheliem waited.

"They . . . you have to promise not to hurt Ori."

"You're in no position to make demands, but know that I prefer undamaged products."

"They're . . . they're southwest of here, hiding in a big yellow barn near a field of cotton. It's easy to spot."

Cheliem's eyes narrowed. "You're lying."

"No, I'm—"

"Bring the boy here."

"No, I'm not lying. *I'm not lying.* I swear. They're hiding just around the corner of the barn. I don't know whose farm it is. There's a line of bushes. It's just behind that."

Cheliem leaned over her. "If I find out you're lying, I will show you all the clever ways Lady Rion keeps her servants in check. And I will start with the boy."

He left the room, calling out, "Gather a search party."

Guards stepped forward, quickly unlocking her bindings and marching her down the hall. Cheliem was already at the bottom of the steps; he didn't glance back as they shoved her into a slightly larger cell so hard that she fell on the stone floor, pain shooting up her knees and her hip. The metal gate closed behind her.

Small hands pulled at her arm. She looked up at Ori, his face streaked with tears.

She pushed herself up to a seated position. "Hi, Ori," she said. "Are you all right?"

He nodded. "This is my fault."

"No, it's not." Miren fought to keep her voice even. "This is Cheliem's fault, all right?"

Ori wiped at his face. "All right."

She held him in a hug. They were in a windowless cell, nearly too dark to see. The stone floors and walls were slick.

She sensed movement in the corner of the cell and pulled Ori closer to her. "Who's there?"

Ori tried to squirm out of her grip, but she didn't let go. "That's my uncle," he said.

Miren looked between Ori and the shadowed figure. "Your uncle? That's Cale?" She stood and crept forward a few paces.

She saw dark hair and familiar cheekbones. He was younger than she had expected, perhaps twenty years old. He seemed shorter and stockier than his brother, but that could be because he was slouched against the wall, hunched as though in pain. Even in the faint light, she spotted several bruises along his arms, and she could see that one eye was nearly swollen shut.

He turned his head in her direction. "Ori knows you." His voice was a heavy rasp.

"Yes," she said, crouching in front of him. "I'm Miren. I know your family."

Ori plopped down next to his uncle, looking oddly calm.

"You helped them escape?" Cale asked. She couldn't tell if he was incredulous, or if his bruised eye was warping his expression.

"Not exactly," she said.

"What did Cheliem want with you?"

"He's looking for . . . Ori's parents."

Cale tilted his head up to look at Miren. "What did you tell Cheliem?"

Miren glanced out of the cell, but the guard was down the hall, sitting in a chair by the stairs. She leaned forward and whispered. "I lied. I told them some place close so the others would see the men searching. But Cheliem is going to hurt Ori when he realizes I was lying, so we need to get out of here now."

Cale straightened, his eyes wary and confused. "You lied?"

"Shhh! Of course I did."

"Why?"

"Because I panicked. I didn't know what else to do. Hopefully Liviya is with them and will figure out what happened when she sees the search party."

"My mother's here too?"

She nodded, glancing through the bars again. The guard was still out of earshot.

"But who are you?" he said. "How did you get involved in this?"

"Your mother and I have a deal. It's a long story." Miren suddenly felt exhausted. She slid down the wall and sat on the floor. "What happened to you?"

He eased himself back onto the floor, wincing. "Rion. What else?"

"Why? What does she gain by doing this to people?"

He shrugged. "Fear of pain, possibly?"

Miren huffed a frustrated sigh. "You know what I'm asking."

He glanced at Ori, who was trying to tie the laces on his boot. "When I heard that Arten and his family managed to escape Cheliem's estate, I tried to do the same. Didn't even make it to the coast before the guards caught me."

"You tried to escape on your own?" she said.

He nodded. "Thought I could surprise them, but I guess Rion was expecting me to pull something like that. It's not the first time I've been down here."

Miren leaned forward and whispered. "Do you know how to get out?"

"Of the dungeon?" He glanced at Ori again. "No one has ever escaped here."

Miren stood and walked over to the door. The lone guard leaned far back in his chair, blinking slowly.

"You still haven't told me how you know my family," Cale said.

Miren didn't look at him. "It was . . . coincidence, really. Hard to explain."

"Well, we're not going anywhere."

So she told him — how she and Davri left Crescent Bay to pursue her sister, how they ran into Liviya at Cheliem's estate. She explained the deal they made: Davri would help get them safely out of Kaleo, and in return, Liviya would give them information to help them find Kesia.

"But now Cheliem is telling me that there *is* no record of a recruited Fire Singer — there hasn't been one in months — and that Kesia must be in Avi'or as a — as a slave. How is that — does Avi'or have slavery? I thought they didn't have anything like this — this horrible servitude system."

"They don't," Cale said. "It's why our family came here in the first place. Common story. But there are big companies in Avi'or that rely on cheap labor. Very cheap. Maybe they use Singers."

Miren turned away. She had spent all this time searching, and it was all for *nothing*. She wasn't even in the right country.

Kesia Kesia Kesia.

Where are you?

A jangling of keys caught their attention. The door swung open, and Miren saw five armed guards.

"Cheliem wants to see you," one of them said. "All three of you."

TWENTY-EIGHT
MIREN

CHELIEM PACED ACROSS THE LUSH CARPET IN THE CENTER of the parlor, hunched and red-faced. His head shot up like a predator's as soon as they entered. Lady Rion lurked in the back corner, arms folded, her expression unreadable.

The guards forced Miren, Cale, and Ori into a line. A heavy kick knocked Miren to her knees. Cale fell beside her without resistance, his injuries stark in daylight. Ori whimpered, and Cale placed an arm around him.

Miren trembled. *He's going to kill us.*

Cheliem turned and raised his arm; a pistol glinted in his hand, pointed at Ori.

"Don't!" Miren cried.

"We had a deal, Miss Miren," Cheliem growled.

"I'll tell you, I'll tell you!" she cried. "They're in the next farm over, the one with the blue barn. I swear!"

Cheliem aimed a kick at her gut. She coughed and doubled over, her vision blurring.

"And what good is that information to me now?" Cheliem snarled. "You think they didn't see my men looking for them? I'm sure that was the whole point of your little trick. Very clever. Give me the boy."

Miren looked up as Cale pushed Ori behind him. Cheliem aimed another kick at Cale's stomach, and he doubled over as well.

"Careful, Cheliem," Lady Rion said gently. "That one is mine."

"Pardon my presumptuousness, milady," Lord Cheliem said, his tone pleasant as he grabbed Miren's hair and wrenched her upright. "I could shoot you now, you know that?" he hissed loudly in her ear. "I could lodge a bullet in that grimy little head and throw you in a hole in the ground and no one would find you—no one would even think to look for you. You understand?"

Rion said, "Not on the carpet, Cheliem, please."

Cheliem released her and glanced at Rion. "Maybe if we put the child in the town square for a few hours," he mused. "Do you think that will work?"

Rion dipped her head. "I think that would work just fine, Cheliem," she said serenely. "The threat of violence is often more potent than the act itself."

"And yet I find myself using both to great effect." Cheliem straightened his sleeves. "What if I put the child in the center of town and threaten to hang him if his parents don't turn themselves in?"

Ori ducked against Cale's shoulders.

Rion shrugged. "It would be difficult to explain should the capital hear of it, don't you think?"

Cheliem returned to pacing, the pistol swinging wildly in his grip. Miren pushed herself upright, still shivering from the blow to her stomach. She swallowed against the taste of bile.

Cheliem pivoted and waved the gun at Miren. "What's their plan? How do they plan to leave the country?"

A door opened behind Miren. "Excuse me—" said a servant.

"Not *now*," Cheliem barked.

Lady Rion raised an eyebrow, but Cheliem didn't seem to notice. "Yes?" she said.

"Pardon me, milady, but there is a visitor."

"Another visitor," Lady Rion echoed. "Just what I needed. Who else has come to inconvenience me?"

"He calls himself Lord Davri of Crescent Bay. He wishes to speak to Lord Cheliem."

Silence swept through the room.

Davri?

"What is he doing here?" Cheliem swiveled to look at Rion.

"I'm sure I don't know."

Cheliem glared at Miren. "Is this a trap? Are you planning something?"

"No, I—I didn't know." Miren stammered. Was it a trap? Where were the others? Was Davri alone?

Rion headed for the door leading to the main hall. "We may as well find out, Cheliem."

Cheliem's eyes darted to Miren and Cale. "It must be a trick. They've planned something."

Rion sighed and paused by the door. "I do not remember you being so easily disturbed. It is not becoming."

"I'm not letting this one out of my sight." Cheliem pointed to Miren.

"Then bring them with us." Rion swept out of the room.

The guards yanked Miren and Cale to their feet and shoved them after the nobles, Ori still clinging to Cale. Miren caught a questioning look from Cale but shook her head; she had no idea what was going on.

In the entrance hall, flanked by two armed guards, stood Davri. His blue eyes found Miren's and held them, as though trying to tell her something. She waited for some kind of sign, but he looked away.

"Give me one good reason why I should not have you arrested right now," said Lord Cheliem.

Because these guards are not under your authority. Davri bowed and extended a hand to Rion. She took it and let him gently bring it to his lips. *Thank you for seeing me on such abrupt notice, Lady Rion.*

"I must admit some level of confusion, Lord Davri," she said.

"Lord Cheliem here has leveled some startling accusations against you."

I can only imagine.

"Is this your friend?" Rion gestured at Miren.

Davri nodded, careful not to look at Ori.

"She was found snooping around Lady Rion's estate. Would you care to explain?"

Davri gave Cheliem a questioning look. *I assume you already asked her yourself?*

Cheliem looked away, his ears turning red.

Davri patiently waited for his attention. *I have come to offer you a deal. If you release Miren, as well as that boy and his family from your contract, I will willingly report to the nearest military drafting center and give you the bounty.*

In the silence after Davri stopped signing, Miren swallowed. "Davri," she said. "What are you—?"

Davri continued, *Officially, I am exempt from the draft, but I would be willing to give up my title in this exchange. I will even take a new name if you wish.*

"That is a generous offer," Rion said. "I think half a Singer's bounty would make today's efforts quite worth it."

Cheliem froze. "I beg your pardon?"

"Well, whose men would be escorting Lord Davri to the drafting center? I believe I am entitled to some compensation for today's events. Do you disagree?"

Davri's lip twitched slightly. *I would certainly not begrudge you that, milady.*

"No," Cheliem said. "No, I—I would not begrudge you that either."

Davri's gaze flitted between them, his expression careful. The truth struck Miren with a jolt: *This is a ruse.*

She glanced at Lady Rion, worried that Davri was being too

obvious, but the woman tilted her head with keen interest. "What a brave young man," she said with no hint of sarcasm. "It is an honor to serve one's country."

Davri nodded. *I have avoided my responsibility for too long.*

Miren thought it must be easier to lie when signing.

As a lord of the Fifth Circle, my father has never known great wealth or renown, Davri signed. *Perhaps this is my chance to bring honor and dignity to his house.*

"How very noble of you," Lady Rion said.

"Davri," Miren said. "Don't do this. Please."

"Don't speak in the presence of your betters," Lord Cheliem snarled.

Please watch your tone with my future sister-in-law, Davri signed sharply.

"My, what a dramatic situation this is," Lady Rion said, almost looking pleased. "Well, there's no reason to wait on this, is there, Cheliem?"

Cheliem tugged at his coat. "I'm afraid there is, milady. I left the contracts of service back at my estate. It seems, Davri, you'll need to come with me to retrieve them."

Rion's gaze sharpened. "I think it would make more sense for Lord Davri to remain here while you retrieve the contracts. I can work with the local guard to remove the many wanted posters while you're gone."

Cheliem glared at her. "I'd prefer he stay with me, actually."

"I'm sure you do."

It seems logical that I stay with Lady Rion, Davri signed.

Miren glanced at Davri. Was this the plan? To get Cheliem to leave?

A door slammed, and everyone whirled as a servant barreled into the room. He was streaked with dirt and wore tattered clothes—a worker from the fields.

"Pardon the intrusion, milady," he said, panting, "but the crops are on fire."

"On *fire?*" Lady Rion shrieked.

"Yes milady, we don't know how—"

"You idiot! Get out there and put it out! All of you, help!" she shouted at the guards. She pointed to Cale. "You! Go with them."

The guards looked at their prisoners uncertainly. Cale handed Ori to Miren, his face stricken.

Cheliem whirled. "No, *no!* This is a trick! This happened to me—"

I will come! Davri signed to Rion.

"Thank you," she said. She and Davri hurried after the guards.

"You foolish woman!" Cheliem called. "This is a part of their ruse."

But no one stopped. Miren and Ori were alone with Lord Cheliem.

He lifted his pistol. "What is happening?"

Miren pushed Ori behind her. "Lord Cheliem, I don't know what's happening."

"What's the plan?"

"I don't *know.*"

Cheliem took a step closer, training the pistol inches from her forehead. "I *know* this is a ploy."

"Please, I—"

"I will shoot you now if you don't tell me." Lord Cheliem pushed the barrel into Miren's forehead, the icy metal biting into her skin. She closed her eyes.

"Stop!" Ori wailed.

"Give me the boy," Cheliem said.

Miren swallowed. "No."

The man raised an eyebrow. "Give me back my servant."

"He's not yours."

Cheliem lunged around Miren to grab Ori's wrist. The boy cried out in pain.

Miren kneed Cheliem in the groin.

The lord cried out and doubled over. Miren yanked the gun out of his hand and pulled Ori away from him. She trained the gun on Cheliem. "Don't come closer."

Cheliem put a hand on the floor to steady himself, then stood. "I'll see you hanged for that," he said.

Miren didn't lower the gun. "Don't move."

He coughed. "You're going to shoot me? You know the punishment for killing a noble?"

Miren didn't move. "Go stand over there." She motioned to the corner.

"I will not be ordered around by a *peasant*. Give me my property." Cheliem started toward her.

Miren flicked off the safety. "Don't come closer!"

He didn't stop. "You're going to have to shoot me."

A shot rang out.

Miren aimed the barrel at the ground, terrified that she had just shot him, but the gun hadn't kicked; she hadn't pulled the trigger. Cheliem stumbled. He caught himself and put a hand to his side as bright red began to stream down his coat. He looked up as two more shots found home in his chest. Then he collapsed, unmoving.

Liviya stood in the doorway, a pistol in her grip.

She looked to Miren. "Let's go!"

Miren grabbed Ori's arm. "Come on, Ori."

Impossibly, they hurried out the front door, seeing no guards to stop them. A monstrous pillar of smoke bloomed from the other side of the estate.

"Davri — he went to put out the fire —"

"I know. He's going to meet us."

"Meet us where?"

"At the river."

Liviya ran to the left, in the opposite direction from the fire. On the north side of the estate, the rise dipped for about fifty paces before reaching a sheer cliff that wound from east to west as far as the eye could see, though there was little cover on either side.

Liviya angled down toward the cliff and ran alongside it, heading west. Below them, the Crown's Seam tumbled, the river's surface white and roaring.

"How do we—how do we get down there?" Miren asked.

"Keep going!" Liviya said.

Ori tripped; Miren pulled him upright. "I can't run!" he cried. Miren paused to scoop him up and scrambled after Liviya.

The path continued downward, but they were still in plain sight of the mansion.

"Does Davri know where we're going?" Miren asked.

"Yes, keep running!"

Just behind a dip in the land, Hana sat crouched next to something under a tarp. She gasped when she saw them. "Ori, Ori, Ori!"

Miren let Hana take Ori from her arms, and the two clung to each other.

"Ori, don't *ever* do that again!" Hana said.

"I'm sorry, Mama—"

"You are in *so* much trouble."

Miren looked around. "Where's Arten?"

Liviya ran past them and grabbed an edge of the tarp. "Miren, help me with this."

Miren hurried over to the other side. A small fishing boat sat underneath the tarp.

"You got a boat," Miren said.

"Help me get it to the edge."

Miren didn't understand—it was still a drop of fifty paces from the cliff to the water, but she helped the other two women half-carry, half-push the boat to the edge.

Liviya climbed aboard. "Everyone get in. Stay close to the front."

"But how are we going to get this down to the water?" Miren asked.

"Davri's coming." Hana tucked Ori between her and Miren. "He'll get us down there."

At the sound of footsteps, Miren's hand went to Cheliem's pistol, but it was Davri and Arten and Cale who ran toward them.

"Time to go!" Arten said. "Davri slowed them down a bit, but they're coming."

The men took their spots in the boat, Davri at the stern, with Arten's steadying hand on his shoulder.

"How are we getting down there?" Miren said.

I can do it, Davri signed as he began to Sing.

His Voice wasn't loud, but it carried. Miren heard it briefly touch the faint trace of water that lingered in the air before it reached the river down below. It would be easy for the guards to find them now.

For a few moments, nothing seemed to happen. Hana glanced at Miren with a question in her gaze, but Miren was listening: the Song wasn't trying to reach for the water. It was a Song of slowing, of holding back. But wasn't that the opposite of what they needed?

She understood as soon as she saw the water crest over the cliff.

It stood like a tower, steadily rising as Davri held back the current and coaxed it toward them. Miren held her breath as the water pooled around the boat, filling the space underneath. She could almost feel the amount of effort it took to hold that—like trying to slowly roll a boulder down a hill—but Davri's Voice didn't waver.

She clutched the side of the boat as the bow angled down the tower of water.

The world rushed past.

They splashed hard into the river as Davri's Song released its hold on the water, and the current pushed them forward. The boat tilted dangerously, but Davri didn't stop Singing, though his Song shifted to one of encouragement, steadying the rapids beneath them. She thought it would be too much effort to maintain all the way to the coast, but the Song wasn't trying to control the current—Davri was just nudging it in clever ways. His Song steadied as the current pushed them due east, the estate quickly growing smaller behind them.

The coast came upon them faster than Miren expected.

They shot into the calm waters of the bay, docks and port towns stretching across the coast in both directions. Behind them, a jagged face of rock stood twenty paces high. Miren was soaked and shivering, and so was everyone else.

Davri's Song sputtered to a halt. He leaned over the side of the boat and vomited.

"Whoa, easy." Arten kept a firm grip on his shoulder. "You all right?"

Davri nodded, straightening as he wiped his mouth.

"We need to get away from the coast." Liviya shifted in her seat and wrestled out two oars from the bottom of the boat. She handed one to Cale. "Start rowing."

He took it. "Good to see you too, Mother."

Liviya paused with such a baffled expression that everyone laughed.

And there was plenty of awkward shifting and almost tipping over the boat as everyone insisted on hugging each other. Arten ruffled his brother's hair. Ori fussed until his father pulled him into his lap and kissed Hana. Liviya held up Cale's arm and inspected his bruises while he insisted he was fine.

Miren caught Davri's gaze. He sat slumped against the stern of the boat, looking exhausted but pleased.

"That was incredible," she said. "That was—how did you slow them down?"

Froze their legs together, he signed, grinning. *And some of the barrels of their guns, where I could.*

Miren let out a disbelieving laugh. "Don't look so pleased with yourself."

His grin widened.

"What happened to you?" Arten said to Liviya. "Where did you go?"

Liviya held up a hand. "Someone saw me lighting the fire in town, so I had to hide for a while. I spotted a boat in a cornfield, and it took a while to track the owner down and convince him to let me buy it and to buy a horse and cart to transport it, especially with the coin I had on hand. As soon as I got back and found out what happened"—she looked at Ori sternly, who ducked his chin—"we devised a plan to get you out."

Davri signed to Liviya, *How did you get past Cheliem? He didn't follow us?*

Miren and Liviya exchanged a glance. Liviya said, "He won't be a problem anymore."

Davri's eyes widened, but he nodded.

Miren remembered what Cheliem had said, and her relief quickly soured.

"Davri," she said. "We have a problem. I don't think . . ." She swallowed. "I don't think Kesia is in Kaleo."

Davri shook his head as if to clear it. *I don't understand.*

She explained what Cheliem had said, staring at the water as the boat bobbed and swayed in the current.

"I'm sorry," Liviya said. "I never thought—I never even *considered*—"

"But you can come to Avi'or with us," Arten said. "You have some idea of where to look now, right? You know more."

A small flicker of hope flared in Miren's chest. *Kesia, Kesia, Kesia.* Davri caught her eye. *What do you want to do?* he asked.

"I want to keep looking," she said. "We have to find her."

He nodded. *Then we go to Avi'or.*

"We have supplies enough for four people," Liviya said, "so we'll need to ration, but we could do it. Rion will likely have the Crown's Guard on alert for us, so we can't double back. We should take advantage of our head start."

I can do it, Davri signed. He picked up his Song again and pushed them east into open water.

TWENTY-NINE

KESIA

KESIA WOKE TO THE HUM OF VOICES AND THE CLATTERING of hooves.

She lifted her head, feeling an ache in her neck that was different than what she was used to. There was no collar in place to keep her from tossing and turning on the hard ground.

She sat up and coughed against the acrid smell of garbage around her. As the sky lightened, the mounds of refuse lining the alleyway were thrown into relief—rotted food, broken furniture, shredded clothes. She felt coated in grime, her hair matted and clinging to her cheeks.

Even at this early hour, the city was bustling. People, some dressed in tailored garb, others in flowing dresses or simple work clothes, shoved their way through crowds.

She closed her eyes and lay back down, willing herself to sleep a bit longer. She had been dreaming something pleasant.

In the months that had followed their mother's departure, the sisters had had no word of her. They received letters from their father, but even those came only rarely.

The sisters didn't discuss what the silence could mean. They avoided talking about the war as much as they could. The longest discussion they had was when they wrote a letter to Father, telling him where Mother had gone, and that Kesia, though she survived, had lost her Voice to cloud fever.

Kesia always felt Miren's presence in a room. Her sister tended to hover.

At night, Kesia stared at the fire she had just lit for dinner with the small, dulled spark rocks that Haro the blacksmith had given them. The coming winter promised to be brutal. How would they survive, just the two of them? How would they make it without Song?

A faint noise, like someone inhaling. She looked up, but she was alone. Miren was tending to the lighthouse. Kesia listened but heard nothing. The first lesson Mother ever taught her was to listen. *Before you Sing, you must first hear the Song.*

Ever since the Singer Draft, the village had not celebrated Sky-flame. It was a terrible, gut-wrenching decision, one that made Kesia want to weep, but anyone who might have led Skyflame was away at war. The villagers would rather live without Singing than risk losing their children to the draft.

Only when Kesia had lost her gift had she come to love it.

Kesia knew that the village had slowly grown used to life without the help of Singers, but the absence of Song had robbed them of more than just a means to work. People spoke less. They hardly smiled, and when they could be bothered to gather for a night of songs and tales, it felt forced—less of a celebration than a reminder of what they had lost. Even Miren's voice, always bright and clear no matter what song she sang, had grown quieter and less certain.

I want to Sing, Kesia thought. *I want to Sing.*

There—she heard the Song. She hadn't heard the Song since being sick but wondered now if she simply hadn't been listening in the way her mother had taught her. She opened her mouth, willing the air to pull sound from her throat.

Notes drifted through the air. She felt a tugging inside her, and a candle was lit. Kesia stopped before the Song was finished, feeling winded, but the candle flickered happily.

"Kesia?" Miren called. Footsteps thundered down from the lighthouse, and the cabin door slammed open. "I thought I heard—"

Kesia smiled widely. She hadn't really believed that she missed Singing this much, but the fire seemed to fill her with a warmth that she had forgotten.

We don't need more spark rocks, she signed.

"You can Sing!" Miren gasped and opened her arms. Kesia hugged her. Miren was laughing, and it was a tight, desperate sound, but the sisters held each other. When they parted, there were tears on both their faces.

Write Father! Kesia signed happily, reaching for a pen.

"Wait!" Miren grabbed her arm. "We need to be careful. There's still a draft."

Kesia gasped. She had almost forgotten the war. Singers were still being drafted. They had heard rumors of new Singers being found in cities and taken to war as soon as their Voices manifested.

A sudden wave of loneliness caught her. She was the only Singer in Crescent Bay, except for Lord Darius's reclusive son, but he hardly counted. Besides, he was exempt from the draft.

Miren said, "We can't tell anyone."

Kesia stared at her. *Not even Father?*

"What if Father's letter gets intercepted?"

They won't know who we are.

"What if the military reads them?"

Kesia frowned. *You think they do that?*

Miren bit her lip. "It's possible," she said.

Tell me what you know. I'm old enough to know about these things, Kesia signed angrily.

"I don't know for certain. I'm just—suspicious." Miren lifted her hands. "Please Kesia. Don't tell anyone you can Sing."

How can we keep this a secret? Kesia signed, glancing out the window. *Winter is nearly here, and everyone is worried. The village will need me*—

Miren sobbed. Kesia was shocked to see tears rolling down her sister's cheeks. Miren never cried. Ever.

"Please," Miren begged. "Please keep it a secret."

Kesia's chest ached. She sometimes forgot why Miren was careful, that protection was her way of showing love. Kesia might lose her life, but Miren could lose her reason to live.

Fine, Kesia signed. She came over to give Miren another hug.

"Thank you," Miren murmured. They stood like that for another moment. When they stepped apart, Miren wiped her eyes and retrieved the spark rocks from the floor.

Finding the courage to leave her alley, Kesia walked along the streets amid the constant bustle of the city. On the western side, she found an open market, with booths full of piled fruit and bundled vegetables. She spotted a woman selling carrots. When the woman's back was turned, Kesia tugged at a bundle and hid it under her coat.

No guilt came with the action, nor when she took a loaf of bread from a bakery, or slipped a copy of a newspaper from a stand. She hadn't yet untangled herself from last night's violence against the elderly couple, Gemma and Axel, who had taken her in and then tried to collar her. The fury of it burned in her as she wove her way through the streets, flaring as passersby gave her a wide berth or a disgusted glance. Finally, a fire that didn't steal from her.

She nestled into another alley and stuffed herself with stolen food. She fumbled with the newspaper, a bundle of thin sheets that left her hands smudged with black ink. The lettering was difficult to read, but she flipped through the pages until she came across a sketch of a faintly familiar, heavily charred house with bold words above it: "Couple Loses House in Mysterious Fire, Claims Singer Attack."

She read through the article three times. The couple claimed they found a young woman who had broken into their shed. She had said she was Kaleon, and they had apparently assumed she was a member of the Kaleon military who had escaped Avi'ori custody. They had tried to apprehend her while she slept, but she woke and set their house on fire, then fled. The writer of the article, however, seemed disbelieving, highlighting the couple's age and a few choice words from disgruntled neighbors.

Either way, the article was a sign that she was in the city. Which meant workers from the factory might be looking for her.

She needed to leave.

She continued exploring the streets and stumbled upon the train station, where a billowing steam locomotive waited for passengers. She risked a few moments to study the detailed map encased in glass on the platform.

She was in a place called Peladah City, a large port on the southern coast of Avi'or. She noticed some railways that wove through different cities, but it wouldn't make sense to take a train, even if she had money for a ticket. She needed passage on a ship, but what vessel other than a pirate ship would be heading to Kaleo during a war?

She did her best to memorize the map and then left the station, feeling exposed. If Nadav and Parviz were looking for her, then surely they would check the docks and train station. Her best option was to remain hidden and keep moving. Even now, away from Amos Steel and free of her collar, she was still trapped.

As she walked, the pieces of the collar clinked in her bag. She wanted more than anything to be rid of it, but the memory of the old man approaching her, collar in his grip, stopped her. Each time she spotted a dumpster or trash-ridden alley, she couldn't will herself to pull it from the bag. She pressed her hand against the bag to keep the collar silent.

All day she wandered, afraid to ask questions or ask for coins, as she saw beggars doing on street corners.

The sudden scent of sugar and maple pierced the dirty air, and her stomach leaped in response. Her bag had emptied of food sooner than she had expected.

She noticed a wooden sign that read BAKERY. Just outside a painted window, a woman sold pastries and buns to a large, muddled crowd. Kesia eyed a glazed pastry, laced with swirls of white and brown, sitting on paper. Etela's bread had never looked like that.

Kesia edged into the crowd. She slipped the pastry from the tray and scurried away.

"Hey!" the woman called.

Kesia kept on walking, the bun sticky and warm in her hand.

An angry hand pulled her around by the shoulder. The baker looked livid. "You didn't pay for that, you little rat!"

Kesia cowered under her glare. Attention was the last thing she needed. She shoved the bun at the woman, who shook her head vigorously.

"I don't want it back. I want money, girl!" the woman yelled. "Five coppers."

Kesia backed away, trying to meld into the crowd, but the woman followed, dragging the attention of everyone else with her.

"No money, eh? Big surprise there. Bet you wouldn't like the peacers finding you like this, would you?"

Kesia shook her head, confused at the word *peacers*.

"Here, here!" someone called.

A young boy jogged up and dropped brown coins in the baker's hand.

The baker glanced at him, then back at Kesia. "Well, keep your friend's hands out of trouble, then!"

The baker stomped back to her stand. Kesia stared after her, but the baker's smile was in place as she returned to her customers.

The boy who paid for the pastry was a full head shorter than Kesia, his lanky form covered by an oversized, stained white shirt and crumpled trousers. He wore a bulbous hat that was so large for him that it covered his ears.

He smiled widely and held out his hand. "I'm Zuriel."

When Kesia said nothing, he sighed and shoved his hands in his pocket. "Well, you're *welcome*."

She turned and hurried away, folding her hands in her coat.

"Hey," the boy said, and she cringed. "You could at least say thank you."

She shook her head, edging away from him.

"What, you don't talk? Oh! Are you a Singer?"

Zuriel waited for her to sign an answer, but Kesia kept her arms tucked in her coat. Though his voice sometimes skipped deeply like a man's, he couldn't be older than twelve.

"You might as well eat that," the boy said. "I paid for it."

Kesia thought the pastry far more trouble than it was worth. She tried to hand it to him.

He shook his head. "I don't want it. I don't much like honey."

Kesia bit into the treat. Warm, syrupy cream leaked from its center. She couldn't imagine disliking anything about this pastry.

He frowned. "Why is a Singer living on the streets? You could probably get a hundred different jobs."

She shoved the pastry into her mouth and quickened her pace.

"Your clothes are really . . . different," he said. "You're not from around here, huh?" He gasped. "Are you Kaleon?"

She broke into a run.

"Hey, wait!" he chased after her. "We don't see a lot of Kaleons, is all," he said. He had a bounce that added an extra *tap* to his gait.

She slowed back to a walk, already feeling winded. Running attracted too much attention, but this boy would not leave her alone.

"I mean, there are some here, but not many," the boy continued. "You lot talk weird."

Kesia glanced at him but said nothing. She hadn't heard a single Kaleon accent since arriving.

"I hear you folks in Kaleo own people like property."

She shot him a look of mute horror before she could stop herself.

"It's true!" he said, though he sounded less certain. "I heard you trick people into signing contracts that force them to work forever. They think they'll get money at the end, but they just get trapped in debt."

Davri had mentioned the practice to her in passing, though his father had never done it. It was devious, but it surely held no comparison to the slavery she had experienced. Parviz had been telling the truth, she realized; the Avi'ori people truly had no idea what was happening at Amos Steel.

Zuriel looked smug. "Do you think all Avi'ori are stupid?"

Kesia's fingers twitched to respond, but she kept her hands in her sleeves. She didn't need to defend herself to a child, no matter how many coppers she owed him. She sprinted past him and down another street.

"Hey!" he called after her.

She gritted her teeth, wondering how terrible jail was compared to this. She could think of no way to rid herself of him without causing a scene.

She slowed. If he so despised the thought of Avi'ori workers being taken advantage of in Kaleo, would he listen to her about Amos Steel? Would he care?

Her hesitation had allowed Zuriel to catch up with her. "You

Kaleons think you're so much better than everyone else," he sneered. "I did something nice for you, and you treat me like a scarffer sewer rat!"

Kesia took off running again. No, she decided, she couldn't trust anyone. She swung around the nearest corner, looking for a place to hide.

She spotted an alley nearby and bolted for it. Just as she reached the entrance, the strap of her bag snapped, halting her. Something metallic clunked on the ground.

She whirled. Zuriel stood holding her bag. Between them, on the ground, sat the collar.

Kesia lunged for it, but the boy was faster. He snatched the collar up and studied it, frowning. "What is this?"

She reached for it, but he was stronger than his size suggested. He pushed her away with his free hand. "What does this do? Where did you get it?"

Kesia felt true panic. If anyone saw, or if this boy reported the collar, then Parviz and Nadav would find her; they would know she was alive and track her down, drag her back to the compound, slap on a new collar.

A Song would spark the boy's sleeve. Not enough to hurt him, just to distract—

A smoking apartment, the sound of alarm bells piercing the night. A pirate clutching his blistered arm in pain.

Kesia stumbled back and caught herself on the alley wall, feeling sick. She pressed a hand to her mouth as though the Song might escape.

"Hey, are you all right?" the boy asked, a note of apology in his voice.

She waved him away. *Go*, she signed. *Leave.*

He gasped. "You *are* a Singer!"

She froze, but he looked confused, his fury melting away. "Are you part of the Kaleon military?" he asked.

Was there harm in telling him?

No, she signed. *I escaped from Amos Steel.*

He stared at her like he didn't understand. "Escaped? Like . . . like you were a planter? Avi'or doesn't have that." His eyes narrowed. "Did you sign a contract?"

No! she slapped the word loudly, and Zuriel looked shocked. Her anger felt unstable, as if she might melt into tears at any moment. *There are many Singers there who are treated as slaves, forced to work without pay, lighting fires and melting metal—*

"How did they keep you there?" he asked.

Her eyes flickered to the collar in his hand. She reached for the top of her shirt and pulled it back, revealing the raw skin left from the collar's chafing.

Revulsion rippled across his face. "That's . . . that's not . . ."

He held the collar away from himself, as if he couldn't decide whether to drop it.

He looked toward the street, then back at Kesia.

"You . . . would you come to my house?" he asked. "I want you to talk to my grandpa."

THIRTY
KESIA

KESIA SHOOK HER HEAD. NO, SHE WOULD NOT GO WITH this boy. She pushed past him and ripped the collar from his hand.

"Hey, wait!" Zuriel grabbed her arm and spun her around. Kesia twisted from his grip, drew breath for a Song—

He gasped and stumbled back.

Kesia snapped her lips together, shame washing through her. The Song twisted inside her like poison until she pushed it away. *What is wrong with me?* she thought.

"I—I just think you should talk to my grandpa," Zuriel said again. "He doesn't trust the big companies. He thinks they're doing something illegal. We argue about it all the time. Amos Steel makes steel so cheaply." He gestured at her. "I guess now we know why."

Kesia slipped the collar in her bag. Zuriel shoved his hands in his pockets.

Not safe, she signed. *They might be looking for me.*

"Then you shouldn't be wandering the streets," Zuriel said.

I can't trust anyone, she signed, swallowing tears. He believed her, but he was young. Older minds were more difficult to change.

"You can trust my grandpa!" Zuriel insisted. "And my mother will take care of you. We have food. At least just come for a little while."

She had nowhere to go, and she was too scared to risk visiting the docks. There was no way for her to go home now.

"Come on," Zuriel said, heading back toward the street. "Just stay close to me and keep your head down. No one will notice us."

Kesia followed Zuriel, surprised when he took turns down alleys and dark, littered spaces between buildings. Looking up, she saw lines of drying clothes above the alleys and potted plants in the windows. Metal stairs zigzagged up the side of the buildings, all the way to the roofs.

Zuriel leaped for one set of stairs and pulled. A ladder slid to the ground with a roar of metal. "We'll go this way," he said. "Fewer people will see us."

Kesia wasn't sure that was true, but she scrambled up the stairs after him. Her chest heaved against an invisible collar. She grabbed the rail to steady herself.

"Hey, are you coming?" Zuriel called, already a flight above her. "We don't want anyone to spot us."

She nodded and continued up the next flight of stairs.

On the fifth floor, Zuriel curled his fingers under a window and shoved it open. "I use this way all the time," he said, glancing over his shoulder. His excited grin faltered. "What's wrong?"

She shook her head, her breathing finally steady.

"Don't worry, it'll just be Grandpa. Mother isn't home yet from work." He leaned through the window and tumbled in headfirst. "Grandpa," he called. "We have a visitor!"

Kesia stuck her head through the open window. She saw two beds pushed against opposite walls. Clothes littered the floor and hung off a mantel. Zuriel hurried to the door and paused, waiting for her.

"Zuriel!" a voice shouted from another room. "Did you come through the window, again? You know your mother hates that."

Kesia wiggled her way in until she could drop and roll onto the floor. She untangled herself from a pair of trousers, wincing at the smell.

"We have a guest!" Zuriel said again. He motioned for Kesia to hurry. She straightened her skirt and stepped into the hallway.

A man sat in a small parlor reading a newspaper, a cane propped against the arm of his chair. His shoulders were hunched, and he was mostly bald but for wisps of white hair behind his ears. A wire frame was set on his nose and ears, holding two shards of glass in front of his eyes. He stared at Kesia through them, and his eyes looked unnaturally large.

"Hello," he said.

She nodded, her hands clasped in front of her.

Zuriel nudged her. "Say hello," he whispered.

She glanced at him, her heart thrumming. *Hello, sir,* she signed.

The man pulled the frames off his face and sat up. "Zuriel," he said, "why did you bring this girl through the window?"

"Because she's being hunted!" Zuriel cried. Kesia startled at the word. "She—she escaped from Amos Steel!"

The man didn't move, his expression blank with confusion. "I don't understand."

"Oh, you don't listen." He pushed Kesia forward. "Tell him!"

Kesia stumbled, stiff with fear.

The old man folded the newspaper and set it on his lap. "Please sit down," he said.

Kesia went to the nearest chair and sat on the very edge of the seat, imagining herself darting for the door. Her bag slipped down her arm. Zuriel sat next to her, looking eager.

"I'm Dar," the old man said. "What's your name, young miss?"

She glanced at Zuriel, who nodded encouragingly. She spelled, *Kesia.*

The man watched her with a steady gaze. "Kesia," he said aloud. "Is that right?"

She nodded.

"And what is this about Amos Steel?"

She lifted her hands, and once she started signing, she couldn't stop. She told of the pirates coming to Crescent Bay, of being sold, of working in the factory and later on the airship.

They're building a huge airship, which can really fly, but they need me to keep the furnaces hot.

"A what?" Dar asked.

Air ship. Kesia made the signs distinct. *It's like a large egg on its side, and it has air in it. It's a very big secret.*

"Red skies and seas," Dar muttered. "I heard whisperings about them making prisoners of war work at Amos, but I never imagined pirates dragging Singers from their homes."

"But what about this airship?" Zuriel said. "I've never heard of anything like that."

"There were rumors," his grandfather said. "But there are always rumors. I just didn't think they'd be so daring about it. How were they able to fly the thing without us seeing?"

It's on the other side of the hill, Kesia signed, pointing south. *You wouldn't see it from the city.*

"But someone must have seen," he said to himself. "They must have done their tests around their private cove."

A lock clicked, and the front door swung open. A woman in a dark blue dress swept through, brown tendrils of hair peeking from an otherwise tight bun.

"Mother," Zuriel said. "This girl was a slave at Amos Steel!"

"What?"

Kesia recounted the story, watching the woman's face tighten as she sank onto the couch. She glanced at Dar, whose face was grim.

"I can't believe it," Zuriel's mother said when Kesia had finished the story a second time. "You were right, Father. I can't believe you were right."

"I never thought it was this bad, Tisa," Dar replied. "But it makes sense, doesn't it? Cheap labor means more profit, and this explains a lot."

"How did they control you?" Tisa asked.

Kesia glanced at Zuriel. He nodded, but he looked less eager now. "Show them."

Kesia reached in her bag and withdrew the collar.

Tisa gasped audibly. Dar looked sick.

"Unbelievable," she said. "How many of you were there?"

About twenty, Kesia signed.

"Why don't you just march up to the factory and burn it to the ground?" Zuriel asked.

Kesia shook her head, feeling tears prick her eyes. She had imagined it before, but most of the Amos Steel buildings were made of brick and metal, which took far too much Singing to melt. Besides, bullets were faster than her breath.

"Zuriel, don't speak like that," Tisa said. "Kesia, you are welcome to stay here until you decide what you want to do. You can share my room. I have some old dresses that will fit you."

Kesia's throat closed. They said they would help her, and she marveled at how easily she believed them. *Thank you,* she signed.

THIRTY-ONE

KESIA

KESIA CLIPPED THE FINAL PIECE OF WET LAUNDRY, A FADED blue shirt of Zuriel's, onto the line mounted just outside the window. A whole web of lines crisscrossed the alley, most of them laden with damp clothing that flapped in the wind.

In the apartment building directly across from them, a plump, smiling woman waved from a window. Kesia waved back, nervous that a stranger had seen her, but the woman was already gone.

For three days—three quiet, merciful days—she had been staying with Zuriel's family. She had made an effort to blend into their routine. Mornings were all chaos. Tisa would shake Zuriel from bed at least twice before he finally staggered to the kitchen for breakfast. The newspaper was delivered to the doorstep. In a whirlwind of shouting and shoveling food and looking for misplaced socks and hats, Tisa and Zuriel would leave.

The metallic oven intimidated Kesia, but Tisa was a patient teacher. By the third morning, Kesia was cooking salted pork and baking cornbread for breakfast. At Dar's prompting, Zuriel retrieved the newspaper and read aloud. The first few words startled Kesia like cold water.

"'Amos Steel and Co. Boosts City Economy,'" Zuriel read. "'Leading experts report that the overall condition of neighboring businesses has improved significantly since Amos Steel's founding ten years ago.' Sure, I'd wager my earnings for the week that it has!"

"Read another article," Tisa said, glancing at Kesia. "Please."

Zuriel flipped a few pages. "'Yesterday, the mayor oversaw the raising of the Sky Pillar in the town square in preparation for tomorrow's Star Song Festival.' It's almost here!"

"Oh, is it that time of year again?" Dar said.

"Don't tease, Father," Tisa said, kissing Zuriel's head. "This is the big year."

Zuriel grinned. Kesia sat down with a plate of pork. *Star Song?*

"It's the biggest holiday of the year," Tisa explained.

Zuriel was practically jumping in his seat. "Every year, the town gets together at night and lights the Sky Pillar. They set up four stations around it, one for each element, and everyone who's twelve gets to participate and try to Sing for the first time!"

Kesia signed excitedly, *That's Skyflame!*

Zuriel looked puzzled. "Sky fire?"

We call it Skyflame in Kaleo, Kesia explained. *We climb a hill and build a large fire—*

"This is a festival. We all gather—"

"Zuriel," Tisa said. "Don't interrupt."

Kesia smiled. *Yours sounds much bigger.*

"It's huge," Zuriel said. "You should come with us!"

Kesia paused. Going outside felt like an unnecessary risk.

"You should keep reading," Dar said to his grandson. "I want to hear about the coastal trade agreements."

Zuriel groaned and flipped through the pages. He looked up. "Hey! You know what we should do? We should go to the newspaper and tell them about Kesia!"

Kesia flinched so hard that she dropped her knife, smearing the table with butter. She signed apologies as she reached for a rag to clean it up.

"Zuriel," Tisa warned.

"It's perfect! That way we can let the people know what's

happening without endangering Kesia! Once the people hear about it, they'll get really mad, and Amos'll have to let the other slaves go!"

In the silence that followed, Kesia searched for reasons why that wouldn't work. She would have to show her face; nobody would believe her; they would assume she was part of the Kaleon military.

But when she thought of Ayla Singing fire on her own, those excuses felt cowardly.

Dar cleared his throat. "I don't think it's that simple, Zuriel. The Council employs Amos Steel to manufacture much of their steel. If the company uses Singers as slaves —"

"Then the Council might already know," Tisa finished. "They might not want that information to get out."

"But the paper isn't run by the government," Zuriel said.

"But the people who own the paper might be," Dar said. "We don't know what the Council would be willing to do to keep this a secret."

"But if the people know, then the government would have to stop!"

All eyes turned to Kesia.

Tisa stood. "We can discuss this later. Zuriel, you're going to be late to work."

After Tisa and Zuriel had left, Dar took his place in his chair with the remains of the newspaper, and Kesia cleaned up the kitchen.

A few hours later, the dishes had been washed and put away. The pantry had been organized. Beds had been made and laundry hung out to dry. What else was there to do?

Tisa and Zuriel spent most daylight hours at their jobs. Tisa was a secretary for an office — Kesia didn't fully understand it, but Tisa often came home complaining that she had been sitting for too long. A boy Zuriel's age was expected to attend school, but he held a job at a factory across town. "School is boring," he had said by way of explanation.

Kesia began sweeping the floors. She couldn't shake the belief that if she was idle, she would find herself slumped against the wall of an alley, or worse—back in the Singers' quarters of Amos Steel.

She knew she was being irrational, but when she stopped working, she thought about terrible things: Singers who were still slaves. A young Fire Singer forced to do the work of two. A sister who might or might not still be alive. Parents who were at war. Davri alone in his study.

At least she could help around the house.

Dar's newspaper dipped slightly. "Kesia, why don't you take a break?"

Kesia nestled the broom in the crook of her arm. *I will sweep the kitchen floor first.*

"You already swept it," he said gently. "Sit down."

Kesia hesitated. He had clearly given her an order, however kindly. She returned the broom to the closet and took a seat on the couch.

Dar stared at her for a moment. "Why don't you read a book?"

Kesia nodded, feeling relieved. Reading a book was a leisurely activity, but at least it was keeping busy.

She stood and walked over to the small shelf against the far wall. Twelve volumes stood in formation; she had never seen so many in one place. Davri had once offered to sneak her into his father's library, a rare sign of rebellion from him, but Kesia had refused. Any extra attention from Darius had seemed too blatant a risk—both because she was a Singer and because Darius would not approve of his son courting a commoner.

She ran her finger over the thick, well-worn covers, marveling at how so much information could be held in such a small casing. She found one Tisa had recommended: *The Only Star,* a romance between a rich blind man and a peasant woman born mute.

She opened the book and began reading, but soon her attention was drawn to the window, to the crowded streets. Was Dar right? Was slavery really such a far-reaching conspiracy here?

A rippling snore startled her from her thoughts. Dar had fallen asleep in his chair, the newspaper crumpled in his lap.

She stood, grabbed a shawl to cover her head, and left. She had been on the streets after her escape and hadn't been spotted, but somehow being out in the open felt more dangerous now. Rebellious, even. But she hadn't seen a single Amos Steel worker outside the factory since her escape, and now that she was clean and in different clothes, she was less likely to be noticed.

She traveled the streets with no particular destination in mind. She thought of Davri, of the hours they paced the beach together or sat on a shelf of rock, keeping to the north end to avoid the villagers' attention.

She had never been able to explain to Miren why she wanted Davri to know about her Voice. It wasn't just her affection for him. Being a Singer was lonely, and being the only Singer in a village was lonelier still. Even here, in this bustling city, she was alone.

Another street. She didn't realize where she was heading until she was less than two blocks away.

Amos Steel.

She stopped across the street from the great incline of the southern hill. The same, well-worn path snaked up the facade in switchbacks, giving way to the plateau at the very top. The brick walls of the factory buildings were red-brown, like drying blood.

A woman shouldered past her; Kesia had stopped in the middle of the sidewalk. She stepped aside, her heart hammering.

There were more Singers in that compound than there had been in Crescent Bay at any point in her life. Even when Kesia had lamented the loss of her speaking voice, her mother had never referred to Singing as anything but a gift. When the king had decreed that Singers be drafted, people were furious. Singing was no longer a way to serve one's community; it was now a weapon of war, a reason to hide.

Kesia saw figures making their way down the incline, slowly growing larger.

There were five of them, about fifty paces away from her now. She recognized them all. Two had worked on the airship.

Kesia's whole body shook with fear. The ghost of a collar pressed on her throat, making it difficult to breathe. *In. Out. In. Out.*

She turned around and ran.

THIRTY-TWO

KESIA

YOU HAVE TO GO TO STAR SONG!" ZURIEL COMPLAINED THE following morning. "I'm singing tonight. And the food will be incredible."

Kesia sat at breakfast. Fried pork, spiced eggs, and rolls with butter covered the table, but her appetite hadn't returned since yesterday's trip to the factory. When she had gotten back to the apartment, Dar had still been asleep. No one knew she had left, and she felt reluctant to bring it up.

But the fear occasioned by seeing those men hadn't left her. She had hardly added to last night's dinner conversation. No one had pressed her, though she caught Dar staring more than once.

Now, as they sat around the table, Tisa was stirring oatmeal in a pot. Kesia had gone to bed early and woken late, but she still felt unrested.

She signed, *There might be factory workers at the event.*

"Nothing's going to happen," Zuriel said, waving a hand dismissively. "It's all going to be so crowded that no one will notice us."

I can't risk them seeing me.

"We'll give you a hat, and you can have your face painted. There's a stand for that. Come on, I know you want to go!"

Kesia did want to go to the Star Song festival. From the parlor window, the city of Peladah seemed to have transformed overnight. Banners of bright red and gold were strung between lampposts, brushing the tops of carriages. Ribbons streamed from roofs, and flags waved from open windows. She thought of the Skyflame ceremonies of Crescent Bay. Miren would likely have a few things to say about the noisy festivities—Skyflame was a celebration, but it was also sacred—though Kesia thought the fanfare added excitement. She imagined strolling the streets of Peladah with Davri, admiring all the bright colors, glad for the thick crowd as an excuse to hold hands.

"A crowd is the best place to hide," Dar said. "It'll be all right, Kesia."

A sudden blare made Kesia jump. She rushed to the window. A collection of brightly clad musicians marched down the center of the road, tooting horns and beating drums of various sizes.

"The festival officially begins at sunset," Tisa explained, "but people always like to start early."

"See?" Zuriel said. "It's going to be amazing! Please come."

Kesia allowed herself a smile and nodded. *I'll go.*

Neither Tisa nor Zuriel had to work today, so Kesia spent the morning in the kitchen with them, cooking every kind of sweet the boy could name. While the rolls were baking, Kesia settled by the window and watched the people pass. They wore bright colors of fire, red and gold, as well as white and even some blue.

Zuriel flopped down next to her. "Wait'll you try the food," he said. "There's a dozen booths all surrounding a *huge* fire. They roast beef and chicken and vegetables with this ginger sauce, and there's another booth with spiced rum that actually lights the drink up when you buy it! The trick is not to blow it out right away, because the rum tastes best when it's hot."

In the afternoon, after they had gorged on sweets, they rummaged through the closet. Tisa pulled out clothes in shades of red and gold, with patterns that suggested fire or stars.

"People only wear blue and white if they're a Singer or are

participating in the ceremony," Tisa said, digging in the back of her closet. "I have a lovely white dress in here somewhere, but that's probably not the best idea."

Red is fine, please.

Tisa chose a yellow skirt and blouse. Kesia wore a red dress and shawl to cover her head. Zuriel donned a blue coat with white trim, and even Dar pulled a fiery ensemble from his closet.

At sunset, they left the apartment and joined the crowd. Tisa, Zuriel, and Dar greeted their neighbors cheerfully, but Kesia stayed a few paces back, hoping not to be recognized. She still felt anxious being in the open, but everyone was so enthusiastic that she couldn't help but be excited.

The streets were lined with booths, their bright signs advertising face-painting, food, and drink. The little family waded through currents of people, taking turns supporting Dar by the arm until Tisa decided that only Kesia was equipped to keep up with Zuriel. "Just make sure he doesn't get trampled," she said.

Zuriel skipped along, stopping at booths and eating more food than Kesia thought possible. At one point, he gestured in excitement as the crowd split to watch a performance.

Two looming structures circled each other. They were puppets, each featuring a large cut-out head with a long snout and serpentine eyes, and a tail that extended over the heads of three more performers. One puppet was aqua, shimmering like the scales of a fish; the other was dark brown with a square flank. They twirled and danced around each other in an elegant display of battle.

"The two beasts," Zuriel explained over the noise of the crowd. "The beast of the land and of the sea."

She had heard of the creatures, but they had never celebrated the beasts in Crescent Bay, and certainly not during Skyflame.

When the clock tower chimed eight times, the crowd began to surge.

"It's time, it's *time!*" Zuriel cried.

The crowds led to an enormous plaza. Unlike the rest of the city, the circle of cement was barren. A single pole in the center was adorned with a glass sphere. Red-and-gold ribbons connected the sphere to the four corners of the plaza.

People fought for spots toward the front, and an excited hum floated through the air. Kesia could almost imagine the great flaming structure of Skyflame. *We're so similar, and yet we wage war,* she thought. *We both celebrate Singing and both abuse it.*

At some unseen cue, four people stepped into the center of the plaza: two men and two women, each wearing white clothes with ornate blue patterns that artfully depicted their element. Just as with Skyflame, they each carried a symbol of their element as well: stones, kindling, ribbons, and a pail of water. The crowd hushed as each Singer placed their element at the end of a ribbon. The Fire Singer, an older woman with long braided hair, Sang to light the four connected ribbons. The fire flared and climbed the ribbons until it surrounded the glass sphere on top, which glittered like a star.

Kesia marveled at the similarities to Skyflame.

A bell sounded, and the quiet shattered as children dressed in blue flooded the square. Each rushed to one of the four elements and started singing. The adult Singers tried to impose order, but the children were too excited to heed them properly.

Kesia gaped, appalled. This was *nothing* like Skyflame.

Zuriel had gone still. Tisa stepped up beside him with Dar and wrapped an arm around him. "Any advice for Zuriel?" she asked Kesia.

Zuriel looked up expectantly. Kesia thought of her mother's wisdom before her own Skyflame ceremony. *There's no way to prepare, really,* Kesia signed discretely. *If you're not chosen, don't be discouraged.*

"Chosen?" Zuriel said. "I thought it was just luck."

Kesia shrugged. Her mother had always used the word, and she had never questioned it.

They watched as the children finally resigned themselves to waiting in lines around each of the different elements. There was a crowd for Earth and Fire, though Kesia noted that many of the children who failed there hopped into the Water or Air lines.

The sight distressed her more than she expected. If this was how the ceremony was conducted, it was a marvel that Avi'or had any Singers at all. The children treated Singing like candy—something that could be had if one begged hard enough. She felt a fuller appreciation for her mother's training.

Unexpected applause startled Kesia. A girl had managed to make the ribbons flutter with a quick trill, and now she was beaming as her parents cheered.

"There are usually more Singers than this," Zuriel muttered, disappointed.

Another ten minutes went by, and Zuriel still didn't join the other children. Kesia glanced at Tisa with a question, but Tisa just shrugged. Perhaps he was intimidated by the crowd.

Children were already leaving the center of the plaza, looking disappointed and embarrassed. The four adult Singers simply watched with solemn expressions. The elements remained undisturbed.

They're just singing nonsense, Kesia signed. *They need to listen.*

"Listen to what?" Zuriel asked.

This was another lesson from her mother, but she didn't feel the small pulse of warmth that usually came with those memories. *Just listen,* she signed.

More children spilled into the plaza, singing random syllables or sometimes shouting at the elements as if they could intimidate the water into splashing or the ribbons to stir. Some parents watched with a smile, but others looked worried, even angry. The Singers overseeing each element stood idly, looking resigned to the chaos.

Kesia glanced at Zuriel, but he seemed intent on something. Before she could ask him what he was looking at, he stepped into the plaza and headed for the pile of stones at the far end. A few boys yelled at him for cutting in line, but he didn't seem to notice.

Zuriel stopped in front of the stones, as the Earth Singer who stood beside them waited, looking mildly curious. Over the din of the crowd and screaming children, Kesia felt more than heard Zuriel's Voice.

It started as a hum, a rumble below her feet. The pile of stones tumbled over each other and then rose into the air.

The children's shouting faded so only Zuriel's Singing was heard. A few rumbling, uncertain notes, and the stones clattered to the ground.

A beat of silence. Tisa's hand covered her mouth.

The crowd erupted into applause.

THIRTY-THREE

MIREN

FOR FOUR DAYS, MIREN STARED OUT AT THE WATER.

Her back ached from sitting for so long on the hard, wooden seat. There was hardly enough room in the boat to sit unencumbered, let alone sleep. They took turns huddled in the prow, whispering apologies as they elbowed and kneed one another.

Miren's eyes hurt from the bright light reflecting off the water. Her lips were dry and cracked, and her cheeks were hot from the constant sun. She kept hoping they were nearly there, the Avi'ori mountains slowly rolling closer as the hours passed. But the shoreline never came into view.

While Davri Sang, the group signed instead of speaking, sometimes whispering to Ori when he didn't understand. Any interruption, however slight, felt like an unnecessary burden to place on the Singer.

Miren could hear Davri's fatigue through the Song, but he rarely took breaks except to eat and sleep. At those times, the others would take turns rowing, keeping silent as Davri slept. The currents of the open water were rough and unforgiving, and the muscles in Miren's back and shoulders screamed for relief. More than once, she was convinced that they were even farther away from Avi'or than when they had started.

Liviya's insistence on angling southeast added time to their travel, but her decision turned out to be wise. Occasionally, they heard the faint booming of cannon fire. Sometimes, they even saw a line of towering, triple-masted vessels facing a smaller number of what must be steam-powered ships, long and metallic, heavy steam billowing from fat towers that rose from the deck in place of masts. The Avi'ori ships were clearly faster and held heavier firepower, judging from the ringing explosions, but they were often outnumbered by the Kaleon naval craft.

Once, they heard cannons at night, far nearer than they'd anticipated. In the dark, a line of Kaleon ships had managed to creep close to a smaller Avi'ori fleet and open fire. Everyone had begun to panic quietly until Davri awoke and launched into Song. For the next two hours, they sailed almost due south in an effort to avoid any more skirmishes.

Now, as Miren stared out at the water, she thought she saw the faint outline of civilization: buildings of varying heights and girths were scattered along the base of the mountain range. As they grew closer, she spotted more structures along the mountainside, with thin switchbacks snaking up the foothills. She even saw a building far up on a cliff on the southern end of the mountain range. The Avi'ori coastline at last.

She tapped Liviya on the shoulder. The woman looked up, squinting, the wrinkles around her eyes stark in the pale sunlight.

Docks? Miren signed.

Liviya considered, then shook her head. *We'll be charged for docking,* she signed. *Better to find a beach.*

Miren glanced at Davri. He was staring straight ahead, his gaze glassy as he focused on his Song. Liviya gently patted his knee and explained where they should head.

He looked past her, as though just noticing that they were near the coast, and nodded once. Miren's concern for him had grown over the last four days. She had never seen a Singer work this hard or for this long. She had heard stories about sailors who Sang their ship through horrific storms or fought back wildfires on land, but those tales never gave specifics about what the strain did to the Singer. Could it kill them?

And what of Kesia? What was she going through in comparison?

As they came nearer, the mountains grew, and so did the buildings.

This was a city, larger than any she'd seen in Kaleo.

Everyone in the boat straightened at the sight of land, eager despite their fatigue. Liviya wordlessly directed Davri past a cluster of docks to a short span of beach at the northern end of the city.

The curling surf pushed them the rest of the way ashore. Miren braced as they hit the sand hard. Cale and Arten jumped out and pulled the boat up until the bow was on the sand.

Liviya climbed out of the boat as if she were angry. Arten carried Ori to shore. Hana held her skirt up in a vain attempt to keep it dry.

Miren was so stiff that she nearly tripped as she disembarked. She turned back to the boat to retrieve her pack and noticed Davri still slumped over, dark circles under his eyes.

"Davri," Miren said, her voice rasping with disuse. "Are you all right?"

He didn't sign, didn't move. He just stared at the sand, his shoulders hunched. For a brief moment, he looked like his father, the overhead sun giving his features sharp shadows.

He took a breath and pushed himself out of his seat. She held out a hand, but he waved it away, struggling to find balance.

He got one foot over the side before the boat tipped and dumped him out into the surf.

"Davri!" She lunged into the water and hauled him up. He coughed up a mouthful of water, but another wave shoved him off balance, and he went under again.

"Someone help me!" Miren cried.

Cale crashed back into the surf, followed by Arten. They pulled Davri upright and slung his arms over their shoulders, half-dragging, half-carrying him to shore. Liviya waded in and hauled the boat up out of the water.

Miren noticed onlookers for the first time. People were scattered around the beach, some hitting balls back and forth, others lounging in the sun. Many of them seemed to be relaxing, though the beach seemed a strange place to do so.

Silently, their group trudged through the sand, half-soaked and sunburned, Arten and Cale still supporting Davri.

Unlike towns Miren had seen in Kaleo, there was no gradual shift between the city and the rest of the world here. The beach ended abruptly in stone walkways that lined cobblestone streets.

Arten and Cale led Davri to a relatively quiet street corner and sat him on the edge of the sidewalk.

Miren hurried to kneel in front of him and gently chafed his hands. His eyes fluttered as if he were fighting to keep them open. His head bobbed in what might have been a nod.

"He's exhausted," Cale said, kneeling on his other side. Cale's bruising was stark in this lighting. His swollen eye was more open than it had been, though it watered slightly at the corners.

Miren seated herself next to Davri. He smelled of sweat and salt-water, but she probably did too.

"We need to find a place to stay," Liviya said, glaring at a couple of passersby. She waited until they were out of earshot before adding, "I'll ask around."

"I'll go with you," Arten said. The back of his shirt was stained red-brown; his wounds must have reopened while he was rowing.

Liviya frowned. "Hana should go with me. She looks the most presentable."

Miren thought they all looked like homeless beggars, but Hana collected her matted hair in a bun and followed. Cale and Arten took seats beside Miren and Davri, Ori grumpily leaning against his uncle.

"Skies," Cale said. "We made it."

Miren stared at the city with renewed attention. Buildings twice as tall as any she had seen before stood sentinel along every street, some of them open for business, some with windows that scaled the whole facade. A boy shouted and waved a gray newspaper, his words hardly distinguishable to her through his accent.

The air was stiff and unmoving and heavy with the smell of dirt and horse dung. Unfamiliar spices wafted from different buildings. Even the clothing looked odd. Almost all the women wore colorful skirts, often lined with lace or artful patterns. Many men wore coats despite the warm weather.

Davri's head drifted to Miren's shoulder. Miren stiffened, but his eyes were closed; he likely wasn't even aware of what he was doing.

A long, hot hour later, Liviya and Hana returned and led them to a tavern a few blocks away, passing busy streets thronged with carriages and people on foot. Davri insisted he was fine, but he quickly proved he couldn't walk on his own. The men supported him on either side, while Hana and Miren took turns carrying Ori.

As they walked, they saw people dressed in bright reds and golds, with a few in white and blue. Banners hung from lampposts and outside windows. Troupes of musicians marched down the center of the street with no regard for traffic.

"Hey," Cale said, "I think it's the Star Song festival."

"I think you're right," Hana said, pointing at bright banners.

"What's Star Song?" Miren asked.

"It's like your Skyflame," Cale said. "All children who are twelve years old partake in the Star Song ceremony in the city plaza and try to get a Voice." He saw Miren's incredulous expression and grinned.

"The ceremony I grew up with in a farming town is much more like how Kaleo does it, but the city tends to be a little" — he sidestepped a pair of giggling girls in bright yellow dresses, their faces painted with gold swirls — "louder."

Miren stared at the ever-growing crowd, amazed that Skyflame was so different here. "Where is the city plaza?" she asked.

"It's a few blocks over." Hana pointed to the left. "We saw it earlier. It's pretty crowded now."

Miren considered making a detour, but her worry about Davri overruled any curiosity.

Liviya and Hana led them to the tavern they had found: a tall, narrow building painted dark red. Miren counted five rows of windows. A sign above the door read HORIZON INN.

Inside, they were greeted by a roar of conversation and clinking dishes. Unfamiliar food smells made Miren's stomach tighten with hunger. A plump woman with short hair and an impressive nose sat behind a counter. Just beyond was a staircase.

The woman glanced up at the group and gasped. "What happened to this one?" she cried.

Liviya and Hana carefully explained that Davri had injured himself during a construction project near the docks, but he would be fine, and no, he didn't need a doctor, just rest. Miren kept quiet, realizing that now she was the one with a foreign accent.

Liviya paid; the woman handed Liviya three sets of keys and returned to her perch.

The staircase was too narrow for three people, so Cale heaved Davri up the steps on his own. They came to a room with two small mattresses with maroon blankets and wooden chests at the foot of each. Hana and Miren stripped off Davri's shirt and boots and settled him in bed.

Like in a dream, Miren looked up and found herself seated on the floor beside Davri's bed. The others had gone down to eat. She didn't remember the excuse she'd given, though she thought the bed too plush for her ragged self. Besides, she didn't want to sleep.

Davri breathed evenly, his jaw slack. She was struck with how hard this trip must have been on him. He had lived a life of ease. Had he ever once complained during the journey?

Four days of Singing. Could he have damaged his Voice?

Miren groaned. Her mind was inventing scenarios just to torture her. She was surprised—and wryly annoyed—that she cared this much. Kesia would be happy to know that she did.

Where was Kesia?

Miren pulled the map from her pack. She had all but ignored the right side of the map, but now she stared at the expanse of Avi'or. The country was slightly larger than Kaleo, but most of it was mountains and hills, the cities crowded by the coast and in the valleys. Railways wove through nearly every city. Trains were a fast way to travel, right? Perhaps searching here wouldn't be quite as taxing as it had been in Kaleo.

She took note of the coastal cities, whispering their names to herself: Mishaliv, Vori'alis, Peladah, Ganav. The words felt strange in her mouth. She guessed this city was either Peladah or Ganav.

But how could she search an entire country? What trails could she follow when the men who had taken her sister worked outside the law?

A knock at the door. The light outside the window was still a bright afternoon yellow, though she felt that she had been sitting for hours.

She pulled herself up and opened the door. She had expected Hana, but it was Liviya. The woman looked refreshed, her face cleaner. Her voice was soft as she asked, "How is he?"

Miren stepped aside to let her see. "Still sleeping."

"Then that's what he needs."

Miren nodded. Somehow, she felt responsible for his condition, but she couldn't reason out how.

"Come downstairs and eat," Liviya said. "They have stew."

"I'm fine."

Liviya arched an eyebrow. "You can't do anything for him now. He just needs sleep."

Miren bristled at her tone, then relaxed. She was too tired to be offended, and she knew Liviya was right. She followed Liviya out and gently closed the door behind her.

Liviya led her downstairs and into a dining area of round tables crowded with patrons. Against the far wall, two musicians wearing yellow-trimmed red shirts sat tightening strings on lutes and tapping drums. A woman wearing a pale yellow dress, her dark hair arranged in impressive curls, held a cluster of clinking bells.

Not far from the stage, Cale and Ori took turns flicking a long splinter across the table at each other while Arten and Hana chatted, each of them holding a glass of wine. Miren was struck with how relaxed they seemed, then realized—they were free. The odds against them had been incredible, but they had done it anyway.

Why couldn't she achieve her impossible goal too?

They looked up and smiled as she took a seat.

"Hey, you're awake," Cale said.

"How do you feel?" Hana said.

"Fine," Miren said. Hana raised an eyebrow, and she added, "Tired. Worried."

"Davri will be all right," Hana said.

"I've never seen any Singer do half of what he did," Arten said.

"He's always been talented," Miren said, remembering the Sky-flame ceremony when he had earned his Voice. Everyone at the table nodded in agreement.

A server came by and took Miren's request for stew with a brisk nod.

The troupe of musicians began playing a quick, cheery melody. Miren turned to watch, surprised that the other patrons ignored them. She studied each table in turn, but no one gave the performers more than a passing glance. The performers didn't seem bothered by this, either.

Miren looked at the family and found them all staring at Liviya.

"What's wrong?" Miren asked.

Liviya said, "I don't like to owe debts."

"Mother," Cale groaned.

Arten sighed quietly. Hana gave a faint smile.

Liviya shifted in her seat. "All right, I'll say it another way. Thank you for saving my family."

Miren forced a smile. "Davri saved your family."

Liviya shook her head. "Arten and Cale told me what you did for Ori. I . . . I could never have imagined someone doing so much."

Miren nodded. "You're welcome," she said, and she meant it. As worried as she still was, she could be relieved for this family as well. She caught Hana's gaze and smiled. "I'm glad you're all safe."

Ori flicked the splinter in her direction, but she placed it back in front of him. "Maybe later."

"You might remember," Liviya continued, "that you and I made a deal before all this."

Miren nodded numbly. Right. The deal.

She didn't want to ask the obvious question. It felt like too much effort even to say the words. "What information would you have given us?" she asked instead.

Liviya looked startled. "What does it matter now?"

"It doesn't," Miren said, surprised at the sharp words. "I was just curious."

Liviya slumped in her seat. "I would've told you of a few specific locations where I thought she'd be headed, and the most likely paths the recruiters would take."

It wasn't a complete answer, but that didn't matter. "Do you know anything about where she might be?" Miren asked. "Do you know about these factories?"

"A bit," Liviya said. "There are dozens of factories in Avi'or. Far more than in Kaleo."

Miren winced. "Any that would need a Fire Singer?"

She addressed the whole group, but they turned to Liviya. Most of them hadn't seen Avi'or in nearly a decade.

"If I bring my map down," Miren said, "will you mark them all?"

"I can certainly do that," Liviya said. "Or I could just go with you."

Miren stared, not understanding until Hana leaned forward. "We want to help you find your sister, Miren."

All at once, Miren realized that she had never thought to expect anything from them. Their deal had been voided the moment they learned that Kesia wasn't in Kaleo. The family was safe. There was nothing holding them here.

Nothing, and yet every one of them was looking at her with more kindness than she could bear. Ori flicked the splinter in her direction again. Miren took it and stared at it, finding she couldn't meet their gazes.

"That—" She swallowed and tried again, her vision blurred. "That's kind of you."

Hana smiled, but the others glanced away as though suddenly interested in the musicians, giving her a moment to collect herself. Miren followed their gazes and found herself humming with the performers; she knew this song: "Across the Sea," one of her father's favorites.

Welcome brother, welcome home.
We've missed you these years three.
Welcome brother. Tell us of your
Love across the sea.

The drummer took the next verse:

My dear sister, pleased am I
To see you bright with glee.
Lovely sister, listen while I
Tell of 'cross the sea.

It was easy for Miren to pretend that she was in Crescent Bay, that the village had gathered around a large fire as they often did in the summer to play the same songs. Miren and the other children would dance around the fire while the adults clapped. If there was a line of harmony unclaimed, Miren would pluck it out and sing as loud as she could.

Miren had not sung like that in years. A part of her balked at doing so in front of strangers, but she was almost too exhausted to care: the song was familiar, and singing came naturally, offering warmth and comfort. With ease, she found the upper harmony and sang, letting her humming become words as the drummer continued:

They sing of air and water, and they
Whisper to the earth.
But my sweet love, oh yes, she sings of
Flame and fire and hearth.
She's fine and fair like fallen snow,
Her hair like golden wheat.
But, oh sweet sister, how it aches
That she lives across the sea.

The drummer and woman singer smiled at her, encouraging. The lute dipped with different chords than Miren was used to, giving the song a slightly more cheerful tone, but she had no trouble adjusting, harmonizing with the singer.

> *Wait, wait, wait for me,*
> *My darling dearest, please.*
> *Hold your heart dear, hold it high,*
> *For your love across the sea.*

The lute gave a triumphant arpeggio for the final verse.

> *Hold your heart dear, hold it high,*
> *For your love across the sea.*

Miren was startled when applause erupted around her.

"Miren, that was beautiful," Hana said.

"I didn't know you could sing," Arten said.

Miren clamped her mouth shut. She felt like a dam was crumbling in her, a barrier she had constructed so slowly, she hadn't even realized it was there. She had built walls in her mind. She had needed to focus on surviving. On keeping Kesia safe. Everything else had seemed frivolous, indulgent, selfish.

She thought she knew the exact moment it had started: when Kesia had become ill with cloud fever. Miren remembered believing her sister would die, and her mother would be drafted, and she would be left behind, all alone. But Kesia had recovered, though her Voice had not. Or so they had thought for a time. She didn't want to care about Liviya's family, about Davri. She didn't want to miss her parents or her village or the wonder of the Skyflame ceremony. She didn't want to enjoy singing like this. She didn't want to *want* anymore.

But at least, she thought, she wasn't alone.

The tears were hot and fast, and she couldn't stop them. *Kesia,* she thought. *I miss you so much.*

Hana wrapped an arm around her, pressing her cheek against Miren's head, and Miren let her.

THIRTY-FOUR

KESIA

Relax, Kesia signed. Nothing will happen that you don't intend.

Zuriel nodded, his lips tightly pressed together. They sat cross-legged in the middle of the parlor. All the furniture had been shoved to the edges of the room so that only a small pile of stones stood between them.

After earning his Voice last night, Zuriel and his family had been swarmed by onlookers. Kesia had retreated to the far side of the crowd and waited, watching. People asked him questions and congratulated his family and offered him positions at various businesses. The ceremony wasn't finished, however, so the fanfare had died down quickly, leaving Zuriel looking dazed.

"Be patient, honey," Tisa said now from the kitchen. Both she and Zuriel had been given another day off from work. "You won't get it all in a single day."

Zuriel signed, *I know,* his hands clumsy, but Tisa had her back turned.

The most frustrating part, Kesia signed. *Eventually, they will grow used to it.*

Zuriel shrugged and bit his lip.

Kesia smiled. *Also, your skill will grow more quickly than she knows.*

When the crowd had finally dissipated last night, Tisa and Dar had congratulated Zuriel with hugs and two bundles of sweet fried dumplings. Kesia learned that Avi'ori Singers had a good future ahead of them as factory workers. They could do the work of ten people, so their skills were in high demand and they could earn better pay.

But this morning, there was tension in the way Tisa scrubbed dishes and Dar held his newspaper. Perhaps Kesia was a reminder that there were far more dangerous futures for Singers too.

Per custom, an Earth Singer from city hall was scheduled to come by today and teach Zuriel, but Kesia had offered to give some advice before the Singer arrived. She separated one stone from the pile and placed it in front of her. *Lift,* she signed. *Listen and lift.*

Zuriel stared at the stone and waited, but his focus seemed too deliberate. He opened his mouth, then closed it. *Nothing,* he signed, rubbing his forehead.

Kesia let out a breath. *Let's take a short break.*

A knock sounded at the door. Dar's newspaper drooped. Tisa fumbled with the last of the dishes.

"He's here," she breathed, wiping her hands on her apron. "Kesia."

Kesia nodded and left the room. They had all agreed that an Earth Singer employed by the city shouldn't know of her presence here. She took a book from the couch and hurried into the back room.

She pressed her ear to the door and heard a click. "Hello, thank you for coming!" Tisa said in greeting, her cheerfulness sounding forced.

Kesia curled up on the bed and opened the book.

A few minutes later, an Earth Song rumbled through the walls.

The book slipped from Kesia's hands as the Earth Song filled her mind.

It wasn't the same Earth Singer from the factory, of course, but her body sweated with the memory: the grating work Song in her throat, the constant heat of the fires, the clanging metal. She was there in the factory, her metal collar pressed against her neck and shoulders.

She buried her face in the pillow, fighting the feeling that she was about to fall from a cliff. She thought of Miren and Davri.

I'm sorry, I'm so sorry.

These past few days had felt like another life. A pretend family, a celebration of Singing. Even with the threat of discovery, she had been as close to content as she ever expected to be again. She had stopped worrying about Miren and Davri and home.

She wasn't even sure if her sister was all right; she couldn't wrench her mind from that image of Miren's limp form on the ground. She thought of Davri locked up in his father's estate for the rest of his life, bent under the heavy gaze of his father and the silent judgment of his mother.

Thoughts of home were no longer a comfort, as they had been in the factory. Now, in a warm house with food, the memories were excruciating. Even free from the collar, she was still trapped here.

Miren, I'm sorry, Miren Davri Miren . . .

Kesia must have fallen asleep. When she opened her eyes, the patch of sunlight from the window had moved across the floor.

She heard voices.

". . . hasn't been trained. He hasn't even had his voice for a full day. Why would you do this to him?"

Silence followed, perhaps the Earth Singer signing a response. Dar's voice added something, though Kesia couldn't make out the words. More silence.

A minute later, Tisa cried, "He's twelve years old!"

More silence, murmuring. Kesia pressed her ear to the door but couldn't hear more than a random word or two. A few minutes later, the front door closed.

In the living room, Kesia saw Dar hunched in his chair, his elbows on his knees as he stared blankly at the floor. Tisa stood by the door, her expression tight, as if she were holding back tears. Zuriel sat on the floor in the center of the room, the stones scattered in front of him.

He glanced up at her as she entered and handed her a sheet of paper.

Dear Mr. Zuriel Eichel,

On behalf of the High Republic Council of Avi'or, we would like to offer our deepest congratulations on your receiving a Voice. Such ability is greatly prized and cherished throughout Avi'or.

Considering the great gift that has been bestowed onto you, the Council has summoned you to report to the Peladah Bureau of Military Affairs by tomorrow afternoon.

The Council thanks you in advance for your service.

Sincerely,

Bureau of Military Affairs

Kesia cupped a hand over her mouth. Zuriel was staring at the floor now, his expression blank like his grandfather's.

War. This boy was going to war.

In her mind, she heard gruff men calling orders on the deck of a navy vessel, the *boom* of a cannon firing mere paces away, the scream and stench of dying soldiers, the sudden roar of the surf. From her time on Edom's pirate ship and in the factory, she could picture the burn of rope around her wrists, the ache in her jaw from the gag, the terror of drowning.

"We'll figure something out," Tisa said quietly. "All right, Zuriel? We'll think of something."

Zuriel just stared at the stones.

Kesia realized with a jolt that though the family was distraught, they weren't surprised. *Does this happen often to Singers?* she signed.

She was looking at Tisa, but it was Dar who answered. "In order to work in Avi'or, a Singer needs to go through a test and get a license to practice from the government. It's illegal to hire a Singer without a license.

"There isn't a Singer draft like you have," he continued, "but the military can basically stop you from getting your license unless you agree to serve for a number of years. Or they can at least make it very, very difficult. Zuriel has to go to war, or he can't work. He can't even go to school, even if we could afford it."

"It was always a possibility," Tisa said, "but I've never heard of a Singer being pressed into service right after getting their Voice. Earth Singer or not, he's too young."

Dar nodded firmly. "Much too young."

Kesia didn't know what to think. It sounded like the Kaleon Singer Draft, only with more steps. At least the Kaleon king had been blatant with his cruelty.

"Then he'll just stay home," Tisa said. "He won't go to work or school. We'll figure something out."

But Kesia could hear in her voice that she didn't believe it, and Dar didn't speak up in agreement. Kesia knew that Zuriel's pay made up nearly half of their budget.

Kesia remembered how the Singer draft had gutted their village, how it had torn the gift of Singing from them in a single day. Even through the haze of her cloud fever, she remembered her sister shouting at the men who escorted her mother to the ship.

"I'm going down to city hall." Tisa marched across the room to retrieve her bag. "They can't do this."

"I'll go with you." Dar heaved himself up.

Tisa pulled Zuriel into a hug and kissed his forehead. "Don't be scared, Zuriel. We'll figure this out, all right?"

Zuriel didn't respond; he continued to stare at the floor.

Tisa gave him another kiss and glanced at Kesia. "Stay with him?"

Kesia nodded, and the two adults left, the door slamming behind them.

Kesia glanced at Zuriel. She thought of asking if he was all right, or if there was anything she could do, but everything sounded more insulting than helpful. So she just sat.

He gestured for the paper. Kesia watched him read over the words.

Finally, he looked up. *This is wrong,* he signed.

Yes. Hopefully your mother and grandfather can change this.

He shook his head. *The Earth Singer who came by today. He told me of all the amazing things I can do. I can help build things. I can patch ships. I can help crops grow. I don't want to kill people.*

She nodded.

But Zuriel continued. *The war is not helping anything. The war will just go on until we all kill each other.*

He met her eyes, looking angry and determined and far older than he had yesterday morning. He signed, *I want to help you free the slaves at Amos Steel.*

Kesia blinked, not understanding. And then she did. *No. Too dangerous,* she signed. *You can't. You don't know what you're saying.*

We can do it together! Zuriel signed. *I can undo locks and open gates! I can open the collars. I thought you wanted to help the others.* He paused, taking in Kesia's lack of response and desperate expression. *Are you all right?*

Kesia shook her head. Memories flooded her, the tangy smell of metal and the roaring hiss of steam and the pressure of her collar, that wretched collar.

Too dangerous, she signed. *You can't do this. You will be arrested.*

That's why we should plan—

Or they may just kill you to keep the secret.

Not if we're clever!

What about your mother? Your grandfather?

They would agree if it was anyone else doing it, he signed. *This is the right thing to do! I want to help people.*

Kesia bunched her skirt in her fists. She wasn't sure she could put into words what she was feeling. Fear was a heavy buzz in her mind. She forced her hands to relax so she could sign. *When they brought us to Amos Steel, we met two men. Parviz and the Earth Singer, Nadav. Parviz warned us that we were his property, and that there were severe consequences for trying to escape.* She swallowed. *A few days later, I tried to escape.*

Slowly, she pulled up her sleeve and held out her arm.

Zuriel gasped sharply.

The heavy line of bruising had faded to yellowish-green, though the huge bruise just above her arm still held a tinge of purple. Burn marks had resolved into angry red scars. She pulled up her second sleeve and showed more of the same, with a heavy gash still crusted red that ran across her forearm.

Zuriel's face twisted with horror.

Kesia pulled down her sleeves, feeling shameful. She had never wanted him to know any of this. She recalled his look of revulsion when she had first showed him the collar. But he needed to understand how foolhardy this was.

He wiped his eyes. *It's so evil.*

It is, she signed. *But these people are ruthless, even to someone your age. I know you mean well, but it is too dangerous.*

But he was shaking his head. *That just means I'm right. If I don't do this, no one will help them. We can help them.*

Stop it! she signed. *Please! I do not want to see you get hurt.*

Then help me. If you tell me about the factory, we can make a plan!

What if I tell your mother?

He glared. *I'll just do it anyway.*

Kesia covered her face with her hands. She couldn't bear the idea of him doing something so stupid.

But he was determined. Kesia thought of the day they met, when he wouldn't leave her alone until she let him help her. If she refused to help him, he would go in blindly. If she told Tisa, he would go when everyone slept. If she agreed now, at least he would keep her apprised of what he planned to do. The faces of Ayla and the other Singers flashed into her mind.

Fine, she signed, her hands trembling. *I'll help you.*

THIRTY-FIVE

MIREN

THE NEXT MORNING, MIREN WOKE AND FOUND LIVIYA already gone from the room. It took her a moment to remember where she was. An inn, in Avi'or. She put on her boots and headed downstairs to the dining area.

It was far less crowded now. The performers were gone. Only a few tables were occupied with customers hunched over cups of coffee or bowls of porridge. Miren spotted Liviya at the same table they had used last night, her map spread open in front of her.

Miren took a seat. "Good morning."

Liviya waved a hand and tapped the central coast of Avi'or. "This area of the coast is mostly larger cliffs, so there aren't many port cities, and anything north of here is close to the warfront. Since you are from the southern end of Kaleo, it makes sense that the pirates would have taken your sister directly across the sea to the nearest port city." She traced her finger from Crescent Bay straight to Peladah City.

"Are we in Peladah, then?" Miren said.

"Yes. This is the best place to start."

"But does it make sense for pirates to come to a populated area like this?"

"Every city has its own seedy corners. The question is where would they take her next?"

Miren studied the map. An entire country stared back. "Do you have any ideas?"

"I have some notion of where to look for information," Liviya said. "Do you know the name of the ship?"

"Oh." Miren took a moment to recall the words emblazoned on the hull. "*Darkcrest.* The captain introduced himself as Edom."

"Good. I'll go to the docks today and ask around."

"I'll go with you," Miren said.

Liviya shook her head. "Not with that accent, no."

"What? Why not? I thought Kaleons were welcome here."

"They are legally, but there's still . . ." Liviya's voice trailed off. "Well, we're at war, you know."

Miren did know. "So, I can't talk to anyone?"

"You can. You just might not get a great reaction."

Miren echoed in her best Avi'ori accent, "You might not get a great reaction."

Liviya smirked.

Miren winced. "That bad, huh?"

"You're dipping your *oh* sounds," Liviya said. "Don't drop your jaw so much."

Miren groaned, embarrassed. "Maybe it would be simpler to pretend that I'm a Singer."

"No, keep practicing," Liviya said. "It's a skill worth having."

Cale entered the room, hair disheveled, a sleepy Ori leaning against his shoulder. He grumbled something unintelligible as he approached.

"Good morning," Liviya replied. "Sleep well?"

"Yep. Still sleeping, actually." He slipped Ori into a chair and fell into the one next to it, rubbing his face. "Is there food?"

"There will be," Liviya said. "I ordered eggs and pork for everyone."

Miren leaned forward. "How's Davri?"

"Still asleep."

Arten and Hana joined them just as plates of eggs and bacon and a basket of buns were brought to the table. Miren put some aside for Davri.

"I'm going to need coin today," Liviya said. "How much of Davri's money do we have?"

Miren grimaced as she produced her pouch. "Eleven silver and eight copper."

"That won't even cover tonight's stay," Liviya said.

Cale glanced at Arten. "I guess we'll need to look for work, then."

"Maybe Miren and I can make a deal with the innkeeper." Hana glanced at Miren. "Are you all right with that?"

"Yes," Miren said. "We need the money, right?"

"We do." Liviya stood. "I'll be back by the end of the day. Don't cause trouble."

Hana went to the kitchens and returned a few minutes later with the innkeeper.

"Everyone," Hana said. "This is Bina. She's agreed to let us work for our stay."

Bina eyed the group, looking far less affable than she had yesterday. "You all are new to town with no jobs, is that right?"

They nodded.

"Well, it won't be a problem for you two, I think." She pointed to Cale and Arten. "Plenty of factories around here. Amos Steel is the largest employer in the city. Start there." Bina looked to Miren. "You'll work around here. Ever served tables before?"

"No," Miren said. "But I can cook."

Bina raised one eyebrow. "Kaleon?"

Miren glanced at Hana, but the woman shrugged. "Yes," Miren said.

Bina looked Miren over. "What are you good at?"

Miren raised her chin. "Well, not sewing. But I can cook fine. And clean. And care for chickens."

It turned out that the correct answer was cleaning counters and washing dishes. After Cale and Arten left, Ori was given a pencil and paper and sat at a table in the corner while Hana served customers.

When the morning meal was finished, Miren cleaned the kitchen floor. She scrubbed without complaint, the sudsy water quickly soaking into the knees of her trousers and pruning her fingers.

Perhaps an hour into her work, the door opened.

"The floor's still wet," she said. "I'll finish in—"

Davri stood in the doorway, his shoulders slumped, his hair crumpled to one side. He kept a hand on the door frame.

"What are you doing here?" she said.

Helping, he signed, and he Sang.

Miren startled as Davri's Voice filled the room. It was still a rich and resonating tenor, but now a heavy rasp colored the notes. The water on the floor shifted and collected itself, in tune with the swelling, shifting melody, pooling into the center of the room. Then it gathered itself off the floor and bounced into the bucket next to Miren.

"Well," Miren said. "Thanks. But you should be in bed."

He waved a hand and leaned against the counter. *Thank you for the food.*

Miren nodded, feeling the enormity of all that he had accomplished to get them to Avi'or. She knew there were things she needed to say to Davri, but now that they were alone, she couldn't find the words. She wrung out her rag in the bucket. "Liviya and the family have agreed to help us find Kesia."

Hana just told me, he signed. *That's very kind of them.*

Miren nodded, but Davri was frowning.

"What?" she said.

Davri glanced at the door. *What if the search for Kesia leads us to another city?*

"Then we go to that city."

All of us?

Miren draped the rag on the side of the bucket and stood. "You don't think the family will come?"

Do you think they should?

Miren paused. "You want them to stay behind?"

If Arten and Cale manage to find jobs, should we force them to leave?

"We're not making them," Miren said, feeling childish. "They offered."

They finally have the freedom they've been fighting for. They could save up to afford a home. Ori could receive an education.

Miren's chest ached with it. "So we just . . . leave them?" She wanted the words to sound like a betrayal—*leave them*—but instead they sounded like a lament.

Davri just looked at her sadly.

Miren stared at the floor, pulling at a loose thread in her shirt. Her worry for Kesia was at a pitch so high she could no longer hear it. At least in Kaleo, she could fathom some idea of what Kesia would experience in the navy. But Avi'or was different, a void of unknown possibilities in her mind.

Dragging Liviya's family along with them didn't feel right. She couldn't pinpoint what had changed; it wasn't that long ago when she had hoped to leave the family for good after their first river trip had gone wrong.

You care for them, Kesia would say. *That isn't a bad thing.*

No, but it was dangerous. Was she putting the family's safety over Kesia's? Was some part of her resigned that they might not find her? Would she spend her life wandering Avi'or?

Davri caught her attention and signed, *We'll find her.*

Miren took a shaky breath, her throat preparing for tears even though her eyes were dry. "All right."

Bina was so delighted to find a Singer helping that she offered to cut the price of their rooms.

"We could never afford a Singer's pay," she said. "This is wonderful!"

She led Davri around the inn to fix leaking pipes and irrigate the garden out back and clean up an unfortunate mess in the water closet. After the midday meal, he was assigned to help Miren scrub the dining area floor. It only took him a few minutes to spread the soapy water, but the effort left him leaning heavily against a table.

Miren clutched her mop with both hands. "How are you feeling?"

Davri gave her a knowing look. *Much the same when you asked me a half-hour ago.*

"I'm just asking."

You worry too much.

He didn't seem critical, just observant, but she didn't feel like being observed. She leaned down to start mopping and said, "Well, there's plenty reason to worry."

He clapped softly. She suppressed a sigh and glanced up at him.

We will *find her,* he signed.

"You said that when we were wandering around all of Kaleo."

And now we're closer than we have ever been.

"That is a very . . . optimistic way of looking at it."

He shrugged, and his gaze slid past her. *Liviya is here.*

Miren turned as Liviya marched into the room and took a seat at the table. She said, "*Darkcrest* was docked here in Peladah about two weeks ago for four days."

"What?" Miren said.

"I went down to the docks and asked the dock master. Had to spend some coin, but now we have confirmation."

"Did he say where the pirates went when they were in the city?" Miren said.

"No," Liviya said, her voice growing hard. "He insisted he didn't know."

"Do you know where they went next?" Miren asked.

"No," Liviya said again. "But at least now we know for certain that they were here."

Miren sat down in a chair. "What does that tell us?"

"It tells us exactly what we need to know," Liviya said. "Let's say that I'm a pirate, and I have just found one of the rarest types of Singers by sheer luck."

Miren frowned and glanced at Davri, but he seemed genuinely curious. "All right."

"Now let's pretend that there were a number of places I could take her. If I had a prize as valuable as a Fire Singer, one of two things could happen. Either I tell all potential buyers about what I had and coax them to bid against each other, or — I sell as soon as possible."

Miren frowned. "That doesn't make sense."

"Who's to say there wouldn't be other pirates willing to raid my ship and steal the Singer as soon as they heard about her? Keeping her long enough to encourage a bidding war might be too much of a risk. It might be better to sell her quickly."

Miren shook her head, not understanding, but Davri gave a sharp clap and signed, *You think Kesia is here in Peladah.*

Liviya nodded meaningfully. "If there is a buyer in Peladah City, then I think your sister is here."

Miren looked at Davri, who looked back at her with an arched eyebrow. She shrugged. Hope fluttered in her chest like a caged bird, but she vowed not to indulge it. What if they were wrong?

Then I'll go to the next city, she thought, *and then the one after that.*

But there was no rallying power in those words; the thought just made her ache.

Liviya and Davri stared at her with a mix of excitement and pity. She said, "What do we do?"

"We need to find out who the potential buyers in the city are," Liviya said, tapping a finger on her knee.

"Hey!" Bina appeared in the kitchen door, hands on her hips. "If you all want dinner tonight, you'd better have this floor sparkling in the next hour."

Miren and Davri pushed themselves to their feet. "I think she's just trying to get as much work out of us as she can," she muttered.

Davri smirked in agreement but began another Song.

By the time the evening meal had been served, Miren's back ached as much as it had when she'd helped row the boat across the Sea. Her knees were bruised and stung with splinters, and her hands felt dry like paper. She staggered upstairs and would have missed the meal entirely if Hana hadn't brought up a tray.

Just as the sky was growing dark and everyone had begun to worry, Cale and Arten stomped into the room, looking sweaty.

Hana jumped to her feet. "There you are!" She kissed her husband.

Ori leaped up and waved his arms until his father rubbed his head and Cale threw him over his shoulder.

"What took you?" Liviya said.

"Long workday," Arten said. "They were getting ready for some inspection or other."

"Inspection? Who?" Hana asked.

"Amos Steel." Cale snatched a roll from the tray and bit into it. "We're employed."

"The first place we went to hired us without much issue," Arten said. "Even though we have no factory experience. Apparently they always need workers."

"Factory work is almost as difficult as farming," Cale said, but he looked delighted about it.

"And they pay pretty well," Arten said.

Miren glanced at Davri, remembering their earlier conversation. They had only been in Peladah for a day, and the family was already growing roots.

Arten took a seat on the bed. "We heard something today. The factory foreman mentioned that Amos Steel has a contract with the military. A work program for prisoners of war." He glanced at Miren. "Singers."

Miren stared. It took her a moment to understand. "Singers? They have Singers working for them?"

"Prisoners of war. At least that's what he thought. We tried to ask more questions, but one of us"—Arten glanced at Cale—"was a little obvious."

Cale groaned through a mouthful of bread.

"Where is Amos Steel?" Miren asked.

"South end," Arten said. "It's on a plateau at the very edge of the city. You can see it from the street."

Hana's gaze traveled between Arten and Miren and Liviya. Arten stared at his mother, who crossed her arms. Davri looked ready to jump from his seat. They all seemed convinced, but Miren wondered what the odds were that Kesia would be in the first city they came to, or the first place they thought to look.

Could Kesia really be so close?

Surely it was too convenient, too improbable.

So why was her heart racing?

Liviya uncrossed her arms. "What do you say, Miren?"

Her voice just above a whisper, Miren answered, "Let's take a look at this Amos Steel."

THIRTY-SIX

KESIA

WELL INTO THE AFTERNOON, WITH TISA AND DAR STILL gone to speak with a council representative, Kesia and Zuriel sat cross-legged in his room amid a sea of sketched maps and schedules and written descriptions, arguing about what they should do.

It's so dangerous, Zuriel, Kesia signed. *You might not be helping anyone.*

But I have to try.

What if they catch you?

They won't. I'm an Earth Singer now.

As if to demonstrate, he Sang, and the collar lifted into the air between them clicking open and closed. Kesia winced at the sound.

There isn't enough time to plan a proper escape, Kesia tried again. *You have to report to the bureau tomorrow.*

That's why we have to do it tonight, Zuriel signed, still Singing the collar open and shut. *If we don't, who will?*

Just after sunset, Tisa and Dar returned from city hall looking harrowed.

"Eight people," Dar grumbled. "We had to talk to eight people before we found one who could answer our questions. Skies and seas."

What did they say? Kesia asked.

"We finally spoke to an assistant council representative," Tisa said. "She explained that they have a shortage of Earth Singers, and they've started recruiting as early as possible. They assured me that

Zuriel wouldn't be put into combat," Tisa said. "They want his help with manufacturing ships and . . . weapons."

Kesia straightened. *That is good news, right? He won't be fighting?*

"If it's true," Tisa said. "But either way, he's still a child. It shouldn't be like this. It shouldn't—" She took a breath. "You're going to be all right, Zuriel. I promise."

Zuriel nodded, looking distracted. *I'd like to practice with Kesia a bit more tonight.*

Tisa stared, blinking. "All right."

Kesia could see the hurt on her face as Zuriel retreated back to his room. She thought of telling Tisa and Dar about Zuriel's plan to break into Amos Steel tonight, but she couldn't bring herself to form the words. What would they do if they knew? What would *Zuriel* do?

She followed Zuriel into the room and closed the door. He held a piece of paper in front of him, one of the maps of the compound that Kesia had drawn at his request.

This was her fault.

If she had not come here, Zuriel wouldn't even know what was happening at Amos Steel. He wouldn't be practicing with that wretched collar. He wouldn't be planning to get himself killed tonight.

He glanced up at her, questioning.

She took a seat, but her mind couldn't focus, even as he asked her questions and studied her maps. She felt a rising fear, a slow-rolling realization that something terrible was going to happen.

Zuriel picked up the collar again.

She stood. *Restroom.*

Zuriel nodded, his brow knitted in concentration as he began to Sing.

Dar sat in his usual chair, a newspaper in his lap. Tisa stood in the kitchen over a pan hissing with hot oil.

Kesia signed, *I'll be right back.*

"Is everything all right?" Tisa asked.

She nodded and left the apartment.

The city at night was almost a different world. The lampposts that stood like sentinels were alight with small flames, casting the streets in an orange glow, reminding her faintly of the lighthouse in Crescent Bay.

She walked quickly, heading north. A few men hollered at her, but she clutched her shawl and quickened her pace. She turned and continued on until the buildings and streets gave way abruptly to the dark, glimmering expanse of the sea.

She had never seen the docks at night. Ships never left until dawn. It was possible she might be able to stow away.

She paused in an alley. Ships of varying sizes bobbed in the water, some with large, cylindrical columns in place of masts.

She had no supplies, no money. She had no idea which ships were going where. But she couldn't stay and put Zuriel's family in danger. He couldn't rescue the slaves without her help. She couldn't save him from the military, but if she left, she could keep him from doing something that might ruin his life. He would report to the bureau and be stationed somewhere far from the conflict.

But she didn't move.

I want to help people, Zuriel had signed.

Wasn't that what her mother had taught her since receiving her Voice? That Singing was a gift, a way to serve the community. Work, yes, but joyous work.

I thought you wanted to help others.

She thought of Cari and the morning the pirates had come to Crescent Bay.

Before that day, she hadn't Sung in years. When they had learned that Kesia's Voice had survived cloud fever, Miren insisted they keep it a secret: no Singing, not even when they were alone.

Kesia had resented it, but she had complied. Even now, Kesia was not convinced Miren understood what she had asked, but her sister had been so insistent that Kesia couldn't bring herself to Sing, even when she was alone.

So why had she Sung to save Cari from the pirates?

It had been instinctive, and the Song had come to her immediately. It took no thought for her to light a pirate's sleeve on fire to save Cari, or later, when she was in danger, to set fire to an elderly couple's living room. She wanted to blame the pirates or the war, but maybe Kesia herself was the monster.

Singing in defense of Cari hadn't felt evil.

It had been the right thing to do.

I want to help people.

But she had never thought that she could. She had never been strong. Or at least, there had always been someone stronger. Her mother, her father, Miren.

But that day at Crescent Bay, she hadn't stopped to consider it. She had just done it.

Kesia stepped farther into the alley, away from the docks. She headed back to the apartment.

THIRTY-SEVEN
MIREN

Liviya led the way through the streets, heading due south.

Despite the late hour, the city was bright with the orange glow of streetlamps on every corner. The remnants of the Star Song festival still littered the city. Miren saw grubby banners crumpled along curbs and streamers tangled around lampposts, too high to reach. A few people still wore bright yellow and red, but the foot traffic was much lighter than it had been the night before.

Miren walked with Davri; Cale and Arten were close behind. They had not even been in Peladah for a full day, and already they had found a clue. After weeks of traveling in Kaleo for a scrap of information, the contrast felt unreal. She fought the urge to fidget with the pistol at her hip, the one she had taken from Cheliem's estate during their escape. The loss of her father's revolver felt like a wound.

Miren glanced at Davri. "Are you sure you want to come?" she murmured. He still looked pale, and he had dark circles under his eyes.

He frowned at her. *You're not doing this without me.*

Deciding who would go tonight had not been easy. Hana had insisted that Arten could remain behind if they had Cale to guide them inside the compound, but he refused to let his brother and mother go without him. Arten tried to convince Liviya to stay and was met with surprising vitriol. Miren thought Davri should remain behind on the grounds that he was still recovering from their trip across the sea, but he maintained they shouldn't be without a Singer. Ori insisted he should go because he wanted to, but he was unanimously overruled.

They were still blocks away when Amos Steel came into view. A large, walled compound stood at the top of a wide plateau, dark and featureless. A winding path zigzagged up the side of the hill, faintly lit by scattered lanterns.

It loomed over them as they approached, its dark silhouette looking spectral against the night sky. They didn't slow until they were across the street from the base of the path.

"We shouldn't go up this way," Miren said. "We'll be spotted."

"We'll go around the plateau," Liviya said. "Look for a less visible way up."

The group quietly followed, keeping to the sidewalk until the streets gave way to docks, and they could hear the gentle roar of the sea. The coastal edge of the plateau was a sheer cliff face that angled inward over the water. Around the edge, the surf pounded against the sheer walk, leaving little room for a pathway along the shore. There was no way to avoid getting wet.

"Should we wait for low tide?" Cale said.

Davri held up a finger and pointed at himself.

"Let's at least wait until we're out of sight before you Sing," Miren said. "We don't want you tired before we even get there."

"I thought we were just observing," Arten said.

"We are," Miren said. "But I feel like we should be prepared."

The group followed Liviya, wading through the churning surf at the base of the cliff. It wouldn't be so difficult in the day, but night hid jagged rocks and pits under the water. Miren nearly twisted her ankle on a sudden dip in the ground.

Once they were around the cliff, the rock gave way to a beach. The group stumbled onto dry land, soaked and shivering. Davri Sang to each person in turn, drying their clothes, his Voice still raspy but his tone strong.

Miren looked around. It was dark here, save for the faint moonlight that coated the ground and brushed the trees. The beach ended abruptly with a thick tree line that spread back up the rise toward the compound like black specters. In front of them, the land split into a cragged, uneven valley, the compound still visible on its plateau, which now stood to their left.

When everyone was dry, they started up the rise.

This side of the range was far less friendly. The group sidestepped the underbrush and pushed back tree branches, tripping on jagged stones.

Partway up, as the trees thinned out, Miren paused. Davri was trailing behind, breathing heavily. She kept pace with him the rest of the way, biting back her worry.

Finally, the land leveled, and the walls of the compound rose into view, a massive line of brick that extended into the blackness. It was far taller than Miren had expected—she didn't think they would be able to scale it. Metal spikes stood at attention along the top.

"Now what?" Arten whispered to Liviya. "Just walk around it?"

"A good way to start," Liviya said. "See if we can get a peek over the wall."

"Are we going to try to get in?" Arten asked.

Liviya slid him a look. "If the opportunity arises, maybe, but we're just looking for information tonight."

Miren opened her mouth, then closed it. She wanted to know if Kesia was here. But she also didn't want to risk Liviya's family any more than necessary, and it was tormenting to think of this dragging out over several nights.

"Why would there be a gate on this side?" Cale said.

Everyone turned to look. Miren noticed a stretch of wall where the spikes were missing. She realized that it was a set of metallic double doors.

Liviya looked to her sons. "Did you see this gate when they hired you?"

"No," Arten said. "They kept us in the buildings near the front entrance."

Davri snapped for attention. It was too dark to see his signs, but Miren saw him point to the ground behind them.

Miren looked around, not understanding, but then she noticed a faint strip of even ground leading back down the incline, farther inland than the way they had come.

"There's a path," she said.

The sudden shriek of metal pierced the air.

Everyone whirled as the metal doors opened, and light poured out. A small crowd of men, maybe eight total, congregated around the doors, some of them carrying lanterns, all of them carrying weapons except for two in the center.

These two were well dressed in black trousers and coats, dress shirts. One was slightly taller; the other held a dainty-looking cane. They were both smiling amiably until they noticed Miren's group.

For a single heartbeat, everyone stared at each other.

The man in the middle shouted, "Spies!"

"Run!" Liviya cried.

Gunshots exploded against the night.

Miren pounded down the rise at a run. The ground tumbled past her, too dark to see, threatening to trip her at any moment. She leaped over a bush and ducked as another gunshot blasted behind her.

Remembering Davri, she glanced to her right and tripped.

The ground slammed into her, and she rolled down the incline, into rocks and brush. She pushed herself upright and ran for the nearest line of trees.

She risked a glance back. The men were still giving chase. She heard thundering footsteps behind her, more shouting, more gunfire. Miren tripped again, landing on a bush, rolling off it onto the ground. Her gaze caught a small hollow in a tree, and she ducked inside. It smelled of moss and damp earth, and the ground beneath her was uncomfortably wet, but she didn't move.

More shouting and a couple of gunshots made Miren's stomach tense.

She waited until it was quiet, and then she kept waiting. When she finally poked her head out, the night was still. A faint breeze rustled the trees; an owl hooted softly from somewhere far off. She thought she heard a voice, but the sound was too distant for her to be sure.

Miren's throat tightened. She should not have let this happen. She shouldn't have let the family come. She shouldn't have let Davri come. She should have come by herself or figured out another way to learn more about Amos Steel. First Kesia, and now them. Why couldn't she keep anyone *safe?*

Miren crawled out of her hiding place, wincing at every rustle of brush and snapping twig. She noticed lights moving on the other side of the valley, but she didn't hear any more gunshots.

She continued forward, hoping that the others had also managed to hide. Then the trees ended abruptly at a footpath. Looking around, she didn't see anyone. She could go left, toward the coast, or turn right and continue farther down the path.

She turned right.

She walked for longer than she expected, surprised and worried that she hadn't seen anyone else. Miren thought they had all run for safety, but she wasn't sure. Had the others been shot at the top of the rise? She almost turned back at that thought, but then she heard something: a ting of ringing metal, or a faint wind-like sound that might have been a hiss of steam, or just a breeze.

She continued forward, and the path widened to reveal an enormous building with a domed roof. A set of double doors in the front opened and closed as someone walked inside. Miren crept closer, but the trees were thin around the building. Men were milling about the entrance and might see her.

A hand caught her arm.

She whirled and bit back a squeal, fist raised.

"Hey!" Cale leaned back, hands up. "It's me."

She let out a breath. "Don't do that!" she snapped.

"Sorry, sorry," he said. "Have you found anyone else?"

"No," she said. "Do you think they went this way?"

"I'm not sure. I just ran."

"What is that building?" she said.

"I don't know," he said. "But guess what I heard?"

She waited, but he didn't continue. "Are you really asking me to guess?"

"Fire Singing! I heard Fire Singing coming from in there."

THIRTY-EIGHT

KESIA

KESIA LAY AWAKE, HER PULSE LOUD IN HER EARS.

They were going to Amos Steel tonight.

Saving Cari had been impulsive—she'd had no time to consider her actions. But now, with a plan drawn up in advance, the hours marched by like a funeral procession, reminding her of how foolish this was, and reminding her that to succeed, she would likely have to use Song as a weapon. She imagined leaping out of bed and insisting that Zuriel not go. Instead, she thought of Ayla and the other Singers as she kept running the plan in her mind.

Can we do this? she wondered. *Can we really do this?*

Later, soft footsteps creaked down the hall. Kesia glanced at Tisa, but she was sound asleep, folded neatly under a thin blanket. She imagined waking the woman, watching her sit up, signing, *Your son might die tonight. It might be my fault.*

Kesia sat up, feeling every creak and bend in the mattress. She reached for the clothes Zuriel had lent her: dark trousers, a coat, and a cap.

She crept to the door and cracked it open. The parlor was dark, but she saw a figure on the couch.

Zuriel stood as she entered, dressed in similar dark clothes. A bag hung from his shoulder, hiding her collar inside. There were so many ways this could go wrong.

Without a word, they left the apartment.

The streets were quiet. No one took notice of them.

They didn't sign as they walked, a precaution. In her mind, she saw Ayla and the other imprisoned Singers, starved and exhausted and gaunt. She and Zuriel were two of the rarest types of Singer in the world. There was no one more capable.

They arrived at the base of the hill sooner than she expected, the winding path ghostly in the glow of streetlights. The factory was a rectangular silhouette at the top of the plateau.

A long, quiet hour later, they arrived at the far end of a brick wall spanning the length of several city blocks.

Cold gusts of wind snatched at their clothes. Kesia glanced back at the city. The streets were a crosshatched pattern of orange-and-yellow lights illuminating the ebb and flow of people.

Zuriel headed for the wall, and Kesia hastened to follow. There was a faint glow, but it wasn't enough to sign by.

A muted clank of metal—Zuriel pulled the collar out of the bag. Kesia wished they could have left it behind—a rock would work well enough for this—but they would need the collar for their plan. She reached out a hand until her knuckles brushed the metal. She shivered and took hold.

They hadn't had a chance to practice this maneuver: both of them held the collar in one hand and braced a foot against the wall. Zuriel took a long breath and began to Sing; as the collar lifted them both, they walked up the wall like mountain climbers.

Zuriel's Song was quiet but steady. Kesia realized his Voice had grown strong in a short time.

They reached the top and paused, careful to step between the spikes at the top as they crested over the wall. Factory buildings sprawled in all directions. Oil sconces sent scattered, ghostly light at random angles, but Kesia was sure that no one was in the warehouses.

As soon as the ground was close enough, Kesia dropped, followed by Zuriel, holding the collar. He was breathing hard, but he signed, *All right.*

They dashed between the nearest buildings, Kesia leading the way. Then they huddled against a wall as faint footsteps approached around the corner. They hid in the shadows while a guard ambled past, rifle in hand. Kesia sucked in a breath, ready to Sing, but he didn't even glance in their direction.

Kesia looked at Zuriel. He stared at her, looking nervous. She had not been expecting a patrol—she had never seen men patrolling when Katzil escorted her to the airship early in the morning. The plan had been for Kesia to Sing a building on fire in the hopes of drawing out Nadav and following him to the Water Singer barracks. Then Zuriel would collar him and free the Singers.

But the presence of a patrol meant they couldn't spare the time it would take to light one of these buildings on fire; they would be overheard and caught. And if there was no fire, then there would be no Nadav, which meant they would have to find the male Singer barracks on their own.

And with the possibility of running into Nadav still hanging over them . . . Panic mounted in Kesia's chest. It wouldn't be difficult to climb back over the wall. They could still turn back.

Zuriel signed, *We can start with the female Singers barracks. One of them might know where the Water Singers are kept.*

Kesia bit her lip. They had hardly begun, and already it was obvious that they were not prepared to do this. But she knew Zuriel would never turn back now, and they were still the Singers' best and only hope.

She nodded and led the way toward the factory building where the Singers worked, pausing to check for patrols. They spotted two more guards with rifles before they reached the right building.

Kesia tried the handle and was surprised to find it unlocked. It creaked heavily as she pushed it open, but they slipped in and pushed the door closed behind them.

The refinery was eerily quiet now, the metallic pathways criss-crossing above them like massive spider legs. The large furnace was a mass of black in the dim light from the windows.

Zuriel nudged her, and she led him to the metal stairs, forcing herself to go slowly. It would be very easy to get lost with the building so dark.

She came to the hall where the female Singers were housed and crept forward. It was pitch black away from the windows, so she Sang a small flame just above her shoulder. A large metallic door appeared out of the shadows.

Zuriel Sang, and the door clicked loudly and swung open.

She stepped through the doorway and changed her Song to light the room. Despite the late hour, the female Singers rose slowly from their mats, likely believing they were to begin work now. Kesia clapped loudly.

We're leaving tonight, she signed. *We're escaping.*

They gaped at her.

Zuriel launched into another Song. Several of them jerked back, terrified, but they all stared in awe as, one by one, their collars clicked and fell away from their necks.

Kesia clapped again. *Get up! We're escaping tonight! We must go!*

They pushed themselves to their feet. In the ghostly light of her fire, they all looked hollow and gaunt, their cheeks sunken, their shoulders bony. Was that how Kesia had looked?

One woman signed, *They told us you were dead.*

Kesia shook her head. *I escaped. I've come back to help you.* She looked around, realizing someone was missing. *Where is Ayla?* she signed. *The other Fire Singer?*

An older woman with frizzy hair signed, *We don't know. We think she is working on the project you used to do. They talk of deadlines and inspections. The Fire Singer is taken sometimes at night now and brought back before morning.*

Kesia's breath caught: Ayla was working on the airship. She ached at the thought of leaving Ayla behind, but there was no time for detours.

Zuriel looked at her, questioning.

She couldn't save everyone. This would have to be enough.

We need to find the men, Kesia signed. *I don't know where they are taken.*

A blond girl waved for attention. *Downstairs, I think. Down the far hallway.*

A few other women nodded in agreement. Kesia felt a small flutter of relief. That was one problem solved. She motioned for the women to follow.

They thudded down the metal stairs, but Kesia didn't slow. With a group this size, there would be little chance of stealth. They would just have to hope they could get to the wall and Zuriel could Sing a hole before anyone noticed them.

Kesia paused at the bottom of the stairs, and the blonde girl pointed to the left, farther into the building. Kesia motioned for her to lead the way, keeping her fire low and away from the women.

Then she slammed into the blonde girl, who had halted at the hallway. Kesia looked around her. Before them, lantern held between them, stood two men.

One was a Water Singer, hunched and gaunt, a dark beard spilling around his collar. Kesia recognized him as the Singer who once gave her water after she collapsed.

The other man was the Earth Singer, Nadav.

He glanced up, the lantern casting dramatic shadows over his features. His eyebrows sharpened in surprise.

The women around Kesia froze. For a long moment, no one did anything.

Slowly, with lantern still in hand, Nadav signed, *Return to your barracks.*

Kesia looked at the women. They looked horror-stricken, some of them quivering. A couple retreated back toward the stairs as if to obey.

Kesia caught Zuriel's gaze. He stood behind a taller woman, a hand on his bag with the collar still in it.

She nodded and launched into Song.

A wall of fire exploded between them and Nadav like a sudden sun, briefly blinding her. The women flinched back, but Kesia moved the fire closer to Nadav, blocking him and the Water Singer in the corridor. The Water Singer next to him flinched away, eyes wide.

Kesia watched Nadav's gaze find her, just as Zuriel threw the collar through the flames and Sang. His Song caught the collar and it continued forward, opening like a set of jaws and snapping around Nadav's neck.

Nadav staggered back, his hands pulling against the collar. Kesia let the wall of fire die, feeling winded, but Zuriel immediately switched Songs: he unlocked the Water Singer's collar, then opened the heavy metal door behind the men and ran inside.

Kesia stared at Nadav, a Song on her lips ready to set him alight, but he just stood there, still clutching at the collar. She realized that he probably had no idea what it was like to wear one. He noticed her and paused in his struggling.

Don't move, she signed.

He signed, *Are you going to kill me?*

She froze, uncertain. Should she kill him now, like this? It would not be self-defense. This would be murder.

Could she do it?

She thought of the couple whose house she had burned down.

Yes, she could. She heard the Song she would need as its melody twisted and coiled in her mind.

She shivered.

Zuriel emerged from the male Singers' barracks with the Water Singers in tow, all of them collarless and wide-eyed as they saw Nadav. Kesia counted nine of them.

Zuriel's Song latched onto Nadav's collar and dragged him toward the barracks. Nadav struggled, his feet sliding along the floor, unable to find purchase. Zuriel tossed him in the room and closed the door, locking it with a final note.

Kesia looked at the group. Some of the Air Singers who had scattered came back, still looking frightened.

Kesia picked up Nadav's lantern and handed it to Zuriel. She summoned her own flame and signed, *Time to go! We're going to make a hole in the compound wall and escape.*

The Singers just stared. Kesia beckoned for Zuriel to come, and the two headed toward the entrance at a jog. Still looking stunned, the Singers followed.

The doors slammed shut in front of them.

Kesia whirled at the sound of Earth Song. Nadav marched toward them, his neck unencumbered, his Voice loud and echoing, his arms laden with collars.

He tossed up one and sent it flying at Zuriel. It clicked around the boy's neck.

Kesia lunged for Zuriel, but the collar was locked tight. Zuriel clawed at it, eyes wide with panic.

Nadav sent another collar at a younger woman Singer and locked it around her neck. Everyone scattered, but Nadav was too fast, and Singers were collared quickly.

Kesia sucked in a breath to light his clothes on fire.

His eyes darted to her, and an open collar soared toward her. She tried to duck, but he redirected it at the last moment, and it slammed into her neck, cold and biting.

She staggered and fell to her knees. The collar was stiff and unyielding just as she remembered, but it felt so much worse. She crawled forward and found a table to lean against, sucking in air. *In. Out. In. Out*—a rising panic was threatening to choke her.

A Water Singer's voice jumped to falsetto as ice began to crystallize around Nadav's mouth, trying to stop his Song. Before he could finish, Nadav pulled a knife from his belt and sent it flying.

The Water Singer jerked as it hit his chest, his Song cut off. Nadav pulled the knife back to himself and caught it as the Water Singer slumped to the ground.

Nadav flung the knife at a woman running for the stairs. The knife sliced at her leg, tripping her and sending her sprawling before it plunged into her back.

An Air Song sent a gust of wind at Nadav, forcing him to stagger back a few paces, but he didn't stop Singing. Another collar floated into the room. His Song had managed to grab it from the barracks without his even being able to see it.

Kesia clutched the table edge, shaking. He was too strong, too skilled. He would catch as many Singers as he could and kill the rest. She had done nothing for anyone. She was enslaved again. She had gotten these Singers killed. She had brought Zuriel here to die.

She spotted Zuriel on the other side of the room, looking around. He picked up something long and metallic—a set of tongs—and barreled toward Nadav.

Nadav turned just in time to step away from Zuriel's attack, which was stiff and not fast enough. Nadav shoved Zuriel to the ground and then deftly snatched the tongs from his grip.

Kesia pushed herself upright, feeling too slow, her vision fuzzy and unstable. Zuriel needed help. Someone needed to help him. She gritted her teeth. She didn't think she could save him, but if she didn't try, who was she?

Kesia reached out blindly across the table until her hand found something solid and cylindrical. A handle to a tool, maybe. She picked it up, feeling the heft of it, and ran straight at Nadav.

She expected him to turn around, but he was too focused on His Song. The set of tongs rose and pointed at Zuriel.

She swung her weapon at Nadav.

It was a mallet, the handle made of a compressed wood, but the head was large and metallic and heavy. She felt it connect with Nadav's skull and crack something.

He staggered a few paces and fell forward. She swung the mallet again. And again.

She didn't know how many blows she landed before a hand grabbed her arm. She whirled and raised the mallet, but another hand caught it before she could swing. It was another Water Singer, the man with the gnarled beard who had helped her that time she collapsed.

He held her arm, staring at her with a mixed expression.

Her whole body was tense; it took her a long moment to release the mallet. It thudded to the floor.

He released her. *You did it,* he signed. *He is dead.*

She looked around. Besides Nadav, she counted five unmoving bodies, all Singers. Five people she couldn't save. Five people who died because she came here.

The Water Singer stepped past her and knelt over Nadav's body. He rummaged through the Earth Singer's pockets and produced a small, metal object. It was a key, shaped with a small disk attached to the end.

This is how he got out of his collar, he signed. As though to demonstrate, he beckoned Zuriel and inserted the key into his collar. The collar snapped and fell off.

Zuriel nodded, shivering as he inched away from Nadav's body. Kesia found herself unable to look at the mess she had made. A few notes from Zuriel unlatched the collar around her own neck. She caught it and inhaled a shaky breath.

Slowly, in the dim light of a single lantern, the other Singers stepped forward. The Water Singer undid their collars. A few signed their thanks. When he was done, he turned back to Kesia.

You told us you were going to get us out, he signed.

Kesia nodded, struggling to regain a sense of urgency. Nadav was dead; what else were they running from? *Zuriel will Sing a hole in the wall,* she signed.

Zuriel staggered toward the exit and Sang the door open.

Kesia forced herself to the front of the group and led them toward the nearest side of the surrounding wall, the eastern edge of the compound. Zuriel Sang again, and a small fissure appeared in the wall and slowly widened, chunks of brick falling out of place.

She glanced back at the rest of the compound. The buildings that had once held so much terror now seemed almost ordinary to her. Nadav was gone.

She remembered Ayla. Now Kesia could save her.

Zuriel's Song ended.

She clapped for everyone's attention.

She half-expected them to scurry through the hole anyway, but they all stopped and looked at her.

Please, Kesia signed. *There is one more Singer. I know where she is, but I need help freeing her.*

The Singers paused, glancing at each other.

Where is she? asked an older woman.

She is down the other side of this hill. Kesia pointed south. *They have been building a flying ship there, and they need a Fire Singer to power it. If we take her and destroy the building, we can keep Amos Steel from taking other Singers as slaves. Or at least we might slow them down.*

A pause. Kesia knew this was much to ask of them. *You do not have to,* she signed. She glanced at Zuriel, who still looked pale and shaken. She wasn't sure how she would undo locks without him, but she couldn't bear asking him to risk himself further. She patted his shoulder. *You can go with them. It's all right.*

Zuriel glanced at her, his brow pinched with fear. But he shook his head. *I won't leave you.*

She smiled at him.

The burly Water Singer signed, *I will go with you.*

The blonde girl stepped forward. *I will too.*

Kesia nodded. *Thank you.*

What about the rest of us? a lanky, older man signed. *What do we do?*

Kesia nearly shrugged and signed, *Whatever you like,* but she saw all eyes turn to her with fear. She had no idea how long these people had been trapped here. She realized they were looking for someone to tell them what to do.

Take a boat from the harbor, Kesia said. *Sail back to Kaleo. Find your families. You're free.*

The Singers glanced at each other again, like they didn't quite believe it.

An older woman signed to Kesia, *What is your name?*

Kesia, she replied.

We will always remember you, Kesia, she signed. *Thank you.*

Almost in unison, the Singers echoed their thanks, bowing their heads or even smiling before climbing through the hole.

Of the twenty or so Singers they had rescued, four remained with Kesia and Zuriel.

Kesia signed, *Let's go.*

THIRTY-NINE
MIREN

MIREN FOLLOWED CALE AROUND THE BUILDING, STAYING close to the tree line. The workers had gone inside and shut the front doors behind them. Miren could better hear the sound of their work—the clank of metal, the hiss of steam, the roar of what might be a furnace—but she did not hear Singing.

As soon as Cale had said that he heard Fire Singing, she had demanded that he lead her as close as they could get to the building without risking detection. But now, as they continued on, her anxiety about the others grew. She glanced into the wood, hoping to see Davri or Liviya or Arten. She hadn't heard any more gunshots, but that could mean anything, right?

"Do you really want to do this?" Cale whispered. "We have to find the others."

"I know," Miren said, but she still didn't turn back. Kesia might be in that building. She might be right there. "Are you sure you heard Fire Singing? How close did you get?"

"Closer than this." Cale continued on. Miren bit back her frustration. They were moving away from the coast, and likely farther away from the others, but she couldn't bring herself to turn back. She had to know.

Finally, Cale stopped and crouched behind a bush, motioning for her to join him. They could see the back of the building from here and the faint outline of another set of double doors.

"How did you get this far so fast?" she asked.

"What do you mean? I just kept running," he whispered. "I thought if I went straight down the path, I would lead them away from everyone else."

Miren glanced at him, then away. She couldn't decide whether he had been brave or foolish.

Cale continued, "I dashed around over this way and noticed the doors in the back. They were closed like that when I first saw them, so I don't think anyone really uses that entrance."

"They could be locked, though," Miren said.

"It might not be. You can't see this place from the coast or the city. Maybe they rely on the fact that no one knows it's here. Besides, I've seen workers come in and out of the front door, so we can't go that way."

Miren stared at the door. Was it worth the risk? They wouldn't be able to sneak over there. They would have to run across the clearing and hope they weren't seen.

There were likely still men looking for her and Cale.

But Kesia might be there.

"How fast can you run?" she asked.

He looked at her. "You can't mean that."

She stared at the hangar. How long would it take her to run across the clearing? Ten seconds? Twelve?

She knelt into position to lunge.

"Miren, what if they—*Miren.*"

She shot into a sprint.

Footsteps thundered behind her. She sped up, expecting a pursuer, but Cale's form raced past her. He was incredibly fast. Miren tripped twice in her haste to catch up, terrified of being seen or hearing more gunshots.

Finally, they reached the hangar and crouched against the wall, just paces from the back door. If someone walked out of that door, they would be caught.

"That was so stupid," he said, panting.

Miren fought to steady her breathing. "You didn't have to come."

"You know, that's how I was caught the first time I tried escaping Rion's place."

Miren rubbed a stitch in her side. "You just ran?"

He shrugged. "Thought I could surprise them."

She glanced past him. The doors were still closed. She stood up and walked around him.

She reached for the door, her heart still pounding.

Kesia might be inside.

The handle gave way under her grip.

She leaned forward to look.

"Hey," Cale warned, grabbing her shoulder.

She shrugged off his grip and poked her head inside.

The entire building was one large cavernous room. Metal beams arced high above along the bottom of the curved roof and down the walls. Set along the walls were a dozen or more work benches, all of them littered with tools and papers and fluttering oil lamps. Men in work clothes stomped around, barking orders, many of them with strange, bulbous lenses strapped over their eyes or perched on their foreheads. Most of the men's attention was focused on the enormous structure in the center.

For a moment, Miren believed it was a building within a building, an elongated ovoid structure with metal beams crisscrossing along it like a frame. The giant structure was, impossibly, balanced on a single, much smaller metal carriage of some kind attached to the bottom.

She didn't understand until she saw someone disembark from the carriage and the whole thing bobbed slightly.

It was floating.

Cale tugged her out of the doorway. "You're going to be seen," he whispered.

She pointed. "They're building something. I don't—I have no idea—"

Cale frowned and took her place by the door.

"Skies," he said softly. "It's a balloon, I think, but I've never heard of anything this big."

"That thing—it's supposed to fly?"

"I think so," he said. "This has to be Amos Steel's operation, right? There's a path from the factory that leads right here."

"But why?" Miren said.

"Maybe they work for the military? Imagine them taking that thing to war." Cale rubbed the back of his neck. "I suppose that would be one way to get past Kilithis Bay."

Miren shook her head. A way to fly . . . her mind didn't have room for such a revelation. How high could they go? High enough to see over the mountains?

She remembered Kesia. "You said you heard Fire Singing? You think she's on that . . . balloon? The carriage part?"

Cale risked another glance. "I don't see where else she could be."

Miren's heart thumped. What if it *was* Kesia? And she was just a few paces away?

She risked another peek. She saw no sign of anyone but workers.

Kesia might be in that balloon thing. Kesia might be paces away from her.

She had to see. She had to *know*.

Kesia Kesia Kesia.

She stepped through the doorway.

"Wait, Miren!"

She ran to the nearest workbench and ducked underneath it, then glanced back at the door where Cale still stood, watching her. He looked baffled and terrified, and she couldn't help but sympathize. That had been stupid—very, very stupid.

She risked a glance around the side of the workbench. The men were turned away, and she darted to the next bench, then the one after that, waiting for the inevitable shout or gunshot. She risked a glance back to the doorway, but Cale was no longer there.

Finally, she reached the workbench nearest the door in the balloon's carriage, which was still about twenty paces away.

She could feel her heart pounding in her throat.

She ran, her breath loud in her ears.

The stairs were narrower than she expected. She tripped and barely caught herself on the railing before scrambling inside.

The interior of the carriage was even more confusing than the outside. On the left was a curved metal desk littered with a slew of buttons and levers and little displays of numbers. Beyond that, a window pointed toward the front of the building.

She glanced out the window. The workers were huddled around two men and some guards. She recognized the same two men from before, dressed in suits, smiling pleasantly as the workers looked on nervously.

Miren stepped away from the window and turned.

A door stood just in front of her, metallic and heavy-looking. It was cracked open; a dusty, dry heat emanated from the space.

Fire Singer—

"Kesia," she called to the figure inside.

Hair too dark, frame too small. Her arms were littered with scars and what looked like burn marks.

It wasn't Kesia. The Voice that Cale had heard hadn't been Kesia's.

The girl stared, wide-eyed, her eyes sunken, her arms bruised, her clothing in tatters. She shifted upright, the chains on her wrists clinking as she moved, and signed. *Who are you?*

Miren shook her head. It didn't matter.

But this girl needed help.

She crept forward, feeling the heat from the furnaces. The girl flinched back.

"I won't hurt you," Miren said. "I—I want to get you out of here."

The girl turned her wrists so Miren could see the keyholes in each cuff.

Fire Song would take a long time to melt the metal chains, but Miren didn't see any tools. "Can't you Sing?" Miren asked.

The girl pointed to her collar.

A chill ran up Miren's spine despite the heat. "All right." They would need tools, then. Even if Kesia wasn't here, she couldn't let the whole trip be a failure. "I'm going to find something to get you out," she said. "I'll be back."

The girl's eyes widened, but she didn't sign.

Miren crept toward the doorway to the carriage. The men were all congregated around the entrance to the building. Miren couldn't see what they were looking at, but she gingerly took the stairs and ran to the nearest work bench.

After a moment, the crowd at the front door parted to reveal two figures on their knees, their hands above their heads.

Davri and Liviya.

Miren muffled a gasp. She strained to hear what the man in the center was saying.

". . . much better for you if you answer my questions."

Davri and Liviya stared at the ground, both silent. The men must not have realized that Davri was a Singer or they would have gagged him.

The man in charge gestured, and a guard smacked the butt of his rifle into Davri's head.

Miren bit back a squeal as he fell forward on the hard floor. The guards pulled him upright again. Even from this distance, Miren could see Liviya clench her jaw.

"You're a very strange pair for Kaleon spies," the leader continued. He pointed to Liviya. "You especially. Is Kaleo running out of able bodies as well as Singers?"

A few of the surrounding men chuckled, but Liviya's expression remained cold.

Miren fumbled for her pistol, but it felt clumsy and useless in her grip. Even if she had perfect aim, she'd never be able to shoot them all.

What could she do? Was there a way to signal Cale? She looked back, but she couldn't see the door from this angle.

"Refusing to speak may lead me to believe you're both Singers," the leader said. "And I suspect you may know what we do to Singers here."

She held the pistol in both hands, ready to jump from her hiding place.

And then she heard a Voice of Fire.

FORTY

KESIA

KESIA LED THE GROUP TO THE SOUTHERN END OF THE compound, feeling unsteady on her feet as they wove through warehouses at a jog, but she didn't slow. Even with just six Singers, she realized, it was possible they could take the men at the hangar and rescue Ayla.

Oddly, Kesia didn't see any of the guards she and Zuriel had spotted when they first arrived. Perhaps they had been dismissed? Or had something happened? Had they been called to the hangar for some reason?

She spotted the gate that led to the hangar and looked at Zuriel. He hummed a few notes, and the lock clicked open.

Outside, the moonlight highlighted the trees and path in a faint silver. Perhaps they should try to remain hidden, but Kesia didn't feel the need. She Sang another small flame over her shoulder to light the path in front of them.

The Water Singer came beside her. *Won't they see us this way?* he signed.

She nodded once, still Singing.

He stared at her, his expression difficult to read under his wild beard.

I will extinguish the flame when we get there.

He nodded.

Another Singer, an older man with a hunchback and a square jaw, signed, *What is your plan?*

She glanced at Zuriel. *We need to take their weapons away first,* she signed. *Water Singers can trap them in ice. Air Singers can throw them off-balance long enough for Zuriel to take their guns. They will be afraid. Once they stand down, Zuriel can go in and unlock Ayla's collar.*

What if they don't stand down? asked the younger Air Singer.

I will take care of them, she signed. *But without their weapons, they will fear us. Can you do that, Zuriel?*

Zuriel nodded, though he still looked worried.

Kesia continued down the path, and the hangar came into view.

She heard gasps from behind her at the sight of it. At night, the building looked like a great, hulking worm, with light pouring from the doorway like an open maw.

A crowd of men were gathered in a loose circle inside the door, surrounding someone or something.

She paused, uncertain, spotting at least three men with rifles on their backs.

She snapped to get Zuriel's attention. *Can you reach them from here?*

He shook his head.

Then we need to get closer. She turned to the Water Singers. *I think we should split up. You two freeze the men in place as best you can. Air Singers, keep them unbalanced. Agreed?*

The blonde girl nodded, though she looked frightened. The dark-haired woman next to her looked grimly determined.

The bearded Water Singer signed, *What will you do?*

I will distract them, Kesia replied. She looked to Zuriel. *I'm trusting you to take their guns away quickly.*

Zuriel stood tall. *I'll do it.*

Then let's go.

The other Singers split off, approaching the doors from either side. Kesia doused her small flame and took a deep breath, then marched forward.

The crowd shifted, and she saw two figures on their knees. One was a sturdy woman with a dark rope of hair hanging down her back. The other was a younger blond man. Parviz stood over them, a pistol hanging casually in his hand.

Kesia marched straight ahead, feeling a sudden fury. She realized how foolish it was to fear this man. Nadav had been one of the most impressive Singers she had ever seen, but Parviz relied on others for his power. Without the guns or collars or guards, he was just another man.

But he was responsible for what he had put the Singers through. He would pay for his crimes.

Kesia took a breath and Sang.

Fire ignited the nearest man's sleeve.

His companion shouted, and the man patted frantically at his arm. Kesia Sang another man's shirt alight, then a third man's pant leg. Screams pierced the air.

Parviz was the first to see her. His brow rose in surprise, and he lifted his gun.

It flew from his hand. Kesia heard Zuriel's Song fling it into the darkness before switching to the guards' rifles.

Two Voices of Air sang in unison, and a sweeping gale surrounded the men, kicking up dirt and making them stagger. High-pitched Water Song encased a few men's feet in ice.

A bang sounded to her right.

She flinched, worried she had missed someone, but it was the hunched Water Singer. He no longer Sang but instead wielded a captured rifle that he aimed carefully.

The two figures kneeling in the center jumped to their feet. The woman lunged for the nearest rifle. The other one, the young blond man, began Singing, a piercing falsetto that summoned ice around the nearest man's legs, tripping him.

Kesia knew that Voice.

She remembered days on the beach, sitting on a shelf of rock as he built a small house of ice. They would sign to each other for so long that Kesia's arms would feel tired afterward. She remembered a small boy with bright hair at Skyflame, Singing as swirling water in a pail froze in place.

He turned and saw her. Blue, blue eyes. He looked slimmer than she remembered, his cheeks less round, his jawline more prominent, but it was him. Davri was here.

He ran toward her. In the midst of violent winds and gunshots, Davri caught her hand and drew her into a fierce embrace. He had hardly touched her before, always so carefully polite, so reserved. She had struggled more than she cared to admit about whether he had been holding himself back, or if his feelings were simply not that strong.

Now he pulled away. *Whatever you're planning, do it quickly,* he signed.

He launched into Song again, his Voice even stronger as he proceeded to finish encasing the man in front of them in ice. She instinctively reached for him as he walked away, anxious to keep him in sight, her mind full of questions.

But Ayla still needed help.

Kesia ran for the airship, feeling as though she had wings. She dashed past a man chipping at ice that encased his comrade and another struggling against an Air Song that pinned him to the ground. Her feet pounded on the hangar's concrete floor; the airship loomed above her as she approached.

A hand grabbed her and yanked her back hard. She opened her mouth to Sing, but another hand clamped over her mouth.

"You are far more trouble than you're worth," Parviz's voice rumbled in her ear. "I suggest you don't struggle."

Kesia froze, feeling a knife pressing hard into her neck.

"All right, break it up!" Parviz shouted over her shoulder, sounding calm despite the chaos. "Or I spill this little girl all over the floor."

Davri stopped Singing and held up his hands. Kesia struggled against Parviz's grip in anguish. Davri didn't know what he was doing—he didn't know what would happen to him if he were caught. The older woman lowered her rifle slowly.

"Here's what's going to happen," Parviz said. "The rest of my men are going to tie up all you little rebels. The Singers will be gagged. Then we're going to march back up to the factory and introduce you to your new quarters. You there. Blonde one. Unfreeze my men, would you?"

Davri stared at him, arms still up, his gaze flitting between Parviz and Kesia.

Kesia signed, *No*, but the knife bit into her skin. She felt blood trickle down her neck.

"Don't make me say it again," Parviz called.

Davri slumped, looking defeated. He began to defrost the nearest guard.

"Remember, little Singer?" Parviz whispered in her ear. "Remember when I promised you would die here? Remember that?"

His whole body jerked from behind her.

The blade disappeared from her throat.

His grip on her mouth loosened and slid away. Kesia turned in time to see him fall sideways to the ground, blood spilling from a bullet wound to the head, his eyes wide and sightless.

Kesia turned.

Miren stood there, a pistol in her hand.

Miren!

Miren whispered, "Kesia?"

Kesia raised her hands to sign but couldn't think of words. She staggered forward.

Miren's gaze slid past her. She raised her gun.

Bang.

Miren staggered back. The gun fell from her hand and clattered loudly on the concrete floor. Bright red bloomed on her shirt.

Kesia whirled.

Katzil stood there, a rifle trained on Miren. Before the airship captain could turn it on Kesia, she Sang a fire at his hand. He cried out and dropped his gun.

He staggered back. "You don't—you have no idea," he said. "You don't know what you've done."

Kesia marched toward him, pain and fear and fury and tears blurring her vision, her mind a roaring white inferno.

More shots rang out, and Katzil's body jerked with the bullets. He looked down, his face slack with surprise, and crumpled.

The sturdy older woman stood a few paces away, a rifle in her hand.

A light thump sounded behind Kesia.

She turned and saw Miren on the ground, blood spilling between her fingers as she clutched her chest.

Kesia and Davri ran to her and fell to their knees. Davri began a soft Song, trying to cool the skin around the wound and slow the bleeding.

"Kesia," Miren grunted, her voice tight with pain. "We found you. Kesia, Kesia—"

Quiet, don't speak, Kesia signed, her chest tight. Perhaps this was a dream. Perhaps her mind had finally broken, and she was still in the compound, pushing carts and heating rollers.

Miren was here. Davri was here. They were here together. They had come for her.

More footsteps approached behind. Kesia whirled, a Song ready, but Davri grabbed her arm. *They are friends!* he signed.

Behind her was the woman who had shot Katzil, flanked by two younger men who might've been her sons.

"What happened?" the woman said, dropping to a knee by Miren's head.

"What do you think?" Miren slurred.

The woman took the end of her shirt and ripped off a long strip of cloth. "Cale, help me tie this."

"Yep," he said, kneeling beside the woman.

The woman glanced at Kesia. "You're who we came here to find, aren't you?"

Kesia nodded, stunned.

"Liviya," she said, pointing to herself. "My sons, Cale and Arten."

"There's a girl." Miren pointed feebly toward the gondola. "Collar, chained up."

Kesia looked around, but Zuriel was already running toward the gondola, followed by Arten.

"We need to go," Liviya said.

"What do we do?" Cale said. "Climb back up to the factory? We don't know who's up there. What if they called the peacers?"

Zuriel jumped from the gondola, followed by a familiar small form who staggered down the stairs. Kesia waved, relieved, as Ayla ran straight to Kesia and embraced her.

Ayla pulled away and signed, *You came back? To save me?*

Kesia smiled and nodded.

Ayla's attention drifted behind her. Kesia turned to look. Bodies littered the entryway, some of them alive and frozen in place, most of them still on the ground. They couldn't risk going back to the compound.

Her eyes caught on the airship.

She snapped for Ayla's attention. *Is the airship ready to fly?* she signed.

Ayla nodded. *Furnace is still hot.*

And is there water in the boiler? Kesia asked.

I don't know.

She turned to Davri. *Can you be sure that engine has water in it?* She pointed toward the back end of the ship near the port side propeller. *Use the pump in the corner.*

Davri looked to her. *Yes, but why?*

We're taking the airship.

His jaw dropped. *We're taking* that?

Miren can't walk, and I don't know another way out of here except back up toward the compound.

He nodded and ran off.

She glanced back at the bodies. Some workers, some guards. She noticed a blonde Air Singer unmoving on the ground, but the other three Singers were nowhere to be seen.

Guilt flooded her. She wished she had asked for their names. Too many people had died tonight, and she couldn't undo that. But at least the other Singers had escaped.

"It really flies?" Arten said.

Kesia nodded and gestured for them to board the gondola. Miren tried to climb the few steps, her knuckles white on the railing, but stopped. Kesia's heart twisted.

"I've got her." Cale bent and scooped Miren up. Her head rocked back, and she cried out in pain. He sidestepped into the gondola and set her down against the far wall.

Kesia climbed up last, making a quick head count—eight people aboard, including herself. She shouted a Song into the furnaces, and the room burst with heat and light that pushed against the engines, waiting.

She looked to Zuriel. *Last tether!*

He nodded and hummed a note. The tether released with a heavy clatter.

The airship rose.

The furnaces were still warm from Ayla's earlier Song. The ship rose quickly, the dark interior of the hangar giving way to the darker expanse of the valley outside the window.

At Kesia's mark, Ayla Sang at the furnaces while Zuriel Sang coal into them. Zuriel stumbled in his Song, not accustomed to Singing against another Song; Kesia pointed to the shovel hanging in the corner.

Arten and Davri stood at the panel of buttons and levers. The wheel started to move, and Arten grabbed it. "I don't know how to do anything."

Kesia clapped for their attention, still Singing. *This shows how high we are. That wheel steers us. That controls the propellers.*

"How do we land? Where are we going?" Arten said.

Just go up, she signed.

She wasn't entirely sure how to steer, but that wasn't her main goal. She wanted the city to see the ship. Once Amos Steel's secrets were in the open, she would figure out their escape.

The hills to the north slowly crept by, and the sprawling, lighted expanse of the city appeared. The streetlamps flickered like fiery stars. She thought she saw a crowd at the base of the hill outside Amos Steel.

The airship was no longer a secret.

Davri was staring at the gauge. *We're very high.*

She nodded, realizing she didn't know how to land, or where they should go. Maybe they should head to the other side of the bay, then try to get away from Avi'or.

Thunder crackled through the gondola, shaking them like stones in a jar. Everyone stumbled to the right as the craft tipped violently.

Kesia caught herself against the wall, nearly falling into Cale, who held Miren upright.

"What was *that?*" Liviya cried.

Miren clutched her shoulder, her face tight with pain. "Cannon fire?"

As soon as she said it, Kesia knew she was right.

The airship began to fall.

Kesia pulled herself back into the furnace room doorway. Zuriel was on the floor, lying on his stomach, clutching the doorway to avoid falling into the furnace.

Kesia gulped a breath and continued her Song, but it hardly touched the furnaces—a pipe or something had broken and was now expelling all the air. There was no pressure, nothing there to fill with heat.

But the air warmed anyway, and power filled the engines. She didn't understand—she didn't have the strength for this, but she noticed a soft doubling of her Voice and glanced at Ayla. She was braced against the wall, kneeling, but her lips moved in Song. She looked up and nodded, her brow knitted in concentration.

Davri stepped around Kesia and shoved open the gondola door —cold night air roared in, leeching at the already paltry fires. He began to Sing.

Kesia couldn't see what he was doing, but she heard the intention: he was trying to pull the water of the bay upward to meet them, to soften their fall.

They shared a glance. Their Voices were competing—it couldn't be helped—but their Songs made a strange harmony.

Zuriel crawled out of the furnace room on hands and knees. Kesia reached for him and pulled him the rest of the way. *Sing! Slow us down,* she signed sloppily with one hand.

His eyes widened desperately—to Sing something this large was too much to ask, and too many Songs were already happening at once

—but he opened his mouth and rumbled a note to slow the airship's descent.

Kesia renewed her effort in the furnaces. She couldn't be sure—it might just be her own fatigue making her dizzy—but she thought she could feel the airship slowing.

Arten released the steering wheel and moved to help Miren. "We have to jump!" he cried.

He and Cale each took an arm and hoisted. Miren yelped in pain, but there was no time to be gentle. Kesia grabbed Zuriel's arm, and he nodded.

Davri stepped aside to give everyone room. Kesia and Zuriel came forward and clutched the side of the doorway. The dark expanse of water flew toward them.

Kesia jumped.

She heard Davri suck in a breath at the wrong moment in his Song.

The water sped toward her. She tucked in her arms.

For the second time, Kesia plunged into the bay.

The pain of the impact shot through her, but she knew immediately that she wasn't injured. Cold clutched at her, stinging her eyes as she pried them open. The water was black as it shoved and spun her around. She kicked and thrashed, her mouth shut tight, unsure if she was even swimming upward—

Her head broke the surface. The airship hadn't sunk yet, but it was starting to, the balloon slouching as air wheezed out of tears in the material. The metal frame was fractured or bent in places, but it was the engine that had been dealt the worst damage.

A head popped up over the water, indistinguishable in the dark. Kesia swam over and thought she saw the outline of blond hair. Two more heads bobbed up a few paces away.

"Is everyone up?" Arten called. "Cale?"

"I'm here. Miren? Davri?"

Davri Sang the water to push him and Kesia closer to the others.

"Davri?" Cale called. "Is that Kesia with you? I can't see."

"Where's Mother?" Arten said. "And Miren?"

Kesia's stomach tightened with worry. She was exhausted, but she sucked in a breath and Sang a fire over her head.

Cale and Arten looked around in the new light. The balloon was almost completely submerged now, its sinking making a slight current Kesia had to fight against.

Zuriel and Ayla splashed over, looking shaken but unharmed, followed by Liviya. Kesia gasped in a breath to continue her Song, the light flickering. Where was Miren?

"There!" Cale called swimming away. "I think I see her!"

Kesia moved her flame closer to him in time to see Miren's head sink below the surface. Davri launched into a Song, and the water swirled around Miren and pushed her back up, her eyes fluttering as Cale came to support her.

A boat was coming toward them. Kesia stopped Singing, struggling for breath—she was exhausted, and now she had to tread water while she Sang—but if she could cause a sail to catch fire, she could slow the vessel down.

But it wasn't a naval ship, and she saw figures waving at the bow, holding oil lamps. The Singers they had rescued, their melodies filling the sails, were heading in their direction.

FORTY-ONE

MIREN

PAIN THRUST MIREN IN AND OUT OF CONSCIOUSNESS. SHE was on the deck of a ship; people were hurrying about as Air Song filled the sails above her. Then she was in a small, wooden room while someone wrapped her shoulder, a thick paste stinging the wound like acid. Gentle hands gave her water and dabbed her forehead with a wet towel. A familiar Water Song cooled her wound. A hand held hers and squeezed.

Kesia.

She opened her eyes.

She was in a small, dingy room with a circular window set in one of the wooden walls. She lay in a bunk, a faded orange blanket at her feet, as though she had kicked it away in her sleep. Her wound was bandaged, her right arm wrapped in a sling. She felt a light sway and realized that she was on a ship.

She remembered a face hovering over her: hazel eyes, curled hair, a spattering of freckles.

She got up, bracing herself against the wall, and left the room.

The hallways were narrow but clear, the wooden floor fresh and smooth under her bare feet. Her head felt heavy; she braced her good arm against the wall to steady herself.

"Kesia," she called, but her voice came out cracked and hoarse, her mouth dry. She swallowed and turned to find a ladder. She climbed painfully, one-handed, and pushed open the latch above her head.

A cool wind threatened her balance on the ladder. She pulled herself onto the deck.

Three masts towered overhead, each with sails that billowed like clouds. The deck was crowded with Singers, most in rags. Some were huddled in small groups, while others signed, explaining how the sails worked. Three women Sang a chorus of wind into the sails, directing them due west. Davri and another man were standing at the bow, Singing as they signed about the best way to propel a ship this size.

Kesia stood at the helm next to Liviya, smiling.

Liviya spotted Miren, then gently nudged Kesia and pointed.

Kesia's mouth dropped in a soundless cry, then she hurried down the main deck. Miren smiled through her tears as Kesia nearly fell into her arms.

Kesia Kesia Kesia.

Davri grabbed them both in a bear hug, lifting them off their feet until Miren couldn't take the pain in her shoulder anymore. "Ow! Ow! Down please!"

Davri signed a sheepish apology.

Cale and Arten and Liviya hurried over as well, asking how she felt.

"I feel like I got shot," Miren said wryly.

They all exploded with laughter.

"She's fine," Liviya said.

Miren asked, "Where did this ship come from?"

"Stolen," Cale said cheerfully. "The Singers who escaped saw us fall just as they boarded it." He indicated a few of the Singers gathered on deck. "I think some of them really are prisoners of war. They certainly know a thing or two about ships."

Miren noticed that Arten stood slightly apart from the rest of the group. She glanced around and realized that two people were missing.

"Hana and Ori?" she asked.

"Still in Peladah," he said. "There was no time to double-back without risking everyone here."

Liviya and Cale shared grim looks. Miren suspected they had fought about it. "I'm sorry," she said.

He shook his head. "It might be for the better. If they don't connect her to us, then she should be all right. And it's not as though Kaleo is exactly welcoming to escaped planters. I can blend though and send word that we're safe."

Miren nodded, feeling that she should say more.

Liviya said, "The city is going to be a lot more distracted dealing with the fact that Amos Steel's secret is out now."

"Yes," Cale said. "We've been talking. Hopefully all that chaos was enough to get peacers into Amos Steel to see the rest of the evidence. It might be enough to expose what Amos Steel has been doing to Singers."

That would be incredible, Davri signed.

Unless the government knows about it anyway, Kesia signed.

"Even so," Liviya said. "They won't be able to keep it a secret from the rest of the city. The people will know, and they won't stand for it."

Miren wasn't convinced. It seemed too easy, too neat. But one could always hope.

The Earth Singer boy, Zuriel, came up to her and signed an apology, his chin ducked, his expression fighting tears.

Miren studied him, confused. "Why are you sorry?"

It was my job to take the guns from everyone, he replied. *I must have missed one.*

Miren looked to Kesia for help, but she just smiled sadly.

"Hey, listen," she said. Miren waited until he looked up at her. "This is not your fault at all, understand? Unless you pulled the trigger, it's not your fault."

He looked somewhat relieved, but not completely.

Cale ruffled his hair. "Come on, help me furl this sail before the Air Singers break it."

Zuriel took the hint and followed Cale away. Liviya and Arten drifted back to the helm. It was just Miren and Kesia and Davri.

Miren gave in to her shaky legs and took a seat against the wale. Kesia and Davri crouched in front of her.

Miren asked, "What's the plan?"

Kesia and Davri glanced at each other. *We're going to Crescent Bay,* Kesia signed. *We're going home.*

Miren wasn't sure *home* was the right word; it no longer felt like a place. Home was right here. Home was away at war. "We may have some problems," she said.

I know, Kesia signed. *Davri told me what happened. He thinks he can persuade his father to help these Singers.*

Miren frowned at Davri. "What about what happened at Rion's estate?" Although Liviya had pulled the trigger, they were still partly responsible for Cheliem's death.

I don't know. Cheliem has no heirs, so I'm not sure what will happen to his estate. Rion might seek compensation from my father for the fire and Cale's escape. And considering the way I left . . . Davri grimaced. *I don't think he'll be keen to do me any favors. We need to convince him that helping the Singers is in his best interest.*

"How will we do that?" Miren asked.

I have some ideas, Davri signed. *Still figuring it out.*

The Singers had nowhere else to go. Kaleo wasn't safe for Singers, but neither was Avi'or. The best place for them would be as far from the conflict as possible, and Miren knew of no other place as isolated as Crescent Bay.

Davri and Miren told Kesia what had happened on their journey. Of Cheliem and meeting Hana and sailing rapids. Much of it sounded implausible in the retelling, but Kesia seemed impressed.

I . . . I don't know what to say, Kesia signed. *I'm so glad to see you. Thank you so much.*

"You should be," Miren said, suddenly anxious to lighten the conversation. "I've been stuck with this one for how long? Three months? A year?"

Davri rolled his eyes. *Your sister snores.*

"I do not!"

She never believed me when I told her, Kesia signed.

"I can't believe this," Miren said, but the two Singers were shaking with silent laughter.

Miren watched as Davri caught Kesia's gaze and held it. They were attentive to each other but careful, pining but uncertain. Miren felt . . . hopeful? Wary? She didn't know, but she resolved not to push them. The whole possibility of a connection between them seemed very different now that she cared for both of them.

Toward afternoon, Miren found herself sitting against the wale at the bow of the ship again. Kesia came and sat beside her.

Miren took her hand. She began to hum, from memory, a song.

Kesia smiled and joined in. A small fire appeared in the air in front of them, a flame without a candle. Their voices matched perfectly. Miren dipped underneath, adding harmony. She couldn't remember the last time she had done this. She felt tears stream down her cheeks, but she would have to let go of Kesia's hand to dry them, so she didn't.

They watched the sky darken, the sun taking its time to slip behind the Kaleon mountains. Gulls called loudly overhead. An Air Singer had started Singing the wind into the sails until Liviya called to her to stop. "We have a heading! You're going to strain the mast."

They watched the Singers work, or pretend to work, or happily avoid work as they celebrated their freedom. Someone had found food supplies and cooking equipment. One Singer had taken charge of a large pot of stew. Another was lathering a thick coat of balm around other Singers' necks, where the collars had been.

Miren almost expected to wake up. Even the throbbing in her shoulder wasn't enough to convince her that this was real. She kept glancing at Kesia, still unsure if this impossible journey was over, if everything really had turned out this well, if she and Kesia had managed to find each other.

And then Kesia glanced at her and grinned, and suddenly Miren felt silly for questioning it.

They had done it. They had really done it.

Kesia signed, *What do we do now?*

Miren knew what she meant. What would Crescent Bay be like? What would they do with the Singers? How would they convince Darius to keep them a secret? What were Davri's plans, both about his father and Kesia? What about the horrors that trailed after them, the sights that would haunt them? What about their parents, still off fighting a war? What about them, sister and sister? They were different now than they had been before; how would things be between them?

"I don't know," Miren said, pulling her sister close. "But we'll figure it out together."

ACKNOWLEDGMENTS

Many people shaped this story into something worth sharing, and I'm so glad for the chance to thank them (I hope I got everyone):

To my intrepid agent, Richard Curtis, for taking a chance on me, for helping me fulfill a lifelong dream, and for answering all my dumb questions. Perhaps not in that order.

To my lovely editors, Anne Hoppe and Ruth Katcher, the iron that sharpens. Thank goodness that no one will ever know how much better this book is with your guidance. Truly, I could not have asked for better people to work with. And to the team at Clarion: the cover you designed was my desktop background for months.

To Dr. Kate Evans and my fellow students in that one 2012 Fiction Writing workshop at SJSU. Your notes (which I still have) on that early, early draft were wonderful encouragement, and you were quite right—this was not a short story.

To my Aunt Donna for braving an early draft. Thank you for your insights and enthusiasm.

To my refreshingly excitable writing group, Cierra and Massiel, for their thoughtful notes and reactions. Now it's your turn.

To my first and greatest champions: My dad, John, for reading a lot of bad early drafts and being kind enough to only point out typos. My mom, Rebecca, for answering the question "Do you think I'll ever get published?" every time I asked. And to my sister, Rachael, whose boldness and terrifying willpower may or may not be in this book.

To my Lord and savior, Jesus Christ. Your blessings abound (and are freaking me out a bit). May I run this race with perseverance.

"Sing to the Lord a new song, for he has done marvelous things." (Psalm 98:1a)